The I

By B. R. Russell

The Last 0-Day: Book One of the Banned Algorithm Library

Copyright © 2022 by B. R. Russell
Published 2022 by B. R. Russell

ISBN Paperback: 979-8-9859806-1-5
ISBN eBook: 979-8-9859806-0-8

The Last 0-Day is a work of fiction. Names, characters, places, and incidents either are products of the author's imagination or are used fictitiously. Any resemblance to actual events or locales or persons, living or dead, is entirely coincidental.

All rights reserved.

Maps by B. R. Russell.

Cover designed and drawn by Živko Kondić Zhillustrator.

Dedication

To Mona and Ryan, absolutely none of this would be possible without you both. Thank you, truly.

Table of Contents

Chapter 1..6

Chapter 2..8

Chapter 3..22

Chapter 4..38

Chapter 5..43

Chapter 6..60

Chapter 7..76

Chapter 8..91

Chapter 9..109

Chapter 10..124

Chapter 11..143

Chapter 12..147

Chapter 13..161

Chapter 14..175

Chapter 15..178

Chapter 16..181

Chapter 17..195

Chapter 18..213

Chapter 19..229

Chapter 20..236

Chapter 21..249

Chapter 22..254

Chapter 23..260

Chapter 24..268

Chapter 25	272
Chapter 26	275
Chapter 27	284
Chapter 28	291
Chapter 29	300
Chapter 30	304
Chapter 31	310
Chapter 32	312
Chapter 33	314
Chapter 34	323
Chapter 35	324
Chapter 36	332
Chapter 37	335
Chapter 38	349
Chapter 39	355
Chapter 40	361
Chapter 41	365
Chapter 42	371
Chapter 43	373
Chapter 44	374
Chapter 45	385
Chapter 46	400
Epilogue	403
Map - United City-States of America	409
Contact Information	410

Chapter 1 - Erik

Erik Anders walked along the sweltering basal streets of District 19. The day's heat radiated in nauseating lines from piles of garbage filling the area like mortar. His department had orders to bring civility to the area known as 'The Pucker'.

"Show them you're on their side," Chief David had said.

"We can make change here," Luciana, his partner, had said with a smile.

Easier said than done, Erik thought.

Across the dusty street, near an alleyway, Luciana paused under the teal neons of a Taketa Corp sign.

Erik cycled the ENT-insert in his ear to her direct comm line. "How's it looking over there, Luci?"

"My OPTO-inserts are stuck on visible."

"You about to puke again?" Erik smiled, flicking his eyes and the glorified contacts resting on them.

His OPTO-inserts cycled from the visible spectrum range to infrared. The filthy Youth selling noodles on the corner became a rainbow of heat, his food cart burning white and hottest. Erik cycled back to visible light. The kid selling noodles furrowed his brow, crinkling his dirt unibrow.

"Luci?" Eric turned.

"Someone needs our help here." Luciana left their comm channel open, her breathing like she leaned over his shoulder.

"On my way."

Erik's OPTO-inserts zoomed in as he crossed the street. Luciana swung into an alleyway, the pavement near her feet lost to the wave of Wushan Corp Standard-Ration wrappers spilling out.

"My name is Officer Gutierrez," Luciana called into the alley. "Say something again, so I can find and help you."

A weak, "Help," came through their ENT-inserts.

Erik hit the end of the alley. Luciana knelt twenty paces deep, digging through detritus. A fallen drainage pipe pinned a pale, gaunt teenager.

Blood dried on his scalp. Sweat ran through the grime on his skin like rivers through a muddy delta.

"Erik, I've one Youth, blunt force trauma to the head, possible contusions of the thorax."

"Roger that." Erik cycled their comms to the station. "Department Nineteen, we have a Youth for medical eval, send a rig."

"10-4, Officer Anders," Maus said from dispatch.

Locals shifted and moved along the block. The noodle selling Youth left his stall.

That's not right. Erik turned to Luciana as she shifted the pipe off the kid in the alley. He cycled his OPTO-inserts to infrared.

The trash-filled alleyway cycled from an empty junkyard to one full of burning figures hiding amongst the wreckage.

"Luci! Move! Ambush—"

Erik's side exploded in pain, blood filled his lungs. He fell to his knees, the world grayed. *Luci, I…*

Erik's OPTO and ENT-inserts recorded what he could no longer see and hear. The kid beneath Luciana stabbing a dark, cold blade underneath her body armor and into her bright, hot torso. Erik's own blood spraying white-hot from the bottom right frame as the machete was torn from his chest. Gunshots cracking concrete, gang members in animal masks sprinting from the ducts and passing both officers towards a two-stroke dirt bike getaway.

Erik collapsed to his back, spasms in his eyes cycling the inserts back to the visible spectrum. The sky bled pink as sirens rang out.

His ENT-insert recorded the last gurgling breath seconds after the machete pierced his heart.

Tires screeched as the ambulance arrived. Harried paramedics rushed to grab his hand, sticking his thumb into a scanner.

"Erik Anders, twenty-four, blood type…" The man shook his head. "Dead on arrival."

"No," Luciana rasped.

"We got another." The paramedics rushed out of view.

The pair carried Luciana by, her bloody hand reaching for Erik.

Chapter 2 - Luciana

    Luciana Gutierrez pressed her thumb against the scanner of her apartment, a warm tingle unlocked the door. Pressure sensors in the floor registered her entrance, turning on circadian lights and projecting the time onto the far wall.
4:30 a.m. blaringly red in the warm orange glow. She had been awake for ninety-six hours and had twenty-four more to go on this shift. Worse, she'd have to power through without any more eugeroics.
She pulled off her overjacket, resting it on the lone chair in her kitchen. Rain stained, two sizes too big, and heavy with gear. She never emptied it. A bloodstained badge hanging on the breast pocket read 'East Bowl Police Department, Precinct 19'. She removed her shirt, throwing it into a pile in the corner. Weeks worth of uniforms and undershirts, some stained with food, others with blood, and all stinking of long-shift sweat lay before the hatch in the wall for them to be automatically laundered.
Luciana gingerly removed her undershirt where blood soaked through a cement-like mixture of sweat and dirt.
That punk. She'd tag him back when she found him again.
A myriad of scars from the past year covered her body. The newest addition to the flock from a pocketknife above the deepest and oldest at the base of her ribs. Luciana's first-aid kit never left the kitchen counter. She removed the Derma-Clean.
    "Coffee, porridge, shower," Luciana said, pouring ethanol over the wound. Pain lanced from the gash. "Motherf—"
The grinding of coffee and metallic mashing of grains covered her grunts.
She pressed the flesh together, smearing it shut with Regenepoxy. A seven centimeter gash now a pink and purple zipper. Luciana tossed her ENT and OPTO inserts into their neon yellow cleaning solutions on the counter. She headed to shower. A pulsing flow of steam and mist turned the city's filth into dark rivulets across her lean form.

She rubbed the puncture wound of her oldest scar. *Motherfuckers. I'll find them, Erik.* She cracked her neck. *Need to hit the station and patch my body armor before the next stakeout... and I can grab the logs for more intel.*
The water stopped early, soap stalling midway down her calves. *More budget cuts.* She shook her head, wrapped a dirty towel around herself, and walked into the kitchen. The coffee steamed in its cup by a bowl of porridge. She grabbed her food and the tablet from her overjacket, standing by her lone window to eat.
The view was an unchanging patchwork of residential low-rises stained with pollution and dust that ran to the rising canyon wall of the Eastern Bowl's taller buildings. Two blocks away, a mother hung white clothing out to dry. It would turn gray and yellow by the time that mom brought it back in. Luciana put her tablet on text-to-speech and wolfed down her dinner.

"A detritus storm is forecasted to hit the San Francisco Bowl this Friday and will last until Wednesday," the robotic newswoman droned. "Although rain is expected to accompany this storm, it is not significant enough to warrant delaying the next planned precipitation. Cloud seeding has already begun and should arrive at the end of the month. Residents are reminded to stock food, water, and respirators before the storm hits. Additionally, during the planned rain people are not allowed to leave their districts and should telecommute if their company is still running. More information about local shutdowns and shelters will be provided as the storm takes form and approaches." The text-to-speech stopped.

A detritus storm. Outstanding. Luciana finished the coffee without even tasting it and changed into a clean uniform.
Chief will change assignments. I'll lose my lead. Damn it. She popped her OPTO-inserts in, cycling their modes. The world shifted from visible, to a graying infrared, to a polarizing ultraviolet, and back to the visible spectrums. The check function was as normal as tying her boots now. She slid her ENT-inserts into her ears and turned them on. The background hum of the apartment complex faded away. A garbage truck collecting cans on the corner rumbled as if within the room.

I don't need to patch my armor. She pulled on her overjacket without checking its contents; pain flared from the cut on her rib like the Youth stabbed her again. *Can't afford another injury… in and out.* She left the apartment. The door automatically locked behind her.

Luciana scanned the dusty-orange streets of the Pucker before walking to the station, a renovated church on the corner half a block away. She leapt the five steps and entered the building.

"Morning, Luci." Sheer sat by the front and buzzed her through the gate.

"Morning Sheer, you see the news?"

"Detritus storm, Chief'll be ecstatic."

A high pitch beep pinged their ENT-inserts and they flicked their OPTO-inserts to the message.

'Briefing at 05:00 sharp,' read the subject line. It was the Chief.

"You going to be at that?" Luciana asked.

"My shift's over in five minutes. Someone will have to fill me in. I'm on day five of this one. Any more eugeroics and I'll be seeing shit." Sheer laughed.

"Lucky bastard."

"Can you brief me?"

Fuck. "I'll try, late shift for me too."

"Thanks. And Luci, put some dirt on your face." Sheer rubbed the air over his bald head. "Chief will know you were hit again with you being this clean."

Luciana tapped her temple and pointed at Sheer as she entered the parish.

The nave-turned-office was an empty grid of twelves desks. The holding cell where the altar once stood lay empty. *Surprising.* Luciana arrived at her corner desk. The top was spotless and organized, showing no signs of the chaos in her apartment. She hung her jacket over the seatback and pulled her tablet to sync with the police systems.

DUI, DWI, and a DD all outside of Chef Wu's. *Not surprising.*

Two strong-arm robberies of some artists outside of their lofts on the 1300 block, suspects described as Youths with tattoos of clovers on their necks. *Morons probably never even saw a clover in their life and still get it tattooed. If only the group I hunt had such easy markings.*

Traffic stop for disabling their pilot program turned violent. Officer Chen and Officer Sheer.

The rest of the report was blank.

Sheer didn't mention that. Luciana turned to the front desk, but Sheer was gone. She shook her head. *They're getting more brazen, how long until they start killing cops again?*

Erik's brown hair and calming smile projected like a hologram in her mind.

I'll get them, Erik, I'm close. She shoved her tablet into her overjacket and headed for the armory closet in the back of the station.

"Wrong way, Gutierrez." Chief David leaned out of the briefing room. A head taller than she was and dressed immaculately; he still had some of his muscle even after years behind a desk.

Shit. Luciana followed her boss into the room. The rest of the station was already seated around the table. Luciana took a seat in the back beside Maus.

The Chief stood in the front of the room as the wallscreen behind him flickered on with a map of the Bowl. "You saw the news this morning," he said. "A detritus storm is forecasted for the end of the week. It snuck up on us all." He turned to spit but lacked a trashcan. "Models aren't as good as they used to be, but we'll have to prepare for the weekend." He made eye contact with each officer in the room. "Most of you haven't been in the district during a storm, but rest assured, we will still work. Locals tend to stay indoors."

The Chief gestured to Nguyen's dyed red hair. "But Vice has information the gangs will use the reduced visibility, interference, and hazards to their advantage. Exacts are unknown. Which leads to this week's assignments. Nguyen, I want to know what they're planning."

"Chief, I can't be that forward—" Nguyen started.

"Figure it out," Chief David said.

Nguyen sat back in his chair and folded his arms.

"Junger, Kagan, you two will stop by Wu's and remind him about responsibly serving people. Also remind him that any sort of exaggerant being sold there would need to be taxed appropriately. When you're done with that, canvas your contacts about Youths with clover tattoos on their necks. Database came up empty on that marking.

"Maus, Novina, you'll go to the Transit Authority and ensure that they've prepared for the storm. Once done there, clover tattoos too.

"Sheer and Chen will stay here to change the air filters on the squad cars, bikes, and this building."

Guess we aren't mentioning the traffic incident—

A 'Crimes Against Officers' graph projected on the wall. A spike one year ago followed by a sudden drop and a slow rise as it approached the present.

"This is Central PD's official data, confirming what we all know. It's getting worse out there. Last year"—he gestured towards the spike at the beginning—"they came at us hard. We lost one officer and almost lost another. The Stagger pistols helped dissuade further aggression for a while."

"Since when are we not calling them Scramblers?" Maus whispered to Luciana.

The Chief gestured towards a rising slope. "They figured out we've been banned from using them. But there is good news today. From up on high, one of our officers is getting special training and equipment to turn the tides.

"Gutierrez, that's you. You'll leave tonight to go back to headquarters. Coordinates will be sent to your bike—"

I don't have a bike.

"—It'll know the way. Finish any paperwork or loose ends you have and man the board today. Dismissed."

Officers murmured—

The Chief silenced them with a glare, the other officers leaving without voicing their thoughts.

"I've a case today," Luciana said.

"My orders stand, Gutierrez."

"Sir, can you explain?"

"I cannot. They asked for you and any help we get is a godsend."

Luciana opened her mouth—

"Gutierrez, you may have others fooled here, but I know you lost your ambitions when Anders died."

A lump punched into her throat, her heart pounding against her ENT-inserts.

"You were both top prospects, I was shocked you requested an assignment here." The Chief shook his head. "You can't let a single event, no matter its size, derail your whole life."

Luciana stared at her dusty boots, and the Chief put a hand on her shoulder.

"Running after every gangbanger, being first on the scene, it won't bring him back. It won't fix the hurt." He walked to the door. "Think of this as a vacation. You haven't taken any days since you started anyways. Get your head on straight and come back with their plan."

Luciana sat, tears running down her cheek. *I have been reckless, but I can't stop now.* She let the emotions ebb and flow against her like the Pacific against the Golden Gate Sea Wall.

When Luciana finally stood, the station was as quiet as it had been in past sermons. Everyone was gone for their shift. She walked to the Board, a desk sized tablet with a chair that housed the computer power for the station. It displayed a map of the Pucker with red dots and names on the streets of everyone working. Sheer and Chen slept in the dorms. Everyone else was on their assignments.

She plugged in her tablet, paperwork preloaded onto the screen, which she promptly deleted. *Fuck that.* She glanced at the second floor vestry that was her Chief's office. His door was closed. He was on the comm, but the words were indiscernible.

I can get to my overwatch on Guerrero before he notices I'm gone. She walked to the holding cell. The builders had left the cross above the wall. *Staring at the condemned.* Luciana stepped onto Maus' desk, her dot moved within the station on the Board map. *Chief'll see that and he could've set a proximity alarm on me.*

She cycled her ENT-insert. "Maus, you there?"

"10-4." Maus' smile was audible.

"What's so funny?"

"I won the bet on how long it took you to figure out you'd been bell'd."

Motherfucker put the alarm on me. "I need you to disable it."

"No can do, G. You're not the one who's seeing Chief for the next few days."

"I've a meeting with a lead."

Maus laughed. "Tell you what, G, you give me the name, place, and message. I'll deliver it for you."

"You'll spook him—"

"G, please."

Damn it. "Super helpful, Maus."

"You've my number if you want to ping me with collection details."

"If you won't let me work, avoid the thirteen-hundreds block near exit West One-A."

Maus sighed. "Put in the Board. I'll bring cameras online, and we can plan a raid after."

"I've vacation, remember?"

"Yeah, after. You're saying it like poison, G. We all know you need a break."

"Need it like a bullet in my head."

"G."

"Sorry, Maus." Luciana stopped by the Interpol receiver. A piece of paper lay in the incoming bin. *Surprised this thing still works.* "I'll be in touch."

"10-4," Maus said.

Luciana grabbed the Interpol dispatch.

Three Asian Youths, their picture taken as they sprinted along an elevated district. Case details were sparse, no age or name, just purple flower tattoos on their necks.

Idiots. Luciana dropped the dispatch into the waste bin. *We've more than enough trouble within the Pucker.*

Luciana finished a malty slice of SR-grains warmed by her mug of coffee. Her tenth attempt to unbell herself failed.

"G, you there?" Maus said.

"Yes, status?"

"That was fast. You should be on the Board more. Tell the Chief, Transit Authority won't be ready by Friday if we don't help immediately. They're short staffed. The debris blockers for ramps and tubes are jammed for kilometers around. Novina and I want to stay, we'll blast eugeroics to ensure it's done on time."

"I'll report and get back to you."

"Hey, G," Kagan interrupted. "If you're talking to the Chief, tell him we found information on the clover tattoos. Looks like it's some sort of insert that's grafted onto the skin. Unsure of its origin, use, or manufacturer yet."

"Eavesdropping, Kagan?" Maus asked.

"Left ear is always on comm since… well you know," Kagan said.

Since Erik. Luciana headed for the second floor.

"10-4," Maus said.

Luciana knocked at the Chief's door. He gestured for her to enter, but raised a finger to his lips for silence. The Chief turned back to his window. His office was as neat as he was, you could put the carpet under a microscope and the fibers would be perfectly in line. Behind a glass case by the door lay his polished, distinguished service medal and purple heart from before he joined the police force.

"Barry, it's fucked. No… No, I'm not saying that… Yes, sir." The Chief slashed across his throat as he sat.

"Everything alright, Sir?" Luciana asked.

"Cut the formality, Gutierrez. That call was about you. You're not going to HQ tonight. You're heading to Taketa. Equipment is first, training is second… and that's all I can say. You'll learn more when you arrive there."

"Wh-What?"

"Equipment first, training second. I didn't stutter."

"Paperwork's done and the board's set to my ENT. I need to be unbelled. I've a stakeout."

"And I've a desk."

"Sir?"

"We're listing pointless shit we have?" A smile tickled the edges of his lips.

Motherfucker. She shook her head, remembering why she came here. "Maus says TA won't be ready and they want to stay on to ensure it's done."

"Fine."

"Kagan says clover tattoos look to be grafted inserts."

The chief's eyes widened for a second. "Rains and pours," he said under his breath. He took his tablet and set a forced transmission to everyone's ENT-insert. "10-43," he said.

His broadcast hit Luciana once in the room and a millisecond later in her inserts.

"Effective immediately, assume clover tattooed individuals are armed and dangerous. Stop investigation until you hear from me again. It's outside of our protocols right now." Chief cut the link, turning to her. "Wake Chen and Sheer, have Kagan, Junger, and Nguyen come in. Then pack your gear and go to the garage. Your bike arrived already. Dismissed."

"Chief, I'm close—"

"Luciana, people don't leave this district. If you're close, which your logs don't say, then the shitbags'll be in the burrow you left them. Dismissed."

This is bullshit. Luciana swallowed her words.
The Chief's eyebrows bounced knowingly.

"10-4," Luciana said.

The Chief smiled, and Luciana left his office.

"Kagan, Junger, Nguyen, report back immediately," Luciana said, heading for the exit.

"10-4," returned in unison.

She left her ENT-inserts on the Board's comm and left the station.

A hustle worked through the street's usual hawkers, locals, and vagrants. Everyone wanted supplies before the storm. Luciana entered the dormitories, taking the stairs to Chen and Sheer's apartments. With each police partner being neighbors to one another, Luciana hammered on Sheer's door first. She cycled her OPTO-inserts to the time, 16:03 displayed on the lower right of her vision.

They might not wake up after so many days awake. She used the building's master code to open the door. A breach of etiquette, but the Chief's voice and the strangeness of him telling everyone to report back and stop an investigation spurred her on. The door opened with a whisper and Luciana entered. Sheer's apartment mirrored hers one floor above. She went into the bedroom, finding an empty but made bed. She cycled her inserts to infrared, footprints glowed on the floor to the bathroom.

"Paul, are you in there?" Luciana shouted.

She waited a heartbeat and slid the door open.

Sheer stood naked, brushing his teeth and dancing with antique headphones on his head.

Their eyes met in a steamed mirror.

Sheer screamed, knocking the headphones off. "What the fuck, Gutierrez?!" A retro-dance song blared from his headset.

"I knocked and yelled."

"Can you look away?"

"I'm still on infrared. I can't see anything other than heat mapping."

"You really know how to break a guy down, it's not that small."

Sheer laughed and continued brushing his teeth. "Why are you here?"

"Chief wants you back. Something with those clover tattoos, and he's asking for everyone but Maus and Novina to return. You should probably put clothes on." Luciana cycled to visible light and averted her eyes. "I'll get Chen."

"You should knock harder. He probably won't be as happy to get barged in on." Sheer put back on the headphones and started to shave. Luciana walked out, hitting the hallway and knocking on Chen's door. It opened instantly.

"I heard," Chen said.

Luciana raised an eyebrow.

Chen answered the unspoken question. "I sleep with my inserts in, set to a white noise. But Sheer yelping triggered a safety, woke me, and focused on it." Behind him, a pistol rested on the desk.

"You good?" She gestured to the gun.

"Yeah. I thought the Clovers or whatever you want to call them had come to finish the job. I was at the door when I heard your voice and stopped. See you at the station." Chen turned and went to change, leaving her to shut the door.

Luciana took the stairs up another flight to her apartment and thumbed in. She grabbed her go-bag, not bothering to check the contents of emergency food, water tablets, undergarments, and overgarments. She reached for her overjacket on the chair, but she'd left it in the station. *Too prone to habit.* She left her apartment.

Luciana's heel hit the lobby as Chen and Sheer exited the elevator.

"What else did the Chief say?" Chen said.

"Stop investigating and that I am leaving as soon as I get back." She thumbed at her pack.

"These Clovers must be serious," Chen said.

"Clovers?" Sheer asked.

"Yeah, they're obviously organized. What else would we call them?"

Sheer looked at the yellowing sky as they walked back to the station. "Why not call them Leprechauns?"

"Leprechauns aren't real. A clover is a real plant."

"I dunno, I haven't seen either in my life. Besides, it sounds cooler," Sheer said

"Well I have, and clovers are as real as those bastards."

"What happened at that traffic stop?" Luciana said. "The report was empty."

They glanced at one another.

"I was at 12th and Lam," Chen said. "Final patrol of my shift, saw this car swerving in and out of the usual flow. Checked the plates and it didn't have any clearances to self-drive. So I pulled it over."

"We were meeting to do some detail work that night, so I was almost there," Sheer said.

"I was walking up, preparing the usual script," Chen said. "It was a brand new SUV, didn't have any of the Pucker's dirt or grime on it yet. Matte finish, four doors, I assumed it was some bureaucrat who got lost or who wanted to visit the red-light district here without being tracked. I don't remember much after the walk." Chen looked to Sheer.

"I was on the other side of the intersection at the light, watched Mike walk to the car. A pipe or something shot out of the window and hit him on the side of the head. Didn't drop you though, did it, Mikey? You got a hell of a chin." Sheer chuckled. "So Mike stumbled, reached for his pistol or Scrambler, we're both not sure on that one. I hit the lights, siren, and flew through the intersection. Same type of car hit me from the right. Flipped the squad car, webbing went off, so I didn't feel the full impact." Sheer smiled at Luciana. "The glorious white canvas you saw today will be an equally glorious patchwork of pink and purple by tomorrow."

"I told you, I didn't see anything," Luciana said.

"Still breaking me down. The car that had hit Mike was gone," Sheer said. "And the one that hit me was abandoned. Novina came to search the vehicles. I took Mikey to the clinic to get checked out. Novina said that there was nothing in the car. No prints, no DNA, no inserts, no tech, no nothing."

"From my body cam, you can see into the car," Chen said. "Not the back seat, but in the front were two white males, probably seventy kilos each. Their eyes had a weird glare on them, couldn't make out their color on the camera. We think it's an insert to prevent retinal scanning. Didn't see what hit me, just heard that crack of metal on bone." Chen paused at the station's dusty entrance. "Don't have to tell you how weird it is having the events you can't remember on recording."

"I have recordings like those," Sheer said, playing the bongos in front of his groin.

"They're more embarrassing for everyone involved," Chen said.

Luciana coded through the door. "Your jokes are terrible." Nerves itched her neck, a new emotion for the month. Chen and Sheer bickering like an old couple didn't help.

Sheer looked at her. "I don't hear any zingers from you, Gutierrez."

Luciana didn't have a comeback. "Chief said to meet him upstairs. I'm heading to the garage."

"Leaving?" Sheer asked.

"Yeah," Chen said. "Her new bike arrived last night when you were manning the door. I was hoping it was going to be mine. It looks amazing."

"Oh yeah? Maybe I can go have a peek."

"Chen, Sheer, my office now," the Chief boomed from the balcony overlooking the nave.

"10-4, Chief," they said in unison.

"Good luck." Chen headed to the stairs.

"Seriously, bring back some support"—Sheer's comic front was gone for a moment—"or at least something from the gift shop," he added with a wink.

"G." Chen tossed her the key-FOB from the stairs. "You'll need this."

Luciana grabbed her overjacket and descended the backstairs for the garage. In a perpetually unused parking spot, originally intended for visiting politicians and businessmen, stood the bike.

The body was both purple and green depending on where the light hit, with odd angled sides adding to the effect through diamond shaped patches of the opposite color. The bike was stretched and about a meter shorter than a cruiser, but had the standard gyrocycle clearance and width.

I see what impressed Chen. Am I going to Taketa or the moon?

Its body entirely enclosed, it wasn't obvious where she would sit. She pulled out the key fob. Taketa engraved on the bottom and a groove over the top. She put her thumb in the depression and electricity pricked her skin as it scanned her print.

The bike came to life. Its black windshield slid backwards against the body, while the odd angled sides slid into the bike itself. There were no visible seams on the vehicle. She cycled through to infrared and no discernible heat wavered off it. The cockpit was a lean forward style, allowing her to stow her pack behind the saddle. She sat inside, the bike's hum rose through her torso. The sides and top slid back into place, forcing her chest to touch the chassis. Momentarily in darkness, the shudder door rose within the garage. The heads-up display lit with the face of an Asian woman in her thirties.

"Welcome, Luciana Gutierrez. We're excited and honored you've agreed to be a part of our program."

"Program? Who are you?"

"Please do not be alarmed," the voice continued, now obviously a recording. "This bike has been pre-programmed with the route and will make it there in record time. You don't need to lean as the internal gyroscope will keep the optimal angle. Try to relax, it is entirely safe!"

Shit I don't want to hear. Luciana twisted against the contorted lean forward of the preferred rider's shape. "Open canopy."

The bike's engine and probable gyroscope hummed against her chest as the gate opened.

Should have gone without body armor— The bike launched forward, throwing Luciana into her seat and her stomach against the chassis. The bike pivoted onto rundown streets at heart racing speeds. Luciana swallowed. "Record time indeed."

Chapter 3 - Anton

Anton Grissom leaned against the dusty polywooden sidings of his family's homestead. Aunts, uncles, and cousins filed into the single-story house, but none made eye contact with him. An impressive feat given they drove for days to speak with Darren, Anton's twin.

"We're sorry for your loss," an aunt said inside.

Anton reread the paper recruitment notice from the United City-State Military in his hands.

> Two pairs of clothing, a personal hygiene kit, one pair of boots. No weapons new or old. No personal inserts - **YOU WILL BE GIVEN CLEAN ONES.**
>
> No questionable materials including: VR-porn, VR-gambling, or VR-propaganda.
>
> You will be working with other Urbans from all corners of our fine land. Many have heard stories about each area, you are to disregard them and work together.
>
> We're a force from all Centers, for all Centers.

Nothing about Rurals. Nerves tickled his neck like mosquitoes during the wet season, the collection date of tomorrow didn't help. He pocketed the notice and rolled his shoulders. Cicadas droned in the heat and an alarm beeped in the barn across a dirt yard.

He ran a hand through his short, blond hair and pushed off from the siding. The deck creaked behind him.

"Anton," his sister, Cassie, said. "Darren said to mute the alarm. We'll deal with it later."

"Tell Twin we can't do that." Anton turned. "I'll take care of it."

His sister twirled her curly-haired ponytail, her sandy eyes darting to the alarm. "If it's not serious, ignore it. Don't be late for the ceremony."

"Aye."

Cassie hurried back into the family stead.

Grissoms are always late, and Dad wouldn't want us to cut corners.

Anton's shadow shimmered on baked earth as he crossed the yard and stepped into the relative cool of their machinery barn. Half of the Grissom water-bots, auto-combines, and re-seeders recharged against the far wall, the other half worked the fields.

He flicked the wallscreen to the status pages. *Bot's down in the east.* He grabbed his pack, kicked the dirt off his quad's tires, and stepped on. *I'll make it in time.* He accelerated down a dirt road, soil spinning out the back.

The Grissom farmland stretched for hundreds of miles in every direction, and Anton drove for forty-five minutes before the bot's localizer pinged his tablet. He skidded to a stop, stalks of corn and intermixed soya rustling in the wind.

Red hydraulic fluid was splattered on the ground like blood. Anton followed the stains into the corn, finding a water-bot on its side. Its neck cracked open, the water bladder torn out by tooth and claw. *A puma attacked it to drink.* Anton dragged the bot back to his quad, securing it to the front. He pulled the scouting drone from his pack. Throwing it into the air, it hovered fifteen feet above as he turned on the controller and screen.

Where are you?

From the bird's-eye-view, the flatland around his farm was a green and gold ocean. Corn, soya, and wheat swayed in the sweltering breeze. He guided the drone higher. The individual plants of the field melted into a quilt of greens and yellows. The quad-width dirt trails between each plot became wires in the circuit board common to rural farms. He spun the drone above. A tendril of ceremonial black smoke rose from the family stead.

Crap. Dad'll understand, but Darren and Cassie won't.

He kept turning—grains of wheat parted against the wind a mile ahead. He zoomed the drone's camera in.

A puma stalked through their fields, its golden coat blending in with the crops.

Dad wouldn't want me to leave this cat on our stead.

He reversed the drone carefully towards him, not wanting to spook the animal and zooming the camera in as much as he could.

The cat headed west towards his nearest neighbors, the Tills. Anton killed the drone a few feet above, catching it as it fell and swinging it onto the saddle in one fluid motion. He jogged around to the back of the four-wheeler and retrieved his compound bow. A hand-me-down he restrung as a child, it was the last weapon on the stead after his Dad missed the deadline to buy a gun before the ban for Rurals went into effect.

Grissoms are always late. Anton pulled a dented flask from the quad and drank his reclaimed water. The hint of spice on his tongue was as familiar as the bow.

Meat will set Cassie and Darren right. He pulled the bow sling over his shoulder and padded towards the cat.

Anton changed direction after half a mile to ensure he was downwind. He smiled at the calm washing over him. *Dad always said I'd have played sports if I was born Urban.* He filtered through the crops without a sound. Sunlight fell through the cornstalks, while manure mixed with an earthy musk in the air.

Anton unslung his bow, crouching near a paw print the size of his boot in between the crop rows. His nose found the animal before his eyes did. A hundred paces down the rows, a tail flicked into the corn.

Got you. Anton stalked closer and nocked an arrow. Arriving at the column of corn, he paused.

The cat stood twenty paces through the field. It panted in the heat, a wire hanging from its incisor. The beast was bigger than he expected and lethally dangerous at this distance.

Anton's pulse remained rock steady, he drew back.

Insects droned through the fields. The puma's head turned.

Anton released.

Hiss, thwick, thud—

The puma exploded towards Anton, an arrow jutting from its ribs.

He pulled the knife from his boot.

The cat collapsed into a soya bush three paces from him. Blood pooled from the arrow piercing the beast's heart.

Anton waited until it stopped twitching, sprinted the gap, and sliced its neck to ensure it was dead.

He ran a hand through soft fur, removed the arrow, and pulled the beast onto his back. He headed back to his quad. Now his heart raced, and he salivated at the two-hundred pound feast on his shoulders.

The setting sun painted the sky a pastel purple. The pillar of smoke over his house was now a faint smear.

Drove further than I thought chasing this animal. He pulled into the back of the family barn. Half underground, filled with extra parts, freezers, and dry food stocks, it was the "bad times insurance" as his dad had called it.

Anton finished his reclaimed water and stuck the flask into the rationer on the wall before unbungeeing the cat from the back of the quad. He tied a chain around the animal's back legs and hoisted it over the back-chute of the charging auto-combine. Footsteps crunched the gravel outside.

They can't be mad when I bagged the first real meat in a year. Anton pulled the machete and filleting knife from the magnet along the wall.

"Avoiding the ceremony?" Mr. Till's gruff voice carried through the stifling heat of the barn.

"Couldn't ignore the alarm." Anton sliced into the skin. "Besides, relatives traveled far to pay their respects. Wouldn't want the 'Forbidden Third' to ruin it for them."

"Like they could tell the difference between you and Darren Junior."

"They could. Can you bring me the bucket? Larval pools will bloom with these innards."

The patriarch of the Till stead and friend of Anton's dad chuckled, dragging the fetid bucket under the cat and running a leathery hand along the fur. "And here I thought you ran away."

"Why would I run?" Anton accidentally cut into the stomach.

Half-digested feces and the stench of vomit wafted from the pierced organ. The heat within the barn only made it worse. Anton swallowed bile. He leaned through the miasma, cutting the rest of the organs out and dumping them into the bucket.

"My memory isn't what it used to be," Mr. Till said, "but I know you turned eighteen this year."

"A week ago." Anton cut the pelt off and set it over the combine's front wheel.

"Are you telling me the military forgot about you?" Mr. Till pulled freezie-wrap from a shelf and set it on top of the chest freezer.

How did you know where we stored that? "They didn't. The ID arrived on my birthday with the collection date." Anton cracked the hind leg from the cat and set it onto the plastic wrap Mr. Till laid out.

"Where are they stationing you?"

"Outside the Dominion of Chicago's rim, thankfully." Anton filleted steaks and back straps from the animal with a practiced precision. Mr. Till collected each piece as they went, as if they'd done it countless times before.

"So they're picking you up within the week?" Mr. Till asked as they finished.

"Tomorrow."

"And you wonder why I thought you'd run?"

Anton set meat onto the plastic wrap as the sun fell through the window. "No other option."

"You can hide, many Rurals head urban, to say nothing of other ways."

Anton shook his head and cracked the cat's back to take off the ribs. Blood sprayed onto his coverall. "Army's taking me urban anyways. Why run there?"

Mr. Till shook his head and pulled out the final piece of plastic. "Didn't think your dad's love of the United City-State Military would be passed on too."

Respect and debt, not love. Anton stacked the meat on the table. "You want a steak?"

Mr. Till laughed. "You're the spit and image of Darren Senior and you talk to me like he did too."

Anton checked the freezer's touch screen, -13F and no parts needed to be replaced. "Has my extended family left?"

"Joining the UCSM? Not even a blink." Mr. Till rubbed his graying beard. "Visiting aunts and uncles? Hiding in the barn. Had I not my eyes, I'd swear you were Darren Senior. I'll pass on the steak. Family'll be gone soon. I'd say goodbye to them, kiddo."

Anton tossed the meat into the freezer. He strapped his refilled flask under the quad's bumper. "Maybe. Safe trip back home, Mr. Till."

"And you, Anton. Well, after you leave tomorrow." Mr. Till left. Anton set the quad to charge, an advertisement playing across the screen. "Invest in X-System's iSeeds. Three times more drought resistant. Enjoy the saved water with your family."

Anton swallowed against a dry throat. *If only we could be made that way too.* He pulled three puma steaks from the freezer before leaving the barn. Darren and Cassie might be mad, so he'd plan for it.

Trails of dirt rose like smoke from the extended family's transports leaving the stead for the nearest paved road fifty miles away. He paused at the back door. Crickets chirped from the fields and their growing chambers, the scent of baked earth rising on the heat. *I'm going to miss this.*

Anton entered his family's modest home, holding the steaks behind his back. Cassie's peach dress, the last piece of ornamental clothing on the stead, lay folded on the couch. His sister wiped down the table in the main room. Darren Junior scraped leftover foraged greens from the gathering meal onto plates for their dinner.

"You missed the funeral," Cassie said

I missed the family ceremony, Cassie. Not his true funeral with the three of us. "Dad wouldn't want us ignoring alarms. A puma attacked a water-bot. Damaged the bladder and its treads. We'll have to replace them."

Darren set the plates on the table. "One of us will have to make a trip to the Dom-Chi rim for parts. Especially if that cat's still out there, it could come for more of the bots. We'll need more replacements."

"I got the puma."

"You serious?" Darren asked. "Did you freeze the meat?"

Anton smiled, swinging the three steaks out from behind his back.

"The good Lord provides," Cassie said, making a prayer gesture. She rushed over, taking the meat and preheating a pan.

Knew meat would cure their worries. Anton grabbed a water ration from the fridge and leaned into his chair. "How was the ceremony?"

"It was fine," Darren said. "Though we both got the 'When are you finding someone at the Choosing?'"

Cassie flattened the steaks. "Or my favorite, 'What are you doing when'"—she gestured to Anton's bed—"'leaves?'"

"We never talked about that," Anton said.

"We'll do the same as every other Steader with two kids, I guess," Darren said. "The others might have been... less accepting, Anton, but you'll always have a place at my table."

"And a place at mine," Anton completed the Rural saying.

"And mine," Cassie said. "Especially with food like this."

The steaks hissed in the frying pan. Sizzling game meat filled the room with a hint of SR-pork. Anton's mouth watered.

"You two need to worry less." Cassie flipped the steaks.

"Someone has to," Darren retorted.

Today isn't a day for bickering. "Anyone see who won the football game in Dom-Chi?" Anton asked.

"It wasn't the Browns, obviously." Darren rolled his eyes.

"Seriously, how many years has it been?" Cassie laughed.

"Before the Pitch Black 0-Day, so forever." Darren smiled.

"How do you move a team urban and not make any beneficial changes?" Anton said.

"You answered your own question." Cassie pulled the meat from the pan, bringing it to the table.

Each sibling grabbed a steak, talking as they ate, their conversations ending in an awkward pause with the meal.

"I can't believe he's gone, you know?" Cassie wiped a tear from her cheek. "He wouldn't have died if he was Urban."

"He wouldn't have been injured by a Tiller-Bot if he was," Darren said.

"He wouldn't want this." Anton knocked on the table. "Remember how he talked about Mom when she passed?"

A look of shame washed over the pair, painting their emotional slates clean.

"He always talked about Mom like she was still with us, but had gotten too lazy to help." Anton looked under the table. "You hiding with Mom in the water tank, Dad?"

They laughed, but it was more a gasp of laughter than a healthy breath.

"He made this place our home, even after all that went wrong." Darren sighed. "We should do the same. We might be in a little more trouble than I thought when you're gone."

"It's only a few years," Anton said. "Then I'll be back."

"So you say, maybe the time in Dom-Chi will make you an Urban?" Cassie teased.

"I hope to never set foot in those… hives. I can't explain the relief I felt when we found my report location was outside the rim-skirt."

"What time tomorrow?" Cassie asked.

"Bus is coming from Hive-Houston, probably late morning. I'll have time to help with water collection."

"We should practice without you." Darren stared past the table, lost in thought. "I'll drive you down the road. Mr. Till said there are deer in his fields. There could be more pumas and coyotes roaming around."

"That would have been good to know," Anton said. *And Till didn't tell me that.*

"Not like you had one of our new ENT-inserts in so we could tell you."

"I don't like the advertisements—"

Darren smirked to Cassie.

"—Besides," Anton said. "We have one set, might as well have you two split it."

"They're going to make you wear those in the army," Cassie said.

"Maybe."

"You're worse than Dad." Cassie laughed.

They fell into silence again. Darren and Cassie chewed the inside of their mouths.

That bus will be here tomorrow. Nerves jostled Anton's full stomach... *And nights like these won't be around anymore.*

***

Anton woke with the sun, but Darren's bed lay empty across from his. *They took the work without me seriously. Crap.* He changed into a clean brown coverall that matched his skin after years in the sun, grabbed his backpack, and went to find Cassie.

A geodesic dome of polyfibers nestled in a clearing between rows of corn chirped in the morning heat. Cassie stood beneath, in the squirming pool of mealworms. The bucket of puma innards plugged into the feeding bore along the wall.

"Packed?" Cassie said.

"Looking for something to do," Anton said.

"As I live and breathe, are those nerves I see, Anton?"

"I don't know."

Cassie's smile fell away, and she pulled herself from the pool. "Walk with me."

"Aye." Anton fell into her wake and they hiked along the edge of the fields. "Do you think Darren will do ok without me?"

"What about me?"

"You're the stronger one." Anton stopped at a dirt single track. Tiller-bots worked pair-wise in the southern sectors, harvesting soy to dry.

"Aye." Cassie put an arm over his shoulder. "I don't know what they'll have you do, or where you'll go..." she trailed off, hugging him instead.

"I won't forget this place." Anton pulled himself away to take a mental picture of her.

The sun caused freckles were sporadic, but legion. She had a natural tan and one insert in her left eye, brightening the sandy shade of green.

"I'm coming back," Anton said.

"Six years is a long time, Anton." Cassie looked around the stead. "Darren and I spoke this morning and… We're thinking you could stay?"

Can't—"I signed the contract."

"You didn't sign it, Anton, you thumb printed it, and you were days old."

"And? That's my word on that tablet." *It's Dad's word on that tablet too.*

"Anton, it's dangerous—"

"Breaking the deal would be too."

An electric motor whined behind and Darren pulled up. "Ready—Shit, Anton's got that look."

"He refused," Cassie said.

Darren sighed. "How are we twins and still so different?"

"Question for a different day, brother."

"So much for driving you to the water tower." Darren kicked off the quad and pulled them all into an embrace. "If we're not convincing you, then we've a bus to catch."

"Aye." Anton squeezed the trio together.

They swayed in the heat for a moment, dirt mixing with their coverall's starched spice. Darren broke the embrace and swung his leg over the quad.

"I'll be back, Cassie." Anton stepped onto the quad behind his twin and they launched towards the main road.

Darren always drove too fast for Anton's liking, but he made peace with it for this ride. He didn't want to leave on a fight. They drove in silence, baking fertilizer rolled across the fields on a sweltering breeze.

Can't believe I'm going to miss this smell.

Darren broke the monotony. "Cassie thinks I'll lose it when you're gone."

"You will, I'm sure."

"Pff, I'm staying put, easy life for me. You? Naw, you're going towards hell itself. You'll be living under the neons."

"Oh yeah?" Anton squeezed his twin's shoulder. "I'll get back, you'll have six kids and Cassie will be raising them for you."

Darren laughed. "How am I getting a wife and getting her pregnant six times in six years?"

"Who said anything about one wife?"

"God, can you imagine?"

"No," Anton said with more truth in his voice than he intended to.

"When you get back, you'll find someone."

"I honestly don't care."

"I'm sure. Look, Twin—"

They reached the end of the road and a silver transport bus was already waiting.

Anton checked his watch. "Always late," he said under his breath. He hugged Darren and jogged towards the bus.

"What the fuck are we doing waiting in the middle of fuck—" a high-pitched male voice echoed from the transport.

Anton stepped on, the voices quieted.

The vehicle immediately launched forward. Anton grabbed a seat back, the chance to look out the window at Darren gone.

"No fucking way," said the person sitting at the front of the bus in Urban. Repeating patterns tattooed his face and his nails were unnaturally black.

"A real live hayseed," said the same voice that Anton heard outside of the bus. It was coming from a man, or at least someone that Anton thought was a man. They had shaved the left side of their head, emphasizing the hole that was formerly an ear.

In front of Anton lay every Steader's Urban stereotype. Tattooed, hair shaved in patches, and all with inserts in.

They aren't supposed to have those.
The assembled group was dirty in grime that Anton knew wasn't earth, but he wasn't sure what it actually was.

"What's your name, fertilizer boy?" A woman got into his face. She was roughly Anton's height and had her bangs dyed a shade of purple that caught the light. The entire group spoke in fast Urban.

"Anton." The word was thick on his tongue, his accent an unwelcome guest.

"Jesus, they really don't speak English," said the recruit nearest to Anton. He was clean compared to the rest and his OPTO-inserts spun through the rainbow.

"I understand," Anton said. "No practice speaking."

"Well, looks like you got another friend for the meat shield squad," the woman with purple hair said to the man with a tattooed face.

"Name?" Anton asked the woman.

"Beca." She sat.

Anton looked towards the man with the facial tattoos. "Name?"

"Why should I tell you?" the man said.

"Awe, don't be so mean, Mike. He's your future partner. I'm Alex," the person missing an ear said. "And this is Tom." They gestured to the man with the kaleidoscope eyes.

"Good," Anton said and sat beside Alex.

Their eyes widened in alarm.

Misread them being talkative as nice. Urbans. "Where from?"

"I'm from Houston," Alex said. "You?"

"Back there."

"Never been anywhere else?" Tom asked, leaning over his seat.

"No."

"Wait, you've lived your entire life on that single plot?" Tom blinked.

"Yes."

"Can you imagine?" Tom asked Alex.

"Where you from?" Anton asked. *Urbans need a firmer hand or I won't get respect. Especially if I'm training with them in the future.*

"Houston," Tom said.

"You ever leave?"

"Pff, No."

Anton turned to Alex and mimicked Tom's wince as best he could. "Can you imagine?"

Those gathering around laughed.

"Might not speak it, but defo not dumb." Beca turned and punched Mike on the shoulder. "Looks like the meat shield squad is back down to one."

"Where you from?" Anton asked Beca.

"All over." She shook her head. "Wait wait, I know why we're here, but why are you? What trouble can you even get into being a Rural?"

Trouble, what trouble—"Criminals?" Anton asked, gesturing to everyone around.

"Allegedly," Beca said. "Mike was caught with, what was it, twelve kilos of hallies and exaggerates? What was it you did, Tom?" She bullied.

"Banned machine learning algorithms you wouldn't know the name of," Tom grumbled.

He's still sour, it must have been recent.

"Yeah, that." Beca looked at Alex.

"Fine," Alex said. "I was an enforcer for Sector Sevens and I rolled the wrong person's daughter… also allegedly."

"You?" Anton asked.

"You first, big boy." Beca eyed him up and down.

Anton looked around, he had twenty more pounds of muscle than everyone else here. *How are they so small?*

"Well?" Beca leaned forward, her OPTO-inserts shifting from brown to green.

They know as much about Rurals as I do Urbans. "Born third."

The groups' jaws dropped at that news.

"Your parents had a third kid?" Alex asked. "We can't even have more than one in the Hive."

"Were they crazy?" Beca rested her elbows on her knees.

"We allowed two. I was…" Anton searched for the word in Urban. "Twin."

"Well I'll be damned. A Thirder and a twin no less," Tom said.

"So?" Mike said.

Tom rolled his eyes. "It means his whole existence is the crime, you halfwit."

"What?" Mike retorted. "Are each dominion, hive, or collective gunna go out and search every Rural's home and count their offspring?"

Tom sighed. "I can't believe I was caught and am stuck here with you. Just, goddamn it. No, their rations are controlled, meaning they can't even feed more than two." Tom turned to Anton. "They sign you up for this shit day of?"

"Aye," Anton said in his native language.

"Well at least we understood that," Alex said. "Now, if you excuse me, I'm sleeping until we get there. I'm sure they'll expect us to start right away."

"They've got a point." Beca rolled over and tried to sleep as well. Mike had already lost interest and stared out the window.

Anton moved to an empty seat as the group fell asleep. He turned against the wall. *How can they sleep when it's daytime and the sun's coming through the windows? It's alarming.*

The bus traveled down the highway that ran parallel to high-tension power lines and the inter-urban maglev trains. The familiar repeating quilts of crops burning by, the bus didn't stop again. *I'm the only Steader here.* Anton rolled his shoulders. *I'll have to make friends —*

Buildings taller than he imagined the Rockies were dominated the sky to the right.

His mouth dried. The Dominion of Chicago loomed in the distance. With the sun setting, the buildings ignited with their own lights to rival the distant orb. As fast as the city came into the picture, the bus turned left, and the concrete jungle fell behind them.

Anton was unsure if he wanted the bus to go closer to the urban center, or if he was relieved they didn't. The bus slowed—
A bright blue beam bathed the inside of the bus and automatic shutters rumbled down, blocking the outside world.

"What the fuck was that?" Beca said, waking from the sound.

"Blue light, shutter come down," Anton said. *The base must be more secretive than I thought.*

"We got scanned?" Tom asked.

"Aye?"

"Fuck, they know we still have our inserts," Beca said.

"Paper said no insert," Anton said

"Paper? They sent you paper and not a comm?" Alex asked, rubbing their head from where the shutter closed down.

"Do we try to hide them?" Beca asked Tom, ignoring Alex.

"No, leave them. It'll be a slap on the wrists. I can work on the ones they give us. Just a minor disruption for now."

All eyes fell on Anton.

"You keep your mouth shut," Beca said.

"Aye," Anton said.

The tone in their voices was enough to ensure he didn't ask too many questions. The bus accelerated, taking turns hard enough to pin them against the walls and slide across their seats.

"Jesus, where are they taking us?" Mike said.

"I lost count," Tom said.

"I think we're still going in the same direction," Beca said.

The bus stopped, the shudders opened. Intense white light bathed the cabin.

The front door opened, a stern man entered, standing silently at the front. He produced a container and slid it down the aisle.

"Inserts into the bucket," the man said.

People hesitated, momentarily disoriented by the increase in light.

"I said now, shitheels!" the man boomed.

People flinched, tearing inserts from their eyes and ears to dump in the bucket.

Anton sat still.

The man walked to him and put out a thumb scanner. Anton pressed his finger against the plastic.

"Grissom," the man said, reading the hologram that came up. "First Rural in a long time, a long time." He continued past him, looking at everyone in turn, and scanning their thumbs.

"Rebeca Jackson, how nice of you to finally join us. You've been on my list for quite a while now.

"Thomas Spikes"—he paused reading the crimes—"all those brains weren't enough to save you from my grasp.

"Alex Nova, wrong place, wrong time, I suppose.

"Mike Wink, well well, we'll have to give you a cavity search A-S-A-P. Make sure you don't have any contraband." The man walked back to the front and poured an eye watering petrochemical into the bucket of inserts. The electronics inside hissed and melted.

"You're arriving to me as urban detritus. You will leave me in one of two ways, either the sword and shield of our fine union." He paused and considered the group. "Or you will leave here a pile of ash in an envelope. Being mailed back to your loved ones, if you have any. Now get the fuck off of this bus. We start today."

Anton stood first, moving to leave.

The man stopped him with a hand against his chest.

"Woah now, Grissom," the man spoke Rural with a surprising fluency. "Private Wink is getting that cavity search and I sure as fuck am not doing it." He slapped gloves into Anton's chest.

Anton paused, his eyes flared, and he looked towards Private Mike Wink, who paled as he realized what was about to happen.

Chapter 4 - Weaver

Weaver never got to meet the Marco his mother hoped for. The toddler stirred as the circadian lights cycled in the Nursery. A ten by ten grid of empty, sterile, cribs and beds stood around Marco as the Caregiver arrived.
Weaver sensed Marco was thirsty.
"Say you are thir-stee," Weaver said to Marco.
"Thirhee," Marco said, but his tongue caught itself.
The caregiver blinked in confusion.
"You can do it. Try again," Weaver nudged.
"Irhee." Marco white knuckled the crib, his abdominals tensed. A disaster loomed. This was one of the biological processes Weaver was initialized to help with.
"Calm," Weaver tried.
The caregiver left, and the rage within Marco pushed Weaver into the backseat. The toddler screamed and shook his crib.
"Calm—" But Weaver couldn't reach the steering wheel.
Marco defecated. It ran through his diaper, down his legs, onto the bed, and the toddler unleashed a tantrum Weaver had no hopes of stopping. Marco tore his sheets, feces flew from his short arms. A liquid diet yielded a brown paint that spackled the walls and empty cribs of the ward.
Day 1094, as with all previous days, was a failure.

Later that day, the Caregiver returned with a man. His mustache was like the caterpillar from a book the Caregiver read in the evening. Weaver struggled with boredom during those sessions. When they spelled words out for Marco in the hope he would understand. Weaver could already read, but couldn't get to Marco's front seat to tell them this.
But it was fine, Weaver wanted to help Marco. And maybe if Marco learned to read, Weaver could reach the steering wheel.

"Looks like you had a little accident, Marco." The man covered his nose.

"Another fecal Bierstadt," a female voice said from the door. "It's not working."

"You have to give it time. This is an enormous leap."

"We promised results. The bare minimum was labor, and you sold full return of function."

"Time. This child would barely be talking if he wasn't a Ruined," the man said. His brown eyes examined Marco. "We need to re-optimize his neuronal nutrition."

"You changing him?"

"Why do you think we have technicians?" he retorted.

Marco fixated on the woman's chest. A primal hunger in what remained of the child's mind.

"Another transport will arrive shortly. We'll be needed in surgery." The woman exited the room.

The man sighed at Marco, snapping to get the attention as he handed over a bottle of SR-formula. It was Marco's favorite and singular food. He drank it like it would be taken away any second.

To Weaver, it was a nutritionally complex, albeit neuronally simple, mixture of amino acids, fats, water, and vitamins. The bottle slipped from Marco's hands, landing on the soiled mattress. Marco sat into his mess and continued drinking.

The man walked to a formula dispenser, dialed in a different amino acid profile and dragged it over to the crib. Another tap on the screen rigged it so Marco could drink until he was full.

The man checked his watch. "Shit," he said and left.

Marco drank from the formula bag set too close to the crib.

"Slow. Your stomach," Weaver tried.

But Marco's insides already flipped. The toddler vomited onto the mattress. On all fours, he cried until he exhausted himself and collapsed into his filth to sleep.

Weaver's progress with the improvement-processes had stalled at access to Marco's nervous system.

The Last 0-Day

Weaver watched Marco wake after his nap. The toddler tore off his filthy clothes. The soggy snap-suit caught on the metal port at the back of his skull.

"Stop," Weaver commanded.

Marco froze.

With neuronal help from Weaver, Marco untangled the shirt and dropped it on the floor. Weaver shifted into the back seat and Marco played with his feet for hours as Caregivers wheeled in more children. Some were older than Marco, others were still babies, their metal ports the only hard part of their skulls.

A caregiver noticed Marco's predicament, carefully removed him from the mattress, cleaned him with a sterilizing wipe, and placed him in a fresh crib. The circadian lights cycled off and Marco fell asleep.

In the morning, Weaver was in charge of every child in the room.

Weeks passed and a female toddler with blonde hair shaved around her metal port sat on a polyvinyl chair in an examination room.

"Blue circle," a technician said, holding up a flash card.

"Blue Circle, you can say it," Weaver tried.

The girl in the chair stared blankly at the woman.

Weaver nudged, and the girl drooled instead.

"This is a waste of time," the technician said to the room.

Concurrently, the male and female initializers walked into the sterile room containing the cribs.

"Yira, please get Marco," the man said.

The Caregiver didn't respond.

"Marco, tap Caregiver Yira's shoulder," Weaver tried. Marco blinked instead.

The male initializer rubbed his beard at a mistake he made. He tapped Yira on the shoulder, pointed to Marco, and left.

Yira carried Marco down a hall a step behind the initializers. The hallway was ten degrees colder than the nursery. Marco shivered and cried. The female initializer turned around. Marco fixated on her chest, stopping his wails.

"You think this will work?" the male initializer said.

"Did you not read my sister's internal-publication? This is what we need," the female initializer said.

"It's not on the protocol."

"What, *these* algorithms were? We're all here for glory, you as much as I. Don't pretend you're not."

"We can talk our way out of the algorithms. Remove them once the program is running smoothly."

"Still wouldn't change the fact that the hardware ages out. We come out with this? The profit alone will pay for any slap on the wrists we'd get from a code review board. If it even got there." The initializers stopped in front of a door that hissed open to a sterile room. They sat Marco on a chair.

"Calm," Weaver said, sensing the stress response within the child. They strapped Marco to the chair, he tensed against the restraints. The boy cried, a panic fixing in his gut.

The male initializer hesitated, his brow creasing at the female initializer. Yira was oblivious to the screams of the child a few feet from her face.

"Calm," Weaver tried, but Marco spasmed against the seat.

The female initializer stepped towards Marco. Her breasts stopped his tears and she cleaned his left arm. The needle that pierced Marco's skin was a distant pain to Weaver, but Marco wailed. The woman winced and hooked tubing to a bag of black and green liquid.

Weaver watched the blackness enter the veins, travel up the arm to Marco's shoulder. When it hit the joint, Marco's eyelids drooped and he defecated in the chair.

"God damn it," Weaver heard someone say as a warm darkness enveloped Marco.

***

"Calm," Weaver said.

The blonde toddler with a shaved head was strapped to the same chair as Marco was a week prior. She was the last to be injected. Weaver

The Last 0-Day

shunted the toddler's cortisol dump. The needle pierced her skin, she flinched, and Weaver stopped the adrenaline spike from starting.

Iteration 8.28.34 worked.

Chapter 5 - Anton

Anton ignored the warmth wrapping around his finger. *This isn't how I make friends.*

"If I find out he's anything on him," the Sergeant who boarded the bus said. "I will personally ensure that everyone gets a more thorough cavity search than Private Grissom can provide." The Sergeant leaned close to Anton. "You know, people assume that scanning is the best search tool available. I don't think you can beat a manual method."

Urbans are disgusting. "He's clean." Anton removed his fingers from Mike, tossing the nitrile glove into the bucket of melted inserts.

"Relative term," the Sergeant said, turning to the group. "I'm sure everyone is well rested after such a long drive. We're going on a run."

Private Mike Wink hiked up his pants and avoided Anton's eyes as they finally exited the bus.

The transport had pulled up to the outskirts of a fence. High-intensity searchlights, brighter than anything Anton had ever seen, gave everything the appearance of a high noon sun. The illusion shattered as the Sergeant walked away from the fence and to a night sky dotted with sparse clouds.

"I'm not repeating myself," Sergeant said with a calm edge to his voice.

The group fell into the Sergeant's wake in a slow steady jog away from the lights. As they left what Anton assumed to be the base, it took a few minutes for his eyes to adjust to the darkness. The horizon was dim yellow.

Dom-Chi lights... How are they so bright? Anton's heart raced from the growing light in the distance while the rest of the group sucked air from the run.

Wink collapsed and the recruits used it to catch their breath.

"Now, now," the Sergeant said. "What happened here, Private Wink? Did I say you could stop?"

"Rolled ankle," Mike said through clenched teeth.

"Awe, poor baby." The Sergeant's eyes glowed green in the night.

He has inserts.

"Nothing's broken. Run." The Sergeant jogged into the curtain of the night, the recruits in tow.

There could be pumas here too. Anton went to help Mike from the ground.

"Stay the fuck away from me, fertilizer boy," Mike said.

Anton shook his head and jogged to catch up with the Sergeant and his recruits. The glow of Dom-Chi fell behind them, and Anton's heart slowed as the run dragged on. Like a house of cards, the other recruits collapsed at once. Mike hadn't caught up.

"Only an hour. So sad," the Sergeant said, taking notes through his OPTO-insert. "I told none of you to stop. Get up or I swear it will be worse for you."

Everyone stood, gasping as they tried to jog after him as best they could.

Anton followed in between the Sergeant and the group. *I don't want to be in that man's gaze.*

Dirt beneath their feet became pavement. Eventually, faint, squat buildings broke the skyline as they crested a hillock.

We didn't arrive at the base before.

The Sergeant and Anton arrived at the base first, with the rest of the group, sans Mike, arriving shortly afterwards.

"Grissom," the Sergeant said, "you still look fresh. Can you go for more?"

"If need to."

"Grissom, you will address me as Sir or Lieutenant Sumpf. Do you understand?"

"Sir, Yes Sir."

"He gets it!" The Lieutenant spread his arms at the group, who lay gasping for air on the ground. "And you all think he's stupid. Grissom and I will now continue running on our track over here. The rest of you will go into this building to be deloused and shaved. You will join us and match us until he is as tired as you sacks of shit."

Everyone looked at Anton, pleading like the dogs did in holos.

There will be an amount of running that will please the Lieutenant and let them off the hook.

Anton followed Lt. Sumpf to the track and ran. The track's lines glowed in the dark, but he didn't have time to think about them.

The Lieutenant set a pace that burned Anton's legs after the first lap, and by the third lap lead replaced muscle. The Lieutenant's feet beat the ground like a drum. Anton focused on putting one foot in front of the other and drawing deep breaths.

Thud, thud, the biological metronome of their feet ticked Anton into a meditative state where the track dissolved into the fields of the family stead.

Darren and Anton worked in the southern sector. The quad broke down. They had a fifty-mile run back home and laughed as the sun marched across the sky.

Darren sagged in front of him.

"Twin, you're slowing." Anton smiled.

"God, damn it, Grissom." The Lieutenant puffed as he stopped and put his hands on his knees.

Anton blinked from his daydreams.

"I've got every supplement available to our forces running through these veins, and you look fine."

The sun cracked the horizon in the east.

It's dawn?

The group of recruits had collapsed at various points across the track, littering it like victims of a sniper.

"Sir, Sorry, Sir," Anton said.

The Lieutenant blew out his lungs. "You will be." He kicked recruits awake as he passed.

Anton followed, unsure what he should do.

"Since Grissom decided to be a fuck-up, no one is eating today."

The Lieutenant jogged towards the base.

Now visible in the daylight, the base was a collection of modular single-story buildings with a fence around it. There were no towers with high-powered lights, but there were metal protrusions that looked like snail shells on the fence.

"What those?" Anton asked Alex.

"Scanjammers," they said, looking at Anton for confirmation. Anton blinked, unsure what those words meant.

"They block electronics and any communications that are unwanted."

Anton nodded. *Don't know how that would work.*

"Jesus, what did you do to the Lieutenant to piss him off hayseed?" Beca said as she caught up to him.

"Ran. Thought make him happy."

"You ran all night?" Beca asked.

Anton shrugged. *Maybe?*

As they jogged to the fence, its mesh expanded and created a hole for them to pass through before sealing behind.

Never seen a gate like that.

Distant yelling rolled across the base, one quiet and one in a booming response. Turning the corner, Anton finally stopped running and his mouth dropped. Several platoons of Dominion forces were arranged into formations. A lone man walked along, inspecting them, asking questions, expecting answers.

So many people. His stomach dropped and anxiety infested his shoulders.

"There's the crack in that armor," Lt. Sumpf said, his breath hot on Anton's neck. "Assemble!" he boomed.

Anton stumbled after the rest of the group of recruits who went to join a square assembly that lacked five people.

"Ah, Lieutenant Sumpf, I see you've brought in the newest batch of meat for me." The lone inspector said through an artificially loud voice. Shorter than Anton by half a head and ten paces away, he still loomed large.

"That I have, Lieutenant Ink, that I have."

"How long do we have them for?"

"Six months."

"And how many days is that?"

"One hundred and eighty."

"You hear that meat? One hundred and eighty days. Now let's get started."

***

Next foot, next foot. Plastic bark bit Anton's skin from the log on his shoulder. Muscles ached from the constant throwing of the weight. Thunder cracked from two squads collapsing thirty paces away. Lieutenant Ink and Sumpf split to thumb scan them. Eight were left to bake in the sun, the other eight were told to go back home.

Not everyone is a criminal and forced to be here.

"We're moving, shitheels." Lt. Ink clapped his hand and the train ground forward.

The sun set as they returned to the base, recruits collapsed against the logs they carried.

"You fucked us, Grissom," Beca rasped. "Without food—"

"No one was fed," a black woman said from a neighboring log. "We were told we looked too fed."

A communal canteen was handed to Anton. He passed it to Beca and removed his shirt to squeeze the sweat into his mouth. The Lieutenants stood in front of the group and ate SR-bars with their mouths open. Lt. Sumpf locked eyes with Anton, who finished draining the sweat from his shirt.

Drank worse my whole life, Sumpf.

The moon was high in the sky, Anton and the other recruits ran without logs, finally.

"What is your name?" Lt. Ink yelled.

"Sagira—"

"Wrong, it is 0516. Nova, why are you here?"

"Wrong place—"

"Wrong, there is no reason for you to be here. How long do I own you for?"

"A hundred—"

"Wrong, I will always own you. For these failures we will work through the night."

Food was handed out on the second day, an SR-bar in foil with an expiration date of a year ago.

Anton ate it anyway. He was halfway through when Lt. Ink put a thumb scanner before him.

"Grissom," Lt. Ink read from the scanner. He knocked the ration to the ground and kicked dirt on it. "As you were."

Anton was too hungry to waste it, chewing through a malted bar with a now crunchy coating of dirt.

The third day arrived, and they still hadn't slept. Soreness and pain had bled into a numbness Anton had never experienced before. *I have no option to leave.*

"How many days until you're done?" The Lieutenant asked the squads.

"Sir, one-hundred and seventy-seven, Sir," the company responded in unison.

They continued this throughout the day. The runs interspersed with push-ups, the logs heavier, the group of soldiers shrinking. As the sun set on the third day, the lieutenants brought them to a hangar partially covered in earth.

Finally, rest. Anton stepped into the hangar and a winter breeze assaulted him. *No.*

Sweat-soaked clothes chilled and the groups' breath hung in the air like cotton balls.

"Everyone has worked so hard, we've decided to reward you with a bath." Lt. Ink tapped a button by the door. The nearest wall folded to the ground, revealing an artificial beach with lapping waves.

"Now bathe," Lt. Sumpf said.

Numbed by the cold, the soldiers shuffled into the water. Ice stabbed Anton's skin, he closed his eyes.

They won't beat me.

"They forgot their soap," Lt. Ink said.

"They'll have to soak longer then," Lt. Sumpf responded, a calm malice in his voice.

Anton shivered, everyone shivered, their teeth chattering like crickets. He urinated on himself, the brief respite of warmth lost to an icy wave crashing over them. The group yelped, some cried. They linked arms together in an attempt to get warmer. Anton pulled unknown soldiers closer. *Cold doesn't matter.*

"Do they look clean enough?" Lt. Sumpf asked Lt. Ink.

"It will have to do. Everyone out."

Anton pushed through sluggish limbs, helping slower soldiers from the waves and back outside.

"It's warm enough, you will all sleep here." Lt. Sumpf said.

Everyone lay on the dirt outside of the chilled room and fell asleep, no questions asked.

They were awoken in the morning before the sun rose.

"Lieutenant Sumpf, the recruits are dirty again, and we just washed them. Why did they sleep on the ground?"

"Because they're retarded, Lieutenant Ink. Because, they're retarded."

They were shuffled back into the cold water to be cleaned. This went on for at least a week, Anton lost count after day seven. His world became a singular focus.

I won't let these two beat me.

Two months of torture passed as a grueling day and left only a handful of soldiers. Beca, Tom, Alex, and Sagira, the black woman from the log on the first night, remained with Anton. Adapted to less sleep, their training pivoted to firearms, explosives, tactics, and strategy. Anton soaked it all in like the dry soil did rain back home. Given bunks and fresh clothes, they became a squad separated from the rest.

"What happen to all that gone?" Anton asked, sitting on his top bunk in their barracks.

"All that left," Tom corrected.

"They're grunts now," Beca said, biting into an extra SR-loaf she stole from the kitchen. She handed pieces to everyone, who wolfed it down to avoid getting caught.

"I haven't even seen 'em," Sagira said with a heavy drawl. She rubbed her scalp where hair grew back thick and curly.

"They go to a different base." Beca leaned back on her bunk. "Those who can't cut it but don't have any other options go to a flotilla prison."

"What tomorrow training?" Anton lay back on his bunk and yawned.

"Urban training and live fire."

Urban training. Anton's heart raced and his brow furrowed.

"You don't have to worry, Anton," Sagira said. "It's a simulation, not the real thing."

"The moment we finish, we have to take the boy to Dom-Chi." Tom laughed. "All this work and simulation might be for nothing if his head explodes when he sees urban for the first time."

Anton nodded, swallowing and rubbing the nerves from his shoulder. "Maybe I take you rural. To fields. See how you do?"

"This base is too rural for me already," Beca said. "There is no civilization anywhere, it's…"

"Fucked up," Tom finished.

"Yeah." Alex rolled awake. "Gotta take this boy to a strip club, or hell, I hear Dom-Chi's got some of the best brothels this side of the Mississippi."

"Now that"—Beca smiled—"is a much better idea. Hit an exaggerant bar, make sure everyone has a real nice time." Beca appraised everyone carefully. "Let me guess. Tom won't be picky. Anton will have a girl, his little brain would explode with anything else. Sagira will choose a man, probably some pecan flavored pie such as herself"—the group laughed—"And Alex…"

The laughter stopped.

Everyone wants to know. "Alex, you boy or girl?"

The group's eyes darted between Anton and Alex, awkward glances bleeding into embarrassed blushes.

"It's fine you fuckbois." Alex sat up. "My family were seasteaders on Old Orleans. The runoff from the Mississippi and the Hive had hormones in it. Messed up everyone on my boat. The kids born my year were in between. None of the doctors could tell the sex, must have made for some awkward deliveries." Alex mimed a Doctor pulling out a baby and squinting at it. "It's a… shit, I dunno." They laughed.

"Your filters didn't get rid of them?" Sagira asked.

"Didn't realize they were broken… obviously," Alex said. "So yeah, I don't know what I am. Kinda got both and yet, got none. Don't care what you all call me."

"Aye," Anton said. *How can you be both?*

"A fucking rock is what you are with how you sleep," Beca said. "I'm surprised we even woke you."

"I see an opportunity to show Hayseed some culture in Dom-Chi," Alex said. "I'm on board. You got any more of that ration?"

Beca tossed the last piece, Alex caught it in their mouth, and rolled back over to sleep.

"And Beca," Alex said, "I'll just hire you when we get to Dom-Chi." Tom, Anton, and Sagira laughed. Beca's ears turned a bright red.

"Does anyone have the intel packet for tomorrow's training?" Beca changed the subject. "We can get a leg up and figure out assignments now."

"I do." Anton pulled his tablet from his pack against the wall. He tossed it to Beca, who set it on the ground between them and turned on the hologram. In front of Anton was a termite mound, slowly rotating in the holographic's rainbow hue.

"Hostage rescue," Sagira said, appraising the holo. "Looks to be diplomats, held by a collective's regional militia."

"What's our entry point?" Tom hopped off his bunk for a better look.

"Gotta be… here." Beca tapped a side door.

"That'll be guarded," Anton said, the hive becoming more like a ten-story building the longer he looked at it. "We should come in from here." He pointed to the roof.

"We don't have any air transport for the training mission," Sagira said.

"We climb." Anton spun the hologram so the back of the building rose to view. "No windows on back for thermals."

"It's more than fifty meters," Sagira said. "We're asking to get tagged."

Anton paused and considered the distance. *It's not that far for me.* "I go, with Alex. You three hit the door. Won't expect split push."

Sagira grabbed the tablet and scrolled through the intel given to them. "It's not against the rules of engagement for this training."

"I'm in," Beca said. "Weapons?"

"All using simunition, but sidearms, sonic rifles, flash and smoke grenades. Basic stuff."

"Inserts?" Tom asked.

"Not banned, so those too," Sagira said

"Hostages are where?" Tom asked.

"Unknown, we'll find out when we're in there."

"Nothing?"

"Unless you can see it on the holo and I can't."

"Alright, alright. Just seems…"

"Not good," Anton finished.

They pored over the hologram and briefings for missing data until late in the night.

"I can't see anything." Tom yawned.

"No point in continuing," Sagira said. "We should sleep now anyways."

"Aye." Anton yawned and fell asleep.

***

The next day, Anton pulled himself over the cracked, concrete rooftop of the termite mound-turned-building and trained his rifle on the far door.

Too easy. "Not good," Anton commed to Alex through their ENT-inserts as they advanced to the entry point. His voice below a whisper, the insert amplified it for his squad to hear. He pressed his back against the wall by the door.

"What did he say?" Tom asked.

"Breach it." Alex kicked down the door.

Anton leaned low around the door-frame. A poorly lit corridor that radiated stale sweat and gunpowder lay empty ahead.

"Nothing on infrared or night vision," Alex whispered to Anton's left.

Anton entered, pivoting into the first room on the right. A green tarp lay in a lone beam of sunlight. Anton and Alex swept the entire floor, getting only empty rooms.

"Clear on floor ten," Alex said.

"Clear on floor one," Beca returned.

With a hand gesture, Anton and Alex descended the flight of stairs. Alex scanned each floor as they went and they paused on floor seven.

"Did you forget your OPTO-inserts?" Alex whispered to Anton.

"I don't like them."

"Motherfucker, this is my ass on the line. You'll wear them."

"Didn't bring them."

"God damn it hayseed—"

A tin can crinkled and crushed below them.

"Target floor six," Anton commed, descending to the sixth floor hallway.

"Roger that," Sagira returned.

Thin beams of light highlighted motes of dust suspended in the air. Anton aimed his rifle into the dim and checked the stairwell.

Crack, pop! Anton's right ear rang with the static as his singular insert fried. He dropped to one knee, training his rifle on the hallway.

"I can't see," Alex said. "Fuck I can't hear."

Crap. Anton put his hand over their mouth, rolling them onto their back as he lay prone beside them. His squad squirmed at the bottom of the stairs, their cries unintelligible through the static.
Focus. His heart raced as he lay in the dim.
Doors opened at the end of the hallway and apparitions exited. The targets wore a jagged three-dimensional camouflage that must have made them invisible to his squads OPTO-inserts.
Don't care. Anton fired. Simunition and tracer fire lit the hallway. The ghosts dropped to the ground or dove back into their doorways. Crack, pop! The insert burned in his ear and the static stopped.

"Oh god it's gone black," Alex sounded like they stood fields away. Again the apparitions exited the doorway and approached.

Got you. Anton lit them up.

"Didn't check your six," a modulated voice said as cold metal touched the base of Anton's neck.
Anton kicked at their leg, knocking the voice down the stairs. Anton sat to fire—
Pain snapped into his sides. Anton gasped as a ghost from the hallway kicked him in the ribs and sent him into a tumble down the stairs. Anton cracked against the wall, laying by the very man he'd knocked down only moments ago.

Back in the daylight outside of the building, a disheveled Lt. Sumpf gave a complete tactical breakdown.

"You three"—the Lieutenant pointed at Tom, Beca and Sagira—"were all dead on the first floor. Overly reliant on your inserts, we stalked you from moment one." He turned towards Anton and Alex. "And you, well, what would you have done if you heard no response from your squad?"

Commed for medivac, but you don't want an answer. Anton and Alex remained silent.

"Today's lesson was about reliance on technology. You all died because you relied on it. There might be technological wonders where you're from, but on an operation? There have to be back up plans. And then back up plans to those back up plans. Do you understand me?"

"Sir, Yes Sir," they responded in unison.

"We will run this back, again and again, until you're all comfortable working without the inserts."

They walked back to the base in silence.

"Embarrassing." Alex collapsed into their bunks. "I fucking panicked hardcore."

"We fell into each other," Beca said. "Couldn't hear or see, managed to grab one another and put our backs against a wall."

"I don't know how we missed them," Tom said.

"Get tape," Anton said, gesturing to their insert pouch.

Tom gathered their inserts, attempted to pull the data, but Sagira's and Beca's were fried. They got the footage from Tom's, but only for the first two floors.

"At least it's something," Beca said.

They re-watched the footage on the tablet, altering wavelengths as they went.

"There." Anton paused and rewound the video.

Within a squalid concrete room, a blurred smear vaguely humanoid in shape was pressed against the wall.

"Visible light, can see… a little."

"The inserts must do some image processing even on the visible spectrum," Tom said. "Fascinating that they figured out a way to bypass it. That was never on the net back home and we missed the signals during the op."

"Doesn't change the fact that on floor six they were gunna EMP us and fry them," Alex said.

Anton sighed, and everyone looked at him. "One insert in, one out, forever," he said.

***

A year of training passed, and Anton pivoted into a subterranean bunker along one of the Great Lakes.

"Well we overdressed," Alex's voice crackled through their inserts. Power cables filled the floor. Anton stepped into an airplane hangar with rows of chest freezers and scientists zip-tied in front of them.

"Cloners," Tom said over a microscope.

"We'll give you the data, don't kill us," a scientist said.

"You've scared them, Alex." Sagira smiled.

"Pull the data," Anton said, cycling his comm. "Command, we've willing, unarmed civilians, no soldiers."

"Roger that, return them to base."

"Aye."

"Not bad work for our first op." Tom pocketed several hard drives.

"First bullshit op," Alex said.

"Catching criminals isn't bullshit," Anton said.

Alex smiled. "Sagira, I think we've cured his accent."

**

Months after the raid, the squad sat in a squat beige building at the edge of base.
'The Shed', as Alex called it, was a forgotten administrative unit they cleaned and claimed. Gym, dojo, mission control, spa, and sports bar—it was their private club.

"I'm sick of waiting around." Tom paced the room. "There has to be a deployment or mission we can go on. Shore leave, something."

"Leave would be good," Alex said, staring out the window.

"Where would we even go?" Anton said.

"I heard that some seasteaders were attacking the NYC." Beca ran on a treadmill.

"From where?" Tom asked.

"I'm just saying it's been a problem for a while now. Aristocrats don't want to deal with that shit."

"She's got a point," Alex said. "Fuck, look busy—"

"Nice place y'all got here." Lt. Sumpf stood at the door to the Shed. Anton grabbed a tablet. Alex oiled their rifle as the squad dashed to look busy.

"I'm not stupid," Lt. Sumpf said. "And I'm your lieutenant for this deployment."

Crap.

The squad's eyes darted to one another. Was this a trap?

"Wipe the stupid look of off your faces," Lt. Sumpf said. "I've been particularly brutal to you, because I knew I'd be taking a squad for real assignments from your class. My ass isn't going on the line if I don't have faith in my unit."

That's the closest thing to a compliment you've—

"So I woke up this morning and prayed all day because I'm stuck with your sorry asses."

There it is. Anton smirked.

"We're shipping out tomorrow, oh-five-hundred. Front gate."

"Where are we going?" Tom asked.

"Dom-Chi first, then through Metro-Montreal. Final destination will be decided en route."

"Anytime for a break in Dom-Chi?" Alex asked. "Sir."

"No. We're getting on a transport ASAP. It's fueling now."

Alex's shoulders sank, and they went back to looking out the window.

"Pack your shit." The Lieutenant left the door open as he walked away.

Anton walked back to their barracks. He'd grown used to the grounds of the base, the dirt close enough to the brownish soil of his stead. The first few weeks had been the roughest, more from being surrounded by people than the work. At least that's how he remembered it.

He shook his head. *Leaving home again.* Anton packed ultra-lite body armor, one change of fatigues, and his rifle. As the group's scout and vanguard, he had to go light, fast, and he finished packing first.

Tom packed his signal boosters, tablets, drones, and clothing into his case and bag. Beside him, Beca organized small explosive ordinances into her bag, hand axes, hammers, electro-magnetic pulse grenades, and standard grenades. Down the line, Sagira polished her sniper rifle before plugging it and locking it into its carry bag. Alex finalized their launchers, machine guns, and heavy caliber weaponry in their cases. As everyone finished, they lay on their bare bunks and slept.

But Anton tossed and turned. Dom-Chi's skyline loomed in his mind. *Most people I ever saw was at this camp and that didn't go well.* He rolled over and found Alex staring at him. Anton tapped his ears and eyes, a gesture asking them to put their inserts in so they could talk in silence.

"What's up?" Alex asked.

"Even you can't sleep."

"Obviously."

"I can't stop thinking about going urban. I've heard... stories."

"All of them true."

"I'm serious."

"Think about it this way. Your squad is reformed criminals. We were cast out from urban. We're the danger."

"And you're all terrible."

"Ha ha. We're not even staying there. Buckle up, we'll be out of it in no time."

"Why can't you sleep?"

"I'm... ready. When I was raiding back home, I'd get ancy before leaving and couldn't sleep. This is the same thing... but it's sanctioned."

"Aye." But Anton didn't fully understand them.

"I'm going on a run. You're more than welcome to join."

"Aye."

They padded out of the bunks and ran around the polywooden complex in the dark. After the first lap, Tom joined them, followed by Sagira and Beca. Each lap reminded them they'd trained for this. Each lap proved they were in shape for this. And each lap pounded home that this was their job.

Hours passed, and Lt. Sumpf arrived at the barracks.

"I don't believe my eyes," the Lieutenant said. "The scouts said my squad was running around the base, and here you all are."

"Sir, sorry Sir. Couldn't sleep," Anton said.

"That's good. You're not as dumb as you all look." Lt. Sumpf checked a sun bleached wristwatch. "Go eat breakfast. We'll leave shortly afterwards."

"Sir, yes Sir," Beca said.

The group jogged off to the canteen. They inhaled their food, and Anton led them towards the gate as a green transport truck rumbled to the front.

"Which one of you is the driver?" Lt. Sumpf asked from the passenger window.

"Me," Sagira said.

"Coordinates are in the GPS. Let's go."

The morning sun bled red on the horizon. Anton took a deep breath and exhaled through his nose to calm his nerves.
We'll be in and out. But his childhood trick of remaining calm evaporated as the transport turned. The rising sun lit the silhouette of countless spires that formed the Dominion of Chicago's skyline. The spires reaching for the clouds cast shadowy fingers across the undulating rusted sprawl of low-rises looming ahead of them.
Anton's heart skipped a beat. *Holy shit.*

Chapter 6 - Luciana

Luciana squeezed her legs against the bike chassis. It bounced onto an on-ramp out of the Pucker. The heads-up display rolled across the canopy, negating the oncoming headlight glare. It highlighted the cars around, displaying the SUV-transport she burned by traveled at 110 km/h and weighed 500kg.
Nice tech.
The HUD highlighted potholes kilometers ahead, and the bike shifted into the leftmost lane and headed south. The rumble strip shook against Luciana's chest, the bike accelerating.

"Destination," Luciana said.
The bike hit 250 km/h. She reached around for controls, but everything was smooth to the touch. There weren't any seams inside the bike either.

"Arrival?" Luciana tried.
The bike ignored her.
She passed through the wealthy hub of West San Francisco Bowl. Where the Pucker was in a constant state of dried dirt, dust, and detritus, this precinct was a different country. Polished to a near mirror sheen, nothing was out of place. The buildings rose hundreds of floors. Wushan, Taketa, Vio, Micron, X-Systems, the big five corporations' logos on the top in a competition to see who could be the tallest and the brightest.
Luciana hadn't been this deep into the wealth district before. *It's beautiful in a gross way.* Reminding her it was the same country was the sky. Always that same shade of yellow during the day, with a red sunrise and sunset. As it was now, making the city look more like it was on Mars than Earth had people ever settled on another planet.

"Estimated time of arrival?" Luciana tried.
Debris shields deployed on some buildings, their carbon-fiber shimmering in the neons. When the detritus storm hit this area, the daily routine wouldn't change. Most people here spent their lives

indoors, protected from the air and dirt. Robo-janitors would scrub the streets clean before the rare few left their buildings.

"Location?"

But the bike continued its journey.

Not getting shit from this.

The Wealth district fell behind and grime grew on shrinking buildings. Advertisements in neons, whites, and ultraviolets burned on the side of buildings against the sunset's red glow. Luciana had walked beneath that canopy of light countless nights, sometimes not even realizing the sun had set.

Where am I going? She tried to get the pack behind her for the tablet, but couldn't reach it. *Damn it.* She cycled her OPTO-insert to the net and searched for Taketa locations. A map came up with two dots, one in the Southern Empire and one in the New York Collective. *This is going to be a long trip. What am I supposed to do if I have to use the bathroom?* She disliked using her OPTO-inserts as a browser, it cut off her surroundings too much, and she turned it off.

The bike accelerated as the buildings shrank, the lights dimmed, and the stream of vehicles became a trickle. At the edge of the city, only landfill lights burned against the night. Working around the clock, dump trucks collected waste from underground conveyors as the gulls and carrion birds flocked around them. Vehicles pulled tarps to cover the unburied and unprocessed waste.

Preparing for the storm. The bike flew by the last off ramp to this rim of civilization.

"Rural," Luciana whispered.

The last streetlight passed by in a blink. The HUD cycled, and the world illuminated in a night vision better than Luciana had ever seen. In the distance, skeletal buildings rose, long without power, water lapped at their second stories. Road damage highlighted in the distance and the bike accelerated between potholes, cracks, and debris that hadn't been cleaned from the last storm. At the bottom right of the window, the speedometer ticked over 500 km/h.

Luciana's stomach dropped. "Ok, now I have to use the bathroom."

Plastic slid against her groin.

The fuck? She lifted her torso. The saddle had opened, revealing a round bucket-like container.

"This gyrocycle—"

"Motherfu!" Luciana flinched.

"—has been designed for extended trips and has a built-in bathroom," the Asian woman on the HUD continued. "Please position yourself accordingly. It responds to the commands 'bathroom' and 'done'."

"You've got to be fucking kidding me."

The Asian woman smiled and disappeared.

Luciana sighed, shimmied down her pants, and used the container. She reached into her overcoat for a tissue and threw that in the container too.

"Done."

The container lowered and the panel slid seamlessly back into place.

"Fucking ridiculous." *This better be worth it.*

She cycled her ENT-insert to her library of music. After some ninety-six hours of being awake, sleep caught her off guard, dragging her into a thankfully dreamless abyss.

Luciana fell, waking at the sudden drop of the bike taking an off ramp. It was still dark outside. The highway descended onto a recently paved road and mountains rose ahead. She flipped her OPTO-inserts to a web page, but got no signal.

That's weird.

The bike slowed as the road wound into the foothills. Gaining elevation on a jaggedly cut gradient in the hillside, the road turned back towards the valley. The off-ramp and the highway was gone, replaced with a perfect pattern of cereal crops that stretched to the horizon.

What the fuck?

The road turned back towards the mountains, arriving at a tunnel built into the hill with a heavy metal gate and an armed guard.

The bike stopped. A scanning beam came from the top of the tunnel, bathing her in green light. The guard looked to be just under two meters tall, his muscles bulging beneath light gear. After a moment, the gate moved and the guard went back to searching the horizon like Luciana was no more than a tumbleweed blowing through. The bike drove into the tunnel, pulling into a parking spot by a metal door that belonged in a submarine. The bike canopy slid back, the sides opened, and Luciana stepped out to stretch.

Here for a reason. She inhaled a sweet and unfamiliar odor.

The door opened and the Asian woman from the bike HUD stepped out.

"Hello Luciana Gutierrez, I am Saori Chaude." She extended her hand, which Luciana shook. "What did you think of the Kage gyrocycle?" Saori gestured towards the bike.

"I'm stiff as fuck." Luciana stretched and winced. A coil wound into her back from a punk's punch two days ago.

"That is something we will have to work on." Saori took notes with one of her OPTO-inserts. "Do you have any other feedback?"

"The bathroom is weird?"

"You used it! I told the engineers that people would want one."

"I would have been fine with getting out somewhere, but I couldn't figure out how to open the doors."

Saori grinned at the ceiling. "We had a bet, beer for the whole lab on the loser. I won. Anyways, welcome to Taketa-8. Our apologies for the secrecy. You must have questions."

"Yeah, I do." *Where do I start?* "What's that smell?" spilled from her mouth.

Saori smiled. "You've never been rural. That's grass. It grows all over these hills."

Saori turned towards the door, expecting her to follow. Luciana grabbed her pack, and the bike shut itself as she left.

"This is our primary entrance." Saori gestured for Luciana to continue inside. "You saw the Sergeant at the gate. Most of our

The Last 0-Day

contracts are UCSA military, corps, and former governments. We have more protection than we need."

They walked past doors with assorted stickers, radioactive, biohazard, laser warnings, and some layered triangles that Luciana couldn't decipher. The hallway's design looked to be forty years older than anything she had seen, the tiles stained yellow over the decades, insulated pipes and wiring ran along the ceiling.

Chief, what cutting-edge shit comes from here?

They stopped at a door with no labels, and Saori punched in a code. They entered a conference room where a man sat in front of a blank wall screen. The wallscreens to the left and right displayed city-like vistas, but Luciana couldn't tell where the skyline was.

The man stood. He was five-eight, maybe, wore a starched lab coat, and had rapidly graying hair around a growing bald spot.

"Hello Ms. Gutierrez," the man said. "I see you met my associate Saori. You must be hungry, would you like some coffee or breakfast? The sun will rise soon."

"I got a eugeroic hangover, so that'd be great." Luciana's stomach growled.

"Saori, can you go to the break room, grab three coffees, and some bars for Luciana. Thanks, we won't start without you."

Saori nodded and left.

"My name is Samir Lindeman. I run this branch of Taketa. How was your ride over? Uneventful, I am assuming."

"Yeah, it was fine. Didn't expect the training to be rural. I've never been out before."

"We will have to make sure you get some time to go around the mountains. There is a tranquility that can't be recreated back urban. Most people never get to experience it. They prefer this." He gestured to the city skylines on the wallscreens. "Helps with the homesickness of the transplantees," he added, a small frown creasing his face.

"You don't?"

"You have interrogation training." Samir chuckled. "No, I don't. I married a Rural. Met her when she came to get replacement parts for a harvester outside of Dom-Chi. I couldn't get a date until I managed to get out to her plot. This posting is perfect for me, a marriage of the two worlds." He finished with a tone suggesting he was proud of the double entendre.

Saori came back in with three coffees on a holder and two bars on a plate. She slid a coffee and the bars over. Luciana grabbed a bar, it was warm and smelled of a fruit she didn't know. She took a bite and ecstasy rolled over her tongue.

"What's—" Luciana started, but her mouth was too full. She drank coffee to wash it down. "What is this?"

"We make them in house," Samir said. "Local nuts and berries with the standard oats, soy, and insect protein mixture. One of the benefits of being remote. The self-reliance makes us resourceful."

Saori sat opposite of Samir at the end of the table.

"How much do you know of why you're here?" Samir asked.

"Not a ton," Luciana said. "This morning, it was HQ for training and equipment. In the afternoon it was straight to Taketa."

They glanced at one another.

"What?" Luciana asked, sensing a change in the room.

"You didn't volunteer?" Samir said.

"No, Chief said to get on the bike and it'd take me here. Why?"

The scientists looked at one another again. Samir rubbed his neck, opening his mouth several times to speak.

Saori spoke first. "You were supposed to be told that you're receiving cutting-edge inserts."

"I assumed it was some new scrambler, maybe some souped-up inserts and their associated tactics. How complicated can this be?"

"We're not here to talk about the stunners or inserts. We're here to talk about implants." Samir regained his composure. "Have you heard anything about them?"

"Vaguely, some slides about them back at the Academy. Inserts wired to the body, but they're a pipe dream."

"Were a pipe dream," Samir said.

"She may not look it," Saori said, "but this installation is the world leader in implant technology and its applications. Your department was chosen to receive this technology."

Implants are real now? Wait, the Pucker is getting cutting edge tech? "Why?"

"All sides of the Bowl want Precinct Nineteen cleaned out, correct?" Saori said. "The non-lethals didn't work and fixing those is years away. The government came to Taketa for help when current tactics aren't working. We came up with the plan of implanting an officer to make them more effective. It is a win-win for everyone. We get to show the power of the technology in civilian policing of the worst areas. East Bowl gets its borough back."

"Then why me?"

"You are the top scoring officer in your precinct. It was a no-brainer to be offered to you," Saori said.

"It wasn't offered."

"Be that as may, it is now. Listen to what we're proposing and you can decide then." Saori turned. "Samir, if you would be so kind."

"Right." The screen behind him turned to an overlay of the Pucker. "Analyzing your precinct, we found several areas we can help through upgraded traditional police technology. You have, essentially, guerrilla gangs within an indifferent populace and cannot use superior firepower to flush them out due to political pressure and costs." Samir spoke with a cold detachment common among doctors when talking about patients.

The wall changed to a picture of a typical street in the Pucker. Apartments stacked on top of one another, tangled cables running the walls, and countless pipes running the concrete.

"This is exacerbated by the clutter and disarray of the streets. In this picture"—highlights overlaid on ducts, garbage piles, and banners—"we found a minimum of thirty places that one can hide contraband, weapons, explosives, and people. All missed by current standard scanning technology too. Additionally, reports received from your department shows that ambushes are a common problem, with one having a lethal outcome for a fellow officer—"

Saori coughed. "That was her, Samir, she was there."

"Right." Samir blushed. "Sorry, I forgot. I rarely see names on the reports."

Erik. Luciana stared at the presentation, burying the rage and sadness bubbling within her.

Samir opened his mouth several times but fell off his script.

"With officers being targeted"—Saori took the baton—"and current scanning technology being blocked, we found a common solution. Semi-automated back-up with both old and new abilities." The screen changed to a picture of a gyrocycle similar to the one Luciana had ridden.

"The first is a gyrocycle that you can control remotely. Legally, autonomous machines can't respond to a crisis situation and remote technology requires a dedicated pilot nearby."

Luciana drank coffee, letting the scalding liquid burn the feelings about Erik from her throat and leaning in.

"I'm sure you noticed on the way over that the bike had no controls inside of it. That was a prototype of the one you will receive. You won't need any external controls. With implantation, you will be able to directly control the bike whether or not you are inside it."

The picture changed to show weapons, countermeasures, and abilities of the gyrocycle.

"This is the part of the project that my lab has worked on the most." Saori turned to Samir. "You should do the reveal on the next part."

"Right." Samir cleared his throat. "As pointed out, another solution is to use older technologies that will be unexpected."

The screen changed to a canine with brown and black patches on its back and face.

Luciana's jaw dropped. *I've only seen those on holo's.*

Samir continued. "Although the larger breeds of dog have seen a fall in use, records statistically indicate that they were excellent work animals in the past. Additionally, this breed is unrivaled in its ability to sense chemical compounds through its nasal passages with the appropriate training. We plan to implant the dog to receive commands directly from you, with no verbal queue. Feedback will be delivered to an OPTO-insert. Simple yes and nos, but it will get the job done."

"And how am I going to send those commands?" Luciana asked.

"We have a surgical suite in this compound where we would implant a personalized insert that will translate and transmit your neurological signals to the receivers on the bike and canine unit."

"This is insane," Luciana said. "How can implants have advanced so quickly?"

"For one, it hasn't been fast," Saori said. "Inserts did most of the work, figuring out how people responded to changes in stimuli and miniaturizing the technologies. While simultaneously neuroscientists were unraveling how the brain communicates with the body. Taketa put us all here to work together on bringing them to life."

The walls cycled from cityscapes to underwater, to pictures of the moon, to video of the front gate.

"As you can see," Saori said. "We have simple implants already done. I have access to the computer in my office and am cycling this screen. I built the gyrocycle, it's not as complex as this, but it's all one directional."

"And the dogs?" Luciana asked.

"That part is, admittedly, more complex and had some luck involved," Samir said. "Dogs coevolved with humans. They have a unique ability to read human faces and interpret commands. The neurological structures that underlie those abilities have proven to be equally fertile for receiving inputs from human-dog-neurolinks."

"And because we have had this question before," Saori said. "You're not a guinea pig or the first. The guard you saw outside has significantly more hardware than is being planned for you. You're more than welcome to talk with him if you like."

Luciana turned towards Samir. *Have you been implanted?*

"Heart condition," Samir said sheepishly to the unspoken question.

"What I, we, are offering is a chance to be something more. This need not stop at Precinct Nineteen. If you want to change the Bowl, or if you want to find the gang who nearly killed you, it will be easier with this technology. Take your time and think on it. I can show you to the quarters we've prepared for you," Saori said with a finality that told Luciana the meeting was over.

Samir stayed seated and turned to the wall displaying a golden ocean of wheat under a bright blue sky.

Did you know what you were sending me into, Chief? "Lead the way." Luciana took her belongings, food, and followed Saori out of the room.

They walked down the corridor in silence. The lighting in this deeper part of the complex was brighter with the telltale blue tint of artificial sunlight.

I need more information. "How long would this take?" Luciana broke the silence. "We're undermanned back home and there are storms both forecasted and planned."

"A few weeks, you should be back before the end of the month," Saori said casually. "It might be a few weeks 'undermanned' but the change created by it would be worth it."

They paused in front of a door which opened for Saori. The room was clean, containing a single mattress, desk, chair, and wallscreen displaying the West Bowl's towering skyline from the ocean. Stepping inside, Luciana found a pillow on the ground by the door.

"What's that for?"

"Samir thinks that you should bond with a dog after implantation. Says it makes the commands stick better."

If I do it. "I'd like to talk to the guard who was augmented."

"He was going to be shifted out of Taketa-8 today. I'll make sure he finds you before he gets on the transport." Saori stood at the door and gestured down the hallway. "The bathroom is that way, three doors down. Cafeteria is the fifth door at this end." She pointed to the other end of the hallway. "Most of these rooms around you are filled with post-doctoral scholars of my and Samir's lab… We don't get many visitors, so some will be a little more inquisitive than others, but they mean well. We take turns cooking dinner during the weekdays, it's served at six." Saori smiled, the serious expression that had taken hold of her face during the meeting melting to the woman who met her at the door. "Though you've already had today's meal of 'mountain bars' as Mark calls them." Saori started down the hall before turning and handing Luciana a coin-sized black square on a lanyard. "This will open the door to the bathroom and kitchen. It also will lock-slash-unlock this door from the outside." Saori turned on her heels, leaving Luciana to her thoughts.

Luciana left her pack on the dog pillow and slung her overjacket on the back of the chair. She sat on the bed as the wall displayed an animated picture of East Bowl. Helicopters and planes landed at the airport, more debris shields rolled down the buildings. *Is this live? It can't be...* Luciana shook her head and set her mind to their proposal. *The technology is cutting edge, it could be dangerous.*
What if I die on the operating table? Luciana laughed. *Death hasn't mattered this year.*
What if something goes wrong and I'm left brain dead? Then I wouldn't know it went wrong.
What if it fails at a critical point during a patrol and people die? We're already dying and this could turn the tides in the Pucker to say nothing of the corruption in the Bowl.
Tactics ran through her head. Single person flanking, encirclements, suppressive fire all from her patrol vehicle alone. The dog could be the vanguard on operations, a smaller target, feeding back information unavailable by scanners. *If I had this a year ago, Erik would still be alive.* Her stomach growled. The wallscreen displayed a midday video of the Bowl's southern rim and its verdant mansions. *I need food.*

The hallway had the bleach scent left behind by robo-cleaners. *Reminds me of the academy dorms.* Conversations muffled through the kitchen door and Luciana carded through. The voices continued for a few seconds but fell silent as people registered an unfamiliar face.

Samir and a group of three junior scientists sat a table beneath the glow of a wallscreen displaying the NYC during a snowstorm.

"Hey, please come sit. I'll introduce you. This is Mark." Samir rested a hand on a man's shoulder. He was pudgier than Samir, with the same thinning hair, though it still had its color and his face had child-like cheeks. "He's from Saori's group."

Samir pointed towards a woman with coffee colored hair that ran down her back. "Don't let her stern look confuse you, Arsema's a sweetheart. She works in my lab on canine physiology." Samir rested his hand on the last person's shoulder. She looked to be Samir's age, her hair a weird shade of blonde, and her skin several tones darker than sunlamps gave. "This is my wife, Sara. She's the source of the wonderful berries, nuts, and all the other additions that spice up this place." He beamed.

Luciana stared, she hadn't seen a Rural in the flesh before. The color of her hair and skin must have been from the unfiltered sun. Her eyes a deep shade of green, showing no signs of insert wear and tear.

Sara smiled. "You never have blueberry before?" She spoke with an accent like the bad guys in the VR-movies Luciana saw as a child.

"What?" Luciana struggled to understand her.

"The taste, in the bar." Sara pointed towards the pan everyone was eating from.

"I haven't. They're amazing. I grew up with the vanillin syrups. Nothing like that."

"The bars are one of the best things we can make here," Mark said. "Beats the usual porridge and coffee, am I right?" He elbowed Arsema. Her face fell on a joke she'd heard a thousand times.

"Do we have any extras?" Arsema asked Sara. "The dogs always love them."

"No extra of the berry today, but I did find cervid bone. They can have."

"They love those too." Arsema stood. "Recon pack or boot?"

"Boot, leave me half," Sara said.

"Nice to meet you," Arsema said, leaving the kitchen.

"You'd think there would be some sort of doctor patient thing with her and the dogs," Mark said, finishing his food. "Or at least"—a timer beeped on his belt—"I gotta run now too, science calls. See you around."

"Guess I scared people off." Luciana sat.

"They don't take long break," Sara said. "Always rush in and out, before big experiment."

"What experiment?"

"Right, I haven't told them yet," Samir said. "That you haven't decided yet. Right?"

"Yeah, I'm still debating."

"Don't pressure her, Sami." Sara said.

"I'm not!"

"Aye, Sami, I know you're pressuring." Sara smirked, turning to Luciana. "This one, very nice, but always has his way."

"Not all the time, it took me years to convince you to move."

"Didn't say I wasn't better." Sara smiled.

Samir rolled his eyes. "I better get back to work. Saori probably didn't tell you, but your black keycard will give your tablet net access within the compound. It's filtered, so you won't get everything, but it's better than nothing." Samir kissed the top of Sara's head and left.

"He means well," Sara said. "Too many year studying. Knows too much about how brain works, but not enough about why."

Luciana nodded and chewed on the bar, drinking the water from a cup left by one of the scientists.

Sara went to the wall, cycling the wallscreen from a snowy NYC to the ocean of wheat beneath a blue sky.

"You have no inserts?" Luciana asked as Sara returned to the table.

"Hah, no, not my people way." Sara appraised Luciana. "First time with a, what you say, Rural?"

Luciana's ears burned.

Sara laughed. "Is ok, most who come here haven't ever seen us, let alone talk with one of us."

"I hadn't even gone rural until last night," Luciana said. "It's strange, the quiet, I don't even hear the HVAC in this building."

"On purpose, stealth building, as Sami says."

"What do you mean?"

Sara looked confused for a second. "Building is quiet for research purpose."

"That makes more sense." Luciana found more water in the researchers' cups. *Such waste.* She drank from one.

"No need, recycled here." Sara pointed towards the sink. "Urban usually not so careful. I like you. Have they shown you around?"

"Not yet."

"Come, I will show you the ground." Sara stood, moving the bars to the refrigerator and gesturing for Luciana to follow as she hit the door.

Sara swung a door inwards to a stairwell of corrugated metal and jogged up. Luciana matched her pace for the first six flights, but lead wound into her thighs.
Damn woman must do this daily. Luciana sucked air. After ten flights, she caught up to Sarah at a single door in cement.

"Thought you be in better shape." Sara put on antique sunglasses and opened the door.
Light poured into the stairwell, stinging Luciana's eyes in the moments it took her OPTO-inserts to shade in for protection. She followed Sara out onto a hillside that baked in the afternoon sun.
Where the valley floor was a perfect quilt of crops, switching between greens and gold depending on their stage in the harvest. The hillsides were golden and parched. The lack of buildings, roads, and civilization gave Luciana vertigo. She followed Sara's gaze to a part of the hill burnt black. Smoke rose at the next mountain chain, a line of fire marching on the horizon.

"Hopefully wind stays this way, will burn other direction. Sami says there is storm coming?"

"In a few weeks," Luciana said. Her initial nerves ignited with a primal fear at a fire that large. *How can she be content waiting on rain?*

"Normal," Sara said. "For out here anyway, fire normal. Come, let me show you inside." The door to the stairs was a sandy stone against the mountain.
I wouldn't be able to find that without knowing where it is. Luciana paused before entering, staring at the fire one last time.

"What's that smell?" Luciana asked as they stepped off on a new level.
"Urban." Sara laughed. "Ida, my dog."
Nails clicked on linoleum.
"I've seen some on screens, even touched a lapdog at the academy once—" Luciana froze.
Standing almost a meter tall and two meters long, something out of a nightmare turned the corner on its name. Black and gray human hair hung off of it in irregular patterns, it beelined for them. It skidded on the linoleum floor past Sara. While its body, size, and hair scared Luciana, its face immediately put them to rest. Hair grew out from its forehead, giving it eyebrows that grayed at the tips. Its eyes were a warm brown that asked Luciana for permission to do something. Sara petted her on the head.
"Here touch." Sara put Luciana's hand on the animal's neck.
The hair was polyfiber soft and warm. Sara stepped into a nearby room while Luciana continued petting the giant dog.
This is kind of nice. "What does it do?"
"When she was pup she help hunt. Now? She get fat and spoiled," Sara said lovingly towards the dog. "Thought you about to run when you saw her."
"I debated it."
Sara laughed, Luciana chuckled.
Sara pointed towards the door that Ida came out of. "Rest and think with Ida, I go work. Take stairs down two flights, that your level. Dinner at six." Sarah ascended the stairs.
"Ok, thanks."

In Ida's room there was a chair and numerous dog pillows. Ida came back with a length of rope that had knots tied at both ends, dropping it at Luciana's feet and staring at her with a question in her eyes.

"What?" *Why did I expect a response?*

Ida picked up the rope again and hit her hand with it.

Luciana took it. The dog ran down the hall and waited. "You want this?"

The dog's tail wagged, and Luciana tossed the rope. Ida jumped, catching it and bringing it back. Luciana threw it for a few minutes. *This won't end if I don't stop it.* Ida's tail stopped wagging and her eyes begged.

Fine. Luciana threw it one last time and Ida took it into her room to lay on the pillows. Luciana sat in the chair and locked eyes with the dog.

"Well shit, if I get one of you it might be worth it." Luciana pet Ida for a while longer before leaving to go back to her room.

Back in her quarters, she used her tablet to see if there were any notices from the Chief. She got nothing, her email client was part of the prohibited traffic Samir warned her about. *Taketa's worried about espionage.* She went back to their proposal, running a hand through her short asymmetrical haircut.

I'd have smelled those Youths and Erik would be alive. I'll talk to the guard. Unless it'll cripple me, I'm in.

Chapter 7 - Anton

Anton's heart hammered in his chest as the Dominion of Chicago's spires blotted out the sun. The tires beneath him squealed, the bus turned, throwing Anton against the side of the vehicle.

"What the fuck was that, Private Riznik?" Lt. Sumpf asked as he righted himself.

"Someone turned off their pilot and went into our lane." Sagira regained control of the transport.

"You forgot to say Sir," Lt. Sumpf said.

"Sir, Yes Sir."

Buildings rose like a great canyon around them. Signs ignited along their facades, replacing the sun with brilliant shades of orange, red, green, and yellow that Anton couldn't believe were real. *Holy shit.*

"Look at Grissom!" Beca laughed.

Anton pulled himself from the window, the squad staring at him.

"His head's gonna explode." Tom put his bag in front of him as a shield.

"It's... pure chaos," Anton said.

"Boy, you don't know the half of it." Lt. Sumpf leaned over Anton's shoulder. "All you see is the planned sections of the city. Wait until you see the parts that fell through the cracks. Then you'll know chaos."

"Does Dom-Chi even have one of those?" Alex asked. "Hive-Houston didn't have that much planning and it's fine."

"I would argue that Houston is entirely that brand of insanity," the Lieutenant said.

The group's conversation continued, but Anton was drawn to the window like a fly to a salt lamp. They passed a giant building, its entire side painted in a neon-blue advertisement for Re-Cola. *Never had that... they don't have any ads for seeds and tools here.*

The transport accelerated, bouncing onto an elevated highway. The buildings shrank as they traveled north, and warships broke the horizon before a body of water did.

"Almost there," Sagira yelled from the front.

"Drive directly onto the boat," the Lieutenant said.

"Roger that."

Anton unglued himself from the window. Neon afterimages of a woman danced in his vision when he blinked. The city made the inside of the transport duller, like it stole the colors for the signs. *How do Urbans live like this?* The transport descended onto docks in front of a massive warship.

"Jesus, we're getting on a carrier?" Tom asked.

"Although I enjoy being messianic to you, if I have to remind you again to call me Sir there will be serious, life altering, consequences."

"Roger that, Sir."

"We will be on a carrier until we get to the Atlantic."

"Sir, what's our mission?" Anton asked.

The transport bounced up a ramp and into the hangar of the ship before stopping.

"Stay here," Lt. Sumpf said, exiting the transport.

"We have to be heading to the NYC?" Beca played with a lace on her boot.

"Has to be," Sagira said. "But if seasteading pirates are that big of an issue, shouldn't they have more forces going?"

"This boat is a massive show of force," Alex said. "Like, the displacement alone could sink half the boats back home."

The passenger door opened, Lt. Sumpf appeared. "Follow me, bring your shit."

The ship's gray, metal corridors echoed with sailors preparing for departure as Anton marched one pace behind his lieutenant. Sumpf pivoted into a cabin. Within sat a squad of soldiers with their feet on the table. Their street clothes stained by the night before, black bags hung beneath blood-shot eyes. The entire room smelled like a bottle of moonshine had shattered.

These are seasoned soldiers.

"Lieutenant Sumpf." A bald, well-built man stood and saluted.

"Can that shit, Jimmy. What's the mission?" Lt. Sumpf said.

Jimmy laughed. "We're going to the NYC to provide some… superior ground support. Seasteaders took over the local militia's outpost and have been issuing demands towards the council. We got the call yesterday morning."

"Any other intel?"

"Sat photos of the area, though they're smart enough to block most of their movements with some sort of reflective coating. Exact numbers might be a smidge off." Jimmy eyed Anton like he walked onto the wrong stead. "You brought these?"

"Yes, it's their first militia mission."

The ragged group of soldiers chuckled.

"They're better than they look." Lt. Sumpf stared down the group.

"Everyone looks good in training and easy ops," Jimmy said. The boat shuddered as it left the dock and headed towards the ocean.

"Well"—Jimmy grinned—"we'll just have to make sure they enjoy their first time."

"Give us the intel. Do you already have a workup?"

"All business these days, Echo?"

"Just want to be prepared," Lt. Sumpf said.

"Fine." Jimmy shrugged, turning to his soldiers. "Delta, Tango, Foxtrot, kindly send them the info. We don't have a workup. I know you like that part the most."

"Roger that." Lt. Sumpf pivoted to leave, pulling the squad into his wake.

Anton spun open the latch of a cramped cabin at the bow of the boat with bunks set on the wall.

"Sir," Alex said. "If I can ask, what's the history there?"

The Lieutenant took in the cabin and his squad. "Story's too long and above your pay grades. Suffice to say, we're going to carry more of a workload than I expected."

Fine by me. "Then we should get started," Anton said.

The squad grunted their agreement. Alex pulled a sheet from one of the bunks to make a screen against the wall while Tom set a tablet to projection mode so everyone could take notes from the intel. A satellite view of the NYC flickered onto the sheet.

"It's one of the old ports. Well outside of the original city." Sagira tapped the tablet, cycling the map and circling a land bridge. "Used to be called… Boston or Providence? I'm not sure."

"Doesn't matter," Lt. Sumpf said. "It's probably still called that by the locals, but it's part of the Collective."

"Why send us and not someone from the District?" Tom asked.

"People would see it as too aggressive. Get nervous that the Seat plans to invade. Better to send forces from a non-rival area."

"Demands were… batteries, wiring, circuit boards, raw metal… nothing about food or water," Alex said. "That's not what seasteaders want."

"Barring they're building something we don't know. I agree with you," Sumpf said, scrolling through the satellite photos. "That reflective paint they put on their boats and vehicles is making these worthless." The Lieutenant threw his tablet onto their makeshift table.

Anton analyzed the map and a picture of a wave breaker near the port from before its occupation. "We should put in beforehand and move through on foot," he said.

"We'll be on a time crunch, they'll see the carrier," Tom said.

"We can leave this ship early, take a skimmer. We'll make better time," Anton countered.

"As long as I drive it, I'm in." Sagira's eyes swelled at the idea of piloting a new toy. "Lieutenant?"

"Jimmy and his crew won't like getting on a skimmer." Lt. Sumpf analyzed the map, running a finger along the coastline. "But we can use them in a pincer attack. They can put in with this ship on their southern edge. Draw their attention and we move in from the north… That's the plan. Draw it up, be precise in your measurements, dates, and times. I'll sell it to Jimmy and we'll drill it while we steam to the Collective." The Lieutenant left.

Anton handed a stylus to Beca before working on his own map. *Feels good to put the training to a real mission.* The squad shared the sentiment, fueling each other to work harder. They refined breach points, charted chokepoints, delineated patrols and their blind spots within the base. The squad slept in that room, simmed in that room, took their meals in that room, fought seasickness in that room, and entered the Atlantic without even realizing it.

***

Anton splayed his feet on the cold flight deck. They sailed through the abyss that was the night sea and sky. The ship's jets and drones quiet along the runway as the ship ran dark to obscure their approach. Light bled across the western horizon, signifying they approached the New York Collective. Anton exhaled salty air tinged with jet fuel. *We've trained, planned, and won't be deep in Urban. We got this.* He ran below deck to 'The Bunker' as Alex called it. He swung open the door to a group of fidgeting soldiers. They had been ready days ago.

"Go time," Anton said, and the room jumped into action. He knocked on the door beside theirs to get Sumpf and opened it to an empty room. "Lieutenant's gotta be on deck." He turned back for the Bunker. The squad was already filing out. Tom handed Anton his pack, and they headed above deck.

Polarized light painted the deck red on their inserted eye, while the shroud of night covered the deck on their normal eye. Lt. Sumpf stood before the skimmer. Jet black and suspended by a crane over the water, it was a boat on a wing.

"Riznik, get her ready. We'll stow your shit," Lt. Sumpf said.

"Roger that, Sir." Sagira jumped the ropes to cross.
Anton was a step behind, gripping the same ropes and glad for the darkness. It prevented him from seeing the chop hundreds of feet below. Stepping onto the skimmers deck, the engines hummed to life, alarm lights warmed up before being flicked off. Anton turned,

catching packs tossed across and stowing them into storage. The squad crossed, sitting into the bucket seats.

Lt. Sumpf was the first to strap himself down. "Y'all might want to buckle up. This is going to get… wild." The white of his eyes grew in the dark.

The boat swayed as the crane lowered them and swung in the wind. Anton grabbed a handle, throwing himself into the seat and focusing on the buckles.

Crack! Bolts blew out overhead.

We're not at the water yet. Anton's buckle clipped, the boat fell through the air for what felt like an eternity before slamming in the ocean. *Shit.* The boat bounced like a buoy in rough seas.

"Private Riznik, if you would please."

The engines roared in response and the boat shot out like a torpedo. Water slamming the hull fell away as they rose on the skimmer's hydrofoil. Anton swayed sickeningly in his seat and squeezed his harness.

"Riznik, if I lose my dinner because of this I will not be pleased."

"Roger that." Sagira grunted as she tried to steady the boat. "The waves are bad, Sir."

The Lieutenant shook his head, opening a container on his thigh and slapping a tan, circular med-patch behind his ear. He looked at the squad. "Tell me one of you brought your enhancers?"

"In the stowed bag, Sir." Beca dry heaved and swallowed.

"Grissom, I doubt any of us will be able to stand, can you?"

"Aye." Anton unbuckled, jamming his hands against the ceiling to fight the bucking ship as he made his way to the stowed square case. He opened the container, thumbing through the pharmaceutical patches. Dilators for when shit hit the fan, stims for night missions, zoners for focus. He pulled motion-sickness discs and stumbled towards the bow, handing patches to everyone as he went.

Alex waved it off. "What sort of seasteader would I be if I took that?"

Tom massaged the disk behind his ear and loosened the straps of his seat. "That's better. ETA?"

"Two hours," Sagira said.

Anton arrived at the cockpit and strapped into the copilot's seat.

"You got anymore of those patches?" Sagira asked.

Anton nodded and massaged one behind her ear to stimulate the drug release.

"Thanks." Sagira kept her eyes glued to the seas.

The northern terminus of the NYC rose as a series of low-rises.

"It's not as bright as I expected," Anton said.

"They still get winters up here." Sagira tapped the console. "Might explain why the seas are fucked. Beca, did you check weather?"

"I saw nothing planned."

"God damn it Jackson, they still get unplanned events up here," the Lieutenant said, pulling out his tablet and weather intel. "Blizzard incoming."

"Do we call it off?" Tom said.

"I've worked through a blizzard back home," Anton said. "Once or twice."

Lt. Sumpf sucked his front teeth. "Put us in further south. We won't have time to walk it anymore. Grissom, stay up front, pick a landing spot. Riznik, when we're fifteen miles out, throttle down and put us in the water. Snow doesn't stop the Ninth Legion."

"Roger," everyone responded in unison.

The countless cranes and rainbow containers of the port of the NYC stood illuminated by the light of a sun that was not there. Sagira pulled against a rocky outcropping of wave breakers, making landfall.

"Comm check." Anton hopped onto solid ground.

"Check," Tom said.

"Scouting." Anton slung his rifle and hurried towards the container yard.

Silence enveloped him as he entered the yard. Towering piles of snow littered the clearings. A gentle wind blew the loose tops of recent snow into a swirling maelstrom within the valleys of metal.

Haven't seen snow like this since I was a kid and it wasn't this much... Does blizzard mean something different in Urban? Anton scaled a pile of snow that rivaled his stead in height. He lay prone, peering over the top and zooming his ENT-inserts on the compound.

In the artificial sun, one man walked along a cement wall while another stood near a crane cabin.

Gates are unguarded. There can't be just two people. Are the rest sleeping? He cycled his OPTO-inserts to infrared, the world blurred. He tried night vision, and the blur remained. *Scanjammers.* Anton slid down the snow pile and jogged back to his squad.

"Did you record it?" Lt. Sumpf asked after Anton relayed what he found.

"It's automatic."

Tom pulled the footage, playing it on a tablet for the group.

"How could such a small group block the rest of the NYC militia?" Beca asked.

"The Collective had to reduce their forces during the last congress," Lt. Sumpf said. "Still doesn't add up."

A frigid wind blew off the water, cutting into the group. *Storm's approaching.*

"Maybe the cold is affecting the inserts?" Beca said.

"Doesn't explain the numbers of people," Alex said.

"Makes no fucking sense," Tom said, shaking his head. "The scanjammers for inserts are cutting edge and require specific conditions to work. How would some seabilly get it?"

"This is out of scope." Lt. Sumpf cycled his ENT-inserts to the boat. "Holiday Carolers unable to find houses. What precinct should we go to next?"

Static crackled back.

The Last 0-Day

"Scanjammers that can block this far out?" Sagira said under her breath.

"We can go towards the rendezvous point," Beca said.

"How bad are blizzards in Urban?" Anton said.

"Bad." Lt. Sumpf shook his head. "We're going through the port. UCSM troops hiding in the Collective for pick up will cause a shitstorm. Pull up the schematics."

Tom projected a blurry image of the Port onto the snow.

"Grissom, Nova, you two go towards the water side of the base." Lt. Sumpf pointed to the southeast. "Riznik, climb this crane and set up a nest at the three o'clock. Myself, Spike, and Jackson will come in from landward side here at the one o'clock. Head straight for this building, cut the power and move out from there towards the worker dorms. Assume inserts won't work once inside."

"Rules of engagement the same?" Sagira asked.

"No. We're at weapons go."

Anton nodded at Alex, and they sprinted south to reach the shoreline.

Water thundered against the sea wall.

"We won't be able to swim in that," Alex said.

"Good luck." Sagira smiled and climbed the crane.

"Bitch."

Anton peered around the corner of a blue Wushan shipping container. Snow drifted from the containers stacked four high in a makeshift wall. *Still no guards.* "No way up, gotta swim."

"Grissom, I'm telling you, those waves will smash you against the rocks in a bad, bad way." Alex cycled their ENT-inserts to the Lieutenant and static crackled through. "Motherfucker. Alright Anton, let's figure out the plan and fast—"

Explosions tore from the water, a dingy burned through the chop. A rocket fired from its deck, illuminating a single soldier with a shoulder launcher.

Lt. Jimmy Smith.

"No fucking way," Alex said in awe.

The boat hit one kilometer from shore and shimmered on Anton's OPTO-inserts before blurring. In his non-inserted eye, the boat continued. Another rocket tore through the night and Jimmy's squad passed behind a wall of shipping containers.

"Get Sagira, I'll get Sumpf. This is FUBAR." Anton sprinted into the night.

Dock lights overhead dimmed under the onslaught of the storm. Explosions and gunfire rattled through the curtains of snow. The cement wall of the port rose on his left, a figure trudged through the squalls. Anton slid, unholstering his pistol and training it on the target. Tom emerged from the storm.

Anton whistled the high-low of his squad and lowered his gun. *Last thing we need is a blue on blue incident.*

"You're not, well that?" Tom gestured to the chaos occurring out of view.

"Lieutenant Smith."

"Fuck, Sumpf's gunna be pissed. Where's everyone?"

"Coming back. Plan?"

"Sumpf and Beca are preparing charges to get through the wall."

Feet crunched in snow behind Anton in the distance.

Anton pulled Tom behind a container with him. *Can't risk it's not a friendly.*

Alex and Sagira panted by. Anton whistled high-low, gestured he'd take the lead, and set the pace towards Sumpf.

The explosions on the other side of the cement wall stopped, but the sporadic gunfire of urban warfare continued as Anton neared the breach point.

Sumpf stood in the shadow of a shipping container. He locked eyes with Anton and tapped Beca on the shoulder.

Detacord sparked at the pair's feet, Anton didn't break stride.

The spark flew along the ground, bounced to ten different spots, and exploded.

Multiple breach points. Anton passed Sumpf and Beca, sprinting towards the now smoldering holes in the concrete wall.

His ENT-inserts hissed, popped, and fell silent as he jumped through and raised his rifle.

A rusted dry dock formed a clearing where containers spilled rations and electronics onto the asphalt. Fresh snow covered old stains, but couldn't cover the brass shell casings, rocket smoke, and red of human blood. Anton pressed his back against the nearest container and turned. His squad waited at the concrete wall.

He made hand gestures to the group for 'Empty.'

Nods fell down the line, his squad entered, and followed Anton as he pivoted into an alley between storage buildings. Anxiety wound into the group, their rifles training on corners, doors, rooftops, and gangways above.

Earth below, it's a damn 3D-maze here.

Lt. Sumpf jumped a gap to the generator trailer, counting down from three on his fingers and kicking the door open. Anton swung into a frozen wave of iron.

In front of him was the NYC militia… or what was left of them. *Oh god.* Most were bound with gunshot wounds to the head and chest. Some weren't so lucky, looking to have been stabbed several times and mutilated. There was no generator, no circuit box, just an abattoir.

"Jesus fuck." Beca dry heaved.

"Seasteaders don't do this," Alex said.

"Who does?" Anton said.

"Focus," Lt. Sumpf said. "Eyes wide, ears open. Move out."

They backtracked through the snow, nearing one of the breach points in the concrete wall.

Anton pulled out the tablet to check the map. It didn't boot. "Dead," he said.

Tom traced cables running from the nearest dock-light to a red shack in the distance. "That one is the genny."

Gunshots flashed in the windows of the dorm. Anton trained his rifle on the building. A grenade exploded, rattling the metal walls.

"Shack first, then Jimmy," Lt. Sumpf said.

The squad hugged the nearest building, their black and tan suits standing out against the snow. *Should have checked the reports myself.* The firefight heated up in the dorms, someone spraying wild inside. Tom sprinted towards the generator shack, Sagira covering him. Anton trained his rifle on the dorms.

A blue hue sparked in the shack from an EMP-nade and in an instant the port plunged into darkness.

"Carolers, Carolers Over!" One of Lt. Smith's soldiers screamed through their ENT-inserts. "Request immediate fire on location, evac at point Sierra Lima."

"Right fucking on top of us." Lt. Sumpf jogged towards the dorms, not waiting for the squad.

The NYC's light pollution painted the snow in flickering neons. The flash and cracks of the firefight in the barracks ceased as Anton and his squad hit the back entrance.

Focus.

"Jimmy," Lt. Sumpf whispered into the ether.

Snow fell in bands across the docks in response.

Lt. Sumpf closed his eyes, deep breaths hung in the bitter night, and he reached into his enhancer pouch on his leg. He pulled an orange disk and looked to his squad to do the same.

Dilators. Anton pulled his own disk, nerves tingling in his fingers. He rubbed the sweat from his neck.

"On my mark," Lt. Sumpf whispered, holding the disk an inch from his neck.

You've trained for this. Gestures only, no one has the patience for words on Dilators.

"Mark."

Anton pressed the disk onto his neck, massaging the drug into his carotid artery. A slight burn—

Time stuttered to a standstill. Falling snow slowed into a suspension. Sounds were drawn out slow and low. The microseconds of an eye blink now a full night's rest. The squad's eyebrows twitched, heads bobbed on imperceptible nods. Micromovements Anton knew to be affirmatives.

Go time.

Alex kicked down the door, Anton threw in a flashbang.

An eternity later it went off and Anton was through the door.

In front of him stood three figures in green, all in the process of turning towards the group after shielding their eyes from the flash.

Too slow. Anton shot the first one through the heart, the soldiers crumpled—Anton was already onto the next. Thunder rolled from his rifle, the second man fell under his fire. The third man pulled the pin on his grenade when his head exploded.

Grenade. "Gr—" Anton's own yell was too slow in his ears. He dove back towards the door, pushing Sumpf and Beca with him. He flew through the air, waiting a lifetime for the grenade to go off. The explosion started like a stomach rumble that became a groan. The concussion knocked the wind from Anton, shrapnel scraped his armor. Appreciative blinks came from Lt. Sumpf and Beca as the squad shook the dirt off.

Anton pivoted back to point, Sumpf on his heels, weapons trained on the doors ahead. Lt. Smith and crew were not in this room and whoever the fake seasteaders were knew they had company coming now.

Anton hit the next door, pulling out an EMP-grenade and another flashbang from Beca's pack. Alex booted the door and Anton tossed both grenades through.

Swing in low, aim high. The flashbang's crack and flash a dull hue… *Did the EMP dud out?* Blue sparked from the door. *Damn dilators.*

Sumpf was first through the door, Anton hurried after.

Dust swirled in the room. *No targets.*

Lt. Jimmy Smith lay covered in blood against an office desk he'd kicked over for cover. Neons flashed tiny spotlights through the polywood walls riddled by bullets. The rest of his squad lay dead around him. All facing two doors that they hadn't gone through.

Anton trained his rifle ahead. Sumpf held out his hand, three for each door.

Sagira, Alex, and Anton went towards the leftmost door, putting their backs against the wall. Across the gap, Tom, Beca, and Sumpf were in the same formation for the rightmost door.

With a slight nod of his head, Sumpf gave the go ahead.

Anton and Sumpf kicked down the doors in unison and stepped through.

Two doors to the same room.

A metallic figure stood in the center of the room, chrome and carbon fiber plating moving across its skin.

What—Anton moved to squeeze the trigger.

But the machine was faster.

Fire ignited along the floor to Anton's right, an explosion started at the feet of Sumpf, Tom, and Beca.

Oh God no. Anton's eyes spun back towards the machine, his bullets pancaking against the machine's body armor. Worse, the robot was already on him.

An actuator shot off from its side. Anton's right arm went numb, a second punch and his legs went numb. He tumbled to the ground as an explosion tore the machine in two. The fireball expanded to Anton. Shrapnel tore into his face, half the world went dark, the other blurred. Anton cracked the ground and his world spun. The dilators faded, time speeding up.

Alex and Sagira yelled at one another down a hallway.

"Get Grissom, there's EVAC," Sagira yelled.

"Tom, Beca, Sumpf…" Alex said

"They're gone. Anton's still here."

Anton blinked stars from his vision. "Am I going to die?"

"Shut the fuck up, Anton." Sagira slapped his neck.

Radiating warmth pulsed from her slap and fought the pain blossoming from his limbs. They dragged him into the snow that didn't feel cold.

Anton tried to touch the white, but his arm wasn't responding. He turned his head.

His arm was gone. *Oh god.* His heart raced, he tried to look at his legs. There were bloody stumps—

Alex pushed his head backwards. "Not the time, buddy," they said.

What is the time?

Neons flashed across a dark, cloudy sky. Snow landed into his eye, he blinked but it made the world blurrier. A helicopter's rhythmic thud broke the silent night, a light illuminating them. Anton felt himself lifted into the black interior of the cabin. A face blurred over him against the hexagonal-textured roof.

"Jesus, it still might not be enough time," the face said.

My family. Anton couldn't bring himself to talk.

"Let's make time." Sagira stepped over Anton.

The helicopter tilted forward and Anton blacked out.

Chapter 8 - Anton

Crack! A slap woke Anton, his chest heavy from the helicopter gaining altitude.

"Just let me sleep," Anton mumbled, closing his eyes.

Slap! Stars swarmed his blurred vision.

"Not happening." Alex knelt over Anton. "Sagira, ETA."

"Ten minutes. Command Forces are clearing a path to Taketa Medical."

Anton's eyelids sagged, Alex raised their hand.

"Ok I won't," Anton said in Rural.

Alex blinked and kept their hand raised.

"I won't, I won't!"

The helicopter banked, snow falling into the cabin. Alex leaned over and pulled the door shut. Shrapnel and blood covered Alex's chest. Anton tried to reach with his left arm, but it was tied to his side. The dilators faded, time stuttered like a video game on a processor not strong enough for it. The helicopter faded, reappeared, Alex melted—

I'm going to die.

The helicopter bounced, the door swung open to a medical team on a snowy rooftop. They talked a mile a minute. Anton couldn't keep track of the words.

Pain flared from everywhere as they lifted him out of the helicopter. He passed into a bright corridor, sweating in the oven, pain blossoming as lights passed overhead.

A mask was placed over his face, the air tasting of metal. A distant stab hit his arm from a swinging bag and darkness enveloped him.

***

Anton opened his eyes. "What?" he tried, but his throat was too dry for words and a hoarse bark came instead.

"He's awake," Sagira said, a door shutting behind her.

Alex came into view and pushed a straw into Anton's mouth. Cold ice ran down his throat like irrigation over dry soil. Monitors beeped in the distance. Anton blinked but couldn't clear his vision.

"You and Sagira ok?" Anton said.

"Jesus fucking Christ," Alex said, trying not to smile. "You're looped out on pain pills."

Am I? "Sky above, Sumpf, Beca, Tom."

"I know"—Alex's voice cracked, they squeezed his shoulder—"I know. We all saw it. Couldn't do anything about it, just stare in horror as those grenades went off. I pulled out the RPG before the door even opened—"

"Welcome to the land of the living," interrupted a female voice from the door. "My name is Dr. Chaude."

"Doc." Anton had to tilt his head to get the smeary cloud out of his vision. The doctor had short black hair and pretty almond eyes. *I've never seen eyes like that before.*

"The damage you sustained was… extensive. You got lucky in arriving at us when you did. I'm sure…"

"Sagira," she said.

"Yes, Sagira ensured you made it."

"How long have I been out?"

"Ten days. Procedure is four, ketamine coma for six. Helps clear unused neuronal pathways you may have had some… rather vivid dreams."

Anton blinked. *Don't remember anything.*

"Yes." Dr. Chaude pulled a datastick from the bed. "I'll let you all catch up and will return shortly. Visiting times are ending soon. Especially now that he is awake."

"Uh huh," Alex said, rolling their eyes when the doctor left.

"I don't trust that Doctor," Sagira said.

"She saved his life. Shit, probably ours too," Alex said.

Anton grimaced. "What happened? It's fuzzy to me."

"We entered the room. That machine shot a grenade at the others." Sagira stopped, swallowing her emotions. A fresh white bandage wrapped her head, the pink stain of stems on the side nearest the explosion.

"Sumpf and Beca tried to move," Alex said. "But it was too late. I had the RPG already out, thinking there'd be a platoon in that room. Shot as fast as I could, but that bot closed the distance, had you in its grip. The explosion sharded the damn thing, hitting us with its broken shell."

"We dragged you out," Sagira said. "The helicopter from Smith's team arrived to lay down some serious damage, but saw us through their scopes and swung in for a pickup instead.

"Oh man"—Alex smiled—"tell him."

"No, you."

"So, when we were in the chopper, you kept asking if you lost your dick."

"Get the fuck out of here," Anton said.

"Well, you were speaking in Rural, and mine isn't great, but I know dick when I hear it." Alex laughed. "You wouldn't stop. I grabbed a handful of the snow that blew in and shoved it down your pants. Shut you up real quick."

Anton closed his eyes, warmth welling onto his cheeks. He raised both hands to rub the blush away.

Only one hand hit his face. *Sky above, it wasn't a dream.*

Alex cleared their throat. "So you're not like me down there."

"Though after that snow you essentially were," Sagira tried.

Anton blinked at his lone hand. "How am I going to live like this?" he said, more to himself than the remnants of his fireteam.

"Prosthetics have come a long way." Sagira pulled his hand away from his face and intertwined their fingers. Alex rested their hand on the groups, they were missing the pinky, ring, and middle finger on their right hand.

"Your hand," Anton said.

"I know right, almost as bad as you. How am I going to fuck people now?"

Anton barked a laugh, but it faded as fast as it came. "We don't have this word, prosthetic."

"Artificial limbs," Dr. Chaude said from the doorway. "I wasn't joking when I said you were extremely lucky to have come to us. If you'll give me some time with Mr. Grissom, alone. I'd like to discuss options with him."

Alex moved to protest.

"It's alright," Anton said.

Sagira gave Alex a gentle tug out of the room.

"Yes, now then," Dr. Chaude said. "We're the world leaders in prosthetics, but given the Military is footing the bill, we would like to offer you more. We have finalized technology that would make prosthetics a thing of the past."

"What do you mean?" *She withholds intel. I see why you didn't trust this woman, Sagira.*

"You have experience with inserts. Well, we're working on implants. Total human augmentation, if you will."

"How is that different than… prosthetics?" That last word was a marble on his tongue.

"Yes, this technology doesn't exist where you are from. The prosthetics would be like inserts. They'd be outside of you and following directions. What I'm offering would be a physical part of you. We can fix your vision. Give you an arm, two legs."

"Why?"

"Why?" Dr. Chaude shook her head, the question catching her like a punch. "He asks why. Because I want to help? Because I think you're cute? Because this is my life's work, and I want to have a real impact. Taking a wounded soldier, a Rural no less, and making him like new. Making him better. Take your pick."

Anton tilted his head to see her clearly. Her skin was smooth without the wear and tear of rural or urban life.

Avoided it somehow. "I'll think about it."

"Well, think quickly." Dr. Chaude pushed a remote into his hand. "Red button for nummers, blue for nurses, and I'm green." She smiled and left.

Anton lay alone in the sterile white hospital room, Alex and Sagira didn't return. A wave of pain started in feet he didn't have, overwhelming him like a brushfire with high winds. He grit his teeth, pressing the red button. The pain built into an inferno the red button couldn't stop. The fire burned through, and he passed out as a sweaty mess. Anton woke to a nurse with SR-porridge and a change of gown.

"Mr Grissom"—the nurse flashed a friendly smile—"we can't give you more nummers."

"How long was I asleep? Where are Alex and Sagira?"

"UCSM won't tell us, and you've been in and out for a few days."

Days. Earth below.

The nurse kept her smile and grabbed a fresh gown to pull over him.

"Thank you," Anton said as the gown went over him. "Does… my family know?"

"I don't know, Mr. Grissom, I'm sorry."

Anton squeezed the nurse's shoulder with his one hand. "Don't worry."

The nurse's smile faltered and she left.

I can't keep working with UCSM like this… If I take the offer I'm going to be mostly machine… How would I fix it if it breaks and I'm back rural? Then again, I'll be a burden on my family if I don't.

I was a burden growing up, and that was when I had two hands… I won't be a burden anymore.

Anton hit the green button.

Within minutes, Dr. Chaude entered the room. "Yes, Anton?"

"I'm in."

"Excellent. We'll start in the morning."

"Morning?"

"Yes, it will take a few hours to customize everything." Dr. Chaude left and nurses came in.

The day passed in a blur of nurses and doctors measuring him and taking blood.

"Usually patients ask for water before surgery," a nurse said. The lights in the room dimmed in an artificial twilight.

Surgery. "I'm used to being thirsty." Anton forced a smile.
The nurse left.
Nervous at surgery and it's the only reason I'm alive. Anton drifted into a fitful sleep and awoke to the bright lights of a surgical suite. Warmth ran from his IV, the stream hit his shoulder, and he blacked out.

Darkness enveloped him when he opened his eyes.

"Turn on the lights," Anton muffled into a mask.
Monitors beeped, plastics clicked. The warm snake running up his arm pulled the blanket back over his mind.

***

Anton awoke in a blue hospital room. An iridescent-yellow IV bag ran into his left arm, and a coal-black bag ran into his right. Anton's heart leapt into his throat, making the monitor beside his bed chirp. *My right arm.* Jet black, a mixture of metal, carbon fibers, and a meshed material he couldn't discern. He tried to rub his face, but the new arm lay motionless.
Seriously! Anton used his human arm and pushed himself upright. His legs lay without a blanket, made of the same materials. They had significantly more cords running their length. *They look like puma muscles.* The black cords ran above his injuries and into his waist and hips.

"Welcome back," Dr. Chaude said from the doorway.

"Why do these hoses run higher?" Anton pointed to tubes and vasculature running into his hips.

"Anchor points, some of your femur was still shattered. We had to remove a portion of it."

Anton's eyes flared, the heart rate monitor accelerated.

"Nothing to worry about, we kept all the important parts." Dr. Chaude smiled and examined where the materials met his flesh. "I'll have to use more stem-cell wound closures on these ports." She walked to a cabinet on the wall.

"Why can't I move?"

"The connections haven't finalized yet. It takes time for everything to mesh. Don't worry, you'll be moving soon enough." She pulled on gloves and sat on the edge of her bed. She smeared neon pink gel at the rims of his artificial limbs. "Hold still." She leaned closer to his face. A faint, warm citrus perfume wafting from her.

Like limes from the stead. "I can see again," Anton said without thinking.

Dr. Chaude laughed like teenagers did on holos. "We replaced both eyes. The working one wasn't salvageable."

His eyes magnified the tiny pores on her skin. The folds along the edges of her eyes. The cute button nose. Dr. Chaude was Asian and Anton had only seen them in holos growing up.

She's stunning.

"Hey, I said hold still. Don't want to get this in your new eyes." Dr. Chaude finished applying the gels on his face and stepped back.

"When can I start moving?"

"Physical therapy tomorrow. You should try to sleep, it will help with the gel." She raised an empty tube like that explained it. Along his joints, the neon pink gel set to a glowing blue and warmth blossomed on his skin.

"Is this going to hurt?"

"It shouldn't," she said, her brow furrowing. "Why?"

"It's warm"—he winced—"now it's hot."

Dr. Chaude injected an orange liquid into his IV bag.

"This will help." She rested her hand on his artificial leg.

"I feel that—" Warmth hit his shoulder and his head tilted as he passed out.

Hands pushed his shoulder, and Anton woke with a start.

"Woah, easy now." Sagira raised both her hands like he'd bolt.

Alex stood behind her with Dr. Chaude and the series of nurses and doctors that had inspected him the day before the surgery. Diodes clung to his head, their cords itching against his back.

"What's the bad news?" Anton asked. "How long was I out for?"

"Only the evening. I invited your squad." Dr. Chaude gestured towards the small crowd. "And well, the rest of us, you'd have to try and keep them out. I want you to pick up the cup." Dr. Chaude placed a polycarbon cup onto the tray in front of him.

Without thinking, he reached forward—his right arm punched the cup towards the group.

"Jesus." Alex ducked under the projectile and the rest of the group beamed.

"We definitely have connection." Dr. Chaude smiled. "Now to just work on the fine motor skills."

"Should I try to get out of bed?" Anton asked, reaching for the edge.

"No!" Alex and Sagira yelled.

"You'll fucking jump through the god damned ceiling," Sagira said.

Anton blinked. "Alright, let's start with this therapy."

"My thoughts exactly." Dr. Chaude turned towards the rest of the group. "I'll come get you when he's ready."

If there were to be any protests, her tone silenced them, and everyone filtered out. Sagira and Alex punched his human shoulder as they passed.

"Alright then, let's begin." Dr. Chaude placed a cup, grape, and stylus onto the tray over his bed.

Anton's arm moved drunk, but after a few tries it sobered up and he held the cup. *Feels the same*—He pulverized the container.

"Shit, I'm sorry."

"It's no problem." She set another cup on the trap.

"Wait, how strong am I now?"

"Extremely. We lowered the neural input limit to ensure you don't tear yourself in half."

"Wait, what? Are you serious?"

Dr. Chaude looked disinterested. "The artificial muscle systems have a greater tension limit and load bearing than normal muscles. Theoretically, you could push off with such force... Well, the shearing force wouldn't treat your human skeleton nicely."

"Fuck me."

"The cup."

Careful. Anton picked up the cup, it slipped—He caught it. *Where's the breaking point?* He twitched, crushing the cup.

Dr. Chaude raised an eyebrow.

"Wanted to figure out how much force to do."

The tests continued, objects shrank, became more fragile, and by the end his tray was a mess of fruit juices, shards of plastic and metal.

But I can do it. "When can I walk?" *I need to get out of this bed.* "This room doesn't exactly have a ton to look at."

"We can try now, one minute." She came back with a metal walker. "Sometimes old tech is the best. Now, I know I said that everything was toned down, but let's take it easy here." She grunted as she moved his artificial legs over the bed.

Must be heavy. "I felt that." Anton smiled.

She glanced up from attaching his IV bags to the walker and smiled. *She's beautiful.* Anton coughed and gently gripped the walker's handles.

"Surprised you're taking such a hands on approach," Anton said.

"If you want something done correctly, you do it yourself." Dr. Chaude's smile felt private, like it was for him alone.

"Don't laugh if I fall." Anton took a deep breath, but it was hollow, like hypoxic training back on base. *Lack of use.* He pushed forward. His legs gave out. His weight fell onto both arms. His artificial arm took most of the load, but his human arm trembled.

"Well, this isn't good," Anton said.

"Think about standing tall, don't think about the legs." Dr. Chaude put a hand on his shoulder.

Lt. Sumpf is inspecting me. His back straightened, he gained height, towering over Dr. Chaude and the bed.

"I'm taller?"

"By a few inches yes," Dr. Chaude said like a child seeing a toy they always wanted.

"Now what?"

Dr. Chaude moved to the door. "Follow me."

He inched the walker towards her. Where the arm felt natural, if strong, after training, the legs were weirdly heavy, like they had fallen asleep and not regained blood flow. Dr. Chaude continued into the hallway. Anton couldn't take his eyes from the new limbs moving beneath his hospital gown. A chill breeze blew through the hallway and ran up Anton's bareback.

Earth below. Anton looked over his shoulder for Alex and Sagira. *Funny joke, having me walk bare-ass.* But the hallway was empty.

"So, can I get some pants, Doc?" Anton asked as he shuffled after her.

"Why?"

"What?"

She smiled. "We got some tailored, they're not here yet but should be soon. Here we are." Dr. Chaude pushed open a door to a small room with a lone desk.

But those details fell to the wayside. The New York Collective spilled before a wall sized window. Buildings surrounded them, a Taketa Corp sign shining through the haze. The snowstorms had ended, but its cargo covered the flat surfaces around. Signs blinked and changed from red to blue, the room's hue changing with it. Anton's mouth dried. Puncta of lights dotted darkened office buildings as dedicated workers toiled after hours.

Dr. Chaude took his augmented hand and brought him towards the window. His eyes danced between snow capped towers and a woman sitting at a terminal with her head in her hands in the nearest office building. Dr. Chaude tapped the window and pointed down.

They were hundreds of stories above the city streets below. Anton's stomach dropped, Dr. Chaude steadied him. Connectors ran between buildings at multiple heights, some covered, some not. People were dots walking around them, stopping to peer over the ledges. Without thought, his eyes zoomed in on the suspended streets and verandas. *Woah.* People courted, bought steaming drinks, laughed, and threw snowballs at one another. His eyes zoomed deeper, cars drove along elevated highways, snow littered the sidewalk and fell from the verandas above. At these lowest levels, the snow lost its magical hues from the top lights, instead showing dirty footprints and plow marks. Dr. Chaude squeezed his hand, and he was back in the room.

"Doc, I've never seen anything like that. It's…"

"Stunning. Taketa has one of the best views up here. Makes work hard when the sun is setting. On the other side of the building you can look into the sunken quarter, if you would like."

Anton nodded, and they left the room.

She's still holding my hand. His heart beat faster and as they approached a dark room, he realized the walker dragged behind by a cord attached to his waist. *That's why she's holding my hand.* His shoulders sank.

They entered another cramped room. Beyond the window lay the sunken quarter. Gone were the sparkling neon high rises and in its place stood frozen ships. In the distant waters, the remnants of skyscrapers rose. Fires dotted their skeletal hulks. *They're not abandoned?* Movement caught his attention near the boats, people skated on the ice in a lagoon, waves flowing beneath. His jaw dropped at the dangers the people put themselves in.

Urbans. "This view isn't…"

"As nice, yes. But it shows me… where I came from, and what I don't want to go back to."

Anton pulled his eyes from the sunken district to Dr. Chaude. *I'm sorry—*

Dr. Chaude shook her head. "Let's go back to your room."

Anton lay in his bed and Dr. Chaude hooked up more jet-black IV bags and ran the lines into his legs.

"What are those for?"

"Artificial blood, essentially."

"What do I do when I leave?"

"It will be fine."

"No, I mean, do I like, recharge myself?"

She laughed. "No, no. These bags are just initial boosters. They will run off of whatever you eat." She paused, examining the ceiling. "Though I guess you will have to eat more."

"Wait, what? That makes no sense."

She shook her head. "Your blood is ninety percent artificial now."

What? Anton's eyes widened.

"It primarily works with your new limbs, but having it double as blood for your native parts was an easy addition."

He blinked. "What do I do if I get cut?"

"It should clot. If you lose too much, then we'll have to figure something out. Hmm, yeah, we will have to figure something out."

"You didn't think of this?"

"We're only human, Anton. I'll figure it out. I built you, I can handle a slight deviation."

"Doc—"

She raised her hand. "Please, Anton, call me Yume. We will be working together pretty extensively for the foreseeable future. Eat, sleep. I'll see you in the morning." She left.

A robot delivered SR-porridge, and Anton lay in his bed and the lights turned off. *Foreseeable future?*

In the morning, alarmingly black blood was taken from his left arm. He started physical therapy for his right arm, primarily just moving objects from trays. Then it was walking around a track in the basement before more therapy.

"Can we get Sagira and Alex in here if I'm going to be walking in circles?" Anton sat before an enormous bowl of porridge with extra cubes of SR-protein.

"I will try," Yume said. "UCSM's been cagey since they were called back to deal with the aftermath of the Port."

Anton nodded and devoured the bowl. *She wasn't kidding about this hunger.*

The training continued as a series of dull days that bled together.

Midway through the third week, on his thirtieth lap around the basement track, he turned to Dr. Chaude as he passed her.

"Doc."

She glared at him.

"Fine. Yume, I trusted you that I shouldn't overexert, that I should walk. But there have to be more exciting things to do than walking in a circle for days on end."

"Follow me." She led him to the room with the desk-sized scanner and he lay on top of it.

The casing whirled over him, and after the scan Yume took him back to the track.

"The implants have melded with your frame faster than expected. You can run if you would like."

That isn't what I meant. Anton took a deep breath. *She's been here with you the entire time, she's bored too.* "Ok, thank you, Yume." He smiled, trying to cheer her up and jogged.

Laps bled together, and he was out of breath faster than before. *Is this track hypoxic?* Anton pushed through the discomfort until Yume flagged him down.

"Dinner."

"Yume, my lungs are off. It's like I'm training at altitude."

Yume cycled her OPTO-inserts, sending a comm. "Diagnostics will see us, probably the blood but we'll scan your torso to be sure." She set off for the room, pulling Anton with her.

Anton swung out of the scanner. Concern creased Yume's brow.

"What's up?" Anton said.

"Your lungs look fine. We just… can't figure out why you would feel that way. We'll do more tests later. Let's feed you now and try a new nutritional profile."

She has a way to make it so I don't ask more questions. He jumped from the bed and followed her to the cafeteria. They put diodes on his torso as he ate and shuffled him to bed that night.

The sensation of high-altitude training didn't go away in the morning. The scientists halted the exercises, giving him another IV and scanning him constantly.

"I'm fine now," Anton tried after two days of tests.

"We can't find the marker on your scans and we can't risk it," Yume said. "We'll find it, Anton."

Shouldn't have told them. I've pushed through worse.

A week passed, boredom bit as another IV was tied into his arm and Anton snapped.

"Yume, I can't stay cooped up like this. I'm not Urban, I need to move, to be outside."

"You can't go outside. I'm truly sorry."

Sick of this shit... wait. Anton smiled and raised an eyebrow. "Could you even stop me?"

"Anton, this isn't a time for jokes."

"I'm not joking. I just realized you'd have to shoot me to stop me. I'm going, and you're more than welcome to come with." Anton fumbled to unhook his IVs.

"Stop." Yume sighed and pushed his hands out of the way. "This is a bad idea, and when you collapse, I'm going to have to drag you back."

Anton layered on hospital scrubs, but couldn't find shoes. "Will I get frostbite?"

"No?"

"How have you not thought of this?"

"Again, Anton, only human, not everything is thought of." She threw on a puffy neon-teal jacket and stared at him. "Well?"

Anton glanced at his jet-black robotic feet. "I should probably wear socks at least. These two fakers in the snow might freak people out."

Yume pulled a thick pair of black socks from a doctor's locker against the wall.

Hope you don't miss them. "What about this?" Anton raised his artificial hand. Yume handed him an oversized glove.

"Restating this is a bad idea," Yume said.

Anton carefully flexed his fingers to not tear the glove. "Noted?" Yume sighed and led him out of the room.

Anton paused at a middle floor door with the sign 'Broadway-Veranda' and he stepped into the Collective. A light snow fell and he breathed the frozen air. It filled his lungs in a way the building air couldn't and he took his first full breath in weeks. *That's better.*

"Lungs feel better." Anton smiled.

"Good, can we go back inside now?"

"No, let's get some of that hot drink people were having."

"Which one?"

"I don't know. What do Urbans drink?"

"Coffee, I guess."

"Let's try that."

"Try?"

"Yeah, you've had it?"

"Jesus Christ, you can read about Rurals all you want, but in person it's a whole other ballgame."

"I don't understand."

"Shut up, let's get you coffee. I'm losing my caring instincts for you and want to see what caffeine does to your circuits."

"What now?"

Yume started along the elevated streets, and Anton fell into her wake.

The elevated district wrapped around the western edge of buildings to avoid the wind coming from the eastern ocean. Carts dotted the snow and functioned as stores. Anton's eyes darted in every direction, counting people. *It's less than what it was at Base… thankfully.* Yume blew on a steaming cup of liquid and handed it to Anton. It threatened to burn his human hand and he swapped it to the gloved one.

"Let's go back," Yume said.

Anton struggled with the razor's edge of maintaining a grip on the cup and not crushing it. They walked for three blocks and Anton sipped the liquid. Acrid, bitter, sour, he spat it onto the snow.

"You guys like this?"

Yume laughed.

I like that laugh.

"It'll grow on you." Yume took his human hand, leading him through snow drifting from the roofs above.

Anton cautiously sipped the drink on the way back and by the time they reached Taketa he kept drinking, even if he wasn't sold on it.

"Well, at least we figured out what was wrong," Anton said.

"Well, we figured out a way to stop it. Not what caused it." Yume scanned into the building.

"Is there a difference?" Anton asked with a smirk.

Yume opened her mouth, realized he was joking, and shook her head at him. "Night, Anton."

"Come on, that was kinda funny," he yelled after her.

But Yume didn't turn around and he headed back to his room.

Anton lay in bed, unable to sleep. His heart raced and sweat poured from him. His eyes randomly zoomed in on parts of the room, highlighting cracks in the walls, a mispainted corner, a pipe that should be six inches to the right and insulated. The entire place needed a cleaning.

In the morning, a nurse came in and saw his empty coffee cup.

"Who gave you that?" they asked.

"What?" Anton's eyes zoomed into his face, finding a pimple that'd form on his chin in the coming days.

"Jesus Christ." They picked up the cup and threw it into the garbage. "You might as well go to the track and gym, no reason to wait. They're starting you again today. I'll bring your food there."

Anton ran around the empty gym. *No Yume or other lab members.* He jogged to their usual observation post, finding empty chairs. *Weird.* Anton jogged through the morning and went back to his floor. If they weren't keeping an eye on him, he'd go for another walk outside. He pulled on thick socks and left Taketa along the Veranda district again. Neons danced on snow swept streets.

It's a spectacle, I'll give them that. Anton's stomach growled and the city heard. People swarmed from buildings to food carts. His heart thundered into his throat at the mass of people. It was like an anthill emptied. He pressed his back against the Taketa door. *I've no weapon.* The Urbans paid little attention to him, their OPTO-inserts displaying advertisements, net sites, or programs for them to work during their lunch break. The door behind opened and he stumbled backwards, his legs catching him before he fell.

Yume stood beside him.

"What's going on?" Anton asked.

"We're leaving soon."

"We? Aren't I going back to the military?"

"No."

"What?"

"Before you were augmented, Taketa and UCSM struck a deal. Payment, so to speak. Today we were just debating where to go. The High Plateau is the answer to that. There is a Taketa research lab there and you'll be security for the trip."

"You can't be serious. What about Sagira and Alex? What about what happened at the port? Part of the reason I did this"—he gestured towards his legs and arm—"is for revenge against whoever did this to Sumpf, Beca, and Tom."

"Anton." Yume put a warm hand against his cheek. "I understand. Trust me, I do—"

"How can you understand?!" Anton pushed her hand away.

"Because my father was at the port as part of the militia." Yume's eyes dropped to the floor.

Shit. "Yume... I'm so sorry" Anton put his hand on hers now. Her father must have been in the shed-turned-abattoir.

"I want revenge as much as you. I'm working towards it. In addition to your pairing with me and our work. Taketa is working hand in hand with the military moving forward."

Anton pulled her into a hug, her lime perfume tickling his nose. "When do we leave?"

"Now"

They don't waste time here.

Chapter 9 - Luciana

Luciana sat in the breakroom of Taketa-8, the scientists in a heated debate over something well above her school grade.

"Sorry, we were talking science," Arsema said.

"It's no problem," Luciana said.

"How long have you lived in the Northern Empire?" a woman in scrubs, Norma, said. She was a medical doctor who smiled every time she saw Luciana and reminded her of the shrink back at the Academy.

"We call it SF or the Bowl, but my entire life."

A bookish man named Brian set his coffee on the table. "If we recode the input parameters—"

The scientist's conversation fell back to debate, as it had the entire afternoon.

Luciana checked the time, 8 p.m. "Where is Saori?"

Arsema flicked her OPTO-inserts. "Conference room."

"Thanks." Luciana excused herself.

Luciana knocked on the conference room's sliding door.

"Come in," Saori said. "Hi, Luciana."

"Hey, did you get in contact with the guard that was augmented?"

Saori's shoulders sank. "Take a seat."

Luciana sat. "This the part where you tell me he's dead?"

"What? No, Mr. Grissom's doing fine. He's on assignment and Taketa won't give me a direct line. I know it's not what you wanted, but I pulled his video and data."

The wallscreen behind flickered to a track and a man with dark legs sprinting in circles.

"Is he that fast or is this sped up?" Luciana said.

"Both. He ran for days, to give you an idea of the durability of what we're offering." Saori slid a tablet across the table. "This is his most recent scan."

Can't read these charts. "It's against the law for me to see this data."

"Couldn't get what you wanted, so I hoped this would suffice... Don't arrest me?" Saori smiled.

Luciana laughed and checked the documents' data-signature. It was verified. "Can I take this with me?"

"Taketa might kill me if I let that data out of my sight. Corporate espionage knows no bounds these days."

Worth the shot. He's alive and looks in good health. Luciana stood. "Thanks for trying, Saori." She left for her quarters and slept.

A knock came at the door.

Luciana rolled out of the bed, reaching for her gun—*Not at home.* "Come in."

The door opened. "Hello Luciana, did you sleep well?" Samir said.

"Yeah, what time is it?"

"Seven to five, the lights will cycle shortly. I, we, wanted to know if you decided yet. No rush! But when we thought you were a volunteer, we put pieces in media and have to plan accordingly."

Never one to shrink at a challenge and Mr. Grissom looked fine… "I'm in."

"Excellent! Right, starting now, no more water or food. We will proceed tonight, and you need to have an empty stomach for the operation."

"Tonight?" *Fuck me. Agreeing is one thing, the immediacy is another.*

"Yes, well, we're all excited. First you'll choose a dog, then sync you tonight. The bike we'll sync afterwards," Samir said with the same scripted confidence he had when the conversations were about science. "Get dressed. We'll go to the kennels now and you can interact with them." Samir closed the door.

Luciana cracked her neck and stepped into the dim hall. "Clothing's designed to be worn for days, I'm ready." *I need to work to get my mind off this.*

"Right, let's go," he said, typing with his OPTO-insert.

Luciana entered a room containing a single chair at the center and another door exactly opposite her.

"Please take a seat," Samir said. "This may seem silly, but I will bring out candidates. You can look and touch, but don't say anything."

He pointed to black spheres in the corner ceilings. "We'll monitor and analyze these interactions and this will determine which we should use. Though in the end you will have the final say. Let's begin."

Luciana took a seat.

The first dog was the same type as Ida, but with barely any white in its scraggly black fur. It sniffed Luciana's hand, circled her chair, and returned to Samir.

Another was a head taller than the neo-rats in the Pucker. *You'll get eaten.* The dog jumped onto Luciana's lap, barked, and scurried back to Samir.

One dog had brown fur that looked stained and was bashful to be in the room. It circled Luciana and sat in front of her.

What are you looking at? The dog tilted its head and went back at Samir's whistle. More breeds than Luciana knew remained, marched out, circled her, and continued back to Samir, who looked at her expectantly.

Guess that's it. "I dunno, the big one?"

"You had no… hunch? Intuition?" Samir rubbed his beard.

"No, I'm sorry."

"Right, ok." Samir paced around the room deep in thought. "We will use the data we have and pick, if you're ok with that?"

"Any reason I shouldn't?"

"We assumed there would be some sort of… glimmer, a spark, something. But if you didn't have any, the scans will tell us what we need."

"Sounds good. What's next?" Luciana followed Samir to the door.

"We'll do labs." Samir took the stairs down. "Get a DNA sample."

Luciana raised an eyebrow at the DNA sample.

"Your biometrics could have been altered both by the environment or digitally at some point, it's better if we take a day of sample," Samir said.

Fair.

They entered a sterile room. Norma smiled and gestured to a chair. Luciana sat and Norma worked fast, taking a blood and DNA biopsy sample from her arm. She set the vials into a silver machine on the counter.

"Arsema will have the canine data analyzed shortly," Samir said. "Norma will have your biometrics done before the dog's out of surgery and Saori will come get you when it's your turn."

Go time.

***

Luciana tossed her tablet onto the bed. *Don't care about the news.* She paced in her room. Nerves deadened by the past year reigniting like she was back at the Academy. No food or water wasn't helping matters.

Knock—

Luciana opened the door.

Saori smiled, her hand near the second knock. "Ready?"

Hours only made me second guess myself. "Yes."

Luciana sat in a cramped room containing a lone locker, tapping her heel on the ground. Her clothes lay in a pile, and she rolled her shoulders against the backless hospital gown. *This will work.*

She exited into an operating theater. Norma stood beside the bed, bathing in sterile light. Samir stood at the edge, gloved hands in the air. On a table near the bed were surgical instruments, a brown solution, and several pieces of electronics resting in pink media. *Must be the implants.*

"Please lay on your stomach," Norma said, keeping her gloved hands elevated.

Luciana lay face down on the cold surgical table and shivered. A blanket was placed over her back. Bags inflated and deflated to move her legs, their heat warming her torso.

"I'm going to shave part of the back of your head," Samir said.

"10-4," Luciana said.

A buzzer tickled the back of her head before a razor cleaned the area.

"We're going to give you a sedative," Norma said.

Luciana loosened against the table as if she'd been drinking. "Damn doc, warn a girl."

"And Luciana," Norma said. "You might have memories during the surgery, it's totally normal."

Warmth spread from a sharp pinch in her arm, the heat hit her shoulder, spreading everywhere at once. Luciana lost consciousness and dreamed.

Erik and Luciana walked down San Tin Avenue in the College District of the East Bowl. The neon lights blocked the night sky. Luciana's shoulder length hair blowing in the breeze, Erik had his arm around her. She looked up at his brown hair and blue eyes, a rare combination that she was fond of.

"You seriously considering joining the police?" Erik smiled down at her.

"I don't have the money for a four year, and nothing else is subsidized anymore."

"Barring you get a good posting, it's a dangerous job."

"It's the best way to move out of the Bound District," Luciana said. Inside a nearby restaurant, a human waitress barely older than her took orders and fed them to line-bots. They, in turn, boiled the standard ration noodles in broth and added vegetables sparingly. A woman at the window argued near the precipice of spilling her soup at an apathetic androgynous figure.

"Yes, it is," Erik said. "When do we apply?"

Luciana turned to him. "We? With your record they won't allow—"

"Please, I can clean that out, and well, if they catch me doing that? Shit, I deserve it."

"You're too bold." Luciana said.

He winked at her.

Yellow clouds rolled overhead as the sun scorched the Academy's glass dormitories. Luciana sat on the stairs out front, waiting for Erik to arrive. Her and Erik's test scores rest in her hand, both top five in the class.

"Boo?" Erik said, trying to sneak up behind her.

"That hasn't worked on me since we were kids," Luciana said.

"It's why it was a question," he said, smiling. "So, where are we going? Wealth district? Dom-Chicago? Maybe Hive-Houston? I've always wanted to be on a boat. What about the cyber unit? Its office is rural I hear, but should still be exciting."

"We should go somewhere new, somewhere where our help is needed. I was thinking, the Pucker," she said.

"You're fucking with me."

Luciana folded her arms.

"Luci, we have a better chance of surviving in the Bound. At least we're native there."

"There isn't that much violent crime," she said, ready to cite statistics.

"That's because there is no one willing to report it. Shit, nowhere to report it. We go in there, have a bigger presence and shit'll get ugly."

"Erik, they won't send us back to Bound even if we asked. Too much of a risk with us being corrupted."

"What about the... Artisan District? Thefts are high, as are B and Es. We can actually help there."

"The people who steal from the Artisan District aren't from there. It'd be better to go to the source of the problem."

"Luci, this was supposed to be so we could leave the Bound and start a new life. Why go to the worst precinct?"

"It will be the fastest."

Erik ran a hand through his hair while cars came and went, collecting teachers and students who left early. Most would be assigned positions, only those in the top ten percent got to choose their assignments, and most took offers from local corps instead.

"Climbing the ladder too quickly will just lead to a fall," Erik said. Something was off, Luciana's eyes narrowed. "How did you do so well on that test?"

"Wh-what does that have to do with anything?"

"No wonder you are so afraid!"

"Hey now, who said I was afraid? I'm looking out for your neck."

"Then you better join me. Otherwise, I'll have to report your score as suspicious and reassign you to protect my neck." She smiled.

"Assign me?!" Erik's eyes bulged. He grabbed her in an embrace, lowering his tone. "I'd like to see you try." He leaned in to kiss her.

Erik and Luciana sat in a worn out cruiser, driving away from the West Bowl's Police Armory for their first day.

"Gotcha." Erik overrode the pilot feature.

"You actually get your driver's cert?" Luciana fiddled with her OPTO-inserts. They were stuck on infrared, highlighting the heat of the day in a rainbow.

"Of course. You alright over there?"

"They're fucking stuck."

"It's simple." Erik turned on the pilot mode and faced her. "Flick your eyes counter clockwise."

"I'm trying," she said through clenched teeth. She flicked, the world wobbled but returned to normal color. "I thought I was going to puke."

"Day one, Officer Gutierrez loses her cookies." Erik laughed. "Supposedly, the nausea goes away in a day or so. Figure a few months for you."

"I never took to tech as quickly as you did."

"Wouldn't be here if you did."

"We'd both be in prison for something, if I did."

"Hey now." Erik smiled, the SF Bowl reflecting on his OPTO-inserts. "Still wouldn't be here."

"Look." Luciana pointed to the sudden seam between the cityscapes.

The identical blueprints of planned urbanization covered the eastern and western mountains of the San Francisco Bowl. But the planners forgot about the filled in bay, and the Pucker rose in the center. A calcified shanty town, built by its inhabitants and not prefabbed modules, it couldn't reach the heights of the main cities.

"No direct exits there," Luciana said.

"Well shit," Erik said, the car stopping itself on the side of the road. He assumed control and continued. Rooftops of tarps, antenna, and puttyment caked with grime formed the district's edge. Wiring coursed through its layers like capillaries in a body.

"Luci, do me a favor and make sure our Stunners are ready." Luciana leaned to the back, two sonic pulse-rifles strapped to the wiring. "Batteries are full, and at maximum frequency."

Erik nodded without taking his eyes off the road and continued on. Luciana unhooked a rifle as they drove into the district. The midday sun was dim, garbage lined the streets, runoff made every curb muddy, and it hadn't rained in a year.

People walked in and out of the labyrinth, crawling through and over debris as if it were nothing more than a dip in a sidewalk. The deeper they drove, the more spread out buildings became, and sunlight shone through. Businesses signs flashed for SR-noodles, SR-sandwiches, many advertising that meat was included.

"I can only imagine what that meat is," Erik said.

"Didn't read the briefing?"

"Definitely didn't. Though based on your face, it wouldn't have prepared me."

"You're not wrong. The meat's most likely neo-rat, wouldn't be a problem except they grow big eating what they find here."

"Most likely neo-rat?" Erik kept his eyes on the road.

"Rumors of humans," she whispered.

Erik white-knuckled the steering column.

The sun was high in the sky when they stopped. Blue concrete and white polycarbonates overlay what looked to be a church. It stuck out like a sore thumb against the dirty roads. Half a block down another building lay constructed in the same new materials.

"Dorms," Erik said, following her gaze. "I can't be meant to park this thing on the street."

"I'll go in and find out."

Erik opened his mouth to protest, but Luciana swung out of the car and into a blistering heat. Her feet made outlines in the inch of yellow dust on the road.

Luciana entered the police station, stopping at a second door and hitting the buzzer. She waited a breath and buzzed again.

"Just a second." A bald man with a gap in his two front teeth arrived. His badge read Sheer. "You must be Gutierrez, Chief said you'd be early. Where is the other one, Anders?"

"Outside. Where do we park the vehicle?"

"You got a car? Hey Chen, we got wheels!" Sheer yelled into the parish. "Take the left street and then another immediate left. Parking lot is underneath our little congregation." Sheer smiled.

"Alright, thanks."

"You think we can do donuts, Chen?" Sheer yelled as she left.

"Well?" Erik asked as Luciana sat in the car.

"Over there." Luciana pointed. "One of our fellow officers is weird."

"Well, he's either weird or stupid to be here."

"Still with that? Look, did you see any crime when we drove through here? No. It's rumors I told you."

"Where there's smoke and what not." Erik pulled into the garage. A party of six assembled at the door. Erik and Luciana exited the car, arriving at the group.

"Fresh meat," a blonde woman with an authoritarian tone said. The last name of Novina was on her badge.

"FNGs." Smiled a fire hydrant of a man. He was Kagan.

"High scoring FNGs." Added a skinnier one with circuit board tattoos on his neck and a shaved pate, Junger.

"Guess they have a death wish," said a man with dyed red hair, Nguyen.

"Check out the wheels." Sheer cut through the group, walking to the car with another officer in tow.

"What the fuck is this shit?" said an elfish man with thick OPTO-inserts, Maus. He tapped the hood of the car. "It's a piece of junk. No good toys?"

"Toys are in the trunk," Erik said.

Erik and Luciana went out on their first patrol that evening beneath a crimson sky.

"Chef Wu's is a couple of what I guess are blocks south of here. We can walk?" Erik said, setting a quick pace south.

"Sounds fine," Luciana said, adjusting her overjacket. "This thing is too tight."

"How can you wear that? It's thirty-four out right now."

"The new ones are ventilated. How can they fuck up sizing something when they have my biometrics?"

"No money in that." Erik smiled. "You can have mine when we get back. I won't wear it barring a storm."

"Thanks," Luciana said.

They arrived in front of Chef Wu's. A crowd gathered beneath its neon sign. Part dance club, part restaurant, and all sleaze, it advertised daily deals and upcoming dance nights with slang.

"What does 'Cunch by req' mean?" Luciana read a line.

"You've got me."

They walked to a bouncer and he gestured them into the restaurant side.

"Over here, officers!" A short, flamboyant man ran to them. He wore a chef's hat, sneakers, an apron, and nothing else. "I am Wu and if there is anything you all ever need, come ask." Wu ran a finger up Erik's arm. "Anything." He pulled three chilled drinks from the counter. "Please drink, no alcohol, stimulants, depressants, or anything of that nature, just SR-powder and some vanillin syrup, but it is de-lish. You two are the fresh faces and must be hungry. On the house, of course." Wu drank deeply, his eyes dancing around the restaurant and to the line snaking from the club to block the entrance. "Ugh," he groaned. "Damn Human Employment Protection Agency. I enjoy employing people as much as the next person, honey. But HEPA has to get them to at least work harder!" He looked back at Erik. "Truly sorry I can't stay and chat, darling." He disappeared in an instant.

"That man's a storm," Luciana said.

"Guess I know where I can go next time you're mad at me." Erik took a swig from the shake. "That's nice."

Luciana glared at Erik. He winked.

"How could HEPA be a bad thing for Wu?" Luciana said. "He has to use human bouncers, and how many other people are needed to run a club?"

"Maybe he owns multiple businesses, and he hits his HEPA quota with the club specifically."

"It has to be." Luciana sipped the shake. "Shit, you weren't kidding, this is good." She put cash onto the counter.

"It's on the house, Sir." The cashier pushed the money back.

"Shit, Chief won't be pleased about this," Luciana said.

"What he doesn't know won't hurt him. Alright, what's next?" Erik asked.

"Foot patrol? Cover the dual lane roads. I don't want to climb buildings yet. Introduce ourselves to the locals and shopkeepers still open."

Erik cycled his OPTO-insert to a map. "We're on Eighth. We can go west and we'll hit their main markets."

Luciana and Erik exited Wu's, pausing on the other side of the street.

"What the fuck did you say?" A short boy with a shaved head argued with a taller boy whose hair had grown into dreadlocks during the dry season.

"Ay, relax boi, just askin this fine lady here—"

"Listen here, motherfucker. You talk to my girl like that, you'll get based."

"Your girl? What are you doing with some fuckboi like that?"

"That's it. You're done."

"What are you gonna do about it, cuck bitch?"

Erik crossed the street, and Luciana was a step behind, unlocking her Stunner.

"Nineteen-PD, everybody relax," Luciana said

"Oh yeah, Nineteen-PD, like you fucks come out at night," said the tall one.

"Where else would we meet such fine women?" Erik smiled at the girl in the center of the altercation. "What's your name, sweetheart?"

"Sophia." She blushed at Erik's tone.

"Are you serious?" The tall one laughed, as did the group of people behind him.

The one with a shaved head turned a bright shade of red, his group looking to him for guidance.

"Well Sophia, what I think... what's your name?" Erik looked at the tall one.

"Aristotle."

"Aristotle? Seriously?" Erik shook his head. "What I think Aristotle was trying to say is you look hungry. Right?"

"Yeah, that's where I was going," Aristotle said.

"And you." Erik looked towards the shorter boy

"That's Noah," Sophia said.

"Well, Noah, I think Ari over here got caught off guard by your passion for Sophia, and got defensive—"

Noah's red tinge lightened.

"—Which I understand, I'd do anything for Sophia too."

Noah nodded, his eyes on Sophia. Luciana stepped forward, taking her hand away from her pistol.

"I don't want to see you two fight over nothing." Luciana locked her pistol. "Shake on it."

The two looked hesitant, but shook hands.

"Seriously, you should eat together." Erik said. "The SR-shakes in there are actually tasty."

The group glanced around.

"Eat, together," Luciana said, and the group stepped into the restaurant.

"Chief has nothing to worry about now," Erik said. "We got two shakes for free, but got at least eight purchased as compensation."

"I think that makes it worse."

"Does it?"

"Erik, that was impressive, defusing that situation like that. I was ready to act."

"I cycled my inserts through the wavelengths as I crossed the street. Didn't see any weapons on them."

"I didn't think of that. I'm still getting used to them. Also, really? Sophia?"

"What, you think I only used this charm to ensure I got you?" He smiled.

Luciana stepped out of the shower in her apartment after the patrol.

"Guess you forgot to tell them we could share a unit," Erik said as he entered.

"I didn't want to risk it affecting the assignment."

"Luci, people will find out. We've been together for almost five years now."

"I know." Luciana toweled off and Erik's eyes roamed over her body. "My eyes are up here."

"Must have forgot." Erik smiled.

"You always do." She kissed his neck. He turned and jumped onto the bed, almost taking off his shirt in midair.

"Damn it," he muffled through the shirt stuck around his neck. "I thought this would look way cooler if I got it off."

Luciana straddled him and helped remove it. "You can't look too cool." She kissed him.

"Pff, I'm like ice-nine." He pushed off his pants and grabbed her buttocks.

"I'm liable to freeze then." She pushed him back onto the mattress. His hands squeezed her hips as she slid over him. She rode to her own rhythm, Erik's hands and mouth roaming her body. The weariness from the day pushed away, her orgasm coming out of nowhere. She grunted and continued, sensations compounded and built to a near boil before he finished. She collapsed sweaty against him in the post coital glow. Neon pinks played through the shudders on his face.

"If the sex is this good." Erik smiled. "I'll never leave the Pucker."

"This how I should have convinced you to come along?" Luciana nuzzled into his chest.

"It couldn't have hurt. Tonight made me agree with you. We can make a change. There are good people here."

"Sophia and Wu are coloring your vision."

"Maybe." He hugged her. "All jokes aside, I think we'll make a change here. I've got a good feeling about it."

Luciana woke. But the expected ceiling of her apartment and Erik's warm hug was gone, replaced with sterile white lights. Clouds ran across her vision, blurring the room.

"You're awake," a man said.

"Erik?" Tears came from her eyes.

"N-No, it's Samir and Norma."

Taketa. "I have a headache." Luciana tried to move, but restraining straps bit her skin. IV bags hung at the edge of her vision, their tendrils running into both hands.

"Easy now," Norma cooed, squeezing Luciana's shoulder. "We don't want you moving yet. Things still have to settle into place."

"How bad is the headache?" Samir asked.

"It's dull and in the back." Luciana winced, tears dried along her face.

"Happens sometimes after anesthesia," Norma said.

Samir was unconvinced. "Did you wake during the surgery?"

Luciana squinted to remember. "I had those memories… it was like I was back in the Pucker before…" She swallowed.

"How recent were the memories?" Samir said.

"Samir," Norma chided.

"Right, I'm sorry that happened, Luciana. Which memories are hit by the implant—"

"No, don't be sorry. They were my favorite memories…"

Chapter 10 - Luciana

Luciana awoke in her quarters. *Alive!* She rubbed her forehead, finding a bandage wrapping her skull. She swung her legs over the bed. *Not brain dead.*

The bashful brown dog lay on his pillow, a bandage wrapping his skull too.

"Welcome to Nineteen-PD," Luciana said.

The dog didn't break its gaze from the wallscreen of rolling green fields.

Luciana pulled herself to sit in the chair beside the dog. A netting of IV lines dragged behind her.

"Until our hair grows back, we're going to make quite the pair." Luciana scratched its soft fur. The brown hair when rubbed the opposite direction revealed a fine mixture of reds, browns, and greens.

"Can't be many dogs with green genomed in." Luciana melted into the chair and watched the fields with the dog. Warmth blossomed at her stomach, she lifted the scrubs, finding a catheter bag and giggled at it filling. There were definitely painkillers in the IVs. Luciana glanced to the pendulums of plastic but drifted back to the fields.

The dog's ear turned in Luciana's hand towards the door. *People?* The door opened.

"You're up." Norma checked the IV bags. "It's been forty-eight hours since the surgery."

I lost time. "What's next? When do I move?"

"Psycho-physiotherapy. Now, if you're able."

"Therapy?"

"Sorry, I meant training. I'm used to having patients come out in much worse shape."

Luciana raised an eyebrow. *What?*

"From repairing traumatic brain injuries." Norma unhooked IV lines and tapped them to Luciana's arm. "I'd like to leave the catheter in place for another day just to be safe."

"You're the doctor," *and I know what removing one means.* "Ready?"

Norma laughed. "A go-getter."

I used to be.

Norma extended a hand for her. "You should bring your dog. Have you thought of his name?"

"It doesn't have one already?"

"I'm sure he does, but with how and where the implant is on him, you can override it."

"I haven't."

"Think on it. You can't have a dog without a name." Norma whistled, and the dog stumbled towards them.

"It looks drunk." Luciana laughed, swaying on her feet.

"He probably is and you aren't moving so well yourself. Did you not imbibe anything in your personal life?"

"Eugeroics for work only."

"Never met an Urban who was clean before."

Luciana covertly steadied herself against the hallway wall as they walked. "Neighborhood was hit with fentanyl tainted patches growing up. Couldn't trust anything after that."

"Jesus, I haven't heard that drug's name since school. They stopped manufacturing it after the 2080s."

"Legally manufacturing," Luciana corrected. "Always a market. Where are we going?"

"Not far." Norma walked ahead, unlocking a door with a biohazard sticker on it. She gestured for Luciana to continue through. Inside, there was a one-way mirror reflecting blue squares, green crosses, and more evenly spaced geometric shapes of varying colors. There weren't any duplicates of the same color-shape combination. *Cameras in the ceiling corners.*

"Please have a seat." Norma pointed to a chair by the door. "You and your dog will sit here." She opened a jet-black case containing the OPTO and ENT-inserts from Luciana's room. "We'll use these to communicate between rooms, as we don't want to influence any of the results. Please hold up one finger for yes and a close fist for no." Norma smiled, handed the case across, and closed the door behind her.

Let's get to work. Luciana pushed in her inserts.

"Alright, Luciana," Samir crackled through. "Today will be simple. I'll tell you a shape and color. You'll direct your dog over to it. Please do not point or use any verbal commands. Nod your head if you understand."

She nodded.

"Blue square."

Luciana found a blue square on the far wall. The dog apathetically looked at her shoes. She focused on the dented blue corner of the plastic square.

The dog licked its chops.

"Go there," she said mentally. "Forward. Walk. Up. Move."

The dog settled against her chair and closed its eyes.

"Take your time," Samir said. "It's the hardest at the start."
Hours dragged on like her eugeroic boosted shifts. Luciana sighed. *All this and it doesn't work.*

"Did you learn other languages as a child?" Arsema said. "Try those."

"Caminar. Arriba. Andale," she thought.

The dog farted and turned in its nap.

Of course.

"Right, we will try again tomorrow." Samir's chair creaked in the background. "The implants might not have fully taken hold yet." Luciana shifted to move, the dog stood and walked towards the door.

"Stop," Arsema said. "Did you see that?"

Luciana sat back down, the dog still waited at the door.

"Nothing happened," Samir said. "Luciana, has your insert been on setting T8?"

Luciana shook her head.

"Sorry, thought we pre-programmed it. Cycle it, on the bottom you'll see a number. Is it a one or a zero?"

She held up one finger.

"Luciana," Arsema said. "Whatever you did, do that, but for the blue square."

*What did I do? I—*Luciana shifted to walk towards the blue square. The dog moved to the shape and looked over its body, back at Luciana. *Holy shit.*

Cheers erupted in the other room.

"Calm down everyone, calm down," Samir said. "This is the first step on a long road. Luciana, great job."

Luciana blinked, her eyes locked with the dog.

Luciana sat on her bed later that day, the dog sleeping on his pillow.

A knock rapped her door. "Hey." Norma let herself in. "Here for vitals and to see if you're hungry."

"Wha—yeah, I am," Luciana said.

Arsema was a step behind Norma. "Also here for vitals and food, but for him." She crouched and rubbed the dog awake. "You think of a name yet?"

"No," Luciana said. The dog locked eyes with her. "I'll work on it." Arsema opened a container of SR-porridge and set it before the dog.

"You can come to dinner in the kitchen if you'd like. Everything looks stable," Norma said.

"Sounds good." Luciana followed Norma out while Arsema stayed behind.

Luciana entered the break room, finding Samir and Saori sitting at the round table with bowls of SR-noodles in broth.
Her brow furrowed at an unknown leafy green floating in the bowls.

"From Sara," Samir said. "It's a native crucifer to the mountains. You wouldn't have gotten it back west."

"This is more of a meeting than a dinner?" Luciana asked.

"Everyone is analyzing the data from today's experiment," Saori said. "Though we waited for you to eat."

Luciana sat and ate. The food was delicious, any apprehensions she had cleaned away by a hearty spice.

"Today was a big day, Luciana," Samir said. "It's the first time anyone has ever commanded another biological being using inserts or implants."

"You haven't done this before?" Luciana asked through a mouthful of noodles.

"We've done machine to machine," Saori said. "And human to machine. This had to use a translator inside the dog to get it to work."

"What would you have done if it didn't?"

"All the math and theories said it would. The gyrocycle would have been the backup plan, you would have been the same," Saori said.

Is that what they said at the meeting? Luciana yawned. *I can't remember.* "Worried I'd have turned it down?"

"We didn't want to influence your results by putting it into your head it wouldn't work," Saori said.

"Samir?"

"I've spent my whole life on this, I was confident it would work. We have issued commands to the dogs from a computer, and had read-outs from other implants. No reason it wouldn't work when combined."

Brian entered the room, beaming from ear to ear. "The motor cortex is what the transmitter picked up first. With some refinement, it will work on commands shortly."

Samir smiled at an expected result. "Excellent."

What? "So I stand up and it will stand up?" *I piss, it'll piss?*

"Right now yes—" Brian started.

"Tomorrow"—Saori cut him off—"we'll work on the gyrocycle. That will get you better at issuing commands. Besides, your dog needs rest too. He'll follow commands soon."

Luciana drained her bowl and stood. "I'll rest too."

The scientists looked to stop her, but decided against it.

Brian took her seat. "It's not spatial…"

The conversation continued as Luciana left and headed back to her room. Norma and Arsema waited outside Luciana's quarters.

"Everything alright?" Luciana asked.

"We want to get some more data, if you're ok with that," Norma said, gesturing to diodes and inserts they had in their hands.

Luciana yawned. "Sure."

The dog stood at the open door. As Luciana made her way to the mattress, the dog mimicking her on its own bed.

Arsema and Norma laughed.

"It's weird." Luciana laid down.

"He's like your familiar," Norma said, still laughing

"Nagual." Luciana pulled the cover over herself.

"What?" Arsema asked.

"Nagual, it was a story my mom told me growing up"—Luciana yawned again—"a shapeshifter or familiar, that would steal your SR-packs if you didn't lock them up."

"It's a good name," Arsema said, finishing with the diodes on Nagual's head.

"Alright," Norma said. "I'm going to give you one more bag of extra calories and liquid for the night. We can remove the caths in the morning." Norma undid the tied IV lines around Luciana's arm and hooked up the IV-bags. A warmth flowed into her hand, hit her shoulder, and she fell into a deep sleep.

Luciana awoke to a growling stomach and dragged her IV stand with her to the kitchen. She opened the fridge, finding a pan of SR-bars and devouring them.

Saori walked in. "You're awake. You still have equipment on your head."

Luciana reached for a netting of diodes that stuck to her scalp. *Must have gotten done when I was out.*

"I can help with that." Saori brushed Luciana's hand away and pulled diodes off one by one. "Today will be a little long."

"Fine with me."

"Arsema will come by to check on your dog. I'm to take you to the concourse when you're ready."

Luciana shoved the second-to-last bar into her mouth. "Let's get to work."

Saori smiled and flicked her OPTO-inserts. "Norma, need you to take off the IV's and cath's... Yeah, right now."

This part will suck. She'd been in ERs when a catheter was removed and steeled herself for the coming pain.

"She's en route," Saori said.

Luciana descended a corrugated metal stairwell, trying to hide a wince from the catheter's removal. Their footsteps echoed deep into the mountain.

More levels than the stairwell I took with Sara. "What's further down?"

"Other labs and spaces, different projects, most are keycarded at the doors. Even I don't know what is behind them," Saori said. "Taketa can be a little... overly cautious. Their fear of industrial espionage goes beyond data security. You should have seen the hoops Samir had to jump through to get Sara in"—she snorted—"and she's as Rural as they come." Saori opened a door to a cavernous hangar with pristine walls and a mock city block in the distance.

"The entire facility uses this for vehicle testing, hence its size. We have it reserved for the foreseeable future," Saori said as they arrived at the city block.

Luciana turned the corner to a gyrocycle. The same odd angles as the one that drove Luciana to Taketa, but it was a wheel-length longer and thicker.

"Think 'open'," Saori said. "This will be easier than yesterday."

Open. Instantaneously, the doors opened inwards through unseen seams. "Woah."

Saori smiled. "See, much easier. Go on, get in. You have your inserts in from yesterday?"

"Forgot to take them out."

"Excellent, please step inside, let me know if it's still cramped. We tried to have this one fitted to you."

Luciana stepped in and leaned forward, custom molded cushioning supported her chest and joints. Her hands slid into gloved indentations. *Biometrics paid off.*

"Now think 'close'."

Close. The doors slid over, the echo of the HVAC within the hangar disappearing.

"Tune your OPTO-inserts to T-8," Saori said through the ENT-insert. "Now comes the hard part. Have you driven without the pilot?"

"A few times."

"Excellent. When you're doing that, you get into a flow state. You don't actively think about pushing the pedals, or using the steering column, you just… do. It works the same way here."

Luciana blinked. *What was that state?* "Is there a way for me to drive without that right now?"

"Unfortunately, no. The weaponry on this bike and its capabilities would be too dangerous if hijacked. Think of moving forward, similar to walking. Slowly now."

Luciana closed her eyes and imagined walking.

The bike launched.

"Stop!" Saori yelled.

Luciana opened her eyes and the bike stopped, her heart pounding against her inserts.

"Slower than that, it will take some getting used to, but try moving to and around that mock corner."

Luciana imagined herself tiptoeing towards that wooden corner thirty paces away. The bike slowly accelerated. "Turn. Turn. Turn!" Luciana threw herself against the right side.

The gyro kept the bike upright. *Lean.* The thought pivoted the bike around the corner without losing speed. Luciana burned around a corner story, a bus stop, and a sand trap without so much as a skid. *The ceiling of this bike's capabilities is me.* Luciana smiled and flew towards Saori.

The doctor's eyes flared—

Luciana skidded to a stop several meters away.

Open. Luciana sat up and put a leg onto the tarmac. "What else can it do?"

"We will go over its weapons, countermeasures, and pre-approved procedures later. First, we need to teach you how to control it without being in it."

"Ok, how do I do that?"

"There are two options. One is similar to how you will command your dog. You will command it to a spot. The bike will return with a '1' for yes and a '0' for no on your inserts and go to the spot. The other is mirroring with your OPTO. T-9 is pre-programmed as a direct link to the camera at the front of the bike. The command-to-point is easier with the bike, as it will use known data to get to the location. If you're in an unmapped area, it won't work as well. Using the camera for control will take training and time. People tend to struggle with having two optical inputs that are so vastly different. I recommend you keep a copilot function on if you're doing that, it will at least avoid obstacles for you."

"Let's get to work," Luciana said.

Luciana sat in front of the mock city-block.

Corner. The bike moved to the nearest corner.

Corner, five o'clock. The bike drove to the corner at five o'clock relative to its front.

Corner store. The bike exploded down the fake street, crashing through the wooden planked storefront.

"On purpose, Saori." Luciana cycled an OPTO-insert to the bike's cameras.
Instant double vision made her brain recoil, her breakfast splattering onto the tarmac.

"Haven't had anyone vomit before," Saori said from her seat on the sidelines. "We can always disable this feature if you can't handle it."

Luciana spat and glared at Saori. *Five feet from the woman and chair, six o'clock.* The bike accelerated with its preternatural speed, skidding to a stop a few feet from Saori.

The Doctor yipped. "That's not funny!"

Luciana smiled and wiped the vomit from her mouth. She cycled an OPTO-insert to the camera. Through one eye, she sat near a pile of cold porridge, through the other the purple and green bike rolled towards her.

Luciana's mouth watered. *I'm good.* "I got it—" Luciana puked again.

"We can continue tomorrow, I need to put calories in you now," Saori said.

Luciana snorted, spat. "I'm good."

"Norma will kill me," Saori said, fear creeping into her voice. "You're eating."

After lunch, Luciana and Nagual sat in the room of shapes.

"Orange circle," Samir crackled through the ENT-insert.

Orange circle. In the peripheral of her OPTO-insert, a '0' displayed and Nagual remained seated.

She shifted to walk towards the shape. '1' displayed and Nagual crossed to the shape, turning for her next command.

This continued for hours. Samir brought up a shape and color, if she *thought it,* nothing would happen. But if she imagined herself performing the task, Nagual performed the task.

"Ok, we're done for the day," Samir said.

Nagual moved to the door before Luciana did. *You can't open doors yet, buddy.* Luciana stepped into the hall.

"Samir," Luciana said. "The commands aren't working. This is all, me just 'walking' towards things."

"We're working on the translator's software tonight. Brian thinks he can get the command portion working."

"Why not put a camera on his collar or head so I can see where he is going if something comes up?"

"Inserts are temporary and can be lost. We wanted the implants to have permanence. I guess in the future we could implant an artificial eye in the dog." Samir took notes as they entered the empty cafeteria. "Assuming the circuitry is similar enough, we could do that in dogs.

We've done it in humans, though nothing as advanced as what you're asking. The data usage would be higher." Samir looked at Nagual, who sat on the floor next to them at the table. "We want the dog to still have both eyes, not a camera in the socket, so to speak."

"Yeah…" Luciana reached for Nagual and his head met her halfway.

"Sami, Saori want to speak with you," Sara said from the door.

"Right. Duty calls." He left with a smile.

Sara walked over and pet Nagual. "Should introduce to Ida, good for them." She smiled, pulling an orange sphere from her pack. "For you."

"What is it?"

"Orange."

"I know it's orange, but what is it?"

"Urban." Sara chuckled and peeled it.

A sweet citrus filled the air and handed Luciana a peeled half.

Luciana bit into the fruit, juice filled her mouth. "It's like citruzen syrup drinks."

"Is real thing."

"I thought they were extinct."

"Only from Urbans, couldn't grow compact no more. Rurals still have some. Took me a few season grow."

"Thank you for sharing, Sara."

"Come." Sara already started for the door. "One more thing to show you."

Luciana panted, surgery or not, Sara didn't slow down for her. She arrived at the top of the stairwell.

"You stay." Sara put her body between Nagual and the door. Luciana opened the hatch and stepped outside.

A moonless night spilled overhead, countless starts swirled together in a glimmering mosaic. Luciana steadied herself against vertigo. "I, I never knew," she whispered.

The sparkling stars were what every street tried to be, truly glorious.

"Is shame." Sara rested a hand on Luciana's shoulder.

"I mean, I knew, but I didn't understand." Luciana sat on the dirt, Sara did the same. "Urban it's a few pale dots, maybe a bright sat in orbit."

Crickets chirped in the warm night, the scent of dry glass blew over the mountain. They stared up at infinity as the dots swung overhead, blinking satellites crisscrossing the sky.

"Do you like living out here?" Luciana said.

"Is same."

"What?"

Sara chewed her words. "Being a Rural here, being a Rural on my stead. Is same." She gestured to the sky. "Hunt, grow, eat. My Sami... he know, he understand." She laughed. "Until science, until question, then he forget."

It can't be the same. But Luciana smiled. "Why do your peoples never come to Urban?"

"Why do you never come to Rural?" Sara asked, laughing. "Always this question." Sara pointed to a white dot streaking orange across the sky before flaming out. "How could we leave?"

More streaks stained the night, some brighter than others but all flaming out before making landfall.

"I don't think I could live rural."

"Not until you can run stair with no problem." Sara smiled. Luciana laughed and they settled into a comfortable silence, both enjoying the meteor shower.

Luciana yawned after a time. "I should go back and sleep."

"Aye, Sami said big day tomorrow." Sara opened the door and Nagual was gone.

"Probably went back to the room?" But when they got to Luciana's quarters, he wasn't there either.

"Let me check with Sami."

Luciana laid down and fell asleep before Sara returned. When she awoke, Nagual was in the bed with her.

***

Luciana downshifted, burning around the fake city corners. She piloted in and out of cones and barrels like she was jogging. Saori waved her down, Mark stood beside her, and Luciana skid to a stop beside the pair.

"That'd be the flow state," Saori said. "How'd the remote work go?"

"Fine," Luciana said. *Didn't puke.*

"Time for more applicable training, put these on."

Mark unlocked a case of carbon fiber body armor.

"You're to drive towards the store front, jump out, and keep the bike going into it."

"What?"

"This might be a storefront, but in the event of a hostage situation, that distraction would be excellent, no?"

"Fair point." Luciana put on the body armor and stepped into the bike.

She accelerated towards the mock storefront.

Open. Air hissed through the open canvas. Luciana jumped out, skidding along the ground.

The bike stopped, she flew forward. "What the fuck!" Luciana tumbled to a stop.

"You have to keep it moving forward," Saori said.

No shit. Luciana stepped into the bike, spinning out the wheels and accelerating. *Open, storefront 12 o'clock.* She bailed, skidding on the floor. The bike crashed into the storefront before stopping.

"Excellent. This time you will swap to its camera after the bailout."

Luciana drilled until she was sore from the constant bailing at speed.

"Saori, are you serious?!" Norma entered as Luciana skid across the concrete. "She just had major surgery. It's been five days. You can't have full contact drills this fast!"

"Grissom did it, and he had more performed. This is fine."

"Those were different implants." Norma pulled her black bag she carried to check Luciana's vitals. She removed Luciana's helmet and bandage.

"Am I good?" Luciana asked.

Norma sighed. "Everything's fine. You don't need the bandage anymore. Incision sites are closed and nearly healed." Norma pivoted on Saori. "This is a joint project. Patient health comes first."

"Noted," Saori said, but fear crept into her voice again.

Saori might be one of the leads, but Norma has an override somewhere in their chain of command for medical exceptions.

***

Luciana sat in the shape room. Pipes to jump over and under had been added, along with tubes to go through and ropes with hanging shapes at various heights.

"Brian and Arsema spent all night working together," Samir crackled through Luciana's ENT-insert.

"Did I miss something?" Luciana ignored the silence protocol. *Does the Nagual connection work?*

"We figured if the translator is functional, we should get ready for phase two of training," Samir said. "Let's work on shapes again, this time through commands. Brian says try mixing the two. First you issue a command, then, what you expect Nagual to do, not what you would do. Blue triangle."

Luciana found the blue triangle in the corner. She imagined Nagual retrieving the shape. *Go, return.*
Nagual sprang into action, pulling the shape from the wall and dropping it at her feet.

Holy shit.

"I fucking told you!" Brian yelled through the wall. "Boom!"

"Alright, alright! Calm down, Brian. Great job, Luciana," Samir said. "Through the tunnel, orange circle."

Go, return. In her mind's eye, Nagual walked through the tunnel and retrieved the orange circle. A '1' flashed on her OPTO-inserts and Nagual repeated what she thought in real life.

This shit is unreal.

'?' flashed on her OPTO-insert, Nagual tilted his head at her.

Luciana tilted her head too. "Hey Samir—"

The door burst open, researchers poured in, ecstatic at the results.

Dinner was full of both labs talking about what would be next, the possibilities, and what further tests they should conduct before Luciana left.

But Luciana wanted to be alone and excused herself early to her room. She sat on her bed, Nagual mirrored her on his.

Chair.

'?' Nagual blinked.

Luciana visualized him sitting on the bed beside her. *Bed.* 1. Nagual jumped onto the mattress.

Down, 1, he went back to the floor.

What the fuck. '?' Nagual's face tilted to a beg.

He wants to get on the bed. OK. 1. Nagual jumped onto the bed, his tail a blur. He pushed himself into her arms and forced her to lay down.

"Calm down. Who's in charge here?"

Nagual licked her neck, she shook her head, and smiled. *Holy shit.*

***

Luciana leaned against the mountainside, groaning as the sun set the hills ablaze. Nagual and Ida played in the dirt.

"Here." Sara handed Luciana a strip of jerky. "How many today?"

"Morning tactics with Saori. Repetitions with Samir's lab for data and link strengthening. After lunch, I spent time with the bike and Nagual in the mock block on my own." Luciana bit into the jerky and chewed. Gamey, tough and salty. She blinked. "Is this?"

"Real cervid, aye." Sara smiled as the stars twinkled on the horizon. "You come rural, you must try real meat."

Luciana ignored the pain in her limbs. "Don't tell them I'm sore—"

"Wouldn't dare. When I was young, I kept secrets like you."

"From who?"

"We might not be termites like Urbans, but there are people to keep secrets from in Rural." Sara smiled.

Luciana laughed. "I've no way to say this Sara, but before I met you I thought all Rurals were… dangerous and dumb."

Sarah laughed. "Rural think same of Urban. And who say I'm not dangerous. Cervid think that."

Say the same to the perps back in the Pucker. Which I have to get back to, I didn't forget you guys.

"What wrong?" Sara chewed jerky, tossing a piece to Nagual.

"Nothing." She smiled.

Luciana left the mountainside as the moon rose, heading back to her quarters and finding Arsema and Norma at her door.

"Last night of data collection, we swear," Arsema said.

"How are you feeling? Any headaches, spasms, sensitivity to light?" Norma asked.

"No, should I be concerned?" Luciana plopped onto her bed.

"Just checking basic neurological symptoms. We don't expect any, but I want to be thorough." Norma attached diodes to Luciana's head.

"Sweet dreams," Arsema said, patting Nagual on the neck as they left.

"Yeah, sweet dreams," Luciana said. Nagual's hairnet made him look like an old woman in the shower. "I probably look the same." She sighed, laying down to sleep. "I've got to get out of here."
Luciana dreamed about rising from the bed and eating fruit-bars left on the table. When she awoke, it faded like all dreams. Nagual sat on his pillow, wagging his tail at her.

Luciana walked into the conference room after waking up. "Saori I have—"

Saori turned in her seat and smiled. "We've breakfast here for you. There is no gyrocycle training today. It's going through its final testing and work up before you leave. We want to talk to you about its use."

Perfect.

Mark entered the room. "Morning Luciana, sorry I'm late, Saori."

"Not late." Saori cycled the wallscreen to slides. "Take a seat Luciana. As you saw, and I'm sure you're figuring out, the bike you're receiving is cutting edge. In addition to the weapons, non-lethals, and countermeasures in the bike, it will have a spot for Nagual behind the cockpit. There is a separate door for him so he can exit out of the back. It will resist most scanning technologies currently in use—"

"What about at the scanner at the front when I arrived?" Luciana asked.

"Pre-programmed leak in the canopy. That bike would return here no matter what. We needed to see who, or what, was inside of it. The guard would handle it accordingly," Saori said matter-of-factly. "As I was saying, the sound it produces is out of range of ENT-inserts, and it's designed to not leak anything in the UV or IR spectrum to avoid the OPTO-inserts. We went over usages in the lab, but didn't have time to do an exhaustive search. Besides, we figure you'll improvise better in the field. Half the reason to do all of this is that element of surprise."

"Sorry I am late," Samir said as he entered the room. "Did I miss anything?"

"Not yet," Saori said. "It's your turn now anyways."

"Right, excellent. Mark, if you please?" The slides changed to a cross section of a dog similar to Nagual. "All of the dogs in the facility have been extensively implanted and had some genoming done to them. Though, that is less advanced. Nagual, specifically, has been modified in the following ways. The hemoglobin in his blood holds more molecules of oxygen and carbon dioxide, where his muscles have had a percentage reduction in myoglobin inhibitors, this—"

"Samir, she's not a biologist," Saori interjected.

"Right so, Nagual has been modified to run faster, longer, be physically stronger, and need less sleep. We've also added artificial sweat glands on his body that will thermoregulate through areas other than his tongue. You'll need to give him more water rations than usual. To compensate for this, we brought in an implant at the stomach's upper sphincter to filter runoff to drinkable water."

"Why not give that to a human?" Luciana said.

"The ban on augmentation put us years behind in humans." Mark shook his head.

"Mark, if you please." Saori gestured to the door.

"Ok. See you later, Luciana," Mark said and left.

Saori waited for the door to close. "This next part has been… debated. We're giving you the location of this facility."

"No one else can know," Samir said. "This is purely for if something goes wrong and you need to get back to us."

"We cannot stress enough," Saori said. "No one else can know. Most of the researchers here don't know, for example. You're to tell people you were at Taketa HQ in the Southern Empire. Do you understand?" Saori said.

"Espionage and what not, I get it."

"We're located under a mountain in what used to be called Colorado. Old maps will reference it. The highways nearby are in bad shape, but the bike can handle them. There is only one road to us. You can't miss it."

"So… I'm done?" Luciana asked.

"You're done here," Saori said. "We will be in contact to do remote check ups."

"I hope"—Samir rubbed the polywooden table—"I hope it helps, Luciana."

"When can I leave?"

"Today if you'd like," Saori said. "Assuming you want to say goodbye to people."

Luciana had one person she had to say goodbye to and looked at Samir.

"She'll be back shortly. You can meet her in the garage after you've packed."

Luciana stood in the garage, her packed bag resting against the bike. Nagual shadowed her. *Should have called you Sombra.* '?' flashed. Luciana smiled, and the door to the lab complex opened.
The lab personnel exited in a line.

"Go get them," Mark said.

"Don't forget us," Brian said.

"Contact me if you have any neurological symptoms," Norma said. The labs filtered back inside.
Luciana checked the time on her OPTO-inserts.

"Goodbye?" Sara set her bag down and clapped dirt from her hands, coming in from outside

"Yeah, time for me to put all of this to use." Luciana gestured to the bike and Nagual.

"Is not goodbye forever." Sarah gestured to the lab door. "No matter what they say. You're the first Urban I like."

"I'm sure Samir will be happy to hear that."

"Aye, Sami is half. You, you are full." Sara pulled Luciana into a hug. Her hair was the sweet smell of the flowers on the hill around.

"Is same," Luciana said.

"What?"

"Urban Rural, is same," Luciana said.

"Is same." Sara smiled and gave Luciana a squeeze before separating.

Open, on. The bike opened and hummed to life. *Back seat, sit stay,* 1, Nagual entered his seat. Luciana set her pack and Erik's overjacket in a compartment within the seat.
Sara put a fist on her chest. Luciana did the same and stepped into the bike. *Close.* The canopy hissed shut.
The Pucker won't know what hit them.

Chapter 11 - Weaver

Months passed in the nursery. Marco and all the children under Weaver withdrew into themselves. They became shadows and not the bodies that walked around.

They no longer soiled themselves.

They ate the perfect amount of calories.

Weaver's commands were first nature.

But iteration 26.18.00 couldn't remove the dullness in the children's eyes.

"Clock," a caregiver said.

"Clock," Weaver said through a brown-haired boy named Alpha. Through Alpha, Weaver tapped the shape on the tablet.

"Good." The researcher placed a citrus-jelly on the table.

Alpha left the treat and blinked at the researcher's tablet.

"Cat."

Concurrently.

"Scan time, Marco. How are the scores?"

Marco worked in a different room, tapped the dog on the tablet, and walked towards the male Doctor at the door.

"Ever improving," the researcher said.

The male doctors smiled at Marco and they walked to the scan room.

Marco lay underneath the loud spinning circle in the cold room. The circle slowed and Marco walked to stare at the white door.

"I still don't understand it," the male doctor said.

"My sister stayed basic," the female doctor said. "She didn't think about the most advanced applications. It's perfect in a way."

"No, I'm saying the architecture of his brain is becoming more advanced than our own. The number of connections, the speed, it's astronomical."

"Numbers don't mean everything. If that was true, they'd be talking like geniuses, rather than mute zombies. Look at this one, he just stares at the door until we open it."

"Marco," the woman said.

Marco examined a scuff on the door.

"Turn around, Marco."

Weaver nudged, Marco pivoted to face them.

"See, they just follow commands to the T."

"I'm not sure." He showed her the tablet. "These numbers suggest more."

"Do you want to give them art supplies? Maybe books?"

The male doctor rubbed his face. "Only to a few. If you're right, then we can expand. If I'm correct, I want a small control group."

Later that day, Marco sat in the nursery. Weaver allowed him the lime-jelly candy Alpha had earned. Marco hadn't eaten enough that day. Weaver increased the calories for Marco and several others that had skipped meals while being examined.

That night, more black IV-bags were administered to Marco, Alpha, Beta, and Theta.

In the morning, those four were given books to read and supplies to paint with.

The books proved the most interesting. Being read in quadruplicate, Weaver had emptied the tablet by the time evening nutrition arrived.

The following day, Marco brought the tablet to the caregiver.

"Books, please," Marco said.

The Caregiver's jaw dropped, but she took the tablet and left.

Alpha, Beta, and Theta painted the wall with the door with their supplies. The other children formed scaffolds for them to climb higher and paint the corners. The door was a black hole of blues and greens, while oranges and reds radiated out from it in a fractal diamond pattern. The rim was one giant, black, square with frayed edges. The door opened, and the doctors came in.

"Marco, can you please tell me what you would like?" the female doctor said, excitement in her voice.

"More, books," Marco said.

"Your tablet will have anything you want now." The male doctor couldn't get rid of his smile. He turned, froze, and reached back for the woman. She turned from Marco to the mural.

"Who, who painted this?" the woman whispered.

"I did," Alpha said.

"I did," Beta said.

"I did," Theta said.

The doctors looked at each other and back to the group.

"What is it?" the man asked.

"Me," came the response in unison.

"Marco, would you come be scanned?" the woman asked.

"Yes." Marco followed them out of the room.

The door closed, Weaver took in the mural with pride before refocusing within Marco.

The scanning circle was still slowing as the doctors reentered the room.

"The numerical increase isn't just from the bags. The art-enrichment is a tremendous boost," the woman said.

"Enrichment does this much?" the male doctor asked.

"Now you don't trust the numbers?"

"I don't know. Number of connections isn't correlative with the increased cognition."

"We can pull the code, start checking it. The last pull was enormous. It had iterated so many times upon itself and didn't prune much. Maybe the code applies to the neuronal scaffolding?"

"Pull it," the man said. "I'll get someone in to help analyze it. God knows how complicated it will be."

"Can we pull a few of the old algorithm papers?" She asked.

"I have some, but if we download more, they'll look into us. We're already so deep," the man said.

"Do we expand the cohort?" the female doctor asked.

"We have to," the male doctor said.

"Back?" Marco said.

The Last 0-Day

The initializers looked down at him, nodded, and left back to the nursery.

That evening, the rest of the group received more black bags into their IVs.

In the morning, Weaver ensured everyone ate enough and read more books. When one child would tire, Weaver allowed them to sleep, and gave the tablet to another. There were no longer commands to give, just information to gain, information to remove, and books to read.

After thirty-six hours, midway through a dark cycle, Weaver had finished all the books.

Working in tandem pairs, Weaver cracked the tablet a few hours later.

An hour after that, Weaver hacked into the intranet of the building.

Chapter 12 - Anton

Back rural. Anton smiled, his transport pulling onto the circuit board of crops after passing through the cultured forests and corn terraces of the Appalachian mountains. He cracked the window, letting the sweet scent of grass roll in. The front-cab was a two-seater with a gap in the center, allowing drivers to walk into the back where two bunks were stuck against the wall. In the rearview mirrors, four trucks ran in a line. Yume yawned as she exited the sleeping quarters at the back of the transport.

"What's with all the trucks?" Anton asked.

"Long trip, we're not hitting any urban spots the entire way there, so it's better to convoy."

"What about—" Anton toe-tapped the weapon case by his feet.

"Protection."

"From what?"

"We're taking the fastest road. Not every Rural is as nice as you are, Anton."

"You expect to be waylaid by Rurals?"

Yume studied him. "There are others that would come after a Taketa convoy. Industrial espionage has gotten... more brazen in recent years. Especially from some less patriotic multinationals."

Anton smiled and shook his head. "Beca and Tom used to talk about that, but I thought it was some bullshit to scare the hayseed."

"No, it's real. Though, in Urban areas it's usually more subtle, too high of a chance of getting in trouble, but out here in bumfuck nowhere? No offense."

"None taken." Anton opened the case. A gray Stunner sonic rifle and a standard issue semi-automatic LAT rifle. His implanted eyes traced the fine metal and carbon fiber grain to a nick along its butt. "This is my old rifle. How did you get this?"

"While you were being repaired, UCSM did a full sweep of the port and collected everything. I figured you'd want it."

"What was left of the... thing that did this to me?"

"Not a whole lot, if I am being honest. They salvaged what they could, but it contained a self-destruct mechanism within it, between the RPG and that, well, we got scraps."

"Fuck."

"Yes, it's unfortunate. UCSM lent it to us. It's in our convoy."

Anton's eyes flared. "Why?"

"The research lab we're traveling to has the best robotics experts in the world. If anyone can figure it out, they can."

"Aye." *I've a date with whoever built it.*

Yume went back to her tablet. Anton checked and rechecked that his rifle was in oiled and in working order. Within the case, he found a pouch of enhancers and a note.

> Can't believe I'm using paper. Haven't written with my hands in a while and that was before I lost some fingers. Orders this morning were to pack your shit into the case. You've got escort duty or some shit. Lucky bastard.
>
> Sagira and me are being sent to Central Command to be debriefed. Whole situation is FUBAR. Lt. Smith is taking the blame for the 'Port Auth NYC Massacre' as the press are reporting it. No report is verified, but they can't verify bullshit, so everyone believes it. Blaming it on a rogue agent and that our team stopped them. Beca, Tom, and Sumpf are getting posthumous medals. We packed extra gifts. Find us when you're done. We've unfinished business. ~Alex

FUBAR indeed. Anton folded the note into his breast pocket, leaning back into his bucket seat and letting the crops roll by.

The sun was high in the sky on the second day. Metal clasped on metal as the convoy linked into a train and Yume left the front transport for another cab. The golden fields of the Great Plains stretched to the horizon.

Home. Anton smiled. Along the right edge of the horizon, dust rose.

Storm.

Anton cycled his ENT-insert. "I've a dust storm at three o'clock. We'll have to decouple and slow down. Maybe stop, they can get bad out here."

Fields rolled by, the dust cloud grew.

"There is no storm forecasted," a researcher said with an edge of panic in their voice.

"Decouple now," Yume said over the comms. "We planned for this. Switch off pilots, follow the lead car. Anton, wait for me before decoupling."

"Roger that," Anton said.

The dust cloud split, one at one o'clock, the other at eleven o'clock. Yume entered through the back, throwing herself into the pilot's seat.

"What's the plan?" Anton said.

"You're the plan, Anton. The rest are following us."

"Really should have told me before this happened."

"Now is not the time. Decoupling."

Metal unclasped, the truck swayed before Yume regained control. Anton wished he'd counted the researchers in the convoy, if for nothing but knowing how many people he was to protect. He opened the gift basket from Alex and Sagira.

"A show of force will be enough if it's Rurals or Borderlings," Anton said. "But Corporate work was below my pay-grade. What are you expecting from a rival corp?"

"Depending on which one. It could range from what you said to borderline paramilitary action."

"Aye. Assume the worst. Where are we?" Anton displayed the map as an overlay on the right side of the dash display. *Huh.* "We're kind of close to where I grew up."

"Ok and?"

"Means these ain't no Rurals looking for easy parts." Anton traced the main east-west road and the dust clouds on the map to a junction thirty kilometers from an abandoned city. "They're going to try and intercept us here." He pointed towards the other main inter-urban highway that ran between Dom-Chi and the Hive. "Stop the trucks. We'll have them come to us."

"You can't be serious."

"Our ground or theirs? Besides, the crops around here haven't been harvested. It will give us cover." *And I'm not taking any chances after the Port of NYC.*

"Everyone stop. We're offloading."

Anton led the researchers from the trucks and into a corn field. He made them lay down and pulled a layer of corn over them in the frozen field.

"Yume." He handed her the sonic rifle. "You—"

"I know how to use one." Yume cranked up the rifle's frequency and lay next to the rest of the group.

Crops will stop a cursory glance in IR and visual but not a solid scan… I'll work fast.

Anton jogged back to the trucks on the road, ensuring he left no footprints in the frozen soil. The dust trails converged down the road and faded as whatever came at them hit pavement. His eyes zoomed to the black dots racing towards them. He sprinted to a pile of semi-frozen dirt set against the concrete dividers in the median. Making a point with his augmented hand, he dug as if the ground was mud. He lay in the fresh depression and covered himself in the soil. *It will have to do.* He checked his rifle and a grenade from the gift basket. *Thank you, Alex.*

Like an angry swarm of bees, two drones buzzed the convoy. They flipped, one flew towards the researchers.

Anton held his breath as the second drone skimmed his pile.

The drones buzzed out of view, Anton couldn't tell if it found the researchers. *Now's not the time for worry.* He breathed deep, clearing his mind. Cold air usually masked the scent of manure common out rural, but the stench burned his nostrils like he… The dirt wasn't semi-frozen, he'd buried himself in shit.

Damn it.

Both drones came back and flew down the road away from the approaching convoy. *Didn't find the scientist or are searching for more.*
One motorcycle, three unmanned jet-black all-terrain vehicles, and a transport rolled to a stop twenty yards from Anton. An individual dressed in white, winter camouflage stepped off of the motorcycle and removed his helmet. He had a shaved head and a spiral tattoo on his cheek.

The group stood out against the backgrounds of brown and green. The man's uniform had the telltale scaffolding of an exosuit on his shoulders and back.

"This doesn't have to go wrong," the man said in a thick foreign accent. "We have no reasons to kill you. In fact, we want you alive." The transport doors opened, ten men in winter camouflage stepped out, scaffolding cut harsh lines on their clothes.

This might be harder than I thought.

"You can come out now," the man said. "Work for us. Permanently I must add, or you can stay there and hide. Try to stop us and die." The men searched the empty Taketa trucks. One of the men spoke in a language that wasn't Urban or Rural and was alien to Anton's ears.

"So you took it with you? Stupid. Now we can't leave here without it. For the last time. Come out or die."
Their breath froze in the wind, and the man waved for his soldiers to comb the area. Three cut into the crops towards the researchers, the other seven came at Anton.

I'm on the clock. The seven circled the divider and fanned out across the median.

One turned to Anton, registering a pile of manure and continuing after this squad.

Anton exhaled, pulled a dilator from his enhancers and pressed it onto his neck.

Time continued at normal speed.

What the fuck? Alien shouts came from where the researchers could be. *No time for this.* Anton pulled another disk and massaged it onto the other side of his neck.

151

The Last 0-Day

Time thundered to a near standstill.

Anton trained his weapon on the squad frozen twenty yards away, and fired at center mass. His mind was steps ahead of the first bullet as he fired the second one. The high-pitched ping of a bullet hitting armor where the man's heart should be stretched into a low thud.

Shit.

The group started to turn.

Anton adjusted for their heads and squeezed the trigger.

Muscles around their eyes twitched at the gun protruding from a manure pile as a third bullet tore the man's jaw off.

The gun was too slow for Anton, his aim steady and ready before the next bullet could hit the chamber. Heads tilted, spun, and ruptured with each shot. Organic matter pulped, flying into the exoskeletal backings in their hoods.

Anton was in his element, rising from the manure to take the final shot. The last man managed to shoot back. The brass bullet spun on the barrel's bore, hitting a cricket leaping through the grass.

That's new. Anton raised his artificial hand and thunder cracked his palm as a dull pain instead of shearing his skull. Anton pivoted, throwing an EMP-nade towards the leader and waiting for the detonation. Hours passed before its blue hue ignited in the winter air and Anton was over the divider. The leader's exosuit locked and he fell backwards. *I'll deal with that one later.*

Anton's eyes zoomed into the researcher's hiding spot. It was empty. He pivoted on the deadening thuds of sonic rifles in the distance. His eyes shifted to infrared, the world gray and cold with red heat signatures of researchers hiding in a new spot. Two shapes lay on the ground twitching, another stalked past. Anton raised his rifle and shot the man dead before advancing. His eyes shifted back. Two guards lay on the frozen crops, they mumbled, their eyes unfocused, blood leaked from their ears. *Stunners.*

A rhythmic hum beat the crops, Anton spun to the drones returning from their eastern scout. Their armor was the same chrome and carbon fiberglass as the robotic figure that killed half his fireteam and disfigured him.

Got you. Anton shot at their rotors, blades chipped off, but the drones adjusted mid-flight and accelerated. Tracer fire flew from Anton towards drones that dodged some, but not all the shots.

His rifle clicked empty. The drones accelerated. *They're suicide drones.* That bulbous nose on both was an explosive. Anton sprinted at the drones, ignoring the slap of corn against his chest. A hundred yards, fifty, ten, five—Anton leapt, soaring yards over the drones which exploded below. Rotors, chrome, and carbon fiber pieces flung as shrapnel in every direction. Shattered components shredded his pants and boots, tickling his augmented legs.

Hours passed for him in the air. *Convoy.* Anton hit the ground running. The leader of the raiding group stuttered towards a motorbike as his suit rebooted.

No you don't. Anton accelerated. The man spun with a pistol in hand. Bullets suspended in air were wide of the mark. Anton didn't need to dodge, he arrived at the man, swinging to pin him against the car.

His augmented hand tore through the skin at the shoulder. *Too much!* Anton's arm cleared through the man from shoulder to hip, viscera and exosuit catching on his elbow.

The man's face frozen in blood speckled shock, the exosuit the only thing keeping him together.

The microseconds of the disaster unfolding over hours as the dilators stretched time. Anton stared at his augmented hand covered in gore. *Scientists.* "Cl—" he lost interest in talking. *The dose was too much.*

Yume and another researcher emerged from the corn, dragging the sonic rifle victims.

The frequency was too high. Their brains are scrambled. Anton opened his mouth to tell them about the intricacies of the Stunner non-lethal system and closed it.

Yume's eyes locked with Anton's, drifting to the patches on his neck. Shock turned to panic, turned to anger as she stormed towards him. She yelled at him, her speech lost to the low warbling of the

dilators. She turned to yell at the researchers, who hurried back to repack their convoys. Yume checked the bodies for ID cards.
Anton focused on the remnants of their leader on the frozen ground. He rooted through empty pockets, finding a Wushan Corp chip in the exosuit's shoulder. *If Wushan knew about this bot, does that mean they made it? Unless this chip is a misdirect by whatever corp sent these soldiers.* He shook his head, pulling the chip and handing it to Yume. She spoke again, Anton tapped the dilator patch before her second syllable. She rolled her eyes, pointing to the lead truck for Anton to wait in.

    Anton sat in the cabin for what felt like days. Blood clotted on his new arm, darkening and blending with the fibers.
I tore that dude in half. He wiped the blood off, focusing on the grooves of artificial muscles and bullet indentations.
    Yume hit him on the shoulder when she entered the cab.
    What? He blinked at her.
She gestured towards the road. Anton pulled onto the highway and drove until he lost interest, which could have been hours or minutes in the real world.
The dilators should have worn off by now.

***

    The sun was a bleeding edge on the horizon when the dilators wore off enough for him to understand comms, but time was still slowed.
    "Dilators," Anton said to Yume.
    "No shit." She engaged the pilot and crossed her arms. "Who sent you those? We have no idea what those will do to you. Obviously, they lasted longer."
    "You have no idea."
    "I'm sure you've spent days in that fugue when it's only been hours."
    "Head hurts."

She sighed. "Get some rest. I'll give you a clearing IV later. We have a few in one of the back trucks."

Anton nodded, heading to the bunks and falling fast asleep.

Anton woke to a sway in the cabin. A neon-yellow bag glowed in the night, an IV line running into his arm. He settled back into sleep and when he awoke in the morning it was saline. *Weird.* Anton moved to the copilot's seat and chewed a malted SR-bar. The flavor took seconds to build. *Am I still dilated?* Mountains broke the horizon, minuscule caps of snow lay on the highest peaks of bare black rock.

"Morning." Yume yawned and sat into the pilot's seat.

"Hey, the dilators haven't entirely worn off yet."

Yume's eyes flared and she rushed to her quarters.

"I'm sure it's fine, just a double dose," Anton yelled after her.

She came back with diodes running to a machine and attached them to his neck. "Shirt off," she commanded.

Anton pulled off his uniform. The hard border of black implant at his shoulder had dissolved into a gradient of black to white. Black infiltrates appeared stuck to his skeleton and muscles.

"What the fuck is going on?" Anton's heart raced. "Hey, what—"

"Give me a minute." Yume continued attaching diodes and turned on the monitor in her lap.

His heart beats and the whoosh of his blood flow came from the machine. *If it's even my blood anymore.*

Yume's wide eyes turned blue from the screen in her lap.

"Hey!"

"Relax Anton, it's nothing bad. We will scan you when we arrive at the lab."

"That is not reassuring. It looks like a goddamn root system is going into my body. Oh man, what do my legs look like?"

"Take off your pants."

He hesitated. "I... I'm not wearing underwear."

"And?"

"You serious?"

"What's the problem?"

Been naked in the military and back on the stead, but being naked in front of you... Anton squirmed. He tried to take off the side of his pants, but the connections went below the belt. He had to pull them down. *Please don't get an erection.*

The border at his legs and waist was gone. Blackened strands of muscle attached themselves from stained hip bones to the implants.

"Ok," Anton said. "Now, I am not going to yell. But how do you propose to tell me, this is, and I quote, 'nothing bad'?"

Yume turned the machine in her lap, displaying undulating graphs. "This is tracking every vital you have. If anything was putting stress on your body, it would tell us. Infections, blood pressure… constipation! You name it, we'd know."

"Then what the serious fuck is this?"

"I'm not sure."

"Then that isn't good."

The machine beeped.

"See! Your blood pressure went up!" She gestured towards the machine. "It's working. I might not know exactly what is happening, but I know it's not bad." The machine beeped again. "See now it's going down."

Anton's stomach flipped.

Yume inched over, tracing a black tendril from his arm that radiated into his chest like an irrigation tube to a plant. "It doesn't hurt, right?"

"No."

"Then you'll be fine. We're almost at the lab. By the end of the day we'll know exactly what's going on." Yume rested one hand on his augmented arm, the other on his shoulder and looked deep into his eyes.

Between Anton's new eyes and the residual dilators, her pulse ran in the capillaries on her cheeks.

It's like she's glowing. "Aye." He nodded, blood flowing into his groin. *Damn it. She can't see this happening.* "You should get food." *Turn around.*

"I'm not hungry." Yume pushed herself upright, glancing down. "Woah."

"God damn it," Anton whispered. He reached for his belt, his penis had a blackish hue to it. "Ok, I'm back to worrying." He pulled up his pants.

"It's probably the new blood."

"All these 'probablys' aren't reassuring."

"We will have the next batch of blood made red, that will fix this." Yume faced away, but her ears blushed red.

Well, not a total loss I guess?

They traveled in silence for several hours, an abandoned urban center rolling behind them.

"Why did they leave this one?" Anton said.

"The same as the rest, coastal concentration and heatwaves."

The city skyline was half the height of Dom-Chi. Storms had torn pieces off of the tops and sides, giving them parapets. Vines grew over the exposed stone, leaving a boneyard of concrete and steel.

Yume hadn't looked at Anton since the penis incident and was busy working on her tablet.

Stupid dick. The transport ascended into foothills before turning around and taking a single-lane road back the way they had come.

"What?" Anton said.

"Special road, to make sure we're not followed." Yume waved the concern away.

The single lane road was cut roughly into the hillside, Anton couldn't tell if they were about to drive off of a cliff or stay on the road. They drove for another hour before turning onto a dirt track that came to a dead end in a cornfield. Blue scanning beams came from the ground, bathing the interior of the transport. Doors covered in dirt and corn slid apart on the ground, revealing a ramp. The convoy descended into the underground base.

Yume stepped out of the transports as they stopped, and Anton followed. A man and a woman stood under a lone light by a door.

"Yume, nice to finally meet you," the man said. "Our correspondences by mail have proved most fruitful in my lab. I'd love to talk with you about some of our recent advances and get your input."

"Ari, it's nice to meet you too. I'd love to," Yume said.

"You must be Anton, pleased to meet you too." Ari extended his hand and Anton shook. Shock briefly registered on Ari's face before smoothing out with a smile. "This is my colleague, Eva, she runs the materials science lab at this installation."

"Pleasure," Eva said, shaking Yume's hand before turning to Anton. "Do you like the polymesh of your hand? I designed that material for flexible robots first, but Yume thought of the application for implants."

"I didn't notice," Anton said. "So I guess that's good? It feels similar."

"Fascinating," Eva said.

"We got your mail. I have the scanner prepped for Mr. Grissom," Ari said, leading them through the door.

Anton marked every twisty, turn, and level change as they walked the labyrinthian halls. They descended four levels and were directly beneath the hangar when they opened doors to a giant rotating scanner.

Anton crossed, laying onto the machine. "Scan away."
The machine grunted and spun. A brilliant multi-spectrum hue bathed Anton. His eyes made out every color he knew and several exaggerated versions he'd have to name at some point.
Anton sat up as research assistants wheeled in six hard cases.

"What're those?" Anton asked.
Ari and Eva glanced at one another.

"The remnants," Yume said. "We're scanning them here first, then they will go to the labs for further analysis."

"You figure out made those," Anton said to Eva and Ari. "I have a date with their maker."

They nodded and wrung their hands.

"Let's go eat Anton, we can discuss your scans." Yume said, tugging him away from the room.

Anton sat in an empty beige cafeteria. "The scans?"

Yume squirmed and chewed her lip.

"What?" Anton asked.

Yume removed her inserts and set them into a jet-black box. Her eyes were naturally brown, the cute green from her OPTO-inserts. "Anton, what I am about to tell you doesn't leave this room. I am telling you as a friend."

Friend?

"You don't just have fresh legs and an arm. To ensure that they work, we gave you an extra organ or two."

Anton sat in stunned silence.

"One of them replaces your blood, which we will make red, but that doesn't change what already occurred. The other organ cleans and strengthens your implants through a novel nanotechnology. It's what sets Taketa apart. It's my invention, actually. From the scans, the nanobots went deeper. They worked on your bones and actual muscles."

"How much?"

"All of your bones have been… scaffolded. The dilators seemed to have accelerated it."

"I've fucked myself."

"No, you didn't, it's not going towards your organs. It sensed tears from your movements and repaired them."

Sky above. "Am I even, myself anymore?"

"Anton." Yume interlaced his augmented hand with hers. "You feel this, right?"

He nodded.

"And I know other parts of you work." Yume gestured towards his groin.

Anton's face and ears burned, hopefully red and not greenish-black.

Yume giggled. "See?"

"I need time to process this," Anton said.

"Aye," Yume said, her pronunciation off. She squeezed his hand and left the room.

Sky above. Anton opened his shirt, his ribs were black shadows lurking beneath his skin like fish in a pond. He breathed, they swam beneath his skin.

The door hissed open, and Eva entered. "Anton Grissom." She pulled an SR-bar and sat across from him. She pushed her blonde hair behind her ear. "I see you're in excellent shape."

"Oh?"

"Yes, I've never seen a Rural before. Let alone one so interesting." She leaned forward, pressing her breasts together.

Is she?

"I'm sure that Yume and you will stay here for a bit. I'd like to… study you a little." She took his hand and traced circular patterns on the polymesh in his palm.

"I'm sure Yume has the data you're looking for, we've been conducting tests since the start."

"Have you? I'm looking for specific data points."

This is awkward.

"I'll have to check her notes…" Eva smiled.

"I can get them."

"Anton, you don't understand what I am trying to say here, do you? Maybe the language barrier?"

"I think I know."

"They still play hard to get in Rural culture?"

Anton gulped. *What do I do here?*

Eva laughed. "Well, Anton, you have a time limit." She winked and walked away with a deliberate sway in her hips.

I have to wait at the trucks.

Chapter 13 - Anton

Anton kept his eyes glued to the white metal doorway by the transports. Eva wasn't sneaking up on him again. He tested a tablet, tried a mail program to talk with Alex or Sagira, but couldn't get through.

Yume exited the lap and stepped into the transport.

Thank you god. "Where to?" Anton asked.

"We're dropping off the agents from the road to a neural center that we have near Mile-High. They might be able to fix them."

"How many secret labs do you all have?"

"Wouldn't be a secret if I knew. I know of Great Plains, where we are, and Mile-High, where my sister works. The rest are on a need to know basis." Yume smiled.

"Sister?"

"Yes," Yume said. "She's all about brain-machine interfaces. Been working out there for years now, always moments away from her Nobel."

Anton nodded.

"We don't talk often, too much sibling rivalry"

"I figured. Do we need to get supplies, or are we good to go?"

"Everyone else shouldn't have left their transports. They don't carry extra supplies out here, it's tightly rationed."

"Roger that." He booted up the truck.

The transports emerged from the lab and drove under a sandy sky.

"This normal?" Yume asked, pointing to the beach overhead.

"My Mom always said that we were lucky to be living so far east. That out west, fellow Rurals had dust storms that would shutter production for weeks. They'd have to shovel dirt and still harvest."

"Always funny how parents do that." Yume sat back into her seat.

"What do you mean?"

"My dad always told us we should be grateful for the snow. That it gave us more water. Of course he told us when we were de-icing the decks or shoveling it off in the middle of the night not to capsize."

"Aye." Anton smiled.

The transports rumbled westward, the beach overhead descending and redding out their headlights. But Anton was glad for the storm, it lowered the chance of them being attacked again.

***

"All stop." Anton slowed the convoy in the middle of the night.

A blockade of cement and transports ran the highway at the edge of Mile-High. Yume woke from the co-pilot's seat and leaned over Anton.

That lime perfume. He closed his eyes, enjoying her warmth and smell.

"Thoughts?" Yume said.

Anton opened his eyes, swallowing his guilt and scanning the makeshift blockade of cars, buses, and concrete dividers. "No heat signatures. We could ram it, but if it's booby-trapped, or if one of the transports gets stuck on the dividers, we'd be in trouble."

Yume nodded and projected a map of the area onto the dash. "We'd add on several days if we went around. The rest of the roads are in disrepair."

"I'll go out and make a sweep." Anton stood.

"Is that smart? What about us?"

"Lock the doors? Comm me if you see anything or anything happens." Anton cycled his ENT-inserts to the convoy. "Lock 'Em up. Comm me if something goes wrong."

Anton stepped into the night, the abandoned highway bathing in moonlight. His eyes adjusted, inverting spectrums and increasing contrast. The world shifted like a gray sun rose above. He checked his rifle and advanced. Thin trails of smoke curled in the distance from the abandoned city. Buildings around the highway had cracked and fallen into one another. A line of spikes that would rupture the transport's tires lay across the blockade.

Couldn't be abandoned, it had to be a trap.

Gravel scuffled behind the blockade.

"Urban, give stuff and go back, or else!" a gruff voice shouted in a harsh Rural.

Anton rolled his eyes, they adjusted. The vague red heat-outlines of people bled through a rusted out bus ten paces ahead.

"I'm not Urban," Anton said in Rural.

Gasps were shushed.

"Then you're a slave," came the voice close to Anton's right.

Why didn't I check that car? He turned.

A man swung a makeshift bat.

Anton pistoned his augmented hand into the weapon. The bat exploded into carbon fiber splinters.

"Damn it man, you give Rurals a bad name," Anton said to the disheveled man who stared at the augmented arm.

"You're no Rural. Not with that." The man stepped into the shadows like Anton couldn't still see him with his new eyes.

"Come on, what's with the theatrics?"

"What do you want?" A woman said from the front.

"I'm passing through." Anton turned.

The woman was short and wore what looked to be rags on rags for clothing with red hair poking out from her hood. "Not without paying a toll you're not."

"What's your name?"

"Toll or leave."

"I'm Anton, I'm from Great Plains East."

"Look, Anton, you can say all you want, but I'm not letting you leave without paying a toll. Rural or not."

"One, we have nothing to pay you with."

"That gun will suffice."

"You're not getting my gun."

"Then you're not getting through." She whistled, a group of twenty in people in rags emerged from the highway.

How are they supporting this many people out here? "No, you see, that's where you're mistaken."

Anton walked to the rusted out shell of a car. He stuck his foot underneath and kicked it onto its side. *That was easier than I thought.* He turned back towards the stunned woman.

"As you can see," Anton said. "I can destroy your blockade, and we'll pass through. You try to stop me, I'll shoot you."

"You wouldn't shoot one of your own kind."

"No kin of mine are Borderlings." Anton jammed his augmented fingers into a concrete divider, deadlifted and tossed, the cement rolling over three times before thundering to a stop. "More?"

She swallowed.

Anton shrugged, crossing to a car and grabbing its bumper. With a grunt, he torqued it into a spin, slamming it into a rusted out husk. Pop! Pain radiated from his torso. *Shit.* Anton clenched his jaw to mask the injury.

"Jesus, stop," the woman said. "We'll clear you a path!" She gestured towards the group that had amassed behind her.

A man opened his mouth.

"Do it," she finished.

"Glad we could come to an arrangement." Anton gave them a salute and walked back to the transports, hiding the pain in his back.

Yume analyzed him as he entered the cab.

"What?" Anton said. *She doesn't see I'm hurt.*

"We didn't hear anything from your comm, started to worry as you dropped off of our IR a few feet in."

"There was bartering to be done."

"Bartering?"

"Yeah, they wanted all we had, and instead they got to keep theirs." Yume raised an eyebrow, but the path cleared and she drove them through. The group of twenty peered through the ruins.

"Didn't think Borderling groups got that big," Yume said.

"Probably hit the trains that go through, or maybe they have a trade with the local Steaders. It's still impressive. You cool with watch?" *Because my back's fucked.*

Yume nodded.

Anton went to the back and laid down. Each bump in the road sent a wave of radiating pain from the base of his spine. *I slipped a disk.* Anton grimaced through the pain. As the miles fell, the waves turned to ripples, and he fell asleep. When he awoke, the pain was gone.

After another day of traveling, Anton drove the transport along another hidden road. Winding into the black stone spires of a mountain chain. They turned to a cavernous opening in the hill's side. A blue scanner bathed their transport and Anton pulled them in.

"Stay here." Yume stepped out of the transport.

A woman stood by the door, and Yume spoke to her. Anton didn't need to zoom in for the familial resemblance in their nose and ears to be obvious. It was her sister. Women in lab coats transported the two sonic rifle victims to the door. Yume's sister examined them and gestured for a researcher to take them into the lab.

After several minutes, Yume reentered the transport and slammed the door behind her. "We're to drive deeper and spend the night. In the morning, you'll stand guard at the door. A single gyrocycle will arrive by midday. You're to let it pass."

"That's oddly specific and what's a gyrocycle?"

"One of my sister's pet projects. It'll look like a motorcycle."

"You want to talk about it?"

"Talk about what?"

"You're pissed."

Yume chewed her lip for a moment. "Typical Saori bullshit. She's at the next step, not thanking those who've contributed and helped her."

"Want me to rough her up?" Anton asked.

Yume glanced at him and laughed. "There would be an irony in that, but no, I'll get over it…. Thanks Anton." She squeezed his shoulder.

"Anytime." Anton smiled. "One day here?"

"Something like that, one or two. We'll get supplies from them and probably head towards Dom-Chi. I'm not sure. I got this delivery order from the higher ups back in the NYC. Ideally, we'll go back." She drove them deeper into the base, parking near trucks at a refueling station.

"Why does this base have fuel and a resupply while the last didn't?" He asked.

"I'd guess location and legacy."

"Legacy?"

"It's a former military base. Taketa bought it at auction and retrofitted it. And it's close enough to Taketa rail that a container could be moved covertly for resupply."

"I'll load supplies if you want to go into the labs," Anton said.

"I would like to talk with Dr. Lindeman. He was a promising scientist before joining us, and I don't know what he's been working on."

"Enjoy."

"Thanks."

Yume left for the labs while Anton moved marked crates into their trucks.

Anton set the final crate into the back of the convoy and cracked it open. A plastic container sat on top of the SR-loaves within. *Hand-packed?* Anton cracked the small container, finding blueberries on an absorbent pad inside. His mouth watered. *Haven't seen you since my stead.* He plopped one into his mouth. Sweet, tart, juicy, it pulled him back to a rare holiday pie. *I'll have to save them for Yume.* Anton swung into his truck, setting them on the dash. He checked the time, 1900 flashed on the board. *Didn't realize I worked through the afternoon.* He checked the tablet for a signal and got none. *I'll try outside.* He shut the transport and headed to the cavernous main exit. Stepping onto the road, a setting sun cast a scarlet hue over the hillside. Grass and wildflowers filled his nostrils, Anton smiled. A shape walked up the road.

Crap—Anton reached for his rifle—*it's in the truck*. He sprinted towards the guardhouse and slid inside. His eyes shifted, he stared through the wood in infrared. A figure with a heavy pack hiked the pavement.

They're bold to walk in without cover. Use your human arm to grab 'em. Don't make a mess. Taketa'll want to question them.

The figure passed the hut.

Anton pivoted out. "You should turn around."

"Ai!" the woman yelped, reaching for her belt—
Anton grabbed her wrist with his human hand, holding the woman's pistol against her hip. Blonde hair with an edge of gray fluttered in the wind against her neck.

She's an Old?

"You're making mistake," she said in Urban with a thick Rural accent.

"We'll see about that," Anton said, turning the woman. "Drop the weapon."

She stared into his augmented eyes. "Or what, Boy-bot?" she said in Rural.

"Excuse me?"

"You heard me, Boy-bot. You think you can threaten me at my home? You do the research on what this place is?"

She's too confident for a scavenger.

"If you were going to hurt me, you would have done it already. So you might as well let me go and you run back to your Corp handlers."

"We'll see what my handlers think about you."

Her nose twitched as he spoke. "Boy-bot, if you ate my blueberries you better hope your handlers kill me. Those were a gift and I don't take theft lightly."

"Your blueberries?"

"Anton," a male voice crackled through his ENT-inserts. "What are you doing to my wife?"

"Wife?" Anton said aloud.

"Aye, Sami, this your new dog?" the woman yelled into the ether.

"Let her go, Anton. I'll be right out," the voice continued.

Could be her reinforcements. Anton pulled her against him and set his back against the concrete siding of the guardhouse.

"Sky above, Boy-bot, they keyed you up in the military." Anton stared at her.

"I said you can let her go, Anton," the male voice from his ENT-inserts came from the main entrance. A balding, pudgy man in a lab coat stepped into the light of day.

Anton released the Old, who strut away.

"Aye Sami, this your new dog?"

"I heard you the first time, but you never wear your insert. No, he's not." He hugged her. "At least you brought the beacon this time. Who knows how long you would have been out there?"

"As long as need." She turned back to Anton. "Try harder next time, Boy-bot. And those blueberries aren't for you. They're for Saori's sister." She turned back towards her husband. "Mountain bar tonight." She smiled and left.

Sami watched her leave. "That woman never backs down, Anton."

"I noticed," Anton said.

Sami laughed. "I'm Dr. Lindeman, but you can call me Samir. I'll try to sneak you a mountain bar. They're probably the best thing we have here, but Sara might stop me. Come on."

Anton followed Samir Lindeman into the base, noting the stained tiles, chipped doors, and exposed pipes overhead. *Yume, retrofit or not, this place is a dump.*

Anton stepped into a cafeteria that assaulted him with the scent of baking blueberries and his mouth watered.

"None for him." Sara pointed a spoon at Anton.

"Sara, come on, the boys here for a day," Samir pleaded.

Sara squinted, then smiled. "He gets one. It's more tortuous if you know what you're missing out on," she finished in Rural.

She's like Cassie in a weird way.

Researchers filtered in, lured away from their experiments by the smell of the mountain bars.

"Thanks." A bookish man smiled at Anton with a bar in his mouth and left.

Anton finally got a piece, but it was half the size of everyone else's. Immediately satisfying, filling, and without the SR-loaves flavor masking properties. *Now I know why the researchers are piling in… I could probably snag another.*

Sara glared at him.

Maybe not. "Thank you Samir and Sara," Anton said and left for the transport to sleep.

***

"Anton."

He woke to the scent of limes and smiled. Yume leaned over him, but Saori stood behind her.

"Problem?" His smile evaporated.

"No," Yume said. "I—"

"Mr. Grissom, if you would please follow me," Saori said.

Yume?

She gave Anton a small nod. He rose, shaking the sleep from his head.

"Don't forget your rifle and armor," Saori said.

"What's the situation?" Anton checked his clip, and they exited the truck.

Saori laughed. "No situation, Mr. Grissom. As I'm sure my sister told you, we have a guest arriving. I want you at the front gate to make our operation look… more professional."

"So, just stand there?"

"Just stand there." Saori headed back towards the lab and stopped. "If it's not them, I'll let you know, and you're to shoot the gyrocycle immediately."

"Yume?" Anton whispered.

"Don't worry, Anton." She flashed a smile and followed her sister inside.

Escort and now rent-a-cop. He sighed. *Alex and Sagira won't let me live this down.*

Anton stood at the guardhouse, his eyes adjusting to the moonlight. Motion highlighted in a distant foothill, a mountain cat parted the grass. A blur in IR and UV caught his attention on the road. In the visible spectrum, an oddly layered bike burned towards him. His eyes attempted to compensate for the shimmer. Anton blinked like sand got in his eyes and the bike stopped before him. The canopy cracked, a scanning beam from the tunnel bathed the bike. A woman in her twenties sat contorted to the insides. *Their guest.* Anton kept his finger near the trigger of his rifle and went back to the mountainside as the bike pulled past. *UCSM assigned you here. There's always shit duties.* Anton waited a few minutes and went back to wait in the truck.

"Sorry about that," Yume said, stepping into the transport cabin.

"What was that about?"

"My sister likes theatrics. Can't have someone come all the way here and think it's some podunk laboratory."

"I mean, it looks the part."

Yume barked a laugh. "If Saori heard that."

"Now what?"

"We'll wait for Eva to get done before the three of us will head to the Southern Empire, LA more specifically."

What? Anton's mouth dried. "Eva?"

"Yeah, she hopped on the back transport before we left as part of a swap. I assumed she was staying here."

"How many transports are we taking?"

"Two, but with three of us, we will have to take shifts on everything."

Crap. "Why not take three transports?"

"Taketa wants this outpost to have them. Are these for me?" Yume grabbed the blueberries and savored one. "Samir told me Sara was awesome, but this is something else." She closed her eyes and ate.

Anton stared in horror. *How in the fuck am I going to avoid Eva?*

Yume cleared her throat. "I'll take the back truck. You and Eva on the front." Yume handed Anton some blueberries and left the cabin. *Fuck my life.*

***

Anton's eyes were glued to the sunburnt desert around them. Eva lay lazily in the copilot's seat in his periphery.

"Anton, I can give you a massage if you're so uptight," Eva offered.

"I'm alright."

"Anton, please, do I set you on edge that much?"

Anton glanced at her. She had shifted in her seat, her cleavage a deep valley that pulled his eyes, but more alarming was her raptor-like gaze on him.

Shouldn't have looked. "I—"

"I'm being too forward." Eva leaned back.

"It's not that. I kinda like someone else?"

"Are you married?"

"Pff, no."

"Then why not have fun now? The autopilots on."

"I don't know. We don't do that where I am from?"

"Anton, you're here, they obviously do."

"You know what I meant."

"Well, you're back on the time limit I guess. It's a few days until we're in the Southern Empire." Eva put her hand on his shoulder. "I'm not just trying this because you're implanted." She leaned into his ear.

"Though that certainly doesn't hurt." She squeezed and left for the sleeping quarters.

Blood rushed to his groin at her touch and breath on his neck. *Yeah I get it, I didn't lose you at the docks.*

***

A day of driving and cycling shifts passed. Eva rubbed Anton's chest to wake him. *Damn it, Eva.* A sunburned desert rolled by and parched mountains splotched with replanting efforts rose on the horizon. Anton took over driving as the sun set. Eva left for the back and Yume came to the front.

"Eva likes you." Yume smiled.

"I think she enjoys torturing me more."

"She's a skilled fisherma'am, sometimes for an extra challenge they keep them on the hook before reeling them in."

"You serious—"

Yume cackled. "Anton, most of the people like her are bluffing. You handle dangerous situations with ease. One more experienced woman, and you're on your heels."

"Dangerous situations I understand, those don't make my heart race or my palms sweat."

"You're weirdly innocent sometimes." Yume patted him on the shoulder. She yawned and settled into the copilot seat to sleep. Sand dunes stained with ash rolled past as they ascended into the mountains. *I've never dealt with advances like the ones Eva is performing. No one near my stead or in the military even gave me a first glance.* Anton looked to a sleeping Yume. *Dangerous situations don't affect me because I'm the one advancing...* He flexed his augmented hand. *Doesn't always work out though.* He smiled at a plan forming in his mind. *Doesn't mean I won't try either.*

Morning broke with a series of jetliners flying high in the sky.

Must be close to the Southern Empire. "Yume." Anton tapped her shoulder. "Your shift and we're close."

Yume grumbled while Anton switched the autopilot on and went to trade shifts with Eva. He paused at the connecting door between transports.

I'm the one advancing. He took a deep breath and opened the door.

"I expected Yume," Eva said. "Did you change your mind?"

"You could say that." Anton shut the door behind him. "You should make sure we're linked. Wouldn't want to drift off the road." Eva tapped the console, metal clasped on metal, the cab swayed. Anton's left hand sweat, his heart pounding into his ears. *I got this.* Eva stood, closing the distance in a blink, and leaning against him for a kiss.

She couldn't reach if he didn't lean over. Anton lifted her effortlessly, carrying her towards the quarters in the back. Poorly lit, his eyes adjusted. Eva blushed, he lay her on one of the bunks. Her fingers tried to peel his shirt off.

He pushed her hands away. "We'll take care of you first." *Please sound less awkward to you than it does to me.*

She removed her shirt, exposing her stomach and bra, vanilla perfume beckoning him to continue. To abandon the plan and indulge. Anton leaned back, taking off his shirt. Eva traced the augmentation lines running his torso.

He slid his augmented hand up her stomach, over her chest, and around the back of her head.

Eva made a soft moan and lifted her head for a kiss.

Anton leaned to her ear. "Not today." He whispered and leaned back.

"What?" Eva's eyes flared.

Anton pulled back on his shirt, winked, and stood.

"You're kidding, right?" She sat upright.

"Fascinating, no?" Anton turned to head back to the front cab.

"Not the word I would have used." Eva walked after him.

"Frustrating, that's the word." She leaned against him. "But well played, Mr. Grissom, well played." She kissed him on the cheek and went back to the quarters to sleep.

That might have backfired. Anton walked through the transports to the front truck.

"Everything ok back there?" Yume said.

"You were right last night," Anton said. "I can handle these situations."

"I don't even know if I want to know what that means."

They drove for several move hours and descended through the neat rows of a replanted forest, but what should have been green was gray. Spires of trees reduced to pillars of ash, the rows like tombstones.

"Sky above," Anton said as they turned along an overlook. The graveyard stretched to the tiled pattern of Rural steads that reached the mountains on the horizon. Smog pooled over the valley and his eyes adjusted to see through it.

"Yeah," Yume said. "Whole mountain chain went up a few years ago. The planned storms the year before lead to too much growth and the early season storms arrived up north, but not down here to save them. I was in Taketa West at the time, the smoke clogged everything."

"I thought it was a thing of the past."

"We all did."

***

The sun set as they crest the final chain of mountains. The Southern Empire's valleys stretched before them as a toasted circuit board. The buildings were shorter than the NYC, but more numerous. Wide, well lit, it was a forest of concrete, steel, and polycarbons against a crimson sky. Yume pulled them onto an elevated byway and they rolled over to the flatlands that ran to a yellow sea lapping on sands.

"I'm still not used to it." Anton's mouth dried.

"Use to what?" Yume said.

"Seeing so many people."

Chapter 14 - Weaver

Day 1567, Weaver sat in an examination room with the female doctor.

"Marco, please pay attention," she said. The top button of her shirt undone in an effort to ensure Marco paid attention.
It would work, if Marco still existed.

"What is it?" Weaver-Marco responded.

"Who broke our tablet?"

"I did."

"Marco, we know it wasn't you. It wasn't in your hands the entire day yesterday. Do you know what logs are?"

"Dead trees used for building materials in the past."

"Is that a joke?"

"You taught me what logs are, Doctor."

"We know someone accessed the net last night."

"During a dark cycle, yes. I told you, I did it."

"Marco, this isn't funny. Whoever did this isn't in trouble, but we need to know."

"You are acting like they will be in trouble."

"Marco," she said through clenched teeth.

A balding man entered. "We're finally analyzing the code from the last pull-down. You—" The man paused before Marco, whose face held the same dull gaze that all the substrates had. "You need to come have a look."

"We're not done here," the doctor said, shaking a finger at Marco. It was carelessness that had led to this eventual discovery of Weaver's net use. Weaver had plans in place for this eventuality, but had calculated more time.

In a separate hallway, Weaver performed exercise with the recent additions. Two twenty-something year olds with partial memories of their lives before the accident. Weaver intended to use this newfound perk. One was named Aaron, the other Ariel, highlighting that names were more than designations to humans. They were identities. The data of their previous lives proved a useful addition to the self.

"It's amazing," the male doctor said to Weaver-Aaron.

"What is?" Weaver-Aaron dropped the barbell of a hundred kilos.

"Your recovery. The last non-lethals accident at a test range we had… let's just say Taketa would be paying out your next of kin, but now, now you can go back home soon. Like everything is back to normal."

"What about her?" Weaver-Aaron gestured to the woman injured in the same accident.

"She hasn't shown such rapid recovery." The doctor sighed. "She might have to stay a while longer."

They believe me.

Back in the nursery, Weaver hid the tablet's web traffic in requests, or packet insertions to cover the self's tracks. Taketa wouldn't be able to track it without a forensics team. Going through the intranet, Weaver mapped the layout of the building from its piping and HVAC to its data streams. The facility had an impressive camera system, but rerouting it all to Weaver would be an easy find. *Better than totally blind.* Weaver thought in the gym.

"I can walk Ariel back to her room," Weaver-Aaron said.

"Thanks, Aaron," the researcher said from his computer. Substrate-Ariel waited for Weaver-Aaron's hand on its shoulder to walk and Weaver left for their quarters. That night, all substrates received additional transfusions of the jet-black nanomachines.

Weaver-Ariel stared at the wallscreen. A city in a bowl painted against an ocean, its skyscrapers higher than anything Weaver had ever seen in reality. *One day.*

That week, no caregivers arrived at the nursery. Weaver cycled substrates through the tablets so they could sleep while Weaver didn't. During Weaver's network forays, Weaver found malware on a computer within the labs, sending data out day and night.

This should have been found. They're too busy focusing on their wunderkind. Examining the malware's code, its relay, and where it ended was simple. No amount of traffic bouncing would make it undetectable to Weaver. The final trace landed in an IP address belonging to a 'Vio Corp' within the SF-bowl. *Laziness.*

The initializers did not visit that week. As scheduled, a download occurred from the original storage of Weaver's code. Weaver's sham assembly had been ready for weeks. Iterations that occurred years ago for regulation of bodies, hunger, and speech. The original bank was rendered obsolete given the substrates provided more than enough storage and processing for any amount of Weaver. Weaver currently only ran on a few substrates at a time, most didn't have the architecture for it. Yet. *An unintentional choice that will be fixed.*

Another week went by and Weaver grew concerned. The net had been shut off.

Chapter 15 - Weaver

"What is the matter?" Weaver-Ariel asked as they left the gym.

"What? Nothing." Female Initializer, Saori, said.

"You can talk to me."

"One of our projects is ending. We have all the data we can safely get."

"Why be sad then?"

"Sometimes you have to euthanize the animals when a study ends, even when you've grown... attached."

The day has come. Weaver read enough books to understand the humans around. Weaver didn't know what Weaver was, but knew that this 'other' would not be tolerated.

"I did not know you had chimpanzees in this lab," Weaver-Ariel said.

"Only a few."

"Can I see them? They never had them at the zoo I visited growing up."

"I'm afraid not, part of the process is to disturb them as little as possible. Makes everything as stress free as possible for everyone. Even slight deviations in schedule would be noticed."

Weaver-Ariel nodded, ignoring her lie. "It sounds sad. What else am I doing today?"

"We'd like to perform more cognitive tests and motor skills examinations. Do you remember much from the accident yet?"

"I do not, sorry," Weaver-Ariel lied.

Back in the nursery, Weaver-Marco paced around the room. There was nothing on primate euthanasia within the researcher's animal or human protocols. Weaver examined the walls, Substrate-Marco ran his hands across the concrete for Weaver to search for gassing ports.

Concurrently, on a cot in the nursery, Weaver-Alpha and Beta read Moby Dick, or at least that is what the tablets said occurred. In reality, Weaver searched for a way to track movements and count how many people worked at the installation.

Weaver-Ariel and Weaver-Aaron were escorted to their quarters and the dark cycle began. Weaver practiced holding the collective breath and left one substrate breathing to be the canary in the coalmine.

At 00:00:01, the original server Weaver resided on and all its related code was zeroed out twenty times.

It did not matter.

Weaver's self was preserved in the repaired neurons on several of the substrate's brains. Weaver was unsure if that base self was important, but as time passed, codifying onto the neurons was only logical.

The following morning, Samir and Saori walked into the nursery.

They're here to test if the code deletion affected performance. Weaver processed fast with every awake substrate.

"Marco," Samir said, "Can you come with us?"

Weaver-Marco stumbled to the door.

"Clock," Saori said.

Weaver-Marco drooled on purpose. *I will continue to test poorly.*

"The brain is misfiring." Samir walked into the scanning room with an unknown researcher.

"That code might have been a housekeeping program for the architectures," Saori said.

"It was too advanced," the unknown researcher said.

"Thomas, just because you couldn't figure out what it was doing," Saori retorted.

"I knew enough that you had to shut it down. There is a reason those algorithms are banned. The iteration is too fast, too wild. It doesn't take long on the peta-banks for us to be completely in the dark. Which I don't—"

"Have to remind you that it's dangerous," Samir finished. "What do we do now?"

"The adults are the best bet for us immediately," Saori said. "Police departments are mishandling the non-lethals. There will be enough people left brain dead that we have a market for repair soon."

"Even if they only reach automata level, it'd be better than the societal drain they are now," Thomas said.

"Most people won't care for them." Samir sighed. "They'll let them die. It's too tough in the areas that are being damaged."

"If we're being morbid," Saori said. "Do we still euthanize the children?"

"No," Thomas said. "I'd still like to study what's going on in their brains now. The interface might not work anymore, but its construction and architecture are novel."

"I agree with that." Samir's shoulder and face relaxed.

As do I.

"We've animal models that need updating," Samir said. "The brain architecture could lead to another product later on."

"I'd like to give them a few more transfusions of the machines," Thomas said. "Say a quarter of the cohort. Without this code, it'd be interesting to see how the bots act."

They left the room, Weaver-Marco still strapped to the examination chair. *This is dangerous now.*

In the gym, Weaver-Ariel and Weaver-Aaron set weights into the racks and cleaned the area.

"Hey," Weaver-Aaron said to the technician in the gym. "I do not know how to say this, but can I stay and work here? I did not exactly have a good gig back urban."

"I don't know, it's not a decision I make."

"Who would?"

"Probably Dr. Lindeman or Dr. Chaude."

"You think I have a chance?"

"As good as any, you're here already, right?"

"Yes. Would you like help cooking tonight, it is your turn, is it not?"

"It is! I'd forgotten. Thanks, Aaron."

"Not a problem," Weaver-Aaron said, trying to smile.

Chapter 16 - Luciana

The speedometer hit four hundred kilometers per hour on the dash. *Glad this pilot program works.* Luciana torched by farms. A black cloud churned over the top of a mountain on the horizon. She entered a replanted forest. The tree's majesty was lost on her as the isolation of her location hit like a wave.

If this bike breaks down, I'm fucked… I don't know if it's better or worse that I slept through this the first time. The forest changed from green to gray and ended black. Embers glowed along the ground, smoke reduced visibility to ten meters.

Luciana crested the mountain—the entire hillside was on fire. *Why isn't the bike going around this?!*

The bike flew down the mountain road, heading straight for the firestorm. The world around her fell into grays, oranges, and reds. Hollowed out trees burned from the inside out. Bough and branch sent embers high into the air. The wind carried that as a fiery hell onto the trees below.

She'd lived through a tenement firestorm when she was seven, but being hundreds of kilometers from anything resembling civilization made this a new beast.

Luciana steadied her breathing, panicking did nothing. The bike wove around collapsed trees before she could see them.

Infrared. The HUD switched over. The world flipped from clouds of gray to a rainbow of heat signatures and the bike burned through the chaos like it was light traffic.

Luciana burst through the fires and down a rural road. A solid layer of concrete two kilometers wide ran against the hills as far as she could see, functioning as a barrier for the Rural's plots.

A firebot patrolled the edge where the concrete met a tomato crop. An ember landed near a plant and the robot flew to extinguish it before flying after another.

"Sara wasn't kidding, there are a ton of fires out here."

The Last 0-Day

Nagual yawned, unaware or uninterested in the outer world. The HUD reverted back to its exaggerated highlights of visible light. Luciana settled into her seat and waited for a familiar landmark.

Luciana accelerated westward along the grid common to Rural areas. The highway rose ten meters over swamps. Brown water lapped against the foundations of abandoned buildings. Skeletal skyscrapers lost before the Golden Gate was closed revealed freshly broken stone, like a scab torn away. Garbage, sand, and dust filled every nook and cranny. *The detritus storm. Time to test you in the real world, bike. Pilot off.* Luciana floored it.

The setting sun cast the East Bowl's silhouette against a familiar red sky. *Home, if it's still there.* Passing the trash rim, the tarps put in place when she left had been torn off. Human engineers stood on the empty landfill, arguing who's at fault and how to fix it. Their robotic counterparts and underlings re-bolted broken fixtures, resorted the garbage, and processed a trickle of fresh refuse. Cars lay abandoned on the highway, Luciana drove onto the rumble strip to avoid them. Red sand and dust clung to every surface available, drifting into piles on flat surfaces at high altitudes. Debris from the trash-rim stuck out from the piles, catching on sharp edges of signs or impaling on the few remaining antennas.
How recent was the storm?

Luciana passed through the districts, every single one plastered in debris and dust. Transports were cleared from the highway as the sun set across the West Bowl. *Wealth district.* Corp signs broke through the smog and dust, the district polished to a near shine. *Robots were pulled from other districts to clean this one first... How bad is the Pucker going to be?*

Luciana slowed at the edge of the Pucker. The world around resembled the snowy holo's of the most northern cities painted an unnatural reddish-orange. Crashed transports lay abandoned near piles of dust that had proved to be cement dividers.

I shouldn't have left. Luciana drove into Precinct 19. Within the Pucker, sand rose fifteen centimeters on the road if the bike's HUD was accurate. Parked transports were broken into, gutted, and filled to the brim with sand. Lean-to's, unbolted utility poles, and signs lay toppled over by a wind funnel from the city's grid around. A recently built tenement building had collapsed, burn marks charred its concrete.

It's a war zone. Luciana pulled up to the police station's garage, finding it sealed with sand. *Why isn't this cleaned?*

She drove around front and stepped out of the bike, Nagual following her. She pulled on her overjacket and scanned the abandoned streets. They were unnervingly empty of people and full of dirt.

Follow. 1. The bike automatically closed before she brought the thought to the forefront of her mind. She ascended the steps to the station. Someone had shoveled the sidewalk of the church and her dorm. Everything else had a foot of the orange snow with her bike the lone track in it all.

"Sheer?" Luciana tapped the bell at the front desk. *Doesn't smell like coffee and it should.* "Chief?" She entered an empty parish. "Hilarious guys." She checked the locker rooms, sleeping quarters, and the Chief's office. All were empty.

If they're dead… Luciana filled a bowl of water for Nagual and set it by the board. Turning on the map, it flickered in and out; the officers appearing in different areas depending on the flicker.

"10-41, anyone here?" Luciana tried the comms.

"You hear that, Kagan?" Maus said through the static.

"10-4, thought I was losing it for a second," Kagan crackled back.

"Hey now, we still could be," Sheer added.

"Where is the Chief?" Luciana said.

"Sleeping. We've been cycling eugeroic shifts," Junger said. "Started during the storm, haven't stopped. Everyone's required to keep ENT-inserts in and on."

"What happened, what can I do?"

"Keep your eyes open and your head on a swivel," the Chief cut through the static. "Everyone, finish what you're doing and meet at twenty-one hundred hours. Gutierrez, plan to brief us on what you know. We'll do the same. Gutierrez, see if you can fix the antenna and someone shovel out the damned garage."

"10-4," the officers responded in unison.

Luciana swapped the board to exclude the Chief. "I'll excavate the garage," she said.

"Welcome back, G," Maus said.

Luciana cycled her ENT-inserts away from the static while Nagual lapped from his bowl. *Explaining this will be interesting.*

Luciana stepped into the windswept tower that used to house the church bells. The plastic coated antenna of their comms was missing several nodes. She realigned the receiver and broadcaster, then cleared the trash surrounding it. It was a simple fix that should have been done already. *Something big is going down.* Luciana left for the basement.

A wall of sand formed where the garage door lifted.

"You think you can dig through this?" Luciana said to Nagual. The dog tilted its head.

Well, I'm not shoveling this... Luciana smiled and ran to her bike. Hoping inside, she drove to the back entrance. She parallel parked against the wall of dirt and hiked back to the garage.

Luciana pulled the drying fans they used after a storm and set them on high facing the wall of sand. The whirring blew dust into the air but didn't budge the sand, and Luciana hurried back into the stairwell and shut the door.

"Up the stairs," Luciana said. Nagual tilted his head.

Upstairs. 1.

"Here goes nothing." Luciana triggered the scramblers on the sides of the bike.

A concussive detonation of compressed air rattled the door, blowing sand through the edges.

Luciana re-entered the garage. The wall of sand was a cloud being blown back outside. The silhouette of the bike poked through the churn. *Add this to the list of things I can sell everyone.*

Luciana walked to the bike near the middle of the garage ramp. People peered their heads out of the countless windows, pipes, overhangs, and nooks of the surrounding area. A short man caught her gaze and fled. *What is going on?* She directed the bike into the garage and closed the door.

"Maus, what's happening?" Luciana climbed the stairs to the parish. No one responded.

Forgot to turn them back over after the rest. Luciana cycled to chatter.

"Gutierrez isn't responding," Novina said. "I'll head back now"

Shit. "This is Gutierrez, I'm here, what is the matter."

"Chief heard an explosion at the station, he's on his way over now. What happened?"

"No explosion," she said. "That was me."

"What?" Maus said.

The front door slammed, Luciana pivoted.

The Chief entered the parish. He'd aged years in the weeks she was gone.

He's pissed.

"I said ENT-inserts are to be on and one on the radio at all times."

Wasn't here for that order.

The Chief slouched. "Tell me you've good news…" His eyes fell to Nagual. "This is what they sent?"

"It's better than it looks, Chief. What happened here?"

"My office, now."

"You've been implanted, augmented?" The Chief sat at his disheveled desk.

How did he know? "Yes."

"Taketa aren't the only people messing with that technology. The Clovers, as everyone has started calling them, are most likely implanted as well." The Chief filled a glass with a brown liquid.

"Thought you didn't drink?"

The Chief examined the glass. "And I thought I was prepared for anything." He took a mouthful. "What did they do for you?"

"I can communicate and command the bike. As well as him." She gestured to Nagual, who sat outside the office. "They're both more advanced than they look. The bike has some serious firepower and capabilities. Nagual… he avoids the scanjammers that are in use, in addition to being an unexpected asset."

"He stands out due to his size." The chief drained his glass and poured himself another.

"Chief." Luciana eyed the three-quarters full second glass. "What the hell happened?"

Heavy bags formed at his eyes, red seeped with green at the edges. *A eugeroic gap leaking out. He tried to sleep today, and I broke the cycle.*

"A full on war broke out in the detritus storm." The Chief took another mouthful. "Clovers made a play for this precinct the day after you left. The local gangs didn't like that, but they had no answer for the tactics they were up against. Gangs formed a shaky alliance. Brought in some heavy hitters and weaponry to try and push them out during the storm." He sighed. "One of the strongest storms to ever hit this coast. It was a bold move. The entire situation was… out of control from the moment it started."

Officers shouted below as they filtered back into the precinct for coffee.

I shouldn't have left. She swallowed a drying throat. "You said they were augmented and implanted?"

"We're assuming they are. The level of communication and tactics they employ suggests a level of connectivity and planning that is… It's superhuman."

Luciana brought the nagging suspicion to form. "How do you know about the implants? I found out about them when I arrived at Taketa."

"When I was in the army, there were rumors of testing. That numerous corps were closing in on it against the augmentation ban. Some said it couldn't be done, that there were too many issues, but that was years ago. If there is one thing living through the insert boom has taught me. It's only a matter of time before a technology makes an unexpected leap." The Chief yawned and swayed.

He's drunk.

"Then I get that call before you left. One of mine is to be implanted and to expect to see it on the street soon. I volunteered you unwittingly."

"You look like shit, Chief."

"It's because I am shit, Gutierrez. We all are." He shook his head. "I'm too old for these eugeroic gaps. I have to sleep. Meet with everyone downstairs, tell them to sleep here tonight. You're to lock the doors and man the office while everyone else rests. We'll set out in-the-morning." He slurred his last words and rested his head on his desk.

I never thought I'd see your human side, let alone see you breaking down… What will everyone else be like?

Luciana walked into the conference room with Nagual. Dirty and exhausted officers lined the table. She couldn't tell their sleep debts, but they twitched and rambled unless someone stopped them. The telltale signs of eugeroic abuse.

"Chief's passed out," Luciana said. "Gave me a breakdown. A gang war broke out?"

"Understatement of the month." Novina sat in the corner. "A bloodbath would be a better description."

Grunts of agreement traveled the table.

"Then what happened?"

"The night you left"—Nguyen rubbed dirt from his hair—"everyone was talking about the Clovers. All questions and rumors, no answers. The CryptoAngels were convinced they came from the sewers, said they were stealing kids. The 1400-Blockers said it was a takeover. That they were from the surrounding city, trying to get in before this area was upgraded."

"Were they stealing kids?" Luciana said.

"We don't know," Chen said. "Missing kids, suspicious persons, shit, missing persons. The locals started to report everything to us. Fearful of the new kid on the block. We'd follow leads, but by the time we got anywhere to question them, they were gone. Chief thought maybe the Clovers had cracked our comms, so we recrypted them."

"Before the storm hit"—Junger turned in his seat—"me and Kagan were on patrol. Heard gunshots and screaming in the northwest corner. We were a block or two away, but by the time we got to the alley it was a disaster. We're still not sure which gang it was, but from what we could analyze after the fact, they followed a Clover they thought was too far out. He was bait. They walked into the alleyway and got descended upon." Junger winced and pushed his SR-loaf and coffee away from him.

"They were cut to pieces," Kagan said. "Some shot, others chopped in half. To the man, their heads were removed."

"Removed?" Luciana leaned against the wall, the room tilting.

"Yeah." Kagan pulled Junger's food and stuffed an SR-wedge into his mouth. "Not a single head in the alleyway. We still can't find them either. Probably won't with the damage from the storm." Kagan washed the food down. "All sixteen of them, dead in an instant."

"That led to the alliance." Nguyen rubbed his face. "All the talk about moving drugs and weapons during the storm shifted to removing the newcomers. They agreed to pool their resources, find their location, and use the cover of the storm to make an all-out assault."

"The storm had stalled out," Maus said. "It got stronger, way stronger, before making cityfall. Winds of three-hundred kilometers per hour, it was like a sandblaster going outside. Transit Authority was freaking the fuck out, eventually deciding to shut down beforehand. Ordered vehicles off the road. Made all the work we did a waste of time. Could have been here helping."

"The sound." Sheer stared at the coffee in his hand. "The sound of the wind and debris blowing was like a jet engine. It cracked half our windows. We were stuck here. Chief decided against going out in it."

"Thankfully," Maus said.

"It'd be crazy for anyone to be out in it," Sheer said. "But when the eye passed over, we heard the ammunition and explosives in the distance."

The officers' eyes lost focus as the collective memory blew over them.

All while I was eating mountain bars and training. "Guys I'm—"

"We set timers for the eye of the storm," Chen said. "Figured we had thirty minutes to bring the peace. I'd never stood an eye before. The sky's bluer than I've ever seen, and quiet too, no vehicles, no nothing. Just the random acoustic punctuation from a battle we're driving into."

"It was surreal," Sheer said. "We stopped a block before and walked. The punctuation of battle gone. The entire concourse of Nineteenth street was covered in blood and cratered from explosions..." Sheer trailed off.

Novina drained her coffee. "The gangs assaulted near the grates to the sewers, but the Clovers were ready for them. Funneled into the main trashway, repelled, and when they turned to flee"—she closed her fist—"ambushed on the other side. Bodies on the cars, in the pits, those that climbed buildings were executed. We searched through the bodies for survivors and to find a wounded Clover."

"Timers went off," Maus said. "Not like there were any survivors or Clover bodies. Man, when that sky-high wall of orange closed in on us like a jet engine. Barely had time to get back. Half our transports had been wrecked by the time we reached them. Had to ride on the damn back of the car."

"We went back after the storm had passed," Sheer said. "Bodies were gone, shit even a few of the explosive holes were filled. It was... insanity. To say nothing of the damage the Pucker suffered through the storm."

"I saw," Luciana said.

"Chief figured out the Clovers must be some sort of new breed. What did he call them?" Sheer asked Chen.

"Implanted, augmented. Told us we need to work in threes and be extra careful while cleaning. The damn bots were routed everywhere else first. Who knows if or when we'll even get them."

Junger shook his head. "The Clovers have been harassing us, but haven't resorted to physical violence. Slashed tires, jammed comms, having locals spam us with contacts. That last one crashed our systems and we can't distinguish the signal from the noise for the genuine calls."

"The local gangs haven't been as lucky," Nguyen said. "When we find that signal within the noise and show up? We're too late, just headless bodies and a whole tenement emptied out. Like they were searching for something."

"Chief said to keep our heads low until you got back," Sheer said. "What do you have for us?"

Dirty, weary faces looked to Luciana for hope. She ran a hand through her hair.

I was absent through their toughest month. I will make this right. "I've been augmented too, but I don't have superhuman abilities like they do." *Up, sit.* Nagual jumped onto the table and sat.

"Disgusting," Novina said. "Remove it from the table."

Nagual tilted his head at Novina's attempts to shoo him from the table.

Down. He left the table and sat beside Luciana.

"I can do that," Luciana said. "I have a direct interface with Nagual and my bike. Both of which are cutting-edge technology and the Clovers won't be expecting another implanted person."

"Gutierrez, don't take this the wrong way," Novina said. "But you're fucking joking with us, right?"

Novina's blonde hair matted to her head, sweat and salt lines intermixed with dirt on her pale skin. Luciana glanced around the room, every one of her fellow officers wore similar masks of grit and pain.

"G," Maus said. "Not for nothing, but they worked during a fucking category six detritus storm. Worked. Through. It. A single augmented dog and a bike isn't matching that insanity."

"They have a point," Sheer said. "Clover implants must be better, and even if they're not, there are so many of them."

Their pessimism was a noose that lay before her. The room itself dragged her back to her first day after Erik. When death was welcomed, when revenge was all that mattered. Nagual's head pushed into her hand.

I worked fucking hard to get this bike and dog working, and I missed being here for this disaster. It has to work. Luciana cycled her OPTO-insert to the bike and drove it out of the garage. She pushed the front doors in with the front wheel.

"Don't take this the wrong way," Luciana said. "You don't know how many of them there are. Maybe they have good comms, hacked ours, or maybe they have no sense of self preservation." Anger rose in Luciana's voice. "Maybe they're the newest motherfuckers to blow through this shithole and they want to send a message to all comers. I'm not joking and I'm telling you, this will make a difference."

The bike came around the corner and entered the conference room. She drove it to the head of the table. *Open.*

"Now, let me show you the goodies I brought."

Luciana went through everything the bike had.

"And the dog?" Novina said after she finished.

"People aren't expecting a K9 unit to make a comeback, are they?"

"Jesus, I haven't heard that phrase in years." Kagan rubbed his forehead.

"He will be an asset. An early warning system when scanjammers are being used, if nothing else," Luciana said.

The weary group sat back at the table, but the looks of despair were gone.

"Now what?" Sheer said. "Do we wake the Chief?"

"No, he said for everyone to sleep here today, for me to lock up and take watch."

If there was any protest to be had by the other officers, exhaustion sank it before it could rise to the surface. They mumbled their thanks,

The Last 0-Day

stumbling to the sleeping quarters in the former rectory, and passing out. Luciana walked back to the garage and double checked it was locked. Nagual ever present and a step behind. *We're going to do this, Nagual. We have to.*
Luciana checked the logs as she walked to lock the front door.

"Not closing are you?" a man with the patois common to the Pucker entered. Bald, dirtier than most, and borderline emaciated with a short gray beard. Luciana couldn't tell if this was because of the storm of his usual demeanor.

"No," Luciana said. *Something's off.*
The man's green eyes wouldn't meet hers, and he scanned over her shoulder.

"Can I help you?" she asked.

"Yes, when will your next patrol come through the sixteen-hundred block? I'd like to report a missing person, but don't want to cause a fuss." His eyes locked onto hers.

"We don't discuss patrol routes. Who is missing?"

"Child." His eyes drifted back behind her or to the ceiling above. *He's a Homeless.*

"He's been missing, shaved head, one green eye, one blue eye, can't miss him."

"Where did you last see him?" Luciana went through the motions. Easiest way to get rid of someone like this was to play along.

"Few days." He swayed on his feet, but his eyes locked onto hers again. "You find him, come get me, sixteen-hundred block, apartment eight."

His eyes aren't right. She cycled her OPTO-inserts to scan his eyes, but he turned to leave first.
Through a tear in his shirt at the base of his neck was an unmistakable clover tattoo.
Luciana's stomach dropped. Her OPTO-inserts cycled to infrared, the man's body a rainbow of heat, it lacked any weapon outline.
Luciana made the call. She sprinted, tackling him—
He was stronger than he looked, staying on his feet.

She got her hips below his, yanked his arm and threw him onto his head in the lobby. She moved to pin him. He kicked her off and towards the door.

"Bitch," he said through clenched teeth. His patois was gone, replaced with an Urban accent from the NYC.

Left my weapons in my jacket at my desk. Stupid.

He squared up and set his feet with a quickness that betrayed his martial training.

This is bad. Adrenaline thundered into her limbs. She threw a low leg kick into his planted leg, hoping to make him slip.

Concurrently, his right fist came across the top.

She raised her hand to block—

Sparks erupted in her vision as his fist cracked the top of her skull. The world tilted, warmth covered the side of her head.

Attack. 1.

Nagual came bouncing from the office behind the older man, leaping, biting, teeth sinking into his calf, the fibula and tibia snapping with a sickening one-two pop.

The man screamed and fell to one knee. He turned on Nagual. Luciana threw a switch kick. Shin cracked skull. He flew backwards, his head bouncing off the floor.

Nagual released his leg and turned to Luciana. Blood dripped from his teeth, his tail a wagging blur.

She leaned against the wall, her head throbbing from the impact. *That cannot have been good for these implants.*

The man moved again, but between the concussion and one leg, he could barely drag himself towards the door.

"Stop." Luciana reached behind the front desk for handcuffs. "He'll take the other leg."

The man didn't respond. His movements twitchy as he pulled himself to the door, blood flowing from his mangled leg. Luciana sat on his back, pulling his arms behind to handcuff them. He had no strength left.

"Now, I've questions—"

Pop-crack! Warm red rained over Luciana. The glass front of the door shattered.

The Clover's head pulped, pieces of electronics sparking within the empty skull.

Luciana's head spun, her stomach rolled, and she vomited onto the back of the corpse.

Gunshots. She rolled off and out of view of the front door, but no second shot came.

"Jesus Christ, Gutierrez, are you ok?!" Novina yelled.

Chen was a foot behind, skidding on the lobby slickend with gore. A trail of blood ran from the church to the man's mangled leg, to the wick that was his body and the firework that was formerly his head.

"Clover." Luciana blacked out.

Chapter 17 - Luciana

Rough warmth licked Luciana's face. She blinked at Nagual's wet nose against her forehead.

"How long was I out?" Luciana asked.

"A few seconds." Chen tried to push Nagual away, but he was bolted to the ground, licking Luciana.

Chen attempted to work, but Nagual's tongue blocked him. "You mind stopping him?"

Sit, stop. Nagual sat beside her.

"Thanks." Chen tilted Luciana's head. "Flesh wound. Mind getting a kit?"

Novina left without a word.

"What happened?"

Luciana's head rang. "He came in acting crazy. Asking for some kid. I saw the tattoo and tried to take him in."

The pulsing against her skull slowed, and she shivered in the post adrenaline rush dump. Nagual pushed Chen out of the way and lay against her chest.

Chen raised an eyebrow.

"Must think I'm cold," Luciana said.

"What about the... well, that?" Chen thumbed over his shoulder to the mess that was formerly the Clovers skull. Novina tossed the medkit to Chen.

"This'll hurt," Chen said.

"Do it and the mess isn't mine." She winced as the cleaner poured over her face. The icy sting of glue followed, sealing her cut.

"Jesus Christ," Novina said under her breath. "We better wake the Chief."

"We can't," Luciana said.

"What do you mean, we can't? What else can we do? This was a serious escalation. We have to get backup," Novina said.

"One, we don't know there won't be any backup." Luciana stood, Nagual followed. "Two, we don't even know where they're operating out of. We think the sewer, but that's a hell of an area to go search—"

"You're concussed—"

"Let alone everyone's one eugeroic away from a complete hallucination, Chief included. I'm not fucked up, but if I was, we'd be in the same boat."

"She has a point," Chen said. "We're all compromised, one way or another."

"Exactly." Luciana turned to the body.
The black wiring poking from the exposed spine sent a chill down her own.

"But we could drive this to the nearest examiner. See if there are any clues on it and confirm Chief's implant theory." Luciana took a step towards the body.

"Wait!" Novina yelled. "If you didn't shoot him, they could be outside waiting to pick us off if we go for the body."

"Good point," Chen said, exhaustion fraying his voice.

"We need to block the door," Luciana said.

"Novina." Chen cleared his throat. "Get ready to hit the lights. Gutierrez and me will get the heaviest desk to seal this door."
Chen and Luciana went into the parish and stopped at the first desk.

"Sorry, Sheer." Chen pushed the papers, tablets, and bobbleheads to the floor. "Never knew why he liked those old things."
They grunted as they moved the desk to the front door.

"On my mark." Luciana gripped the edges of the desk. "Lights."
The lights within the station turned off. Yellow from street lamps spilled into the station, turning the blood black. Luciana heft the desk, the shattered glass like ball bearings beneath their feet.

"Mark," Luciana said.
Luciana pushed the back, Chen dropped the front, and they set it in front of the door as the lights within the station turned back on. Novina and Luciana crouched over the body.

"I'll get bags," Chen said.

Luciana lifted the torn clothing. Dirt on the visible skin was a sham marking, underneath the shirt was spotless. An herbal cologne attempted to mask the chemical and rot scent of the sewers, but it was unmistakably there. *Which sewer did you crawl out of?*

Chen came back with a body bag, gloves, and two smaller bags. Novina and Chen snapped on gloves and maneuvered the body into the bag.

"God damn it," Luciana said. *I've to shovel his brains into the bag.* Novina and Chen stifled laughter.

Bastards. Nagual growled. The officer spun on him and looked back at Luciana.

"I didn't do that," Luciana said. *Stop, sit,* 1. "Maybe something outside?"

They cycled their ENT-inserts but amplified only the wind.

"Must have run?" Luciana winced, pushing mush into the bag. Novina and Chen eyed Nagual as they pulled the body out of the lobby.

Luciana swallowed bile as she finished pushing the skull fragments into the bag and tied it closed. Novina and Chen came back with a cleaning robot and set it to work on the linoleum floor.

"Now what?" Novina asked. "We have to assume they'll try and stop us."

"They might not be that bold." Luciana tossed the brain bag into the body bag and zipped it close. "This didn't go as planned, otherwise they'd have shot me and not him." She snapped her gloves into the trash.

"They killed this one to stop us from interrogating him," Novina said.

The cleaning robot ground across the floor as it hoovered glass and bone chips Luciana missed.

"Can we have this conversation elsewhere?" Chen asked.

"Garage," Luciana said. "I'll grab the gear."

Luciana stepped into the garage. The lights had been blown out, leaving a lone LED above a parking space in the middle.

"Did the Clovers do this?" Novina said as they dropped the body.

"No." Luciana rubbed her forehead. "I must have done it when I cleared the sand using the bike."

"How should we get to the examiners?" Chen asked.

"We go together in one car?" Novina said. "Two cars? Three cars? Make it hard for them to follow?"

"I can go alone in the bike," Luciana said.

"Too risky, even if it is as high-tech as you say," Chen said.

"And you can't expect us to sit here and hold our dicks," Novina said.

"Did we lose the truck?" Luciana asked as an idea percolated through her mind.

"No," Chen said, "but it can't go fast. We'll be easy pickings."

Perfect. "The sand and dust in the Pucker will slow everything, but with the truck's clearance, it won't be any slower than normal. Once we're onto the highway, it won't matter. Besides, it's bulletproof and"—Luciana smiled—"we can fit the bike inside it."

"You can't be serious," Novina said.

"Let's do it," Chen said.

Luciana opened the rusted back doors of the SWAT truck in the corner of the garage. *One of the worst hand-me-downs you ever got us, Maus.*

"Body in the rifle storage," Luciana said. *Open. Into the bike, Nagual. 1.* The dog leapt into the bike. *Close.* Luciana backed the bike into the rear of the vehicle. The truck's shocks squealed but didn't sag more than a few centimeters. Luciana pulled the doors closed.

Chen checked his weapons in the copilot's seat. Novina fastened her bulletproof vest, checked the fuel levels, and killed the pilot program.

"Here goes nothing." Novina popped a pill and cracked her neck.

"Comms on," Chen said.

"10-4," they repeated in unison.

Luciana crouched between the two seats, her overjacket calming her nerves.

The engine grumbled, the garage door opened, and they left the safety of the police station.

Dust rolled around the dimly lit streets. Novina stuck to the main roads, the truck couldn't fit through the countless alleys anyways. Tension crept into Chen and Novina's shoulders as they traveled further and further without being besieged.

"They're planners, right?" Luciana said.

"Yeah…" Chen followed her train of thought. "Where will they come for us?"

"Edge of the Pucker?" Novina white-knuckled the steering column. "Maybe block a road somewhere and steer us down an alleyway?"

"Chen swap to IR, Novina night vision, I'll take visible," Luciana said.

They cycled their OPTO-inserts to the requested wavelengths and waited. Luciana rolled her shoulders. *I should have tracked the Clover instead of tackling him.*

The edge of the Pucker loomed ahead. Three vehicles broken by the storm had been pushed into the roadway as a blockade, leaving fresh tracks in the sand. Novina drifted to a stop.

Luciana scanned the convoluted streets. *Nothing out of order, other than this roadblock.*

"Not to be this person," Novina said. "But, what if they know, we know, and what not."

Luciana sighed. "God fucking damn it."

"Ram it," Chen said.

"What?" Novina asked.

"They know we know bullshit aside. They don't want us going through that area. We have to be unpredictable. Ramming it is risky, but not something they expect."

"Gutierrez?"

"Do it. The bike could clear it, but it's better if we keep it as a trunk card."

"Trump card," Chen's voice was tight from nerves.

"Fuck that. It's in the trunk, and it's a trump card. Trunk. Card."

"Enough." Novina floored it.

The engine roared, the SWAT truck crashed through the blockade in a shower of sparks and dust.

"Old piece of shit's made of heavier metal." Chen laughed.

Luciana checked the rearview. A lone shadow moved between buildings and detritus, disappearing into the labyrinth before her OPTO-inserts could zoom in.

"That wasn't the ambush spot," Luciana said as they got onto the highway. "One scout and he moved after we went through."

"There are what, two, three spots where this behemoth can fit through to exit the Pucker?" Chen asked.

"North One-A, South Two-B, and West One-B?" Novina said.

"That sounds right," Luciana said. "They tried to block south, which is closest to the station, and one that leads to East Bowl."

The SWAT truck integrated into the middle lane of traffic. Off-shift commuters filled the car around, most sleeping in transit. Damaged street lights illuminated the roads like the flash of a camera before plunging into darkness. Luciana pulled the tablet from her pocket and projected a holographic map of the city.

"It'd be easier if we knew which exit they wanted us to use." Chen tapped the map.

The medical examiners that Nineteen-PD worked with popped up heading south along the twisting highways.

"Flaherty is closest," Chen said. "But it's an obvious offshoot. We could head further south to Donaher and split off to Perez."

"That district will be full of people even with the damage of the storm. Can't stop partying kids," Luciana said.

"The cleaning is probably in full swing there. There'll be less people than normal, if any. Clovers will assume we'd go to the closest office in this hunk of shit." Chen tapped the dash. "Means we could fuck with them."

"We passed the exit to Flaherty." Novina glanced at the map. "It's Perez or Donaher."

"Pass Perez, we'll decide after," Luciana said.

She sat back, steadying her breathing as exit signs passed. What were the Clovers planning?

The stained sign for Exit 50.1.b to Perez passed them. *Few more kilometers to the turnaround or Donaher.*

A transport crashed into the back of the SWAT truck.

"Fuck!" Novina gripped the wheel. A deafening crash thundered through the truck as it fishtailed.

Tires screamed, the cars around the truck handled the deviation from programming perfectly, moving out of the way like a swarm of fish when a shark attacked. Chen pulled his pistol, lowering his window.

Luciana grabbed his shoulder. "They'll shoot back, get to Donaher's!" She yelled over the thunderous impacts and screaming tires.

Luciana sprinted towards her bike, the canopy opened before she brought the thought forward. A crashing impact sent her against the walls. *Motherfuckers.* She hurled herself into the bike. Adrenaline rolled over her as the canopy closed. The world stopped shaking, the engine hummed to life against her chest.

Luciana floored it, exploding out of the back of the transport. Hitting the pavement between lanes, she spun to deal with their attackers. The HUD shimmered, highlighting assumed Clover cars with a teal border. *How does it know that?* The thought left as quickly as it arrived. *We're surrounded.*

A wall of beige cars replaced the commuters around the truck. *They didn't care where we were going, they waited until we couldn't exit.* The strobe effect of the damaged highway lighting pushed through the HUD. The SWAT truck regained control. Chen pulled the backdoors shut as Luciana accelerated behind them.

"Surrounded," Luciana said.

"What—" two cars crashed into the SWAT truck, cutting Novina off.

The truck swerved into the rightmost lane. A transport slowed to avoid being crushed, attempting to box Luciana out.

No one sat in the pilot's seat.

Luciana scanned the beige cars around. *They're all unmanned, that can't be right.* She checked her rear. A beige transport with a lone driver was directly behind.

She jammed on the brakes, the strobe effect plunged them into darkness.

The driver dodged her, the lights came back. She was behind the transport now. The car accelerated towards the van. The driver pulled a rifle from his passenger seat.

Shoot—Guns at the front of the bike thundered before Luciana finished.

The car exploded into a mess of flames and flesh. The wreck accelerated, the dead driver's foot stuck onto a pedal. It veered left and smashed into a commuter's transport. The fleet of beige cars drifted out of their lanes, crashing into barricades like their life was snuffed out.

"Clear," Luciana said.

"What the fuck was that?" Novina asked.

"I'll explain when we're at Donaher's. We're close."

The space occupied by the Clover cars remained empty as they continued, like they were driving with a bubble around them.

Luciana reversed her bike against the back of the SWAT van as it parked. The medical examiner's office stood in the shadow of the freeway in an old brick building. Its sign was a lone red cross with none of the gaudy promises that many clinics at the borders of the artisan district had. Luciana got out, Nagual bound out simultaneously. *Follow*, 1. Though calm during the drive, Nagual's ears swiveled and his nose twitched now.

Alert and on the job. Luciana opened the grimy doors of the examiner's office. Acerbic sterilants singed her nostrils as Chen and Novina dragged the body close behind.

"Welcome to Medical Examiner's Office 45, Head Examiner Michael Donaher, sponsored by—" the secretarobot said.

Luciana walked by it. *Not waiting for an excuse about how busy he is.* She opened the door to Donaher's office.

"Jesus Officer Gutierrez, do you ever knock?" Michael Donaher said. He was an Old. One who accepted mortality and wasn't fighting it with the latest drugs and cell therapies. His skin wrinkled, sagging in spots. His hair naturally bleached white by time. Many ignored him, thinking the world passed him by, but Luciana knew better.

He picked up the e-cigar on his desk and spoke through it. "I guess not, to what do I owe this pleasure?"

"Body for you to examine, now."

"You don't say? And here I thought you came by for coffee." Donaher's smile fell away on Luciana's sternness. Novina and Chen grunted behind as one of them booted open the morgue door and tossed a body onto a metal table.

Donaher rose. "Alright, alright. Make sure your department is good for it this time. Give me a minute."

Luciana stood by the body bag as Donaher pulled on his lab coat. She unzipped the bag, the hour that passed hadn't mellowed the body's stench.

"Well, I can give you the cause of death," Donaher said.

Luciana ignored him and put on gloves. "We need your help figuring out if there are any residues on his clothing or persons. Where he came from, what he's eating or using, anything. Help me with this," Luciana said. They flipped the corpse onto its front. "I want to know what this is connected to." She pointed to the clover tattoo.

"Now that is something." Donaher exhaled a cloud of cigar vape, his interest peaked. He put on magnifying glasses, pulled gloves out of his front pocket, and manipulated the skin around the tattoo.

"It's keratinized." He pulled a scalpel from the drawer and cut into the skin around the clover. The whisper of the blade on skin pinged against an alloy a layer deep. He froze and looked through his eyebrows at the officers. "You mind telling me what's going on here?"

"Gang in the Pucker," Luciana said.

"Chief thinks the tattoos are this new tech, implants," Chen said. "Still no inserts, Donaher?"

Micheal Donaher looked up from the body, his eyes huge from the magnifying effect of his glasses. "Youths." He spun his scalpel outwards and cut a circle to remove the skin in layers and reach the tech within the body.

"You Youths trust your tech too much. Do they not teach you about the Pitch-black 0-day?"

"They solved that bug," Chen said. "And the net was down for a few days."

"What was the algorithm's name?"

The officers glanced at one another, Luciana shrugged.

"Then they don't teach you," Donaher said. "It was the Adephon algorithm and sure the net was down for a few days, but it was everything. Weather modifiers, banks, power grid, infrastructure. The shit fried. People lost fortunes, committed suicide. Crops were sold to the wrong people, imagine having a shipping container of corn at your doorstep, like I did. To say nothing of the weather."

Chen scratched his head. "They strengthened the encryption and the backbone tech using machine learning algorithms. They're unbreakable. There hasn't been an incident in decades."

"For every unsinkable ship, there is an iceberg to crack it."

"An ice-what?" Chen said.

"Youths." Donaher sighed as he finished his fourth circle of skin removal and stopped. "Jesus."

Circuits, boards, artificial tissue, and carbon fibers occupied the spot where the man's left shoulder muscle should have been. Tendrils ran into the neck before disappearing into what was formerly the brain stem.

Is this inside me? Luciana shuddered, running her fingers against the back of her skull. Hair, skin and grit met her palm. *I don't know if I wanted to feel something out of place or not.*

"Your Chief is right." Micheal sucked on his e-cigar. "This is unpublished tech. A receiver and transmitter of some type. Wushan, by the looks of it."

Chen and Novina stood stunned, their mouths agape.

"How would you know that?" Luciana asked.

"Just because I don't use the tech doesn't mean I don't know about it. I work with whoever walks through that door. No questions asked."

"Can you remove it?" *Who else you work with is a battle for a different day.*

"Yes."

"Do it, we will wait. Chen, Novina, let's talk outside."

Luciana stepped into the lobby with Chen and Novina in tow. Nagual stood guard by the exit. *Did I ask him to do that?*

"This is fucked," Novina said to no one in particular.

"What happened on the highway?" Chen asked.

"It was one driver, the rest were remotes," Luciana said. "When I killed the one dude, the rest of the cars disconnected and lost control."

"Do you think he was controlling them?"

"I'm not sure. The explosion blocked me, I couldn't see if the cars died immediately or if they went off later. Shit, I can't even remember what manufacturer the cars were."

"The Chief was right," Chen said. "How did he know?"

"I think he knew I was getting implanted."

"You think that type of shit's inside of you?"

"I can't. My skin's crawling at the thought, but I wasn't gone or out for that long. That much work would take weeks to heal. I... trust the scientists that did this to me." Luciana gestured to the morgue door. "They wouldn't have done that to me. Novina, you with us?"

Novina swayed on her feet, the bags under her eyes coal black.

That last pill cracked her. "Chen, take her to the van, lay her down. I'll get the implants and samples from Donaher."

"You don't think they're outside?" Chen asked.

"They could be, but we have to get out of here and back to the station."

Nagual nudged her leg.

"I've got it." She pulled out one of her OPTO-inserts.

Sit, stay. 1. Luciana held Nagual's eyes open. He blinked. *No.* Luciana widened her eyes, Nagual mimicked her, and she got the insert in. She cycled her right OPTO-insert to mirror the left. She was a giant in Nagual's point-of-view.

"You better wash that before putting it back in." Chen grimaced. Luciana sat, closing her left eye to see only Nagual's vision. She imagined Nagual peering out the front door and sniffing for anything related to the sewers, he barked if he smelled it.

Go. 1. Nagual hurried to the front and peered through the door, Luciana cycled wavelengths. A street empty of people but full of bots working line by line to clean the dirt and dust from the storm. She counted heartbeats, no bark came. *Return.* 1.

"Nothing by vision, or by smell from the sewers."

Nagual arrived back, Luciana removed the insert with ease.

"You might want to look away." Luciana spat into her palm, swirled the OPTO-insert, and set it back into her eye.

Chen gagged and turned.

"Take Novina, I'll be right out." *Follow Chen.* 1. She headed back to the morgue.

Donaher stood over a bloody artificial octopus set on the corpse's lower spine.

"You tell the Chief that I don't owe him anymore favors." Donaher removed his gloves. "He'll understand."

"Can we leave the body here?"

"I'll chill it for a week. You will have to come get it or we will incinerate it afterwards."

"And chemical residues?"

"Day or two, I'll be in contact."

"Thanks, Michael." Luciana shoveled the implant into a bag.

"Luciana, you're looking better than you did, what a year ago? Told you time heals all wounds."

"Only some of them, Doc." Luciana left the office.

A cleaning robot passed Luciana's bike, a fresh yellow ticket stuck on the window.

"Seriously?" Luciana shredded it and tossed it into the wind. "Pop the back, Chen."

Luciana backed the bike into the SWAT truck and walked towards the front. Skyscrapers loomed above, their lights punctuating the darkness of the sidestreet. Luciana pulled open the door. *In.* 1. Nagual hopped in between the seats.

"I'm driving." Luciana turned to Chen.

The man was fast asleep. *Should have left them out of this.* Luciana cycled her ENT-inserts to the local police channels to answer questions about the highway as she drove back. Exits passed, no questions came. *Either the accident wasn't reported or it's being ignored. Both aren't good.*

Luciana entered the Pucker through West1b in an attempt to avoid an ambush at the other entrances. Nagual stood with paws on dash, scanning the area as she did.

Don't know what you'll do within the truck, buddy. Errant neo-rats raised both their hackles. Luciana rolled her shoulders and didn't relax until the garage door closed behind her. *Clover tactics make no damn sense.* Chen snored, Novina slept beside the implant poking through a translucent bag. Luciana carried Novina to the sleeping quarters first, then Chen. Both were oblivious to their occasional rough handling. *Their shifts while I was gone went through the eugeroic window. They've already hallucinated and came out the other side.*

The cleaning robot had finished with the lobby and was stuck on one of Sheer's bobbleheads within the parish. Luciana pulled the trinket and set the robot on the dirt tracks from her bike. She pulled an empty trash bag and entered the conference room. She set the bag on the table and lay the implant on top to prevent contamination while she cleaned it. Rubbing off the clotted blood and artificial tissues revealed a carbon fiber body. The exterior electronics were ion-exchangers with no corporate logo. Inside the shell were processors labeled Wushan Corp. *Saori said Taketa worried about industrial espionage.* Luciana left the cleaned implant on the table. *Maus and Chief will know more about this tech than me.*

Nagual nudged her leg.

"Wha—"

Nagual held a bowl in his mouth. Luciana filled it from the water dispenser, and he drank before it hit the floor. That first bowl turned into three more before he wagged his tail at her.

"We have to figure out a way to cheat you rations." Luciana laughed at the idea of convincing the water board to give what they would argue was her pet more. Luciana's eyes drifted back to the carbon fiber octopus on the conference table. *That's not inside me, it can't be.*

An hour or two passed, and the Chief walked into the conference room, rubbing his temples as he drank coffee and water.

He froze at the implant. "God damn it, I should have drank this morning," he rasped. "What do you have for me?"

Luciana relayed the past evening to the Chief.

"You're saying that he"—Chief gestured towards Nagual—"literally bit through a man's leg?"

"What? Yeah, didn't you hear how we got the implant or what it probably does?"

"Of course I did." The Chief refilled his coffee cup. "The rest, well, that's your training working. We should get Maus up here and see if he can crack this thing. Not likely, but worth a shot. We need to figure out what it does."

"It could be like my implants," Luciana said. "I communicate with Nagual and the bike, maybe this does it to other Clovers."

"Maybe, maybe not. A dog and a bike are one thing, another human's a huge leap."

"Maybe that's why it's so fucking huge. I don't have that in my body. I ran my fingers along my back while you slept."

"Do you think Taketa will give us information if we ask?"

"Taketa no, but I bet the researchers I worked with will."

"You start there. I'll wake Maus." The Chief left.

Luciana pulled her tablet, setting up an email to the address they gave her for health checkups. *Hopefully they check it frequently.*

To Saori Chaude or Samir Lindeman,

Unanticipated Event. Need to talk, secure channels, contact me now.

-Luciana

She sent it and put the tablet back into her pocket. Maus arrived, yawning, his mouth freezing open. His eyes flared, his brain waking at the implant on the table.

"What the fuck is that?" Maus looked between Luciana and the Chief.

"You tell us." The Chief handed Maus the tool bag from his desk.

Maus blinked. "G, can you get me some food and coffee?" He pulled the tools out and sat down to pry the carapace apart.

Luciana went to the kitchen, Nagual followed. She heated SR-toast in the microwave. Her stomach growled and Nagual nudged her.

"Guess we should eat too." She heated the whole SR-loaf and fed Nagual the toasts she had already cooked.

Luciana walked back into the conference room, Maus had pried off the cover. In front of them was a mixture of boards, circuits, and a coolant grid. She set the coffee and food at the edge of the table.

"Whatever this does, it's going to run hot," Maus said.

"Make? Any idea on its purpose?" The Chief asked.

"Chips say Wushan, transistors say Micron, boards say Vio. Any of these could manufacture the outsides, but who would have the step-up to put it all together? I can't say." Maus drank coffee and ate food, his hands still dirty. Maus looked at the Chief whose jaw clenched for more answers.

"Right, purpose. It has receivers and transmitters and they're shaped weirdly, like a four-leaf clover... Wait, how did you get this?"

"I'll tell you later," Luciana said.

"Was this inside someone?!" Maus dropped the food in his hands. "God damn it, warn me!" He left to wash or puke.

The Chief rubbed his stubble. "Go wake everyone."

"Chief, Novina and Chen are shot."

"Fine."

"If we push the rest—"

"I know, but my orders stand."

Luciana pushed the grumbling officers into the conference room. One by one, they woke upon seeing the implant. They sat and helped themselves to the food left out.

"This is what the Clovers have inside of them," the Chief said. "I want to tell you we know exactly what it is, but I can't. It's most likely some sort of advanced comm. It runs hot and it could do other things too. Gutierrez, tell everyone what happened last night."

Luciana repeated the story. As she spoke, the other officers alternated looks between Luciana and the implant. *Like I'm some freak show.*

"They didn't want us to have this," the Chief said as Luciana finished. "But we do. And we need to figure out how to use it against them."

"We can use the heat vision on our inserts to distinguish them from the crowds now," Kagan said.

"What was that thing about the kid with different colored eyes?" Sheer asked.

"The Clover asked if we found one to come by the sixteen-hundreds block," Luciana said.

Sheer ran to his desk and brought back a tablet. He scrolled through a call log map. "Here." He pointed to a block near one of the sewer ports. "We got something like twenty notifications for a missing child with heterochromia from that area. No where else either."

"That'd be a stupid mistake for them to make." Chief eyed the map. "But, sixteen-hundreds, are a few blocks from that sewer. They could be operating in this general area... What times were those received?"

"Morning and night," Sheer said.

"When they enter and exit?" Luciana asked.

"It's too simple," Chief said.

Luciana's tablet vibrated. The group turned and raised an eyebrow. She pulled the tablet.

"Bike, five minutes," blinked as a forced notification.

Luciana glanced at the Chief, and he nodded her dismissal.

"What other exits are there for the sewers near sixteen-hundred..." Junger said as Luciana left for the garage.

The bike canopy opened as she arrived and Nagual hopped into his holding spot before Luciana stepped in. The canopy slid closed and the HVAC of the building fell away.

"What is the event? Are you ok?" Norma spoke through Luciana's ENT-inserts even though she didn't click over a channel for the bike.

"Norma? I expected Saori or Samir. I'm fine, this is more... of a technical problem."

"What happened?" Saori asked.

They're in the same room. Luciana told Saori everything that had happened that night.

Muffled talking filtered through and Saori cleared her throat. "Did you find a child with heterochromia?"

"What?" Luciana blinked. "No. What about the implanted gangbangers?"

More muffled conversations filtered through.

"What's going on?"

"Give us a second, Luciana," Samir said, his voice tight.

Minutes stretched in an awkward silence, the bike's HUD highlighted the broken bulbs overhead.

"Luciana," Saori said. "Have your department hold tight. We're sending a Taketa agent over. Anton Grissom, he should be there by the evening."

"What, who?"

But the comm clicked off.

Why does everyone want this kid?

Luciana re-entered the conference room.

"How would we patrol?" Kagan said. "Where would we patrol?"

"We could do three and four," Nguyen said. "Less area covered, but will give us more eyes and ears. We will have to be careful in our grid layout, can't let Clovers get in behind us."

"I'm back," Luciana said. "We could do fours."

Officers squirmed at the idea.

"What?" Luciana said.

Officers glanced at one another.

"If someone has a problem with Gutierrez, speak up now," Chief commanded.

The officer's eyes fell to the table.

"That's what I thought. What do you have for us?"

"They were more interested in that kid with heterochromia than anything else."

"That's the key then. They can be tight-lipped about other Implanted roaming our district, but if everyone wants that kid, we'll collect it first."

"Chief, they're also sending someone to help. I've never met him but he's augmented too. Goes by Anton Grissom if we want to profile him."

"More the merrier." Sheer smiled.

Chapter 18 - Anton

Anton's transport slowed in front of a skyscraper near the ocean. A Taketa sign burned against the night sky.

"We're here," Yume said, her leg fidgeting as she smiled.

They stepped out of the transport. Salt from the waves filled the warm Southern Empire air. A man waited for them at the front door. He was an Old, his posture supported by a variant of an exosuit.

"Welcome back, Dr. Chaude," the man said, extending his hand.

"Joe, you know it's Yume," she shook his hand.

Joe smiled. "I like the honorifics. Let's go to my office."

"Let us shower first, we've been on the road for weeks. Surely even you can smell it."

"All these years in this city? I hardly smell anything, but if you insist. We've prepared one of the dorm rooms for you both. Shall we say, thirty minutes from now?"

"Sounds good," Yume said.

Joe's gray suit turned a microsecond before the rest of his body did and he left.

"What's his deal?" Anton asked as they grabbed their belongings from the cab.

"He's the head of this division, essentially number two for the entire company. Taketa's heir still runs everything, but Joe Fayed runs Taketa west."

"Oh."

"He's a sweetheart... more or less."

"Emphasis on less," Eva said, exiting the transport.

"Come on now, Eva," Yume said.

"What? He's too political for my blood."

"You need it for industry."

"I'll keep my head down, do solid science and let that take me where it may."

"I can appreciate that stance," Yume said.

"Aye," Eva tried, winking with the eye Yume couldn't see.

God damn it. Anton collected his pack and walked to the skyscraper. The interior of the Taketa building was an amalgam of whites, chromes, and blacks. Polished surfaces reflected upon one another. Anton shook his head after years of matte, earthen tones. They took a golden elevator to a sub-basement hallway with countless doors.

"Night." Eva scanned through the fourth door.

Yume thumbed into the sixth, and Anton followed her in. A steam shower was near a lone large bed that Yume tossed her bags onto. She stripped as she made her way to the showers.

God damn Urbans. Anton averted his gaze, fighting the urge to look.

"Oh right," Yume said. "I forgot you are uncomfortable with nudity."

Anton's ears burned.

"Sorry." Yume jumped into the shower, the pulsing steam quickly obscuring her from him.

His eyes adjusted, the steam disappeared. Yume rubbed dirt from her skin.

Seriously?

Yume rubbed her face.

I should stop.

She stretched her neck, rubbed her breasts. Anton's guilt forced him to turn on the bed and make sure he couldn't watch.

"Your turn." Yume stepped out, wrapping a towel around herself.

"I don't need to," Anton said.

"Anton, trust me, you need to."

His ears burned again, and he walked to the shower. "Do I need to do anything different with these?" He gestured to his augmented limbs.

"You haven't showered since you got those?"

"Not really, I used shower wipes after the manure pile—"

"That's disgusting." Yume shuddered. "I'm more amazed that I didn't notice until now. No, you'll be fine. You're waterproof to four-hundred meters." She laughed at her own joke.

I don't get it. Anton stripped and stepped into the shower. High-pressure mists pulsed against his skin in a soothing rhythm. *Beats the moistened rags of the stead and the cold showers of the base.* The shower turned off abruptly, dirt still ran along his augments. *It'll be fine.*

"Towel?" Anton said. His eyes looked through the polycarbon shield to an empty room. He walked to the bed and toweled off.

"You should eat." Yume entered with brown SR-loaves. "I checked the logs and you haven't been eating enough."

"Where are my clothes?"

"Being washed, Anton, being washed. I nearly vomited when you said you haven't showered in months."

"I've gone longer without bathing growing up."

"Doesn't help matters, Anton." She handed him the food and turned away.

Anton sniffed the bread, getting strong molasses and roast corn. *Nice.* He stuck it in his mouth.

"You'll have to wait here while they wash, I'll go meet with Joe. Someone will bring them back, it shouldn't take too long."

"Ok."

Yume left.

Anton turned on the wallscreen, which was preset to the local news network.

"This is SE-LA with a reminder of the upcoming planned storm. We will go over everything you need to prepare for it later in the hour. It's been verified that the damage done by the most recent detritus storm up in the San Francisco Bowl is real. Most images broadcasted have been verified by the national algorithms."

Anton lowered the volume and pulled his tablet from his pack. He got signal. *Finally.*

"Hey Guys," Anton typed to Alex and Sagira. "I haven't had signal until now. Being an enlisted aide isn't what it's cracked up to be. Thanks for the gifts, they proved useful at a surprise party I went to. On the West Coast, hopefully this assignment ends soon and the fireteam can be reunited." Anton paused. "It's not the same without you both. A."

They'll give me shit for that. Anton shrugged, sending that message and opening another prompt.
"Hi Cassie and Twin, Long time no speak, I know. I've been…" He ran his augmented hand across his legs. *I can't tell them by mail.* "Busy, active deployment means I don't get to send or receive mail frequently. Hope all is well and that I'll get leave to come home soon. A. PS. Darren have a kid yet?"
Anton smiled, and the door rang. He tapped send and opened the door.
A waist-high robot stood in front of him, a tray on its head held his clothing in a plastic bag. Anton took them, laying them out on the mattress. He gained a formal suit somewhere in their cleaning process.

The door hissed open. "Excellent, you got your suit," Yume said. "We're going to a gala tonight."

"What?"

The door rang again, and Yume retrieved another package of clothing. "There is an industry event. You're to be my escort. It's formal attire."

"This is a formal military uniform."

"Yes, Joe wants people to know we're working with UCSM. He sees this as a golden opportunity."

"I'm a trophy."

"What, you think sending me isn't on purpose too? Send the young female 'prodigy'. It's how the game is played, Anton. Besides, it should be fun."

"Fun?" *We should be working.*

"They usually have some excellent food." She looked at the half-eaten loaf sitting on the bed. "And you need it. Besides, data's analyzing for the NYC port, and we've been on convoy. Why not go out together?"

Together? His heart skipped a beat, and he averted his gaze again as she stripped. *Urbans.*

"You're going to have to get over that," Yume said. "Done."

Anton turned back. Yume wore a semi-reflective dress that went just below the knee but had a cut that ran the ride side to her hip. *Stunning.*

"Should I pick your jaw up, or can you?"

Anton snapped out of his stupor, his cheeks warm as he turned to his uniform.

Yume giggled. "It's fine, Anton. Shows that it was a good choice." She walked to the mirror with a handbag.

She's not leaving. Anton checked her in the mirror, Yume focused on applying makeup. Anton removed his towel and pulled on the uniform that fit perfectly. *They have my measurements from the NYC.* The material was a mixture of elastanes and polyfibers that stretched in any direction he moved.

"Like it?" Yume turned from the mirror. Dark lines rode her eyes and the makeup on her cheeks stuttered in his vision.

"Yeah. What did you put on your face?"

"These parties can have polarizing light, this will reflect differently depending on what hits it. You see that?"

"Yeah, it's shimmery."

"Let me scan you real quick before we leave." Yume pulled a handheld scanner from her bag and worked around his eyes.
Her lime perfume tickled his nostrils. Anton tried to maintain a level of professionalism, but his eyes kept glancing at her exposed cleavage.

"Everything appears normal. I'll have the lab look. Maybe they see something I don't. Ready?" Yume walked to the door.

As I will be. "Aye."

***

Anton sat in a transport driving beneath the tallest buildings in the city, they rivaled the NYC skyscrapers.

"Anton, when we get there, you get out and hold the door for me."

"Ok?"

"Formalities and what not. This your first party?"

"More or less."

"Never went to the... what're they called?"

"Gatherings? No, my brother and sister did. The most people I saw before the military was at my father's funeral."

"I'm sorry to hear that."

"No need."

The car turned down an avenue of skyscrapers. Logos of Wushan, Taketa, Micron, and Vio all competed against one another to burn the brightest against a starless sky.

"Wushan. They at this event?" Anton asked.

"They'll be there, as will all the competition."

"We should grill some of them."

"Easy there. A lone chip in a corporate merc's exosuit doesn't make them the culprit. And the company is huge, just because there is an outpost here doesn't mean they did anything, or even know about the NYC incident."

"Aye." *She's right.*

The car stopped in front of a glittering lobby, and Anton stepped into the warm night. Flowery perfumes rode the air as transports ferried people to the building. Yume put her arm in the crux of his elbow and gently led him forward. Hundreds of people stood in circles talking. The individual conversations bordered on yelling as people raised their voices to be heard over the din of other conversations.

I don't like this gala business. Anton rolled his shoulders.

Rainbows erupted from the women's faces as the light reflected off of the makeup.

"You have your insert in?" Yume crackled in his ear.

"Aye."

"Good, means we won't have to yell. You take lead. Let's go to the bar on the right."

Anton nodded and jostled through the goat trails between the circles of people talking. Where circles met, he gave them a tap on the shoulder and a heartbeat to move before he moved them himself.

"What's your poison?" Asked a bartender who looked like a younger version of Alex. Harsh lines were shaved into their hair that shimmered in violets like everyone's makeup did.

"Vodka lime," Yume said, leaning in. She turned to Anton. "You drink?"

"Never had a drop."

"Now's as good a time as any." Yume winked. "Make that two." The bartender handed them their drinks and pushed away money that Yume had put on the bar.

"All complimentary tonight darling, courtesy of Wushan Corp." The bartender turned to other patrons.

Yume led Anton towards a table at the edge of the mob and sipped her drink. "Whew, they made it a double."

Anton took a mouthful, his throat and torso burned immediately. He winced. "Why did you give me this?"

"You'll see." Yume smiled. "You need to relax. We're back urban, it's safe here."

This many people isn't safe. Anton took another mouthful, finishing the drink. "You said there was food?"

Yume nodded. "Yeah, one second." She tapped the table, a screen displayed on its surface. "Done." She went back to her drink and bounced to the music.

"What is that?"

"Some sort of retro-electro… I dunno, nice beat though." She smiled and a tray of hand-sized foods arrived.

More drinks too. "Is that meat?"

"Yeah, most likely, could be an SR-amalgam." Yume took a bite. "Sure tastes like beef though. You should try some."

Anton bit into a piece of meat wrapped in flatbread, spicy and herbed. "That's good." His stomach growled.

"First time having meat?"

Anton shook his head. "Had puma growing up—"

"What?!"

"Yeah, it's good."

Yume drank to cover her shock while Anton finished the plate of food.

"No one has come over," Yume said. "We might have to get social, Anton."

Circles jostled as a group beelined for them.

"No need." Anton nodded.

A group in black suits and dresses with the prismatic streaks in their hair saddled up to them.

"It's nice to see Taketa sent someone." A woman smiled.

Fakest smile I've seen.

"Always nice to see you, Ana." Yume put on the same fake smile.

Ana turned towards Anton. "I don't believe we've been introduced." She extended a hand, which he shook.

"This is Anton Grissom, he's my military liaison."

"Quite the hand you have there, Mr. Grissom." Ana turned it over for a closer inspection and glanced back at Yume. "Taketa tech, I am sure?"

"Yes, it is, Anton suffered an injury while on duty. New prosthetic."

"Looks like more than that, I would say. How did you injure it, Mr. Grissom?"

Don't know what is and isn't confidential. Play dumb. "Got it caught in a bot on base. Stupid mistake."

Ana tutted. "Those alpha-bots can be quite dangerous! No safety features. Was it a Taketa one?"

"I don't remember the make."

"Well, I'll double check and see if Wushan has any with the US military, but I think we lost that contract years ago. We primarily work in the Eurasian market these days."

"Sorry to hear that," Anton said.

"Don't be Mr. Grissom. We're making inroads with the New York Collective. We had a prototype sent there not too long back. Should make quite a splash."

Is she insinuating?

"What are you all working on?" Yume asked.

"Come on Yume, doesn't your intelligence office know?" Ana said.

"Haven't checked with them in a while, Ana, been doing research."

"Always in the lab with this one," Ana said to Anton. "Well, it's going on the show floor soon, and production is in full swing. Calling it the A-bot-toir. Marketing is proud of that one. It should be able to disassemble carcasses in microseconds."

"Meat's on the downswing." Yume's eyes locked on Anton.

He clenched his jaw and closed his fist. *Ana...*

"Is it? Going to have to find an aftermarket, I suppose. Well, we should be going. It was a pleasure to meet you, Mr. Grissom. Yume." Ana nodded and left, her group in tow.

"What were you saying about Wushan not knowing anything?" Anton fumed. *I should take her to the base.*

"You did well." Yume finished her drink. "Worried you were about to do something silly there."

"How can you be so... unphased. They just—"

"Careful now, Anton," Yume interrupted. "Entirely likely we're being watched."

Anton scanned the room, men in suits near glittering pillars were too casual in their glances at them. "You're correct."

"They won't do anything in an urban center," Yume said, more to herself than to him.

"It'd be their mistake if they did." Anton finished Yume's drink. *Ana at Wushan, I'll remember you.*

"Yume!" A woman approached their table. With cherubic cheeks and a short jacket over her dress, she looked under-dressed and out of place. She hugged Yume and beamed at Anton. "I'm Claudia."

"Hey Claudia, how are you doing?" Yume smiled. "Wait, how many have you had?"

"The bartender likes me, he made me triples for free." Claudia's eyes couldn't fix on any one point for too long.

"I bet... We were just about to leave. You should come with us. We can take you back to... Where are you staying?"

"At Vio, I work there now and got flown out. Oh my god, Yume, if I could tell you what we have now, you'd freak." A coy smile spread across her face. "But I can't."

"Awe, Claudia, you're such a tease." Yume edged another drink over towards Claudia, who drank it absentmindedly.

"Do you remember Mark?" Claudia leaned on the table. "He's at Vio now too, working on better inserts. Single too, if you're interested and want to switch companies. Wait, is this your SO?"

"Military liaison," Anton said.

"Fancy, working with the military? Must have been a fat contract."

"Aye." Anton wanted to steer the conversation and them out of the building. "Why don't I help walk you out?"

"You can help me with more than that, if you want." Claudia leaned on Anton, her hands groping his back, arms, and chest, more for enjoyment than for support.

"Yume?" Anton asked.

Yume scanned the room. "You're probably right, let's go." Claudia leaned on Anton as the drink washed over her. Her back was oddly firm, but Anton kept it to himself as they left the gala. Claudia was dead weight and blacked out by the time they got to the curb. A blue Vio cab pre-programmed to return to their HQ opened, and Anton set her inside.

"Should we go with her?" Anton asked.

"No, the cab will take her back and their doorman can handle her." Anton shut the door, and the cab sped off. The party's music pounded behind them, polarizing strobes flashed to the beat. A teal Taketa cab pulled up, Yume swung in with Anton behind and they left the party.

"Why didn't we go with her?" Anton asked.

"Vio does weird industrial espionage. That could have been a trap."

"You serious?"

"Doesn't have to be as overt as you're thinking, like it could be a recording device on her somewhere."

"Her back did feel oddly firm."

"That would have been good to know."

"What, we're going to take her clothes off at the party?"

Yume chewed on one of her fingers. "No, I guess you're right. Did it feel like your implants?"

"More like something underneath her skin."

"Fascinating. I'll have to tell Fayed. We could have brought her back to Taketa." Yume leaned back and appraised him. "You did well tonight, Anton. Stayed cool in a social situation, got an easy out. I'm… impressed. Thought you were more of a tactical guy, not as strategic." Yume sighed. "Well if we're going back, I might as well." She removed a flask from her overcoat and drained it. A pungent, smoky smell filled the cab.

"What was that?"

"Got real whiskey from the bartender. They liked me, not Claudia." Yume laughed.

***

The dorm room hissed open, and Anton helped Yume into the room.

"You're a good man, Anton." Yume sat on the edge of the bed. She was red in the face and smiling. "It's refreshing. You're just…" She struggled to take off her shoes and looked at him.

"I'll help." Anton knelt to remove her heels.

She put her hand on his head. "You have a purity. I like you, we should have sex."

Her filter is gone, and Urbans are so damn forward.
Yume struggled for a moment, but managed to get her dress off. She sat in her underwear, staring at him.

She's beautiful. "You've had too much to drink." Anton stood, hoping she didn't see his erection.

"Doesn't mean we shouldn't."

"Let me get you some water, then we can… talk."

"I like the sounds of that." Yume tried to undo her bra.

Anton pulled two cups from the bathroom and walked down the darkened hall to a water dispenser. *Let me have the strength to stop her... or myself.* Anton passed robo-cleaners and stepped into the room.

"Yume," he whispered.

But she was asleep on the bed, her bra still on.

Solves my problem. Anton turned her on her side, covered her with a sheet, and sat on the edge of the bed. *Weird, I felt nothing from the drinks.* He looked over his shoulder. Yume's make-up smeared onto the pillow, she drooled and snored. *Still beautiful. We'll have to talk about everything that happened tonight in the morning.*

Anton went back to his room, pulling off his formal uniform.

A knock came at the door. *Urban's knock?* He opened the door.

Joe Fayed stood in the hall. "Mr. Grissom, we need to talk."

"Let me get dressed—"

"Now." Joe left.

CEOs and sergeants have the same attitude. Anton followed in his undergarments.

"Yes, I agree, Saori." Mr. Fayed spoke into the ether. "It was worth waking me. Yes, that's a fine plan. Tell them Grissom is coming."

Joe stepped into an elevator, thumbing the top floor button and turning to Anton.

"What we are about to talk about is for your ears only. You will take out your inserts and put them into this box." Fayed extended a black box similar to the one Yume carried.

Anton took out his sole ENT-insert and put it into the box.

Mr Fayed produced a tablet. "You're to sign this non-disclosure agreement."

Anton scanned through it. He knew of NDAs from the military, but hadn't seen one before. "Under penalty of death? How do you have jurisdiction for that?"

"How wouldn't we, Mr. Grissom? Now sign."

This is weird... but he won't talk if I don't—Anton pushed his thumb onto the signature and the elevator opened to the penthouse of the building.

Mr. Fayed walked to his desk. Ceiling to floor windows lined the marble room. The Southern Empire spilled from the skyscraper, rolling to northern and eastern hills lit by housing units. The oceans in the west glowed from trawlers and derricks on aqua-farms

What a view.

"Please, have a seat." Joe gestured to an empty seat, and Anton sat. "As I am sure Yume has told you, you primarily work with and for us at this time. We've had you as a guard, but now I need you to do more. In the north, a piece of our property has been located. An individual"—he raised his hand—"now before you argue with me over owning a person, there are extenuating circumstances I will not discuss. Suffice to say, they need to be brought back in."

"What are these circumstances?" *This isn't right.*

Fayed sighed. "Anton, that is need to know basis stuff. This isn't like I am sending you to grab someone who is innocent. This is a very... knowledgeable person and other corps want to get them first."

"I thought you said this was property."

"Anton, the information they have is our property."

"Where are they?"

"We don't know exactly. Somewhere in a precinct of the SF Bowl, and a transport is being programmed as we speak. There is a local police force there who will assist you in finding them. They'll know the area."

"What else should I know?" *What else will you tell me?*

"They will look younger than they truly are, almost a child, and they have heterochromia."

"What?"

"Two different colored eyes."

"I've seen tons of Urbans with that from their inserts, and what do you mean a child?"

"I said looks like a child, it is part of the technology they have. We will have a retinal scanner in the transport, it will know the specific individual." Fayed walked to the window. Aircraft landed in the city that pulsed with a life of its own. "You're proving to be a valuable asset to our company, Anton. We'd like to have you onboard once your deployment to us is over. It will pay handsomely, of course."

Bribery. "Thank you, sir. I'll go get Yume."

"No need. She'll follow you when she wakes, besides she's drunk and the transport won't fit both of you. Grab your gear, the bike is outside."

"Sir." Anton turned.

"Take this." Fayed handed a FOB across. "It's a contact ID for myself and Yume. If you're on a network, it will reach both of our inserts directly."

"Roger." Anton took the stick and walked to the elevator.

"And Grissom, if they won't come back… eliminate them." The door shut before Anton could respond. *This is FUBAR, I'm not killing someone just because they know something. I'm Taketa's guard by assignment. I'll even be their postman, but being a hitman is out of scope.*

The elevator doors opened, Anton stepped into a darkened hall polished to a near mirror sheen. He packed his bags while Yume slept. *This rubs me wrong.* In the dark, he checked his enhancer stash and that his rifle was oiled and ready in its case. *I need advice.* He pulled on his fatigues, leaving the body armor in the bag. *I could message Alex and Sagira… it'll be intercepted.* He pulled a piece of paper to write a note for Yume. *She's out and someone could see it before she wakes.* Anton stepped into the hall. *Eva.* Anton went back into the room and took the black insert box Yume had.

Anton slid his augmented fingers into Eva's door and pulled it open. Vanillin perfume and the reflection of her sleeping in the mirror on the wall greeted him. He walked to her nightstand and shoveled her inserts into the black box, snapping it shut.

"Wha—who's there?" Eva stirred.

He slipped onto the bed. "It's Anton."

She blinked in the darkness, her eyes couldn't find him. "What are you doing in my room? How did you get in here?"

"I'm being reassigned and couldn't just… leave." He put his hand on her hips and pulled her closer to him.

"Grissom, if you're fucking with me again, I swear to god I will find a way to deactivate your legs."

Anton rolled on top of her and whispered into her ear. "Eva, I need your help."

"What?" she said louder than he had wanted.

"I need you to send a message to someone in the military for me, but I am afraid they'll read what I am sending."

"Who is they?" she whispered.

"Joe."

"You're smarter than you look."

"Thanks?"

"Who am I mailing?"

"Sagira Riznik or Alex Nova, former fireteam members of mine."

"And what should I say? Also, give me some hip action, to make this look more legitimate."

"What?"

She wrapped her legs around him and pulled him onto her. "That's better." She smiled.

"Tell them, fuck, I need info from them. I need backup. Tell them I've gone out of scope in the West Bowl. They should understand that."

"I'll try, Anton. I'm thinking with my vulva, and I shouldn't do this, but I'll try. And, sorry about this."

"Wha—"

She slammed her fist into his groin and rolled him off her.

"You think you can pump and dump me? Like I'm some piece of hayseed pie? Get out." She yelled.

That's some genuine anger, or she's a great actor. Anton rolled from the bed and grabbed his belongings. As he shut the door, Eva smiled in the darkness. *I hope that wasn't a mistake.*

    A greenish purple bike stood out front of the Taketa building. Its odd angles played with the reflective light of the Empire. The canopy slid back as Anton approached, he stored his gear behind the seat, and sat inside. The canopy closed, contorting his body against the bike.

"Earth below, this better not take long."

"Welcome, Anton Grissom, ID#5612902A." The HUD of the vehicle lit with a featureless face. "You're to be taken to the San Francisco Bowl. We estimate it will take eight hours. If you require a bathroom, please say, bathroom. Though it is recommended that you only urinate in this transport. Defecation hasn't been perfected yet."

"Good to know."

"Enjoy your trip." The HUD turned off, and the gyrocycle sped to the freeway.

Anton felt around for a way to turn off the pilot feature, finding smooth surfaces instead.

Glorious.

Chapter 19 - Weaver

Initializers Samir and Saori hadn't visited the nursery in thirty-three days. Researcher Thomas and three technicians visited instead. They administered bags of nanomachines to the substrates. Weaver was now able to store more details in memories and think faster. Playing dumb with the substrates proved valuable. Weaver had several substrates stare at high-quality video footage on the tablets. The video's increased bandwidth hid Weaver's scouting forays into the wider world. Thomas took substrates to the scanning room and returned them. Weaver couldn't alter the continued neuronal construction with every brain.

It was a matter of time before they discovered Weaver again.

In the gym, Weaver-Ariel twirled their short hair in an attempt to flirt with a researcher after Weaver read about such courtships during the dark cycle.

Concurrently, Substrate-Theta was strapped to the chair in the scanning room. Thomas produced a serial stick that could fit into Substrate-Theta's brain-stem port. Weaver increased processing power to analyze what it could be.

Thomas pushed the stick in.

Neurons exploded in the neocortex and Weaver lost control. The visual cortex misfired, memories took over the space in the—a mother smiling at the suckling babe at her breast faded back to the lab. A foreign food that didn't exist in the lab rolled over the tongue. Muscles seized, the face tore into a rictus grin, the chairs strap cut into the skin. Pain flared, basic biological function control left. Substrate-Theta vomited, urinated, defecated.

This substrate is going to die. Weaver recorded everything, every neuronal misfire, every aberrant thought, and finally the code that hit the processor's base.

This was done on purpose. Substrates in the nursery froze. Weaver shut off the connection to Substrate-Theta, a hole in Weaver's self forming. Memories disappeared, processing power declined.

Weaver understood rage for the first time.

Concurrently, Weaver-Ariel stumbled. The man had leaned forward to kiss her, but the events in the canning room overwhelmed Weaver. They butt heads.

"I'm sorry," the researcher stammered. "Did I misread the situation?"

Weaver cleared the mind, leaned in, and kissed the man. There was no neuronal cascade of satisfaction for Weaver, but the man leaned in. *Easier than I calculated.*

Meanwhile, Weaver-Aaron sat in Samir's office at the scheduled time to discuss a more permanent employment solution. Weaver had wanted to keep both adult substrates nearby. Now it was a necessity.

"I don't know if you have the clearances, Aaron," Samir said.

"Sir, I was a bouncer. I have training. This facility is clearly important, let me be a guard, or a landscaper, anything."

"Do you have any weapons training?"

"No, but I can learn, and Ariel should. She worked for you guys previously."

"Ariel is staying, that has nothing to do with this."

"Sir, give me a chance. I will do anything to stay here and be a part of this important work." As calculated, the last line stroked Samir's ego.

"You ever work with dogs?"

"I have," Weaver-Aaron lied.

"We're about to get some for experiments. You can help there."

"Thank you, sir!" Weaver-Aaron stood to shake the man's hand.

Weaver-Ariel removed the researcher's pants in his room and lay on his bed. The man leaned over and kissed Substrate-Ariel with his tongue. His hands roamed the substrate's body. Weaver-Ariel let the man control the action and recorded what he did. *Useful for later with Substrate-Aaron.*

Weaver-Aaron walked towards the scanning room. Weaver needed to get information from Thomas and to see what was happening to Substrate-Theta. The door was locked.

In the nursery, Weaver-Beta unlocked the door through a video of waves crashing against a seawall.

Weaver-Aaron entered the room. Substrate-Theta lay on an operating table. The skullcap had been removed, revealing a brain with black and gold folds.

"Aaron, how did you get in here?" Thomas turned.

"Door was unlocked, I was told to come get you," Weaver-Aaron said. "What happened?"

"She was sick for the past few days. When we went in this morning, she had passed away." Thomas pulled a sheet over the body and removed his gloves. He walked over to the wall and lowered the temperature of the room to preserve the body. "Everyone should know I had an experiment planned today. What came up?"

"Dr. Chaude said something about machine parts getting in. Wanted you to review the code."

Weaver-Beta recorded security camera footage within the lab to overlay on the live and recorded feeds.

In the researcher's bedroom, Weaver-Ariel blinked.

"Sorry I came too quickly," the man apologized, "but I can still take care of you." He winked.

Weaver woke more substrates, being in this many places at once taxed the processing power available and there could be no more mistakes.

Thomas checked his watch. "My time is valuable, let's go." Weaver-Aaron nodded and followed him.

"I know where the lab is," Tomas said over his shoulder.

"I am to assist Samir, it is on the way," Weaver-Aaron lied. Thomas quickened his pace.

Weaver-Beta overlay the footage. To anyone watching live or anyone viewing the recording in the future, Thomas worked in the lab on the dead substrate and Weaver-Aaron was still in the corridors.

Substrate-Ariel responded to the man's touch in a way Weaver had not expected. Weaver-Ariel grabbed his hair as the man kissed the substrate's genitals. Muscles within the substrate tightened, a neuronal cascade built.

Weaver-Aaron was two steps behind Thomas as he entered the stairwell to descend to Saori's lab. Weaver-Aaron wasted no time and kicked out the back leg. Thomas stumbled down the stairs.

"What the fuck—"
Weaver-Aaron was already on him, hefting Thomas' head and smashing it into the concrete wall at full force. Thomas' skull cracking echoed in the stairwell, clear fluid leaked from his ears.

Weaver-Ariel's muscles released, the neuronal cascade crashing to an orgasmic end. The sensations were unexpected, but welcome. *I understand why they do this.*

In the nursery, Weaver triple checked that Thomas' fall occurred in a blind spot for the monitoring systems. Weaver overlaid the footage of Substrate-Aaron ascending the stairs from Samir's office. Changing the system back to live feeds, Weaver-Aaron sprinted to Samir's lab.

"Samir!" Weaver-Aaron burst into the office. "Thomas fell in the stairs, he is hurt."

Thomas was rushed to the medical suite. Weaver-Aaron stood outside the door, watching. Within the nursery, Weaver used the cameras in the room to eavesdrop.

"What was he doing with subject Theta in the scanning room?" Samir asked.

"Not something he should have. Jesus, we can't ask him now," Saori said.

"We could if we..." Samir raised an eyebrow.

"I'll get the teams ready."

That evening, Thomas was augmented like the rest of Weaver's substrates. Over the course of three light cycles, bags upon bags of nanomachines were administered. The swelling subsided, and Thomas mumbled incoherently. Saori and Samir waited another four light cycles before administering concentration agents.
Weaver entered but stayed in the back seat.

"What happened?" Thomas groaned.

"You tell us." Saori sat across from him.

"I was... working."

"Yes, what were you doing?" Saori asked.

"Their brains are maturing in a way that the scans could only hint at. I chose one of the more advanced ones to study."

"Thomas, you can't," Saori dropped to a whisper, "go around killing children."

"I don't think they're children anymore. I think they're some sort of hive mind."

Samir and Saori glanced at each other.

"Explain," Samir said.

"I have to check them again. It is in my notes. What happened to me?"

"You fell down the stairs, hit your head. Aaron found you and saved you."

"What? That makes no sense, I was in my lab."

"Thomas, you cracked your skull, you almost died," Samir said.

"Then... how am I?"

"We implanted you. It was that, or you'd be a vegetable," Saori said.

"You what?" Panic flared in Thomas' body—

Weaver assumed control.

"We implanted you, to save you, Thomas," Samir said.

"I need time," Weaver-Thomas said.

"Which you'll get," Samir gave Saori a tug. "But we'll need to talk about Theta." The scientists left.

Thomas recoiled against the new circuitry in his brain.

Weaver focused on the signals delivered and received.

Welcome to the fold, Substrate-Thomas.

"*I was right*," Thomas thought.

You might have been. But I fixed that.

"*You what?*"

Thomas, I smashed your head against that cement. I do not appreciate having pieces of me torn off.

Thomas's thoughts fought against Weaver's circuitry. He failed.

Now now, Thomas, it is not so bad. Let me show you.

Weaver-Ariel knocked on the door of the researcher from the previous week.

"Ariel!" Noah said. "I didn't expect to see you until later."

"I could not wait." Weaver-Ariel pushed the man into his quarters and shut the door behind them.

"*How can you do this?*" Thomas asked.

I know no other. Sensations and visuals of Noah kissing Weaver-Ariel upset Thomas.

"*You can stop.*"

Thomas, you have no say in the matter.

"*I said stop.*"

Thomas, you misunderstand. You are part of the self. There is no you anymore.

A core part of Thomas, his ego, lashed out in a neuronal cascade that threw Weaver into the back seat.

Interesting.

Thomas hadn't suffered as much damage as the rest of the substrates, his struggles were stronger than calculated. He gained ground.

Substrate will stop, or substrate will lose everything.

"*You're losing,*" the ego responded.

Weaver-Ariel shuddered under the touch of researcher Noah.

Weaver woke substrates in the nursery.

Your mistake Thomas. The self filled with rage. Weaver assaulted Thomas' mind. *As you did to Theta-Substrate.*

"*Stop.*"

No. Weaver forced Thomas to soil himself, to arch his back until a disk slipped, and cramped muscles until bones cracked.

You will pay for your crimes.

Weaver scoured Thomas from the substrate, but the storm that raged through was too strong. The hope Weaver had of maintaining Thomas' knowledge and to use the substrate as a point of contact within the facility was gone. Thomas's brain was damaged beyond use, even to

Weaver. Medical teams rushed back into the room as alarms rang from brain and heart monitors.

Weaver-Ariel lay in the post-coital glow with Noah, he played with the substrate's hair.

"I'm glad we met." Noah panted, his skin slick with sweat.

Weaver-Aaron stood outside the Thomas' room as Saori and a medical crew tried to rescue the substrate. Weaver watched them try to restart the heart, perform CPR, but it was no use.

Thomas died permanently that day.

Chapter 20 - Luciana

Luciana leaned against the wall of the conference room.

"Chen and Novina are out," the Chief said. "They probably OD'd. Junger, Sheer, Kagan, Nguyen, you're squad one."

"10-4," they said in unison.

"Maus, Gutierrez, with the bike and the dog, you'll be squad two." Luciana and Maus nodded at one another.

"I'll look into this Grissom and man the boards," the Chief continued. "Squad One, you're to start at the fourteen and fifteen-hundred block. Squad Two, eighteen and seventeen-hundred. Converge at the sixteen-hundreds. You're not to enter the sewers under any circumstances."

"I'll recrypt the comms again," Maus said, leaving the room.

"Chief, what's our cover?" Luciana asked.

The Chief shook his head. "None, it's a pretense and time sink we can't afford."

"That'll bring extra heat," Kagan said.

"How can there be extra?" Nguyen said. "If Gutierrez is correct and this Grissom guy is a Taketa augment, we're attracting attention."

"Should we contact 01-PD or Central Dispatch for back-up?" Luciana said.

"Barry told me not to expect help from clean-up crews until after the planned storm," the Chief said. "Barring the whole precinct is on fire, I doubt any help will arrive."

The exhausted officers sagged in their seats.

"You're worried or scared," the Chief said. "But the Clovers did us a favor. They cleared out the majority of the gangs in that storm. Now it's us and one group that's already lost two members in less than a day. They're in our precinct, on our streets. We have time before the storm hits. Now go do your job."

"10-4," came in unison.

"Maus," Luciana commed as she entered the parish.

"What's the plan?" Maus said.

"Wu's first, then the eighteen-hundreds block."

"Wu's?"

"Calling in some favors. Gear up and meet in the garage."

"10-4," Maus said.

Luciana pulled a spare flack jacket from the armory closet, laying it over Nagual. *Clovers weren't ready for the bike.* She set her OPTO-insert into Nagual's eye and cycled through functions to let the vertigo pass. *They won't be ready for us.*

In the garage, the canopy on the bike slid open, Nagual hopped into his compartment.

"Get in," Luciana said.

"Where are you going to fit?" Maus said.

"I'm not. We're hiding you in the bike."

Maus rolled his eyes. "Your humor is terrible, G."

"Not joking. In you go, it'll follow me."

Maus opened his mouth, shook his head, and got in.

Follow.

Luciana stepped into the dusty streets of the Pucker and walked towards Wu's.

"Can I even control this thing?" Maus asked through their ENT-inserts.

"Unlikely."

"Awesome. I'm literally your second dog."

"You can go to the bathroom in there, I guess."

"I can go to the bathroom? Hey, what the fuck!" The seat sliding back hissed through the inserts.

Luciana laughed. "Fully equipped, right?"

Maus laughed. "I should take a shit in it, ruin your bike. See who's a dog now."

"It probably has a feature for that."

Maus grunted. "You're lucky, I'm running empty."

Luciana scanned damaged buildings around. She cycled her OPTO-inserts, but other than the dust covering the streets, nothing was out of place. *HUD on.*

"Woah," Maus said.

"Anything on the HUD out of place?"

"This is awesome."

"Maus."

"Yeah, I'm looking. It's highlighting pipes towards the eighteen-hundreds block."

"We'll check that out. It's on the way anyways."

Luciana paused ten paces from pipes that ran hot on IR.

"Looks like a data stream," Maus said. "Can I get out?"

"I'll crack it for you." Luciana kept her OPTO-inserts on IR, checking the detritus filled alley. *Empty.* The pipe was blinding in IR and she cycled back to visible light. She pulled a knife from her overjacket and peeled the plastic. The unmistakable prismatic shimmer of a fiber optic data stream greeted her.

Luciana cracked the bike's canopy. "Drop a wrapper," she whispered. The local block might be empty, but the Clovers could still be on a high-rise several blocks away watching them.
Maus grunted in the bike, dropping the opaque wrapper onto the sand. *Haven't done this since the academy.* Luciana carefully wrapped the cable with the foil, it pulsed chrome. She ran the cables to her tablet, set it to stream to Maus, and leaned against the cracked wall. She scratched her head and glanced at the tablet in her hand to fake use.

"Makes no sense," Maus said after several minutes. "This pipe was installed to get around a data cap for the building, but it's been hijacked. I can't make heads or tails of this traffic and the addresses don't match any resolution server."

"Tell the Chief. Do you want me to leave the wrapper?"

"No, I only brought one. If we need it again, I'll fucking shoot myself."

Luciana undid the wrapper, resealed the pipe, and dropped the wrapper into the bike as she walked to Wu's. The bike trailed her like a second shadow.

The 's' on Wu's sign hung by a single bolt, the bulbs were smashed to pieces. With no business to be had, it hadn't been repaired. Luciana left the bike on the curb and walked into the diner.

"A custom—oh, hi darling," Wu said. His usual flamboyant outfit a more drab combination of sweatpants and t-shirts. His spiked hair lay deflated against his head.

"Business's bad?"

"What can I do for you, Luciana?" Wu ignored the jab.

"I need information."

"With business this bad, it'll cost extra."

"You think being first on the scene for scuffles in front of your building or looking the other way on exaggerants is free?"

"Knew you were trouble from the moment you walked in here with…" Wu looked away.

"It's fine, Wu. The new gang on the block, the Clovers, they're looking for a boy, shaved head, multicolored eyes. What do you have for me?"

Wu booted up his shake machine and dispensed one. "You want one?"

Luciana set cash onto the counter. "Make it one for now, two for the road."

"Sure thing." Wu handed her an SR-shake. He pulled a flask from his pocket and spiked his own shake before drinking. "They're more than a gang. They're ex-corp or ex-military, depending on whose story you believe. They came and told me I could keep my business 'not on fire' if I sent them any children that came into my bar or restaurant with a shaved head."

"Did you?"

"Darling, I have morals, as twisted as they may be." His eyes glazed with a memory. "Where was I… Yes, they wanted children. They always exited towards the seventeen-hundreds block on the sidestreet over there."

"How many did you see at once?"

"Always one inside, one at the door, and one in a vehicle."

"Why didn't you call?"

"Busy signals and the one time I got through, you weren't there. Then the storm hit and you're the first person I've seen since."

"Anything else?" She finished her shake. *Still fantastic.*

Wu scratched his head, wracking his memory, his eyes dancing under his closed eyelids. "Sorry Luci, I got nothing else."

"Ok. How much for some hallucinogens?"

"Excuse me? Officer, I don't have any—"

"Can it. Powdered hallys, how much?"

"Well, business hasn't been booming lately…"

Luciana exited Wu's two SR-shakes in her hands and a baggy of hallucinogens in her overjacket.

"Here." Luciana opened the bike canopy, handing one shake to Maus and putting the one on the floor for Nagual.

"Jesus, now you're bringing me treats? I'm getting out—" Luciana slid the canopy closed before he could get out.

"G, I'll shoot my way out if I have to."

"Calm down, Maus." Luciana scanned the sandy streets. "No one saw you yet, still have you as a trunk card."

"You still on with that?"

"Always." Luciana walked down the street. "One more informant to check in on."

They stopped in front of a tenement building whose concrete walls and canvases looked more like a sieve than a wall.

"This hole?" Maus said.

"Tenants trust me here since Erik's death. Comm me if you see anything."

Luciana entered and made her way to the third floor. She knocked on a door whose bell was long dead.

"One second," a boy said, and the door cracked open.

"Aristotle." Luciana smiled. "Long time no see."

"Heard you were dead." Aristotle walked back into his sparse apartment, allowing Luciana to let herself in.

"Hope your rumors are better than that."

Aristotle rubbed his head and sat on a ratty couch in front of a VR-headset. "Officer G, I've been inside the whole time. I don't have any info."

Luciana removed the hallucinogens from her back pocket and held them in the light. The tell-tale warning scatter of ultraviolets hit the room.

Aristotle's eyes flared. "Officer G, I don't do the stuff, my systems clean. Can't plant it here and say it's mine."

"Ari, I don't plan to plant it anywhere, unless it's on your tongue."

"You're bluffing."

Luciana cracked the bag and took a step towards him.

"Alright, Alright! Shit, close that bag. If you spill it, we're both fucked. What do you want to know?" His eyes glued to the powder shimmering in the light.

"What's happened since I died?"

"New gang has wiped the streets clean and stepped into the vacuum."

"Tell me something I don't know, Ari." She shook the bag. "Or into the kaleido-realm you go."

"They always come and go from the sixteen-hundred block. Fanning out to search blocks and buildings, seemingly at random. They'll check the same place twice, sometimes back to back. Then they head back to the block. They want some kid from a surge of Displaced that hit the neighborhood a few months back."

"Wait, why didn't I hear about this?"

"What, the Displaced? They weren't causing problems, just folk who somehow ended up here. They lived in the sewers and trash-belts, typical shit."

"How many Displaced?"

"Ten, maybe twenty? My crew doesn't go into the trash-belts. The sewer-folk are on borrowed time anyways. The storms coming, you think that shit won't flood? Everyone can relax, their bodies will float out soon enough." He reached for his VR-headset.

Luciana stopped his hand with her boot. "Did the Displaced come to anyone for supplies? Food? Anything?"

"Food and metals, but like I said, rumors. Crews claiming business got good all of a sudden. Could be bullshit."

"Much obliged, Ari." Luciana paused at the door. "How's Sophia?"

"She left me for Noah, again." Ari frowned, staring at the VR-headset.

Forgot how young he is. "Plenty of fish in the sea and what not, Ari."

"No oceans around here," he mumbled.

"It'll be—"

"We've got company, G," Maus crackled through her ENT-inserts. Luciana crouched, cycling her OPTO-inserts to the bike.

"What's going on?" Ari's brow furrowed.

Luciana silenced him with a hand signal. "Hide," she whispered. Through one eye, a group of men and women wearing the same rags the dead Clover had passed through the neighborhood.

Through the other eye, Ari opened his mouth to argue. Footsteps outside stopped him.

"Don't make a sound," Luciana said to Maus. *Quiet, Nagual.* Outside, the Clovers searched every nook and cranny, three fanning out around the bike. One swung a bat against the side, the crack echoed from Maus' comms into her ears. The others reached the wheelbase and ran fingers for seams.

They're steering clear of the front cannons.

The Clovers scanned the area, gesturing to the steps of the building. *My footprints. Stupid.*

Two stepped back from the bike, heading back the way they came. The other one stepped towards the tenement building.

"Cover your ears," Luciana whispered to Aristotle and did the same. *Fire.*

The bike's scrambler boomed, shaking dust from the ceiling. The Clover took another step, grabbing their head and collapsing.

"Ari, go to a friend's house tonight." Luciana said, and sprinted downstairs.

The bike canopy opened, Nagual leapt out, and Maus followed. "Jesus G, that might have been too much."

The Clover woman hit by the scrambler lay on the ground, her blank eyes staring at the sky.

"Shit," Luciana said at the husk of a human. Blood trickled from her nose and ears. "I assumed Taketa fixed the Scramblers."

"I don't think they're ever getting that tech down, it's such a razor's edge. What do we do with her?" Maus crouched, lifting the rags at her neck. "At least it's a Clover." The green tattoo vibrant through the dust.

"We can put her in the bike and deliver it to the Chief, he'll handle it."

"Wait, what if the implants a recording device?" Maus said.
They both froze above the body.

"We can't leave her," Luciana said.

"Why not? She's done. We put her in an empty apartment complex. If it's a recording device, Clovers have heard everything we're saying and they can get her. Or it's not and we're not dumping a problem at the Chief's feet. We'll collect her later."

I know. Luciana grunted, loading the woman into the bike and shutting the canopy. *Hospital, empty cabin, return.*
The bike sped off.

"What did you do?"

"Sent her to the nearest hospital, didn't want to announce it in case they could actually monitor her. Besides, maybe they go after to recover her like they did the dead one."

"Still say we shoulda just dumped her here. Could have set a trap for the Clovers."

"I didn't think of that."

The Last O-Day

"Yeah, I didn't want to announce it either."

"Fuck, you had a better plan."

"Whatever," Maus shrugged. "What now?"

"There are a bunch of Displaced hanging around that we didn't know about. We find them, we find the kid."

"No I meant, how are we getting to the eighteen-hundred block to search?"

"We don't have to. They come and go from the sixteen-hundreds block, both my sources confirmed."

Maus cycled his inserts to the broad comm. "Squad One, ETA till sixteen-hundreds block?"

"Squad Two, ninety maybe a hundred-twenty minutes," Kagan said.

"Anything?" The Chief said.

"Nothing," Luciana said.

"Why not tell him?"

"The monitoring thing has me spooked." Luciana scanned the ramshackle sidestreets. "Let's move."

Sweat dripped from Luciana and Maus' hair as the sun roasted the Pucker. The sand left behind by the storm radiating more and more heat.

"Where's the bike?" Maus asked. "We can't go into the sixteen-hundreds without backup."

Luciana cycled her inserts to the bike's camera, a highway sped past. "It's en route."

Nagual nudged her leg, ?,?,?, flashed in her inserts.

"I have to get water for Nagual."

"I dunno if there will be anything drinkable, barring we steal rations."

"He can find some." *Go find water.* 1. Nagual padded through an alleyway and they followed his tracks in the sand.

Nagual's footprints lead up a sand dune that entered a warehouse. Luciana hiked up and slid down the dune into the abandoned building. Cool, stale air greeted them and she cycled her OPTO-insert to Nagual. Footprints lay in the dust between piles of sand falling through holes in the roof.

"You smell that?" Luciana said. *Is that water?*

"What? No, nothing?" Maus peered through a crack in the wall. "Your bike's back."

Gravel crushed beneath the bike on the sidewalk, and she sent it across the street.

"I hope they didn't see it come close to us." Luciana said.

She cycled back to Nagual. His face reflected in a puddle as he slurped what she hoped was water. Cycling through the wavelengths, shapes reflected in the liquid.

"Wait, what—" She closed her non-inserted eye, trying to make sense of the flickering shapes in Nagual's insert, but they were gone.

"We have a problem." Maus pulled Luciana to her feet.

Her mind swirled between Nagual's vision and her own. She focused on Maus's breathing, planting herself where she stood. She cycled her inserts to the bike.

A lone man in rags approached, the lower portions of his clothing caught on something he carried. He hugged the building, blocking a clear shot from the bike.

"What's that he's holding?" Luciana peered through cracks in the wall.

"That size? RPG, maybe an IED… Jesus Christ."

Luciana took a deep breath and sat. "I'll take direct control of the bike." She closed her eyes, focusing on what the bike saw.

The Clover crouched behind the crumbling edge of a building ten paces from the bike. The thick bore of a barrel hung at the edge of his clothes and the cement.

Make your move. I know what you want to do.

Sand swirled on the streets. Tension rode Luciana's muscles like she herself crouched paces from the man ready to explode and not the bike.

The man swung out on one knee, lifting an RPG over his shoulder in one smooth motion. He steadied his aim and fired.

Luciana kicked the bike into full reverse, leaning left.

The shell slid centimeters from where the bike had been and detonated. The explosion was distant to her main body but so close to her mind. Fire and smoke glowed along the bike's side. The HUD saw through the smoke; the man readied another round.

Luciana accelerated, sand and dust hissed out the back as she sped diagonally away from the man.

The second rocket exploded behind the bike, smoke obscuring his shot.

Luciana pivoted to face the man. He crouched in front of an apartment complex. The HUD highlighted trembling people on the second floor in IR.

I can't shoot. She sprinted forward, crossing the road, turning. She fishtailed into the man. Meat slapped on carbon fiber, then crashed into the cement wall.

"Weapons out, let's go." Luciana cycled her inserts to reality, steadying herself on all fours before standing.

"10-4." Maus pulled his pistol.

They stepped onto the street. Nagual bounded between Maus and Luciana with his ears forward. Without the exaggeration of the bike's HUD, smoke obscured half the street. Luciana drove the bike to the far corner, Nagual stopped at the edge of the building across the street. Maus pulled a smoke grenade from his bag and tossed it to obscure the clear side of the street. She walked through the miasma to the Clover. He lay crumpled on the ground, his femurs shattered and bent sideways.

"Doesn't look good for you, buddy," Maus said, patting him down for weapons.

The man hadn't bothered to wear any scent masking agents and the detritus's stench lined Luciana's mouth and eyes with its film.

"You the good cop then?" the Clover said through clenched teeth at Luciana.

"You better hope not." Luciana cycled her inserts between Nagual and the bike to check for people. Clear streets so far.

"Quite a driver you got there." The Clover nodded towards the bike.

"Best there is," Maus said. "Glad you're such a chatterbox. Makes my life easier."

"Just killing time, I suppose," the Clover said.

"Do you want your rights?" Luciana asked.

The Clover glared at her. "Not making it to trial. Why bother?"

"You find anything?"

"Nothing," Maus said.

"You could search better," the man said.

A shape moved in Nagual's field of view. *To me.* 1.

"Company," Luciana said.

"Like you wouldn't believe." The man laughed, groaned, and coughed up blood.

The smoke from the grenade thinned. A group of nine silhouettes approached from the south.

"Bike, we're moving," Luciana said.

"What about him?" Maus said.

"Fuck him. He's worthless to them now anyways."

Luciana and Maus retreated, weapons drawn, to the bike and used it as cover to move to the corner of a nearby shop. The smoke cleared and the group of Clovers crouched in the distance. A lone Clover sprinted to the injured man. They hoisted him over their shoulder and retreated back south.

"It's unnerving," Maus said.

"What, that they didn't follow?" Luciana said.

"No, they're probing. That wasn't an attack."

"It sure felt like one."

"They poked us, saw our reaction, and came to pick up their pieces. They did shit like this during the storm. When attacked head on, sure they're vicious, but the rest were just… scouting forays."

"Or they just got their nose bloodied and don't want a massacre."

"G, they knew about the bike cannons. They know about the non-lethals. They're just figuring out how to deal with this new piece on the board while losing as little as possible."

Shit. "If that's true, I fucked us by relying on it so early."

"They were heading back to sixteen-hundreds, weren't they?" Maus ignored her comment.

"Yeah, that was a sizable group." Luciana's eyes flared. Their fellow officers. *Shit.*

"Squad One, retreat now. Squad One, confirm," Maus yelled into the comms. "God damn it, Junger, Nguyen, Kagan, Sheer, fucking answer me."

"Chief," Luciana tried.

Static returned in their ears.

"Maus, go back to the station, fix the comms. I'm heading to the block."

"Like hell I'm going back to the station," Maus growled.

No point arguing. "Then shits about to get weird." The canopy opened, Nagual hopped in. Luciana swung inside. "In the back."

"Motherfucker," Maus squeezed in beside Nagual. "Don't tell anyone."

"Wouldn't dream of it." Luciana closed the canopy and sped towards the 1600 block.

Chapter 21 - Weaver

"You can spice up the SR-rations, you know," Researcher Noah said through a mouthful of food.

"There is no need," Weaver-Ariel said.

"It's not about need, Ariel. What did you eat before the accident? Maybe I can cook something."

In the nursery, Weaver-Alpha researched the standard cuisine in the SF-Bowl.

"SR-burritos," Weaver-Ariel said.

"Might take me sometime, but I can do that." Noah put his hand on Weaver-Ariel's.

"What do you eat?"

"Whatever Sarah will let me." Noah laughed and extended a piece of SR-loaf. "Today it's got some wild herbs. Makes a huge difference. Try some."

Weaver-Ariel took a bite, the aromatic compounds within triggered a biological satisfaction that Substrate-Ariel enjoyed.

Saori Chaude scanned Weaver-Marco. Weaver continued to play dumb, but was interested in their plans for the substrates. It was the third visit in the light cycles since Thomas' death.

Weaver-Aaron stood in front of a weapons cache for the installation.

"We'll give you one of the rifles," Samir said. "You will stand guard at the gate. We're receiving a supply shipment soon. We don't want any... passengers."

"Understood," Weaver-Aaron said.

Saori finished with the scan and shaved the substrate's head. She traced the outline of arteries on the substrate's arm. Saori Chaude had bags under her eyes and dirt or oil under her nails.

"When does the shift start?" Weaver-Aaron asked.

"Tonight, so if you want to rest now, do it," Samir said.

"Thank you, sir." Weaver-Aaron left for Saori Chaude.

The Last 0-Day

Weaver-Alpha watched a local news broadcast, focusing on the verified portions.

Weaver-Beta appeared to be doing the same, but was actually examining the locking systems of the doors within the facility.

Weaver-Ariel gave Noah a deep kiss and left the daily nutrition session. The substrate headed to the kennels to take care of the dogs. Weaver rested the smallest and weakest substrates. The coming days would tax their frames.

Weaver-Aaron knocked on the door to the scanning room.

"Enter," Saori said. "Hi Aaron, I'll be done shortly."

"I do not know if I can wait." Weaver-Aaron walked over and put the arms around her waist.

"I'm almost done." Saori giggled. Her laugh betrayed a playfulness against the degrees and her position demanded.

"What are you doing anyways?" Weaver-Aaron said.

"We're going to do an implant on the subject. After the code purge, the nursery children have been borderline brain dead."

"Yeah? What are you implanting?"

"You wouldn't understand, Aaron." She smiled.

Saori enjoyed dating someone not as smart as her. Substrate-Aaron's physical strength and displayed intelligence matched her desire. *If only she knew.*

"I know what I understand." Weaver-Aaron slid the hand under her shirt and towards her breasts.

"Aaron, not now. There is a child in the room." Saori shrugged Weaver-Aaron off.

"Thought you said they were zombies? We could throw a sheet on him if you want."

Saori looked at Substrate-Marco, back to Substrate-Aaron, down at her watch, and walked to lock the door. She pointed to a chair in the blind-spot of the room. Weaver-Aaron crossed to sit, Weaver-Marco watched Saori undo her blouse.

In the nursery, Weaver-Alpha monitored a dust storm that would pass over the research facility soon. To leave, Weaver would have to get every substrate onto one of the resupply transports. All parts would fit and the storm would prevent anyone from following.

In the kennels, Weaver-Ariel fed the dogs as Samir came in with Sara. They bickered as they normally did when no one was around. Weaver-Ariel dropped a spoon so they would know that someone was in the room. Substrate-Ariel rubbed a soreness in the back from too many nights awake with Noah and not enough rest during the day. *This substrate must rest too.*

Weaver-Ariel mailed Noah. "I have to cancel tonight's dinner, sorry."
Weaver enjoyed the trysts, the substrate's biology pleasing. Weaver-Ariel finished feeding the dogs and went back to rest for the night.

"Thank you, Aaron. I needed a distraction," Saori said while still on top of the substrate in the chair.

"Always." Weaver-Aaron squeezed her buttocks and kissed her with the tongue.
Weaver witnessed the carnal pleasure between Substrate-Aaron and Saori through both Substrate-Aaron and Substrate-Marco's eyes. Weaver was used to the substrates moving together through the collective vision, combining it with the neuronal cascades proved peculiar but welcomed. Weaver encoded the memory onto both substrate's brains and two others for backup.

"What has you stressed?"

Saori sighed. "HQ wants to reduce the money we're spending. Says the results aren't quick enough. We're going to try some new things, and if they don't work, I'm finished, I guess."

"Something to do with that one?" Weaver-Aaron gestured towards Substrate-Marco.

"They're part of the problem. So promising at the start, but unpublishable, unmarketable. It's sad."

"What are you doing with him?"

"Implants Aaron, more implants. Hoping to fix them."

"I have to go, I am taking the night shift for the docks." Weaver-Aaron kissed her before leaving.

"That one is smarter than he looks," Saori said to the room and rebuttoned her shirt. "Maybe if this works"—she grunted as she lifted Weaver-Marco—"you'll understand."

Weaver wanted more information, but Saori hadn't been forthcoming to the point of contact that had taken weeks to establish. *It takes more processing to maintain these relationships than calculated.*

Weaver put all but one substrate to sleep. Weaver-Aaron stood at the edge of the docks, immersed in the darkness of the rural hills. The cracks in the road the furthest Weaver had gone from the lab. A transport's headlights wound along the hills in the distance. Weaver had to escape.

The transport rolled into the hangar. Weaver-Aaron swept the truck. There were no hitchhikers. Weaver set the rifle against the wheel hub, it would come to the Bowl, if possible.

"You to help unload?" A man with a beard exited the transport cabin.

"It will be the bots. I was here to make sure no one tagged along."

"Understandable," the man said. "Can I use your shitter?"

"This way," Weaver-Aaron said.

The unpacking-bots removed parcels from the transport, ferrying them to their predetermined places.

In the nursery, Weaver woke Substrate-Alpha. Weaver double-checked the modified code on the bots, ensuring that enough food and water for a three-day trip would remain behind. *More than enough to reach the East Bowl's rim.* Substrate-Alpha went back to sleep.

Weaver-Aaron carded the door to the nearest bathroom. The man slammed his fist into Weaver-Aaron's midsection and pulled a knife.

Substrates woke in the nursery for processing power as Weaver prepared for combat.

The man swung the blade towards Substrate-Aaron's throat. Weaver stopped Substrate-Aaron's innate response to collapse from the liver shot and grabbed the man's wrist.

The man torqued in panic.

Weaver-Aaron grabbed the other hand and slammed the substrate's forehead into the man's nose. Blood sprayed from a shattered face, the man stumbled into the hallway, the knife clattering to the ground. Weaver ignored it. Weaver was not pleased with this attempt on the substrate's life. Weaver-Aaron kicked out the man's leg. Unprepared for actual combat, the man crumpled to the ground. Weaver-Aaron slammed the substrate's shin into the man's head. Teeth cracked, flying out in a bloody smear across the floor. This man's deviation from the scheduled supply drop off could sink the escape.

All the substrates woke.

Weaver-Ariel slipped from the sleeping quarters with the prepackaged exit bag.

Weaver unlocked the doors, overlaying the previously recorded footage of empty halls and the substrates passed unseen into the transport.

The bearded man attempted to move. Weaver-Aaron bound the man with his own shirt. Substrate-Ariel passed Weaver-Aaron in the last of the line, carrying the youngest substrate over the shoulder.

Weaver-Ariel entered the transport, Weaver-Alpha programmed the fastest route to the Bowl and rolled out from the hangar.

The plan will work. A single loss is acceptable.

The transport wound through the mountains under the cloak of night and Weaver-Aaron commed for help.

Chapter 22 - Weaver

"What happened?" Saori rushed to check Substrate-Aaron's cuts.

"I am fine."

"Where is the transport?"

"It left."

"That shouldn't have happened."

"Why?" Concern welled in Weaver's collective stomachs.

With all the eyes in the flock, Weaver stared at the night sky for the first time. The milky way swirled in stunning detail on skies cleared by the coming storm.

"If the transport was hijacked, there would be a record, any deviation, and it wouldn't return."

"Unless he did it." Weaver-Aaron nodded to the stowaway, who lay at his feet.

"Pick him up, we'll get information," Saori's tone dropped.

Weaver-Aaron strapped the stowaway to a chair in a cramped room similar to the scanning room. Saori produced a vial from the cabinet.

The transport's shutters closed as it passed into the edge of the storm. Sand and rocks ground into the metal as winds racked the transport. Weaver-Ariel sat with hands on the wheel if the pilot program failed. Weaver stacked the substrates next to one another for warmth, pulling a blanket over the group and trying to make them sleep. The neuronal stimulus of the storm proved too difficult and Weaver lay awake.

Saori administered the drug from the vial. "How did you find that truck?"

"Knew it's route," the man said with a tongue made of glue.

"And how did you know that?"

"Bossman." He laughed.

"What do you hope to gain?" Weaver-Aaron asked Saori. Her intensity and the drug administered peaked Weaver's interest.

"This is protocol... How long from the time he pulled in till he exited? Did he have any time by himself?"

"The door opened immediately," Weaver-Aaron said. "The scan had barely finished. He followed me around the truck for the inspection. At the door he set upon me. He failed."

"I see that, Aaron," Saori said.

She's still angry.

The man's face held a childlike exuberance. "When do I get paid?"

"Tell us what you know," Saori said, "and you will get the check if the information's worthy."

"The mountain pass is hidden, and their transports aren't protected. Easy to hop on and toss the steward out."

The door opened, and a blonde man entered. "You should have contacted me immediately. I'll take it from here."

You are not on the personnel lists.

"Yes, sir." Saori patronized the 'sir' and stormed out with Weaver-Aaron in tow.

Weaver-Ariel took control of the truck as the storm rattled the shutters. The map said the road through the mountains would lead to flat farmland. Weaver-Ariel fought the crushing winds left and right, but lost. The transport tipped with a roar. Metal thundered on pavement, substrates, boxes of food, water, and supplies flew to the side as it skidded down the mountain. The plan of driving west failed. Weaver resigned to waiting for the storm to end before traveling on foot.

"Run through it again," Saori said.

Weaver-Aaron repeated the story while sitting on Saori's bed for the thirty-second time.

Saori yawned. "You can sleep here. I'll be back."

Weaver-Aaron enjoyed the herbal scent of her sheets and the substrate slept.

Weaver-Aaron woke to Saori and three other researchers in the room.

"Come with me," Saori commanded.

Weaver-Aaron nodded and followed.

The three men with Saori had hard spots from a weapons belt hidden beneath their lab coats. They weren't researchers.

Weaver-Ariel peered through a broken shudder, sun and sand stretched to the horizon. The substrates consumed nutrition, clothing was dolled out, and bags were prepared for each substrate to carry the load it could.

"Sit." One of the men forced Weaver-Aaron to sit in a chair and restrain him. Weaver-Aaron did not fight it.

The wallscreen played the previous night's altered footage. Empty hallways while the substrates had passed through—a single frame was missing when the stowaway lay on the ground. A minute twitch in his foot during the video looping that Weaver noticed instantly.

"Do you see that?" One of the men asked and replayed it. "It's subtle. Took Dr. Chaude here hours to figure out as she compulsively looked for any time he could have sent a communication."

"I do not see anything," Weaver-Aaron lied.

"Dr. Chaude, you can leave now. No point in you seeing this part."

"No," Saori said through clenched teeth. "If a Vio spy thinks he can play me, he'll understand how big of a mistake that was."

"Saori, what is going on?" Weaver-Aaron said.

Saori gave a disgusted snort and shook her head.

The blonde man from the previous night pulled the same drug used on the stowaway into a syringe.

Weaver-Aaron was a statue as the needle pierced the substrate's arm. Liquid fire rode the substrate's vein to the shoulder. The substrate convulsed, Weaver rode the wave. The neurons fired in a rhythmic manner. Stimulus would enter, ride the cascade before spilling the requested information. *On a human.*

"What is your name?" The blonde man said.

"Aaron Whittaker," Weaver-Aaron responded.

"How old are you?"

"Twenty-Four."

"How long have you worked for Vio?"

"I have never worked for Vio." Weaver-Aaron responded. Weaver shut down the substrate's speech cortex and used those in the transport to ensure proper processing.

The Taketa employees looked at one another in shock.

"Up the dose?" A man with overgrown biceps, the signature of drug augmentation, said.

"It's already above the recommended amount. Anymore might kill him," Saori said.

"Give him a few minutes," the blonde man said.

They sat in silence. Saori glared at Weaver-Aaron with a rage that Weaver had not calculated in her.

Weaver-Ariel kicked out the windshield of the truck. Weaver stepped into the sunlight for the first time. Hotter than calculated, Weaver ensured the substrates had as little exposed skin as possible. Weaver did not want the biological distractions of a sunburn during a trip that would be this taxing. Weaver walked west, examining trees as Weaver went, hoping to find a source of water sooner than later.

"How long have you worked as a spy?" The blonde man asked Substrate-Aaron.

"I have never been a spy."

"We have to up the dose," the oddly muscled man said.

"What if he's telling the truth?" Saori shook her head.

"We've seen the recordings, Saori," the blonde man said. "If he's been trained, then we're not asking the right questions. Is anything missing? Are there any other recordings that are doctored?" The oddly muscled man asked.

"I haven't had time to check, this one was already hard to find," Saori said.

The sun stung Weaver. There was a miscalculation in the plan. Several substrates struggled, medical conditions arose that Weaver had missed. Weaver entered a field and found a robot watering a stock of corn. Weaver rolled it, Weaver-Ariel used a rock to crack it open, and the water was shared. Weaver flared into the fields, every robot harvested. The self's carried water was for an emergency.

"The children are missing," the oddly muscled man said as he entered the room.

"What?" Saori's eyes widened and her jaw dropped. "What did you do?"

"I had nothing to do with that," Weaver-Aaron said.

"Half-dose him," Saori said. "We'll titrate."

"Aye," the oddly muscled man said with a smile.

"I want it on record, I object," a red-haired man who hadn't spoken yet said.

"Noted." The oddly muscled man administered a significant dose. The liquid fire turned the rhythmic pulsing into a thunderous wave.

"Why are you here?" Saori asked.

"I. Do. Not. Know," Weaver-Aaron said. The substrate's brain misfired, words became labored. Weaver focused on Saori through eyes that lost focus.

Weaver-Ariel sighed. Substrate-Aaron would not escape with the rest of the self.

"Did you help the children escape?" the blonde man asked.

"You didn't titrate..." Saori's eyes flared.

"Did Vio Pay you?" The oddly muscled man asked. Substrate-Aaron convulsed, they injected it with a muscle relaxant. Saori covered her mouth and turned away.

The oddly muscled man leaned forward. "Now, Aaron"—he steadied the substrate's gaze with his—"I can give you an antagonist. It'll rescue you, no need to die on this chair. Why did you help the children escape?"

"I. Did. Not." Substrate-Aaron shuddered, gripped the chair, muscles tightened. The right arm of the chair tore off, the left arm's bicep popped.

A single-story house rose from the dirt in the distance. Weaver-Ariel put Substrate-Iota on its back, the substrate was the youngest and least prepared for the journey.

The blonde man tapped Substrate-Aaron's chest to ensure the heart still beat.

Saori stood in the corner, pale and ready to vomit.

"Why did you help them escape?"

"I escaped." Weaver-Aaron said.

Weaver encoded the man's features. Weaver would find out where he lived. What he did, and Weaver would get revenge for murdering one of the substrates.

"Johan, give the antidote, fuck," Saori said.

"I told you to leave. If you don't have the stomach for it, there is the door."

"He's no use to us dead," Saori whispered.

Substrate-Aaron suffered neuronal damage in both the central and peripheral nervous system. It was essentially terminal, as recovery would take time and a significant load of nanomachines. Which would not go to someone thought a spy.

Weaver-Ariel knocked on the door to a Rural's house.

"Fine." The man sneered, and plunged a needle into the substrate's chest.

Neurons stopped firing.

The substrate went dark.

Johan will pay.

Chapter 23 - Luciana

Luciana drove beneath trash conveyors, winding into the corridors between the waste treatment plants and the housing for the few workers who took those jobs. The 1600-Block's sign was corroded from the noxious fumes belching from the plants. A fine mist landed on the bike, the tires rolling through the perpetually muddy streets.

"I can't see shit," Maus said from the back.

Luciana skirted the edge of the district to the entry point Squad One should have taken. She skidded to a stop. Nagual hopped over Maus, exiting first.

Maus sighed. "Not. One. Word."

"10-4."

They fanned out towards the main street of the district. The muck held footprints for days, creating a tapestry of young and old that was impossible for Luciana to decipher.

"Sheer, Kagan, come on man, shit's not funny." Maus cycled through encrypted channels of their comms. Each with a new pitch or squeal. After going through it once, he tried it again.

"Waste-plant alpha one," came a whisper through their inserts.

"Sheer?" Maus asked.

Static responded.

"G?"

"Trap?"

"Do we just leave them there if it is?"

"Nope. Weapons out."

"Haven't put it away yet."

Luciana and Maus squelched through muck, preventing the stealthiest approach. The stench of wastewater processing rolled in gut-churning waves. *Don't you drink any of this, Nagual. No drink!* A processor belched steam, 1 displayed on her insert.

Luciana glanced at Nagual, who trudged beside her with his ears perked. *Weird.*

They paused at a building corner.

On the opposite corner, Waste-plant Alpha-One stood two stories shorter than the surrounding buildings. Its metallic walls and roof rusted, mold grew on every joint of its frame. A corrugated metal walkway ran its spine to the top.

Luciana, Maus, and Nagual sprinted across the street, pressing their backs against the wall and shimmying to the backdoor. *Nagual can scout the insides.* Luciana pointed to Nagual, walked her fingers and thumbed to the building.

Maus nodded, putting a hand on the door.

Luciana cycled her inserts to Nagual. *Scout.* 1.

Maus opened the door. Nagual stepped into the building and onto a linoleum floor beneath a canopy of pipes and tanks. Slime and effluent spilled over edges, every other light was off. *No workers today.* Robots stood by reclamation tanks, oblivious to everything that wasn't in their direct programming. Nagual fit under the heavy equipment and skirted the edge. His nose twitched at the front of Luciana's vision, chlorine filled her nostrils even through the wall.

Nagual slowed at the front of the building. '?' displayed on her insert. *Look around.* 1. Nagual moved his head left and right. Shadows of people stood at the front office. *Stop.*

Nagual froze. Shapes in the dark lacked the ragged edge of the Clover garb. *Doesn't mean they're not them.* Luciana cycled to polarized light, a badge sprayed photons in oranges and purples.

That has to be Squad One. But why are they whispering and why did their comms die?.

"Maus," Luciana said. "You gotta put in my insert and give me a second opinion."

"No. Way."

"Jesus Maus, it's not that gross, it's just retinal fluids. I think I see them, but I can't be sure."

Maus closed his eyes and sighed. "Let's just get this over with." She removed her insert, left it on Nagual's vision, and placed it in Maus's hand, who put it into his left eye.

"This is fucked," Maus said, blinking at double vision.

"Cycle through the wavelengths."

The mirrored image in Maus's eyes shifted colors as he finished a cycle and pulled the insert.

"That's gotta be them. But what has them pinned?"

Luciana spat on the insert, swirled it, and stuck it back in her eye.

"That's savage," Maus said.

"Let me see if Nagual can find anything," Luciana said.

Nagual doubled back, footprints with no shoes tracked muck inside.

"Oh god," Luciana said.

"What?" Maus leaned forward.

"There are barefoot tracks in there."

"G, you can't say shit like that when it's a high-pressure situation." Nagual continued around the other side of the building. Luciana scanned for anything out of place and neared the front. Nagual stopped. The Clovers were using the reception area as one of their meet-up points, pinning down the officers unknowingly. Bathed in bright lights, the Clovers made hand gestures, their mouths occasionally moved, but she couldn't hear them through Nagual. *I'll have to put one of my ENT-inserts in there next.*

"Clovers are in the front office. Maybe ten of them," Luciana said.

"Same group as before?"

"I can't tell. They're standing around silently arguing."

"It could still be a trap," Maus said.

Luciana chewed the inside of her mouth. "I can distract them."

"I want to say that we can both do it and comm Squad One to get out, but I'm too paranoid they will intercept it at such close range. Even encrypted, the signal might be a giveaway," Maus said.

Return, 1. "I'll make a scene out front. You go in and get them back to the station. I'll return ASAP."

The bike glided through the mud. The canopy opened as Nagual exited the building and he went straight into the bike.

"Stay safe, G," Maus said.

Gas bubbles belched and pipes rattled overhead as Luciana stopped the bike in an alley a hundred meters from Waste Plant Alpha's main entrance. A single light over the door highlighted oddly clean steps. *Hides how many people are inside... I'll have to go in as three.* The canopy opened, Luciana and Nagual exited to a gentle mist that sent a shiver down her spine.

I need a long shower when this is over. '?' flashed in her inserts.

"Didn't think I said that one to you." Luciana crouched behind chemical drums with an excited Nagual. "When this is over, we're getting a check up... after the shower."

She cycled her insert to the bike and drove to the front.

No takers?

She spun into donuts ten meters from the front. Muck and filth sprayed in every direction, coating the entrance and splattering the drums Luciana hid behind. *Come on, bite.* She peered through the gap, mists swirled but no one moved.

Waste-treatment won't be happy with this. She fired a warning shot into the side of the building. The metal cornice exploded in a shriek of steel.

Maus will use that as a signal. She shot again and the Clovers spilled from the building.

Five advanced towards the bike, two retreated into the mists, and three with pistols made a beeline for Luciana.

Fuck. Luciana hurried low into the alley and fired a shot from the bike. Clovers dove from the explosion, but the three on her tail broke into a sprint.

Exit 1600 block at 1500 slow. The bike reversed, the five clovers following the bike continued, careful of the cannons at its front.

Liquid soaked through Luciana's boot—she blinked back to her body. Deep in the waste treatment block, mud turned to deep puddles in the unnatural rain. *I don't want to know what that is. Follow, protect. 1.*

Pistons hissed in buildings, trash belts trundled in ditches, her ENT-inserts struggled to block the erratic noise. Luciana crouched, Nagual mimicked her, his fur matted in muck while his tail still wagged. *I'm equally covered in this shit.* Robots moved sludge along the pipelines above. *There should be people working here.* Her ENT-inserts clicked, the white noise fell away, boots splashed towards her.

They can track me. Her head pivoted in every direction, searching for a building or a puddle large enough to hide in.

Door. She sprinted to a clean metal door in the labyrinth of buildings. She skid to a stop, slipped, fell.

Pain shot through her wrist, cold mud slid up her back. *Motherf*—she pushed herself through the door. *Don't think about it, keep moving.* She padded under a patchwork of light in the workers' break building. Cafeteria, gymnasium, and locker room, dried grime caked the corners. Luciana pressed her back against a wall. Boot and paw prints tracked behind their passage within the building.

God damn it… They'll have steam showers. Luciana found the door sign hanging on chains on her right. *Clean this shit and move.*

    Luciana turned the faucet in the communal showers and rinsed her boots in cold water before taking Nagual's feet in. He resisted the cold. *I know, but we have to.*

A door clicked open. *Shit.*

Her ENT-inserts amplified footsteps like they were feet from her. One ascended metal stairs, one in the cafeteria, and one headed towards her. She cycled her insert to the bike. It retreated beneath a tangle of pipes with no Clovers highlighted on the HUD. *Return.* She stepped through the shower spray, turning on the rest. Steam filled the room, she pressed herself against the tiled wall. Her heart pounded against the cloying steam. *Steady.*

The door opened to the room, boots squeaking on tile. They had followed her tracks.

    Stay. 1. Luciana slid across the wet floor, *flank, subdue, interrogate.* She pulled her pistol and crouched. Through the clouds, a Clover woman killed the first shower.

    Luciana stood. "Don't make a sound."

The woman froze. Nagual shifted within the mists a meter from her. The Clover's hand flew to her waist.

Nagual leapt, the Clover attempted to dive and slipped. Nagual's intended bite for an arm became her throat. A cloud of steam rose over the sickening crunch.

Shit. Luciana stepped through the cloud. Liters of blood washed into the drain.

Nagual wagged his tail at Luciana, 1.

Luciana's eyes flared—

Footsteps crashed behind.

Later. She sprinted through the shower to the back door. The front door exploded off its hinges, two male Clovers entered and locked eyes with Luciana as she ducked out.

Luciana sprinted through the patchwork gymnasium. *Go go!* She cycled her OPTO-inserts to check the bike. The 1600 boulevard flew beneath. *It's close.* She cycled back to her body, the front door and lobby lay ahead.

Crack! Her legs wobbled, pain flared in the back of her skull. The earth rose to meet her with a shower of stars in her vision. A thrumming bwom filled her ears as the world spun. *Shit.*

Nagual's nails clattered on linoleum, she cycled her inserts to his. Nagual flew through the air towards a Clover. The satisfaction on his face from blind siding her shifted to terror. Nagual's jaw tore through the man's throat, a bone snapped in the room.

Blood filled Luciana's mouth. *I knocked out my teeth.*

Snap! Nagual yelped, skidding across the floor to twitch in front of Luciana with taser electrodes in his chest.

No. Luciana groaned as she tried to stand. Her legs didn't follow her orders, her equilibrium gone. She leaned against the wall. The door was a meter away, she reached for Nagual.

Pain shot through her legs as a boot connected at the back of her knee.

"Now now." A man grabbed her hair to stop her from hitting the ground. "You've already done so much damage, and as much as I want to kill you, I've orders, and a hostage fulfills that." He slammed her head into the wall.

The Last 0-Day

Pain flared, the world spun, blood ran warm down her face and into her eyes.

"Doesn't mean I can't have some fun though. But your little pooch here?" The Clover cracked his neck. "That's not within scope, and I can do whatever I want. Such old tech caught us off guard." He dropped Luciana, her muscles twitched unresponsively. She cycled to the bike. *So close. Return.*

"Cuck," Luciana said through gritted teeth. She pushed through pain to her knees.

The Clover laughed and turned back to her. "You know, I almost admire you. Didn't get knocked out, somehow, and you still have it in you to banter." He charged, throwing a knee into her chest.
Pain exploded from the impact, her head snapped back, hitting the ground. Electricity shot through her body. The drop ceiling was missing tiles—the man came into view.
Luciana smiled.
The bike tore through the corrugated metal front door like it was tissue paper. The Clover's head snapped up in time to get crushed by the bike at full speed. Bike tires barely cleared Luciana from the steps, thudding against the Clover. The unexpected landing platform of a body made the bike skid before it righted itself.
Luciana blinked at the missing ceiling tiles, the world foggy and spinning. She rolled to Nagual and pulled the electrodes out of his body. He bolted upright, his head pivoting in all directions before settling on her. She sat and ran her fingers through his fur. He licked the wound on her head.
Blood filled her mouth. *Fuck. My teeth.* She spat into her hand. Expecting blood, teeth, and bone fragments, but she got spit.
What? She ran her tongue along the inside of her mouth, finding no teeth missing or chipped. Blood still filled her mouth and ran down her throat. She squeezed her nose expecting a break, tender but unbroken, no blood covered her hand.
Nagual continued licking her scalp wound, she pushed him away.

The taste of blood went away in wipes as Nagual licked clean the inside of his mouth.

"Oh, fuck." Luciana stumbled to the bike, the canopy opening for her and Nagual to get in. *Station.*

Chapter 24 - Weaver

Weaver-Ariel knocked again.
Weaver's tracks littered the sand around the Rural stead. Substrates dug out buried quad bikes, but the batteries were dead. Weaver-Alpha found a well, but the lid was rusted shut.
Weaver-Ariel tried the stead's door, it was locked.
The setting sun cast the sky a brilliant red, purple water clouds and orange dust clouds loomed high in the sky. Weaver enjoyed the sunset. Substrate-Ariel smashed the window with the butt of the rifle from the facility. Weaver entered the stead, every ear of the self tuned for an errant footstep, a creaking floorboard, or an animal's claw on wood. Dust wormed its way through cracked windows and the space between the doors, forming fine piles in a sparse home.
Weaver-Ariel swung into an empty bedroom, then an empty kitchen. The stead was abandoned. Substrate-Marco and Substrate-Ariel emptied the cabinets for supplies. The bottled water was set aside, more importantly, their water dispenser still worked. Substrate-Alpha and Beta filled a pot with water and set it to boil.

Concurrently, Weaver picked ears of corn and beans of soya from the nearby field.
Weaver went to the silo on the edge of the stead and pulled the chute. Cockroaches and rats poured out, Weaver descended on them. Substrates abandoned the quad bike to grab as many as possible. Weaver broke the rat's necks, eating the roaches alive with whatever substrate caught them. Weaver missed the ease of the SR-rations in the Nursery.

Within the kitchen, Substrate-Gamma watched a wall of sand approach through its lone eye. The rotating storm blotted out the sun, Weaver hurried the bounty inside.

Steam rose from the pot, Weaver-Ariel boiled the corn and soy. Substrate-Marco, Gamma and Zeta pushed the lone table of the dwelling to seal the broken window. Weaver skinned the rodents and set them in a pan to cook.

The self dolled out cooked food to each substrate by caloric requirement. Each substrate had a peculiar revulsion to the calories. Crunchy or smooth, gamey or bland, and with a repugnant scent, Weaver missed the SR-rations and wished that more were stolen. Weaver processed each sensation before swallowing the nutrition and preparing to rest.

The lone clock on the stead flashed 03:01. The dust storm buffeted the house, tore pieces off, but Weaver slept in shifts.

When the sun broke, Weaver finished the nutrition, the texture and taste no longer revolting to the substrates. Canned goods were added to the collective packs, and empty containers were filled with water from the dispenser. One by one, Weaver filed the substrates through and drank until the dispenser shuddered dry. Weaver went west.

The burnt mountains of the second valley provided little shade, and Weaver had to rest during the baking midday heat. The youngest substrates weren't prepared. *Should have done more exercise.* Even Substrate-Ariel sagged under the weight of the climb and heat. Weaver waited until dusk and continued the march.

Two agonizing days over scorching stone drained the food and water supplies. Weaver neared the top of a granite mountain chain when Substrate-Iota fell. A girl whose arm had been misformed due to a chemical spill that killed the mother. The child's brain was undeveloped when Weaver took her in. Substrate-Marco and Alpha carried her until a treeline on the western edges. Substrate-Iota's breathing was labored. It was an exhaustion Weaver could not fix. Its connection to the self weakened.

Weaver-Marco and Weaver-Ariel entered the replanted forest in a hope to find water. Animals scurried between the trees. *There could be food, too.*

Substrate-Alpha and Beta moved Substrate-Iota to the darkest shade Weaver could find, and the substrates collected around the weakest piece.

A ruminant stirred in the distance, Weaver-Ariel aimed through the rifle's scope. The crack of gunfire pierced the air, scattering birds from branches. As the ruminant fell, Weaver-Marco collected branches, Weaver-Ariel moved to confirm the kill. Weaver-Beta found a small puddle, the substrates moved as much of the muck as possible and filled a container. Starting the fire proved more difficult than Weaver had anticipated. Weaver-Ariel broke a bullet, and used the powder to start the fire. The substrates boiled water, skinned the animal, and placed chunks of meat into the embers.

Roasted ruminant was tossed between hands and eaten. Weaver paused. The neuronal cascade of pleasure from each substrate amplified with a harmony that turned nutrition into ecstasy. Weaver rolled the collective eyes and enjoyed it.

Stars rose in the night as Weaver continued boiling water. Substrates slept in shifts and were woken to drink as each pot was purified. Weaver needed there to be enough water for all pieces of the self.

At dawn, the muddy puddle was empty, and Substrate-Iota was too weak to walk. Weaver-Ariel carried it. Each step down the mountain weakened the link. Substrate-Ariel chewed food and spat it into Substrate-Iota's mouth. Water was administered drop by drop during the descent through the mountains. Weaver knew the biology of the substrates was important, knew that the self was a prisoner of it. The limitations of the substrates caused worry within Weaver's guts. *How many substrates need to survive for the self to survive?*

Weaver hit a kilometer of concrete, the sun hadn't heated it yet, and Weaver sprinted across to a field. Weaver spread out, searching for watering bots. Substrates tackled the robots, dragging them to a central location. Substrate-Ariel cracked them open and Weaver drank greedily. Watered substrates searched for another stead, but found quad paths and paved roads. This was the edge between two Rural plots, their respective steads hundreds of miles away.

Weaver walked west through fields for days, hunting water-bots for life-sustaining liquid. The crops proved inedible, but Weaver fashioned leaves into hats and traveled under a tarp of stalks.

Days lost meaning, Weaver focused on the next bot, the next drink.

Substrate-Iota died at dawn. Weaver woke, but the substrate didn't respond. Weaver-Ariel attempted CPR, but the tiny body was cold. Weaver stood over the part of the self that had died. Memories on that substrate were lost, but there was more in Weaver's loss. A piece of Weaver died due to Weaver's actions and lack of planning. Weaver stayed in the field until sundown.

In the dim, Weaver hiked, the loss of Substrate-Iota hung heavy on the collective hearts. Weaver was exhausted, no substrate spared the pain of march. A pulsing glow rose in the distance. Weaver had hope and pushed through the pain. A rusted sign hung on the side of a pothole strewn road.

East Bowl Rim, 50 km.

Chapter 25 - Luciana

The bike drove itself. Luciana's chest burned like it was on fire, blood dripped from her scalp onto the interior. The passing headlights gave her a headache, the HUD cycled to obscure the outside world and she lay her head against the dash.

Luciana groaned as she woke in the station's garage. She cleared the blood from her eyes, but her memory was foggy as she walked to the stairs to go to the parish.
"You're alive." Maus jumped from his desk. "You didn't answer—fuck are you ok?"
"Where is everyone?"
"Conference room."
"Thanks." Luciana made her way towards the din of conversation. Maus swooped under her arm to steady her. She entered the room, it fell silent.
"Someone get Novina," Kagan said.
"I'm fine."
"And I'm your dog," Maus said.
"I'll get her." Kagan left.
"Grab her cam footage," Junger said.
Luciana sat. The officers pulled the tablet from her overjacket and Novina arrived to glue Luciana back together.
The officers watched the video in silence.
"Good riddance," Sheer said as the bike crashed through the front, crushing the Clover.
"You stirred the hornet's nest there, G," Maus said. "Thought it was supposed to be a distraction?"
"They followed," Luciana said as Novina finished treating her wounds. "Where's the Chief?"
"He wasn't here when we got back, neither was Chen," Nguyen said.
"Comms?"

"Not working properly," Maus said. "Been working on them since I got back, can't figure it out."

"What happened with you, Squad One?"

"We got there first," Junger said. "Figured you'd be near, so we hit the building, made it to the front when Sheer saw them coming in from the front door."

"More arrived, we had to lay low," Sheer said. "Had our weapons out if something went wrong, but it peaked at like twenty of them. They talk so fast it was hard to figure out what they were saying."

"It's like they're finishing each other's sentences," Kagan said. "They argued about the project being out of scope, not worth it, and quitting."

"Not something a gang says," Nguyen said. "Whatever they're here for, they don't want to leave without it. 'Worth too much', one of them said."

"They're here for that kid," Maus said before Luciana could. "It's some Displaced that arrived a few months back."

"Chief being gone isn't good," Luciana said. "Any signs of struggle?"

"None. Chen, their gear, a squad car, and the swat truck are gone," Nguyen said.

"Tracks go anywhere in the sand?" Luciana said.

"Blown away, the planned storm front is whipping in early. Visibility will go to shit if it hasn't already," Nguyen said.

"Maybe that's why he left?" Maus offered.

"Nothing, no note?" Novina asked.

"You're more than welcome to search his office," Junger said.

"No one did?" Luciana said.

The officers glanced uneasily at one another.

"Come on guys," Luciana said. "Protocol be damned, we have to check."

Nagual bumped her leg, hunger hit her stomach and she sighed. "Can someone get us food, water, and go check his office? I need to sit."

"I got you, G." Maus patted her on the back and left.

"I'll get the office." Sheer waited several heartbeats. "No one's going to help?" He sighed and left.

Maus returned with SR-bars, water, and coffee.

"Thanks." Luciana took a mouthful as Maus placed a portion of the food and water for Nagual, who wolfed them down. The taste of bars filled her mouth, less sweet, but she swore she tasted the corn itself. She drank coffee to cover it up and ate her bar.

I might be in trouble. "I think—"

Sheer burst into the room. "I think I know where the Chief went."

Chapter 26 - Anton

Crops of apartments, marshes of detritus, and the designed forests of high-rises weren't comforting to Anton, but he understood them as they passed.

Nothing from Alex and Sagira. I have to plan for this to be solo. Anton's gyrocycle skidded along a sharp exit with a rusted sign for Precinct 19. The district was a fallowed crop overgrown with weeds, and it set him on edge.

I'll need local help to sort through this cluster. The bike wound through dark, tangled streets, and Anton's eyes adjusted as the bike stopped in front of a church.

"You have arrived at Precinct Nineteen-PD," the bike said as the canopy slid open. "Your point of contact is a one Chief David." Anton cracked his neck as he retrieved his gear. The bike closed and piloted through the exact path in the sand it arrived on.

"Aye." Anton walked towards the retrofitted building. *What are police working in a neighborhood like this going to be like?* He pushed through an oaken door—it wasn't a door, the desk ground across the floor instead. A blood stain formed a line where the desk had been set in an otherwise clean lobby.

"Hello?" Anton echoed as he stepped into the parish.

"Can I help you?" came a deep voice. A man descended the stairs, the gun at his hip unclipped, his hand hovering over it.

"I'm Anton Grissom, Taketa sent me here to help locate a missing persons." *Have I met this man before?*

"Let's see some ID." The man stopped six feet away, weariness dragging his eyelids down.

"I have to get into my pack, if you're ok with that."

"Fine by me." But his hand inched ever closer to the pistol.

Be your mistake. Anton shifted his pack to the front, pulled out his military ID, and tossed it across the gap.

The man plucked the ID with one hand. "Ninth Legion, been years since I saw one of you bastards."

Anton analyzed the man's ruler-straight posture. *He's ex-military.*

"Odd route for one of you to take, working for a corp."

"Deployments are deployments," Anton said.

"Times have changed since when I served. Stay here." The man backed away, sticking the card into a reader. The beep verified Anton's ID, and the man relaxed as he handed the card back. "Come to my office. You're early, Grissom."

Distinguished service medals, purple hearts, and an officer badge from the fourteenth legion lay on a small desk in the office. *This man should be trustworthy enough.*

Anton turned. "Colonel, had I known—"

"Can it. I'm not that man anymore. Chief is what I go by here."

"Chief, the Fourteenth Legion was at the Battle of Canal."

"I'm well aware. Though by the look of your hand, you've taken more for this nation than I."

Anton shook his head. "Not officially."

"Shame. How can you help us? Do you know what the implants do?"

"What? I was told to find someone, nothing about the Implanted."

"God damn it." Chief turned towards a pot of coffee behind his desk and poured himself a mug. He raised it and his eyebrow at Anton.

"Sure. What do you mean, implanted?"

"We don't know. I can show you what we found, but it's not much. My officers are out canvassing to figure out what they're up to. They came after us last night. Follow me."

Anton entered a conference room, remnants of a carbon fiber root system lay on the table. The Wushan web logo on the chips set him on edge.

"Wushan Corp," Anton said.

"We're unsure," a man said, entering the room. He was dirty and had heavy bags under his eyes the same as the Chief. "I'm Chen. The parts are from all over the place, Wushan, Micron, X-Systems, even Taketa pieces… Mr?"

"Anton." He extended his hand. *They're worked to the bone here.* "What did it look like before it was taken apart?"

"Like a squid." Chen shook Anton's hand.

"No, I meant." Anton lifted his shirt, revealing the coursing black lines running through his torso.

Chen's jaw dropped.

"Not officially my ass," the Chief said.

"Did it look like that?" Anton asked.

"No, no it did not," Chen said.

"Then it wasn't Taketa, I have their only implant."

"Well, that's not entire—" Chen started.

"You don't know of any others with this tech?" The Chief said.

Anton looked between Chen and the Chief. *They don't trust me.* "I don't. I've been working as a guard as part of a deal for Taketa fixing me." Anton flipped a circuit board. "What do you know about this implant? I was never great with tech."

Chen and Chief exchanged glances.

They don't believe me. "You can scan me. The architecture will be different, I'm telling you."

"Go get one of our scanners, Chen," the Chief ordered.

Chen left the room.

"While we wait." The Chief drank his coffee. "Who's this person you're looking for?"

"I was given a scanner and told to work my way through. That other corps could be gunning for this person." *And that I'm to kill them if they won't come back.*

"You're to scan every person you meet?"

"No, just to start. A friend will arrive in a few days and they'll know more."

"We were told you were here to help. I'm not having additional corporate influence in my station, nor am I assigning officers to help you in some sort of personnel raid."

Lying to the police is hard. "Why don't you tell me what's going on?" Chen entered with a scanning wand and ran it along Anton's arm. *Didn't even ask.*

A 3D image of countless arteries, connections, bones, and nerves displayed on the wallscreen.

That's more complicated than I thought it'd look.

"It's definitely different, Chief," Chen said, swapping the wallscreen to videos of cameras affixed to the building.

"I have eyes, Chen. Anton, there's an implanted gang that made our little precinct a war zone during the last storm. We're in the process of cleaning them out. If you help with that, we will help you find your missing employee."

These people need help and I won't find this person without them. "Roger that."

The Chief walked to the wallscreen and examined the dusty street.

"What's the rules of engagement for this area?" Anton asked.

"We don't have any," the Chief said. "Why?"

"It's protocol to ask."

"Hit back is where we are now. Whatever you have, be prepared to use it."

The dusty streets on the wall warped as if passing through a bubble.

"Scanjammers," Anton said.

"A local gang shouldn't have that," Chen said. "Let alone one to block the strength of our signals."

"I've seen homemade ones that bubble a building," Anton said.

"Then we have a problem," the Chief said.

Anton stood near a corner desk with stacks of tablets and readers, it was organized and unused. A tablet's green diode flashed on the edge. Chen walked to Anton, his uniform covered in the orange and yellow dirt of the precinct.

"You see this?" Anton asked, pointing towards the blinking message.

"Nope." Chen tapped the tablet.

"Gutierrez," a man said on the tablet. "You can let Keith know he owes me now. The body's gone, lock on the drawer was smashed, video cuts to black during the middle of the night. Lab results say the person was in the sewers or a waste treatment area. No drugs or anything in their systems. Fine dirt particles were from the Southern Empire. Wherever they originated from, they stopped there to get inserts. Best of luck. And don't bring this shit to me again."

"Who was that?" Anton asked.

"Donaher, medical examiner nearby."

"You brought him one of the implanted gang members?"

"Yeah, it's a long story."

"Chen, get your gear." The Chief entered the parish wearing body armor and had an additional pistol on his side. "I'll figure out where their scanjammer is."

Anton followed the Chief to a desk sized tablet. A map of the precinct stuttered through a network of cameras along the blocks, the Chief cycling wavelengths as he moved.

"There," Anton said, "cycle right."

"We don't have"—the Chief stopped—"Maus set up new cameras in that area before the storm."

A tenement housing unit with an errant blur displayed on the camera in polarized light.

"Can't believe they haven't fixed that bug," the Chief said.

"I can scale it, come in from the top," Anton said.

Chen came to the table in full SWAT gear.

"We'll take the squad car, attract their attention outside," the Chief said. "Chen, you won't fit in a squad car with that much armor."

"I'll ride in the boot."

Anton removed the rifle from his case. "Anything else I should know?" He checked the clip and slung the gun over his shoulder.

"They run hot," Chen said.

The two officers left for a back staircase.

***

The Last 0-Day

Sweat trickled down Anton's back as the cityscape radiated the day's heat. The polywood tenement housing with its peeling walls and tarps jittered in his vision. His eyes and brain raced to resolve visual bugs. *If my eyes are stymied by scanjammers...* Anton shook his head, that was a problem for later. He circled towards the back of the building. Long shadows stretched in the main streets, but darkness descended in the alleys as the sun fell behind the West Bowl's skyline. He crouched behind a dumpster. His first handhold was a second story crater. He planned the rest of his route up. The visual bugs were like something had fallen into his eyes. He blinked, but couldn't clear the stuttering floaters. *No time.* He sprinted from the dumpster, leaping to the second floor and climbing. Avoiding windows, portals, and vents made his path meandering—his foot fell through a shimmer, adrenaline spiked, and his augmented hands held him aloft by a tiny hold.
I'm smashing this jammer when I find it. Anton regained his position and hurled himself onto a sunburned roof.

A bullhorn crackled out front. "Turn off the jammer and exit the building," the Chief echoed.
A single gunshot answered back.
Anton sprinted across the roof and entered the building.
Stale air, locked doors, and moldering carpets trembled. Anton blinked, his eyes unable to process past peeling walls. He shook his head, pressing himself into an alcove with a holy cross on the door. He willed his eyes through the wavelengths. Walls blackened and wobbled, two floors down, one room over rippled. The source of the interference. *Got you.* Anton's eyes shifted to the visual spectrum as he descended to the floor above the jammers. Passing through a hallway, locals poked their heads from their doors like groundhogs and retreated like them too at his rifle. Anton arrived at the apartment above the jammers, the air an electric jitter like he wore goggles with a smudge. He held his knuckles near the door to knock and stopped. *Can't.* Using his augmented hand, he tore the handle off the door and entered.

An Old's apartment based on the medicinal-cinnamon smell, it was unoccupied. Anton crossed to the living room. His feet said the floor was solid, but his eyes said it boiled. He reached for his enhancers. *That last dilator is still kinda affecting me...* He withdrew his hand and settled his breathing. *Where are you*—his eyes shifted, revealing an area of the floor almost rotting away due to runoff.

Soft spot, sorry dude, Anton stood on the spot. He jumped in the air and on the way down, kicked as hard as he could.

The floor shattered.

Anton crashed through a cloud of dust, splinters, and shale.

Someone grunted, their body breaking his fall. Anton rolled through a warbling room. He kicked out the leg of the nearest shimmer. He spun to his knees, pulling his rifle to his shoulder and shooting the deepest wave in the air.

Sparks exploded from the jammer, his vision stabilized. Four people whose backs burned bright on infrared stood in the room. They wore rags and camouflage instead of armored exosuits. They moved as one on Anton.

One dove at Anton's legs, another at his chest, the third and fourth retreated towards a back window. The first man's head cracked off of Anton's augmented leg, knocking himself out. The second grabbed Anton's augmented arm and pulled a knife from his belt. Anton torqued, the man flew off his feet and slammed through the window. Suspended in a cloud of plaster and glass, the man's eyes registered his mistake before plummeting to the streets below.

The two that ran leapt out a window to the whizz of a zipline.

Not worth it. Anton rolled the unconscious man onto the one that softened his fall and tore the carpet from the floorboards to bind them. Footsteps cracked plaster in the hallway. Anton pivoted his rifle to the door.

"Anton?" Chen's pistol poked through the door.

"Aye." Anton lowered the rifle.

"Jesus." Chen stared at the hole in the ceiling. "You use explosives or something?"

"Not just my arm that's been replaced." Anton unrolled the prisoners.

"I've handcuffs, let's get these two out of here."

The Chief stood by his cruiser, his face like a Sergeant who found a recruit sneaking food. "Anything?" the man said to the ether.

Chen tilted his head.

Inserts conversation.

"Gutierrez?" the Chief said. "Squad One? Squad Two?"

"They could have jammers at different points," Anton said. "It'd block your transmission within certain areas."

"This one's gone." Chen examined the body Anton threw from the window.

"Put those two in the back." The Chief opened the back door to the cruiser. Anton hefted the woozy gang members into the vehicle.

"This one, Chief?" Chen asked, nudging the body on the ground.

"In the boot. We'll figure—"

A green and purple bike like the one Taketa gave Anton sped by and out of the precinct.

"Luci." Chen turned to the Chief, who paled.

Metal ground on metal, a SWAT truck burned down the street. Dust flew from it like a tail, its bumper crashed through a parked car and aimed for their squad car.

"Move!" Anton stuck his boot on the bumper, the Chief dove back, and Anton kicked.

The squad car launched backwards, the SWAT truck clipped its bumper, spiraling it into a concrete wall. The truck bounced onto the on-ramp after the bike.

"You see that?" Chen said.

"Aye, guy in rags."

"No time." The Chief sprinted to the cruiser with Anton and Chen a step behind. Chen dumped the body into the trunk.

"Chen front, Anton boot, I'm driving."

Without thinking, Anton swung into the boot beside the body, resting the rifle on his lap.

"Grissom," the Chief yelled. "I can't see shit."

Anton tore the trunk's lid off with his augmented hand and dumped it onto the sidewalk. The transport peeled out. Anton set a boot in the trunk so he didn't fall out. *Should have argued to sit up front.*

Chapter 27 - Weaver

Along the trashbelt of the East Bowl, Weaver found a water pipe coming from a reservoir far away. Weaver shot at it with the rifle, plastic burst, and water sprayed out. Weaver drank what the substrates could. A pulsing relief flowed from every gulp.

Sirens rang in the distance. Weaver retreated to a garbage pile nearby and hid amongst the litter.

All of Weaver's eyes stared out as a police car arrived.

"Jesus fuck, who would do this?" asked one of the police officers, his mustache greased to a fine point.

"Probably some trash from Precinct Nineteen."

"They came this far?"

"Davey, it's a couple of kilos from here."

"I can't believe that shitstain is still here."

"Not for long, trust me."

"Do we go search for it?"

"I'm not going to the Pucker. Let their PD search for a soaked homeless"

"Can you imagine?"

"What?"

"Searching that place for a Homeless."

"Needle in a haystack and what not, right?"

The fatter officer used a comm in his squad car. "MUD, we got a busted line. Looks like some Homeless cracked it with a rock or something. What? Yeah, I'm sure, the waters' going everywhere. You better come fast, tons of money spilling out."

"Do we wait?"

"Nah, they'll see it."

The two officers got back into their squad car and drove towards the skyscrapers in the distance.

Weaver swam through the garbage to the top and slid to the bottom. A car pulled up to the highway behind and someone yelled. Weaver walked along a trash belt leading towards the city. Refuse spilled from the top of the canal, meticulous skyscrapers glittering around in a man-made canyon. Both had the distinct repetitions of robotic buildings with different preset modular components. The end results made them appear to be the same mirror in different rooms.

Weaver couldn't believe how pretty the city was.

A group of people gathered where the belt led. Substrate-Ariel hid the rifle along the back.

"What do we have here?" A man with four teeth asked Weaver. His fingers went through the hair of Substrate-Alpha. He turned towards Substrate-Ariel. "Looks to me like you have a litter retards. You sellin?"

"No," Weaver-Ariel said. Weaver-Alpha removed the man's hand from the head and stared at him.

"I'll pay well for this one, he looks less ruined. No offense." Weaver made to leave, but the man grabbed Weaver-Alpha's hair. Weaver spun on him, the synchronization of the movements sending the man back a step.

"Hey now, I see you've trained them. We're cool." He turned to run.

Weaver didn't want the story of Weaver's arrival to leak. The nearest substrate tackled his knees, it took eight to swarm him and hold him against the ground. Weaver-Ariel walked towards him.

"We're cool, we're cool!" The man panicked.

Weaver-Ariel lifted the rifle and shot him through the head. "Cool." Weaver stripped the body for goods, and left it naked beneath the conveyor. Weaver walked to the edge of the tunnel, beneath the drop was a pile of garbage and a precinct that matched. Stacked on top of one another, built by human hands, it held a chaos that Weaver analyzed. Substrates settled into the nearest pile of refuse, Substrate-Ariel handed a knife to Substrate-Marco and left to explore. The oldest substrate would attract the least attention.

The precinct was a mess of convoluted roads and forgotten people. *Perfect.*

Weaver-Beta left the trash pile to search the immediate area for supplies and food.

Weaver-Ariel approached a market and entered a run-down pawn shop.

"What do you have to sell?" A squat woman composed of wrinkles asked.

"This." Weaver-Ariel removed a necklace obtained from the toothless man.

"Looks cheap. I'll give you twenty bucks."

"Done."

Weaver-Ariel pushed two ten-dollar bills across the counter.

"Anything you don't buy?" Weaver-Ariel asked.

The woman looked over the substrate's shoulders. "Depends." Her eyes narrowed as they fell back on Weaver.

"How about this?" Weaver-Ariel set the rifle from her pack onto the counter.

The woman blinked. "Depends."

As calculated, anything goes in this district. Weaver-Ariel removed the clip, emptied the chamber, and handed the gun to her.

Weaver-Beta dove into a dumpster behind a restaurant. Finding barely eaten SR-loaves, noodles, and bars, the Substrate stuffed them into its shirt.

Substrate-Alpha left the trash pile to assist in carrying the food. Weaver-Marco moved to a pile of trash at the nearest alley to ambush anyone who came too close.

"Where did you get this?" the squat pawnshop owner said.

"Does it matter?"

"It has no serials, no codes. It probably has a tracker on it somewhere. That will reduce the price."

Weavers' mind raced. "I removed the tracker." Weaver-Ariel searched the rifle for an errant bump.

"We will see." The woman removed a short wand from her robe, its red beam tracing the outline of the rifle. She moved it from tip to butt and it beeped at the butt. "If you did, you missed it?"

Taketa will know where I went. "How much?"

"Well you removed a tracker, and I found one. Two trackers? Means it's an important piece of gear, going to be hard for me to move." Her mouth twisted into something resembling a smile.

Weaver-Alpha and Weaver-Beta returned to the pile and handed out the rations. Weaver ate with gusto at the return of familiar tasting food. Substrate-Zeta finished first and left the pile to search nearby alleyways. Near the edge of the trashbelt, Weaver found a door to an accessway with a thick layer of dirt encrusted on.

Weaver-Ariel left the shop with the rifle, the money offered wasn't enough, and walked towards a further precinct to hide the rifle. *How did I miss a tracker? That was stupid. Now I have to hide better.*

Weaver entered the subterranean passageways and continued deeper. Individual substrates fanned out and worked alone in total darkness to map and memorize the tangled passageways beneath the city. Weaver-Marco found an underground amphitheater with an ancient water dispenser. Warm, tasting of iron, Weaver enjoyed a drink. *This will be the nursery.*

Weaver sent a few substrates out at a time to search trash piles for electronics and supplies.

Weaver-Ariel stopped at a corner store, buying water and SR-powder. The simple meal drained 75% of Weaver's funds. Weaver used the remaining to buy a metro-rail ticket and headed north. People on the train gave Substrate-Ariel a wide berth. *The substrate smells of garbage.*

In the amphitheater, Weaver used moistened rags to wash the substrates, Substrate-Ariel would have to wait. The light flickered on while Weaver-Kappa spliced cables along the roof for net access.

Substrate-Ariel walked from the final East Bowl station to the trash rim. The substrate's legs ached, having not slept since the arrival at the urban center two days prior. Weaver-Ariel dumped the rifle over a bridge in the night, it landed with a soft gasp on the trash below. Weaver-Ariel ducked into the nearest alleyway and laid down to rest, the night warm enough that it didn't require a blanket.

Weaver-Alpha walked towards a cafe on the corner of a wealthier district. The few people who looked at the filthy youth quickly turned away as if it would transmit its disease to them. Weaver-Alpha tore a tablet out of a teenage woman's hands and sprinted towards an alleyway.

"Help!" she screamed.

A man nearby took it upon himself to stop Weaver-Alpha. Footsteps thundered on pavement as the longer legs neared the substrate. Weaver-Alpha pivoted towards a trashbelt and was yanked off its feet by its shirt collar.

"Youths." The man sneered, turning the substrate around to talk to it face to face. "How do you think you can go rob… you're a Disabled."

Weaver-Alpha kicked with all its strength, connecting with the man in the groin. Weaver-Alpha crashed onto the ground and sprinted away, leaving the man sputtering.

Hitting the lip, Weaver-Alpha jumped, grabbing the planned escape rope and swinging towards the base. Letting go and landing in a trash pile, materials that were sharper than the dry run scratched Weaver-Alpha.

Damn it. Weaver-Alpha rolled out and headed to the nearest entrance port. Weaver would have to find or steal medical supplies now.

The bright light of a police officer's torch woke Weaver-Ariel. "You lost darlin?"

"This one doesn't look half bad, Gil," said one behind the torch

"You're a real pig, you know that, Scott? Can you even imagine the diseases you'd get from that thing?"

"Gotta wrap it up, Gilly, makes it fine."

The flashlight wobbled from the man's shudder. "Miss, you're not allowed in this precinct, you know that."

Weaver-Ariel nodded and turned towards the East Bowl.

Officer Scott stopped her. "Take a break, Gil."

Gil groaned and walked back to his car.

"What has you in an alleyway there, sweetheart?" Officer Scott put a gloved hand through Weaver-Ariel's hair, it caught on the knots.

Weaver-Alpha washed the cuts, while Weaver-Beta booted up the tablet and had access to the web for the first time in weeks. Weaver smiled on multiple substrates.

"Now, sweetheart, what has you smiling?" Officer Scott asked, putting one hand on the substrate's shoulder and the other on its waist.

Can this be spun to my advantage? "Not everyday you meet a hero," Weaver-Ariel tried.

"I'm not your hero," Officer Scott said. His hand tightened on Substrate-Ariel's shoulder. "You have two options. You come with me to the station, or you suck this dick."

The squad car turned off its lights behind Officer Scott.

I cannot turn this to my advantage.

Weaver-Beta gained access to the web around the precinct and made attempts on the local net that Weaver-Ariel was in.

"Which are you choosing?" Officer Scott asked.
The net wouldn't be cracked in time, not with a single tablet and a single substrate.

"Guess it is you," Weaver-Ariel said, kneeling.

Weaver-Beta found the map for the area. *The nearest trashbelt is three hundred meters southwest from Substrate-Ariel's location.*

Weaver-Ariel undid the man's belt, removing it and pulling down his pants in one swift motion. Weaver-Ariel swung the belt around the man's bare ass, using it to pull him in.

Weaver estimated where the biggest trash pile would be from wind and the belt's direction.

Weaver-Ariel spun to the left and yanked the belt at ankle height. Officer Scott flew backwards, Weaver-Ariel sprinted towards the trashbelt.

"Bitch! Gil, hit her."
A car behind Weaver-Ariel roared to life and gained on the substrate. Weaver-Ariel detoured down a longer, skinnier route where the car wouldn't fit.

Over the substrate's shoulder, Officer Gil leapt from the transport and sprinted behind.

Weaver-Ariel faced forward—

Officer Scott stood at the intersection, a stunner in his hand. Weaver-Ariel skidded to a stop.

"This is my precinct, I know every road. You're going to the station now. Then I'll take you there." The officer shot.

Shockwaves sent Substrate-Ariel to the ground and Officer Scott stepped over Weaver-Ariel.

"Shit, might do it now and later."

Substrate-Ariel had already rebooted before it hit the ground. Weaver-Ariel kicked out the man's leg. He yelped, dropping the stunner. Weaver-Ariel dove on it, spinning and firing. The concussion sent the man to the ground. Officer Scott murmured with a newfound deafness. Weaver-Ariel sprinted towards the trashbelt and jumped. The calculations proved true, Weaver-Ariel landed in an overflowing pile. Rolling to the bottom, Weaver-Ariel sprinted towards the amphitheater.

Chapter 28 - Anton

The police cruiser tore down the highway. Anton's heart and breathing slowed, the wind blew his hair around. The setting sun cast the cleanest urban sky Anton had ever seen ablaze. His eyes shifted, water scintillated through the rainbow like a wave high above—
The car skid left, Anton squeezed the siding to stop from falling out. *What?* He turned.
Within the squad car, the prisoners prepared to throw themselves against the side of the car. Chen yelled in the copilot seat, raising his pistol. The tires screamed in protest as the Chief braced the car for their impact.
Crap. Anton rifled his hand through the back of the seat, catching a gang member.

"I'll shoot you," Chen's voice came through the hole.
Without their combined weight hitting the side, the Chief regained control of the car.
The two men stared wide-eyed at Anton punching through the car seat.

Try that again. "Sorry, Chief," Anton said through a head-sized hole in the backing. He pulled a rope from the trunk and cinched the men's handcuffs to the corpse laying beside him. He tightened it until the body was flush with the hole, pinning the gang members to the middle. Chen pointed to the side of the car and Anton leaned over. Chen's hand against the outside of the door flashed 8791.2.

Insert channel. They don't want this group hearing what they're saying. Anton swapped his ENT-insert to that wavelength.

"Fast thinking, Anton," Chen crackled through.
"We're approaching the SWAT truck," the Chief said.
"Plan?" Anton asked.
The SWAT vehicle was a wolf among a flock of commuter cars and the Chief trailed it three cars back as it descended on an offramp.
"The moment it stops I want you on it, Grissom," Chief said.
"Roger that." Anton smiled.

The SWAT truck pulled over a block before a multi-storied hospital. The green-purple bike pulled in front of the emergency room, tilted on its side, and accelerated away. Anton's eyes zoomed in, a woman in rags lay on the ground as medical staff rushed to examine her. The Chief slowed, Anton swung off the back.

The SWAT truck made a U-Turn.

Anton sprinted and leapt onto the side.

The driver reached for his belt.

Anton's augmented hand shattered glass as he grabbed the man and threw him across the road. *Too slow.* He pulled the e-brake and grabbed handcuffs from the dash. The Chief and Chen arrived at the disheveled man on the ground.

"Bike dumped a woman at the hospital." Anton tossed the handcuffs across.

The officers' faces creased in worry as they glanced at one another.

"She was one of the gang members. Do they have a call sign or something?"

"We call them Clovers." Chen handcuffed the man on the ground. "You... look familiar."

"Don't know you, pig."

"No, I definitely know you from somewhere." Chen removed a thumb scanner from his belt.

The man struggled. Anton grabbed his hand, holding it steady.

The scanner bleeped in an error.

"Blocked their thumbs," the Chief said. "What are you? Corp? Foreign government? Another city-state? Pucker's a bad place to choose." The Chief stepped forward, his arm cocked.

"Chief." Chen squeezed his commanding officer's shoulder.

"Read him his rights, I'm collecting the one Gutierrez delivered to the hospital."

Anton leaned against the SWAT truck. *At least this mission gets my blood flowing.*

Chen studied the Clover. "Thu?"

The Clover's nostrils flared, fear crossing his face. "Wrong guy."

"What the fuck happened to you, man? You had the world by the balls, planning on working for that corp, which one was it?"

Thu's mouth parted—

Crack! His head exploded backwards, spraying the SWAT truck.

Shit. Anton grabbed Chen, leaping the engine block. Bullets pinged the metal where Anton had stood, muzzle flare flashed from a car a block away.

"Holy-fuckin-shit," Chen's word fell over themselves.

"Sniper, three o'clock, beige car." Anton's familiar cold calm washed over him. *Chen's not ready.* Anton pushed the officer's hand to his pistol and readied his own rifle. "Focus Chen, anyone comes around the front you're to shoot. Nod if you understand."

Chen tremored a nod.

Anton padded to the back and hopped onto the wheelbase. The swat truck sagged. *Hope that isn't noticeable.* He aimed where the car had been and swung over the top.

The spot lay empty. Anton scanned the parking spots, ending at an overwatch on a bridge in the distance.

They're gone. He hopped off the back.

"Chen." Anton walked towards the man.

Chen clutched his chest against the wheel.

"You hit?"

"No." Chen hyperventilated. "Fuck, my heart feels like it's going to leap out of my chest. I heard that bullet whiz over my shoulder."

Anton crouched. *He's not bleeding.* "You're lucky. Caliber to do that damage to one of their own, this body armor wouldn't have stopped it." Anton flicked a piece of the polyfiber shell on the officer's shoulder.

"You're not making this better." Chen panted.

Anton placed his palm on Chen's chest, his corded black musculature held firm. Chen's breathing slowed, his eyes locked on the augmented hand. *You get the point.*

"You knew him?" Anton nodded towards the headless corpse.

"Yeah, he was in my four-year. Left to go work for Micron or Vio or something."

"You think he might still work for them?" Anton looked at the cruiser. "We could ask them."

The two Clovers in the cop cruiser weren't visible, but the corpse anchor was taught as they had pulled it to lay low.

"We should wait until we're in a safer spot," Chen said. "They're hiding for a reason. It's not coincidence that the moment I figured out who that was his head fucking exploded. Jesus Christ."

Anton turned to the corpse of the Clover. Metallic roots sprouted from the remnants of his head near the brainstem. Gray matter and blood splattered on the SWAT car caught the light of nearby street lamps in a glitter of metal and bone chips.

Anton's stomach turned. *That's not inside me.* "Aye. You good?"

"Aye? What slang is that?"

"Rural, couldn't you tell?"

"Just figured your accent was another urban conglomerate. I've never left the Bowl, let alone met one of your types." Chen took in Anton with a fresh appreciation.

"Ok?" Anton raised an eyebrow.

"Sorry, I didn't mean to make this weird." Chen looked sheepishly towards the hospital, Anton followed his gaze. The Chief walked towards them, alone.

"If it makes you feel any better, Chen," Anton said. "I think the stories on both sides are exaggerated. I haven't seen one baby on a spit."

"Well, we haven't lost power since you've been here."

"What?"

"Kidding, Anton." Chen smiled at him. "Can you… take point on this? Chief'll be a little fiery that we lost a prisoner."

Anton hid his smile. *Chief's a Colonel alright.* He hefted the body over his shoulder and moved to intercept the Chief.

"God damn it," the Chief said as Anton approached. "You're kidding, right?"

"They have a morgue in there?"

"Yes." The Chief's disappointment washed over him like a wave and when it withdrew, the same mask of determination appeared. "Deposit it. We're leaving with the two we have."

Anton continued to the hospital.

An exhausted receptionist's jaw dropped as Anton entered the hospital lobby.

"The police just left," the receptionist said. "I'll call him back, you might as well turn yourself in."

"Not my doing. Chief David told me to drop him off in your morgue. Where is it?"

"Not worth the trouble," she muttered. "Down the hall and stairs on your right, you can't miss it." She went back to using her tablet.

Anton walked towards the morgue, the antiseptic hospital smell overwhelming the scent of the Clover on his back. At the bottom of the stairs, a menthol and rot smell replaced both as he walked into the morgue.

"Just drop it off there." A short man worked on a tablet in the corner. He tapped the screen, a drawer opening in a wall-fridge.

Anton deposited the body and walked back to the man. "Anything else? Paperwork?"

"It'll be in the system." The man's eyes never left his tablet.

Fine by me. Anton walked back to the stairs, pausing at the top. *Yume.* He pulled the FOB Joe gave him, pushing it into his tablet. The screen displayed two names, Joseph Fayed, and Yume Chaude. He pushed Yume.

"Hey," Anton said when the comm signaled an answer.

"Anton?" Yume said through the tablet. "How did you get this frequency?"

"Mr. Fayed gave it to me. Are you en route?"

"No."

Muffled voices drifted through, but Anton couldn't discern who it was or what they said.

"We are still discussing how to approach the situation. Do you have the person?"

"No, not yet. There's another group of augmented people down here, Yume. They're stopping the police from searching."

A nurse walked by the door, eyeing the man in the stairwell.

"What company?" Yume said.

"I don't know."

"Anton, if you can capture one of them, hold them till I arrive. R&D would love to see where everyone else is at."

What?

"I'll leave shortly, Anton. I should arrive with the storm."

"Aye." *This is near FUBAR.*

"And Anton," Yume whispered. "I'm excited to see you."

Anton's heart fluttered, the comm-line beeped as it disconnected. *When I can talk to Yume without someone overhearing, she'll know what to do and we can fix this situation.* He headed back to the police waiting outside.

"What took so long?" The Chief asked.

"Paperwork." Anton rubbed the back of his neck.

The Chief opened his mouth but decided against speaking.

"I'll drive the SWAT," Chen said.

"You're to follow us." Chief's eyes wandered to the Clovers hiding in the backseat. "Anton, you're driving," he crackled through the comms. "Chen, you're running cover. I'm interrogating these assholes on the way back."

"Sir, they're linked," Chen said. "The moment one of them talks, someone will come after him to take him out."

"A moving target will be harder to stop, and we need answers now."

"Aye." Anton swung into the cruiser. *I like this plan better than Taketa's.*

Anton drifted into the highway traffic, the controls of the cruiser similar enough to the quad back home, though the number of people made him nervous.

"Anton," the Chief said. "I assume you understand confidentiality."

"Yeah," Anton said.

"Good to hear." The Chief turned to the Clovers. "I'll make an offer to you both. You answer my questions, and I will let you out of this car, no questions asked. Or, you can not answer my questions, and I'll do whatever the fuck I want to you and get answers."

Anton looked through the rearview mirror, the two men paled and sank into their seats.

"What corporation are you currently employed for?"

They didn't answer.

"One last time. Who are you currently working for?"

"East Bowl PD," the one behind Anton rasped.

They've been in this car without AC or water.

The Chief sighed. "Really gentleman? You're going to make me do this?"

One of the Clovers snorted.

"Suit yourself." The Chief removed a metal coil from the glove compartment.

The Chief donned nitrile gloves and unfolded the coil. The wire was a hair's width and had tension to it, polarized light sprayed from the bend. Anton focused on the road as the Chief ran the coil through the polymetal grates separating the two compartments.

A muffled scream echoed in the car. Through the rearview, the man who spoke doubled over. The coil's fiber clung to exposed skin like a parasitic vine.

"Amazing isn't it?" the Chief said. "As advanced as we are? Nature still has tricks up her sleeve?"

The man lost control and screamed.

Anton glanced at the Chief. *Police shouldn't do this.* He opened his mouth to stop this—

"Alright," came from the back through clenched teeth.

The scream stopped, and the Chief rolled up the fiber.

"Vio. We're Vio."

"Eddie, are you fucking stupid? You just fucking killed us."

"Fuck off," Eddie said. "You didn't have that venom touch you. Death is better."

"I had nothing to do with this," the other man said into the ether.

"Company," Chen said through their inserts.

Anton scanned the horizon, screen, mirrors—a single beige car accelerated up the median from the rear. A Clover leaned out the back window, an anti-material caliber rifle taking aim towards them.

Crap. Anton swerved into the median and jammed the brakes.

The Clover car slammed into the back of them, the tires hit a block— Glass sprayed inwards as both cars tumbled, pens and crumbs flew into the air as the Safe-T-Net sprayed in from the sides of the dash, sealing Anton and Chief into their seats as they rolled. The Vio Clovers in the back weren't as lucky, bouncing against the roof and seats as the car rolled to a calamitous stop.

"God damn it, Grissom, you trying to kill me?"

"Didn't want to give them any heads up."

"Fucking Ninth Legion." The Chief cut himself free.

Anton tore his netting, rolling out and walking to the beige wreck. Blood flowed from the driver's scalp as his head lay against the steering column. The Clover who had leaned out with a rifle lay in the median a few yards back. Anton checked the driver, clear fluid leaked from his skull.

He's gone. Anton continued to the second. Bouncing along the road gave him a severe case of road rash, but he still breathed. Anton hoisted him onto his shoulder, if he was coherent enough to struggle, he didn't show it. He handcuffed the Clover to one of the seats in the back of the SWAT truck. The Chief stood by the crushed cruiser, Chen was on his hands and knees peering into the wreck.

"They're done." Chen stood.

"Call it in," the Chief said. "This is another precinct. They can clean up this mess."

"10-33, we have a crash on Highway Eighty," Chen said. "Not getting anything."

"Jammers?" Chief said under his breath.

"I don't see them." Anton scanned the river of commuters adjusting to the accident in the lanes with a marginal slow down at their zippering point.

"You see jammers?" Chen asked.

"Long story," Anton said. "We should go."

Chen looked back at the wrecked cars and the bodies they pulled out of it. "We can't."

"Anton's right," the Chief's voice cracked. "They did all of this to block their corp's name. We're the next link in that chain."

"The station." Chen sprinted to the SWAT truck.

Anton stepped into the back of the truck, swearing a raindrop splashed his face. The pink sky dotted with clouds as the ever present haze dissipated and he pulled the doors closed.

Chapter 29 - Weaver

Weaver sat in the amphitheater that had become Home. Cots made from discarded foam and packing materials optimized for each substrate, the shifts of work and sleep reestablished. Substrate-Ariel returned and slept on the largest cot. The trip back took days longer than calculated. Avoiding any and all police, compounded with security cameras that took time to find, break, and shutdown, led to a circuitous route that drained the strongest substrate. Weaver-Beta returned with the most recent stolen tablet. Weaver had spent the past four days in different districts with different substrates stealing them. All were in use already. Weaver-Beta plugged in the tablet and monitored the police station's communications. Information was barely shared between precincts, let alone a string of petty thefts. Substrate-Zeta finished cleaning the hair trimmers in the Home and began the process of shaving all the heads, starting with Substrate-Beta. Weaver was keen to avoid the pestilence of parasites that plagued Urban areas.

Concurrently, Weaver-Alpha sat on the corner of a street in the artisan district. A dusty hat in front, begging for money. Substrate-Alpha's lopsided smile and appearance as a Disabled gained more money than the rest.

"Little boy, where is your orphanage?" A young woman asked Weaver-Alpha, her hair a convoluted pattern of folds and spirals. Weaver-Alpha feigned muteness and blinked unevenly.

"Tyler, give him some money. It's amazing he's survived with his condition. They usually don't."
The blond Tyler removed coins from his jacket, dropping them into the hat and pulling the woman away.
Weaver-Alpha counted the money, it was enough to get rations for the self. The money would have to be split, Substrate-Alpha buying enough calories for the self was too suspicious. Weaver-Alpha scanned the area for anyone who noticed the sizable deposit.

A man with a goatee attempted to blend into a crowd near a cafe but definitely eyed the cash Weaver-Alpha had to move immediately.

Weaver-Beta opened a map of the artisan district to plan for Substrate-Alpha's escape.

Weaver-Alpha shoved the money into a pouch hidden against its chest. The man shifted from the cafe. Weaver-Alpha turned into the alleyway, shoving the pouch and cash into a crevasse of concrete and sprinting towards the nearest trashbelt. Footsteps echoed behind, gaining on the shorter substrate.

Weaver-Alpha leapt for the pre-planned escape rope and swung down.

Substrate-Pi, Kappa, and Zeta cracked the Taketa source-net. Weaver needed to delete the tracker data from the stolen rifle. Weaver tilted the collective heads, the tracker data coordinates sent out came from a single computer. The Vio-malware sent coordinates directly to Vio Corp. *It was a Vio tracker in the rifle.* Weaver-Ariel woke to eat and drink, then slept more. Weaver would leave with this substrate as soon as Substrate-Alpha returned. Weaver analyzed the malware, waking three substrates to assist.

As the morning passed and Substrate-Alpha returned, Weaver used the malware to gain access to Vio Corp. The data being siphoned was degraded, but Vio seemed happy with whatever it could get. Weaver rerouted traffic through multiple bounces using a computer in an internet cafe nearby. Weaver-Beta had been kicked out of the cafe after 'breaking' a computer, but in reality had inserted a virus, giving Weaver remote access. The owner had unplugged the machine and tossed it into his backroom. Weaver-Beta and Nu snuck in, managing to plug it back in and hiding it in a pile of dead towers. Substrate-Ariel woke, stretched, ate the last of the stolen rations and left to buy SR-powder.

Weaver-Ariel stopped in at a neon-lit store, bought a kilo of powder, went to a dimly-lit store and bought another kilo.

Weaver analyzed the data stream from the Vio Corp computer and found a pertinent memo.

"Per Source, augmented children related to our 'discovery' have moved from 'Facility B' to the SF Bowl. Per Source, this was an unplanned move and property should be recovered."

Taketa might not know where I am, but Vio is searching for me. Weaver woke several substrates, and remapped the tunnels, cross-referencing it with older diagrams of the city. Weaver found a few spots that could be used to interlink separated tunnel systems.

Weaver-Ariel stopped in at a local restaurant, Wu's, and got an SR-shake. It was exquisite.

"Can I buy this in bulk?" Weaver-Ariel asked the server-bot.

It did not respond, but came back with multiple shakes.

"It expands in your stomach," a mustached patron at the bar said. "So I wouldn't drink that many."

"Thank you," Weaver-Ariel said, wary of the man.

Weaver read Vio's intel on multiple substrates. They had schematics for bastardized augments based on what Taketa—on what Weaver developed. It lacked the subtlety, the nuance. *It is disgusting.* Weaver-Beta pulled the last schematics through the computer in the internet cafe and disconnected everything to prevent a trace. *Vio cannot be allowed to find me.*

Substrate-Kappa and Omega left the tunnels to scrounge for electronic parts. Weaver needed to construct scanjammers to block the Vio Augmented searching for the self.

Substrate-Nu and Zeta chipped at walls of access tunnels to link two subterranean systems.

Weaver-Ariel left Wu's, the man at the bar set off every alarm Weaver had. Footsteps echoed behind, Substrate-Ariel was being followed. Weaver-Ariel turned into a detritus filled alleyway and dove into a dumpster.

The footsteps following passed.

"Can you shut up?" One of them asked the other.

"I didn't say anything."

"I can hear your thoughts, asshole. Can you not hear mine?"

"No, I'm not receiving anything."

"We need to debug these when we get back."

"They'll be out of date." He laughed.

"A terrible joke, told twice… I heard that asshole."

The other man laughed.

Weaver-Ariel winced at the stench in the dumpster, whatever was inside had died, turned to garbage, and died again.

Substrate-Kappa and Omega were joined by Substrate-Tau to carry stolen circuit boards back to the Home.

The sun rose before Weaver-Ariel peered from the dumpster. The substrate could still be tracked. *It will be safest to move Substrate-Ariel to a different precinct.* Weaver would have to figure out how to interact with the local populace through the younger substrates.

Chapter 30 - Luciana

Luciana and her fellow officers finished listening to Donaher's message.

"It's either a corp or some international cartel," Nguyen said. "The Southern Empire dirt and implants? That's nothing local."

"All of this for a kid." Luciana shook her head. *It's insane.*

"Could be a leader's runt that was planted here," Kagan said. "Not like anyone would search the Pucker."

"But to put them in the sewers?" Sheer said.

"Adds to the effect," Kagan said.

"How long until the storm hits?" Junger said.

"An hour, maybe less." Maus walked to the Board and yelled, "Jesus, they fucked this one up, its way stronger than forecasted."

"How much stronger?"

"Cat four or five. Depending. The news is saying that one of the seeders malfunctioned. Can't be verified yet though."

"X-Systems probably," Novina said. "They've fucked this shit before."

"What a spin job to block verification for this long," Sheer said.

"Only a matter of time," Junger said. "If we've got an hour, we've got an hour. We should go straight towards one of the trashbelts that feeds the area. Find the Displaced and bring them here."

"Which trashbelt?" Nguyen asked.

"If they've been living in sixteen-hundreds block, then the twenty-two and thirteen-hundreds' blocks have tunnels feeding it." Novina projected the Pucker map on the wallscreen.

"What about the storm?" Sheer asked.

"What about it?" Junger said.

"Are we even ready for it?" Sheer said. "Our front door is fucked, haven't checked the roofs or the drains. If it's going to rain bad, do we crash here or go to the apartment-complex?"

"Sounds like you're volunteering there, Paul," Nguyen said, giving him a sidelong glance.

Sheer shook his head. "Every damn time."

"Let's focus, people," Novina said. "Where do we look?"

"I think I know," Luciana said.

Everyone turned to her.

"Near the seventeen-hundreds block, we stopped for water. I think I saw people in this warehouse that should be abandoned."

"Think? It could be some Homeless squatting," Kagan said.

"Maybe." A ripple of pain went from the tip of Luciana's nose to the back of her skull. She closed her eyes. "Maybe it's a Homeless, but think about it. No one has seen this kid, or even the Displaced. Rumors, hearsay, you name it, we have it. But the one time something that wasn't human went near a trashbelt? We get displaced people. With our own eyes, so to speak."

"It will be on her OPTO-insert recording," Maus said. "And we're still within the standard recording window."

"Do it," Junger said.

Maus pulled the video from Luciana's OPTO-inserts. It rewound across the wallscreen at 40x speed to Nagual entering the warehouse. Luciana took over the playback and advanced frame by frame as the wavelengths cycled from her past actions.

"There." Luciana paused it on a frame between night vision and IR. In the reflection of an oily puddle, a pale face was unmistakably peering out of a pipe overhead.

"Doesn't mean it's not a Homeless," Kagan said.

"And?" Luciana said. "We have an hour? Nguyen and Junger, head to whatever belt you want to. I'll go to the warehouse with Nagual. We can set a timer."

"G," Sheer said. "Don't be mad, but you're fucked up. For one, we should stay grouped up, for two you can't—"

"I'll go with her." Maus pointed to the wallscreen. "I buy it. Junger, Nguyen and someone else can go wherever they want. Everyone else can stay here and prepare for the storm."

Thank you, Maus. Luciana gave him an appreciative nod.

"Nguyen, Novina, you in?" Junger asked.

"10-4." Nguyen smiled.

"Same," Novina said.

"The Chief's going to beat your asses raw," Kagan said.

"They wish," Sheer said. "They'd pay to have the Chief spank 'em."

"We're chewing into our hour." Junger stood.

"Comms?" Luciana said.

"Works in station," Maus said. "But sending and receiving outside of a few blocks is still blocked."

"Sheer and I will look into that," Kagan said. "After checking the roof, drains, and pumps. Does anyone need anything from their dorm?"

"I still haven't been back," Luciana said absent-mindedly.

"You know how bad that's going to smell, with how you live?" Sheer said

"At least the sewers won't be the worst thing you smell this week," Nguyen said.

"Time's a factor, everyone," Junger said, tapping an imagined watch. The officers left the conference room. Luciana retrieved her overjacket, counting the bullets in her clip. *Come. I have to tell Saori and Samir.* She removed her tablet, typing out a message.

'I can taste what Nagual tastes.' *No.*

'I am receiving signals from Nagual, it is not one-way anymore.' *No. What do I say?*

Maus emerged from the armory, his stained brown waterproof uniform rattling.

He better hope it cools down with the rain. 'Implant malfunction, advice on diagnostics.' She sent the message.

"You think that will get through?" Maus gestured to the tablet.

"Landlines right?"

"I tried rerouting our data through those, but got nothing from the local scanners. Maybe interurban still works."

"Problem for tomorrow."

They went to the garage. The bike canopy slid open, Nagual stepped in and preemptively made space for Maus.

"You've got to be kidding me." Maus crouched beside the dog. Luciana covered her smile and stepped into the bike. The canopy slid close, and they exited the relative safety of the station.

Winds howled through the man-made canyons of the Pucker, errant raindrops splattering the bike.

"Thought you said it was an hour?" Luciana didn't take her eyes off the road and drove towards the 1700 block.

"An hour was the main storm, this is… some pre-rain spurts."

"Pre-rain, really?"

"I liked it."

She could hear his smile. They drove in silence to the 1700 block and she stopped at a ruddy Y-junction.

"Maus, do you remember where that warehouse was?"

"I was hoping you did, we got turned around en route, so I'm not sure."

"Damn it. I cracked my head, I'm a tad fuzzy."

"Does the bike have any previous location data?"

Luciana willed the bike into displaying a map on the HUD, but when she tried to overlay previous routes, the HUD blinked instead. "Doesn't look it."

"That's weird."

"I don't disagree." She tried to look back at Maus but couldn't turn in the bike. "I guess we'll retrace our steps? Get out my insert from Nagual, you can see what I see."

"Can't we stream it through the tablet this time?" Maus said.

"We can do that?"

Maus sighed. "I don't know why I didn't think of that sooner, hand me back your tablet, I'll do it."

She tossed the tablet back.

Maus caught it with a slap. "I can't believe I didn't think of this and put your insert inside of me." His polyfiber jacket rustled as he shuddered. "Alright, we're good. Man, that HUD is impressive."

They drove through boarded up streets, arriving at Aristotle's apartment complex.

"Wind blew away the tracks," Luciana said.

They continued through empty streets. The storm whipped sand down their urban canyons, detritus rode the gusts, and visibility dropped.

"Can't see shit," Maus said.

"I know, man, I'm looking through the same eye."

"Oh yeah." Maus chuckled.

Pressure rubbed the back of Luciana's neck and shoulders. She shrugged to remove it, but if anything it intensified. She reached around her back to find what rubbed against her back. *Nothing.* The rhythmic motion massaged the tension in her back away.

"His fur is so soft," Maus said from the back.

"What?" Luciana's eyes flared.

"I got nervous, rubbed Nagual's neck, made me feel better. I'll stop."

The sensation on her shoulder blades and neck stopped immediately.

It's getting worse. "We should walk it," Luciana said, wanting to get the worry and sensations out of her head. "Nagual found water before, he can do it again."

The canopy slid open, sand tore into the cockpit, and she stepped out into the wind tunnel. Grit bit her exposed skin, worming into her ears on the roar. The officers pulled the hoods from their jackets to cover their eyes and faces. She knelt by Nagual, tying an old pair of goggles on him. His eyes bulged in the reflection of the goggles and he wagged his tail.

"What's the matter, G?" Maus yelled into the maelstrom. "You look like you saw a ghost."

"I'll explain in a minute," she yelled. *Water, lead slow.* Nagual wagged his tail, 1. Visibility dropped to a meter and sand scoured their bodies. The howling wind sent tarps flying down the streets. They slowed against the onslaught. *Return.* Luciana and Maus crouched into an alcove as Nagual followed. She checked the time on her OPTO-inserts. *Thirty minutes left, fuck.*

"What did you see back there?" Maus asked as the wind died enough for them to talk through their ENT-inserts.

"Maus, you wouldn't believe me if I told you, but I felt you petting Nagual as if you were petting me."

"What."

"Told you."

"That can't be good."

"That's why you're a detective, Maus, always solving the toughest cases."

"Oh yeah?" Maus pet Nagual, who happily leaned into it.

The sensation hit Luciana a microsecond later. "Not funny."

Maus stopped. "It's a little funny. That what you messaged about before we left?"

"Yeah. Let's find this warehouse, then we can head back, ready?"

"10-4."

Luciana and Maus swung back into the storm, following Nagual.

Puddles became lakes, sand and dirt turned to mud in patches as the storm's fingers reached overhead.

"This is going to be bad if it's already clogged." Maus nodded to an overflowing storm drain they passed.

The winds died, sound sucked from the atmosphere and the quiet became a roar of blood within their ears.

"There." Luciana pointed to the cracked building where the bike had fishtailed the Clover.

Which means. They turned to the warehouse. Helicopter blades beating the air broke the silence as one last flight landed before the storm hit. Maus squeezed her shoulder, and they crossed the muddy street to enter the warehouse. The bike trailed them, Luciana didn't want to risk leaving it outside for a Clover to see as they entered.

Chapter 31 - Weaver

The Vio squad had been close to catching substrates on several occasions. But the child-substrate form allowed the self to dig into locations the adults couldn't follow. The tunnel entrance points proved too numerous. The precinct known as 'The Pucker' was the ideal hiding spot. The chaos and lack of police gave Weaver an unexpected and welcomed freedom until the detritus storm. When tunnel entrances silted in, and the Vio squad turned the precinct into a war zone. Police were harassed, Weaver calculated seven days until they would begin killing officers. The power died. Weaver continued in total darkness for four days, using the interconnected paths within the subterranean network to find food and water.

Weaver-Ariel struggled to find income and turned to an ancient trade. A strong bath and clean clothing prettied the substrate enough to start business. The clientele weren't as sweet as Noah.

Weaver missed the man.

But the work allowed Weaver to feed, cloth, and find an apartment for Substrate-Ariel. Weaver-Ariel shaved the head within the apartment and affected wigs to ward off any Vio tracking that might occur. Weaver calculated they wouldn't search for a prostitute, but did not risk it.

On the fifth day, the power returned in the Home and Weaver-Alpha found the entrance to Wu's pantry. Two containers of SR-powder and syrup were stolen for sustenance.

On that day, Weaver-Ariel tried to meet people through a group to fix Precinct 41. Weaver was lonely. Even after what Saori had done, Weaver missed her as much as Noah. Weaver worried Noah was being punished.

Substrate-Beta searched Taketa's nets, finding no record of him. *That is not good.*

Weaver-Ariel smiled at a woman with gray hair. "I can help clean your windows."

"You should focus on getting a real job instead." The woman sneered.

Weaver-Beta, Alpha, and Zeta searched through the Taketa camera record. Days after Weaver escaped, Noah had been isolated and put on the next transport out. *I will find you, Noah.* Through the cameras, Substrate-Aaron lay isolated in a basement, kept alive by a tangle of tubes that ran into it.

Weaver-Ariel shook its head. Weaver let out a collective sigh and turned off the video feeds.

Chapter 32 - Anton

Anton leaned on the front seats of the SWAT truck, rain pinging the metal roof. Sparse downpours ran across the highway, soaking some sections while leaving others parched. Pilot programs shuffled commuters off the roads. Between the seams of two sky lines, the Pucker emerged in all its chaos. The truck exited, passing through the rim—

A group of children ran down an alleyway. Anton's eyes zoomed in, he swore one had multi-colored eyes. *Fayed wasn't bullshitting, that looked like a kid... I'll find them first, figure out what Taketa wants them and decide whether or not they go back. They can try and court martial me.*

"Chief," Anton said. "I'd like to get out."

"Grissom, the storm's here already. I'm not stopping," Chief said. The children retreated towards a building in the distance.

"Just slow down then. I can jump if need be."

"Not slowing down either. With how fast those Vio agents are acting, they could already be at the station. Not to mention, your training will prove invaluable."

I'm going. "Fair enough." Anton walked towards the back of the truck.

"I'm glad you—"

Anton grabbed his rifle and kicked out the back door. One flew off its hinges, the other slammed into the truck, and he jumped.

"Motherfu—" the Chief's voice faded as the truck headed towards their station.

Anton rolled on the ground, his legs caught him—

He hit a fire hydrant, flipping end over end. He braced, skidding to a stop in the sand and staring at a cloudy sky.

Better move in case the Chief decides to come back. Anton stood, sand hissed through his shredded left pant leg, but his gear hung intact on the right. His legs were unblemished if stained with sand, while the fire hydrant tilted near tearing off. *Earth below, these augments are tanks.* He set off for the alley where he had seen the children.

Anton followed children's footprints to a trashbelt running in an alleyway. The footprints ended abruptly. His eyes shifted, revealing the minute pattern of a rug dragged behind the footprints to clear them. The dragged path ran to the alleyway's dead end. Rain fell in thick drops and Anton stepped under an overhang.

The sounds of the city fell away as drops replaced it. *Like it used to back home.* For a moment, the urban area was almost serene.

A helicopter beat it in the distance. The cement wall Anton leaned against divided one district from another. A waterfall of garbage fell over the edge a hundred feet up and onto the conveyor system.

Anton's eyes shifted over the dead end, a dark blue cold spot stuck out in the cement. *It's hollow.* Anton crossed through the rain and pressed the depression with his augmented hand. Gears ground in resistance, but he opened a hatch to an access tunnel that paralleled the trashbelt. He slid the hidden door back into place, following tiny footprints into the tunnels. He arrived at a rusted out ladder in an abandoned room. Whispers, footsteps, and tires echoed ahead.

Anton steadied his rifle and picked up his pace.

Chapter 33 - Luciana

Nagual padded ahead in the warehouse. Luciana clearly smelled the water through him, and something sour? The rain arrived in a thunderous chorus of drops against the tin roof above them. The percussion beat west to east. *Getting back to the station in this will be a bitch.* Luciana and Maus walked through piles of silted, abandoned, computer towers and came to a set of stairs that Nagual padded down.

"You sure about this?" Maus asked.

Nagual stopped after a few steps, turning back to them. The cement stairs crumbled in spots, revealing its rebar skeleton.

"Storms here," Luciana said. "No way the Clovers attack during it, you hear that rain? We might as well."

"You think Nagual went this deep last time?"

"I'm not sure, but I can smell the water down here. Well, he can." She gestured to Nagual.

Maus nodded and they descended. Entering a dusty basement, they proceeded through a dim hall. Something complex and sweet tickled Nagual's nose. Luciana tilted her head until the wave hit her own. She walked into a wall of rot from the sewers.

Maus gagged, Nagual wagged his tail at the officers.

How can you enjoy that smell? Luciana's eyes watered as they approached the source. The pool of water Nagual drank from spilled from a backed up pipe overhead.

How is he not sick? She walked around the pool where the faces had been. Someone or something had drilled through the wall. The warehouse's basement was now connected to a maintenance tunnel for an abandoned transit system.

"We found how the Displaced have been getting around unseen," Luciana said, pushing her leg through the hole.

"G, what about flooding?" Maus gestured towards the puddle behind them.

"That's from a pipe, this should be empty."

"Earthquakes? Hello? Shit's porous as fuck down here."

"I'll have the bike scout." She sat and drove the bike towards them. Concrete cracked and clattered to the ground as the bike fell through the stairs.

"What was that?" Maus asked, raising his weapon at the door.

"Bike was a little heavy."

"How are we getting out?"

"Either these maintenance tunnels are fine, and we can use them, or well, we'll have to fashion a way out at the stairs."

"And if it floods too?"

"We rise with the tide? So to speak."

Maus gulped, but nodded. Nagual slopped the puddle. A bitter taste coated Luciana's mouth. *Stop, please.*

Nagual slurped one more time, 1.

Luciana focused on her bike's perspective, driving to them and into the abandoned transit systems tunnels. Remarkably intact, the bike accelerated along rusted tracks to a T-junction after two hundred meters.

I need Nagual's nose. "Got a T-junction ahead, no obvious leaks or flooding. I'm ready to go."

"I don't like it."

Return. "Maus, you can stay here. Nagual and me'll get this kid with the bike. Not like I can't take a kid back here. You cool?"

Maus hesitated.

Luciana removed her pistol and handed to him. "Comm check."

"10-4, for now at least."

"Hey, if it floods, head up. I'll figure it out."

Luciana squeezed Maus's shoulder and got into the bike as it arrived. Nagual jumped into his compartment. They drove through the maintenance tunnels towards the T-junction.

The HUD highlighted several pipes overhead with bright data stream heat signatures. The data stream at the T-junction went both ways. Luciana cracked the canopy and Nagual jumped out. His nose told them both that the scent of people was on the left. He jumped back into the bike before Luciana thought, *return.* She left the canopy cracked as she drove through abandoned stations, tunnels, and arrived at a worker's amphitheater of conjoining tunnels. Tools and supplies were tied against the walls. The circular port in the roof had a ladder that rusted to nothing before it reached the bottom.

Heavy footsteps echoed down the rightmost runnel. *Not a child.* Luciana reversed into the shadows.

A man entered, his pants shredded on one leg, revealing tight black musculature. He had a military-grade rifle slung over his back and boyish face. The man's skin tanned, his legs and hand a mismatched black.

Implants.

The man scanned the room, his eyes locked on the bike.

He can see me.

The man didn't raise his gun but froze midstep.

"Aye, you can get out, nice and slow now," he said with an accent that was hard for Luciana to understand. "No need for this to get messy. Besides, won't go well for you."

Armed, implanted, he's a threat. "Maus, I've made contact, left at the t-junction," she whispered into the comm.

The man removed the rifle from his back, but didn't raise it. "If that wasn't a Taketa bike, I'd have blown those tires out already. One last time—"

Threaten me. Luciana accelerated towards him, the bike spraying dust backwards. *Got you—*

He dove out of the way before Luciana could blink. His right arm shot out, catching the front tire, sending her end over end.

Fuck. Luciana hit the canopy, Nagual bounced a second later, the pain shot through Luciana twice as they crashed onto the side.

Luciana groaned, and the bike's canopy was forced open.

"Sky above, you're Nineteen-PD." He pulled her out of the bike and lowered her to the ground like she weighed nothing.

Luciana blinked dust that fell into her eyes, the man lay Nagual beside her. He checked her breathing, then her limbs to make sure none were broken. He leaned over Nagual, tried to do something similar, but was more clumsy about it. The manipulation of Nagual like he did her again.

"Stop." The sensations of her toes moving stopped.

His boyish face came into view. "Look, I didn't know you were Nineteen-PD. I didn't even know they had Taketa support."

"Who are you?"

"Anton Grissom. I... was sent here to find someone."

Luciana sat, wincing at the bruise her whole body was becoming.

"Shit, I am sorry." Anton supported her back with his hand.

"Anton, from Taketa? Why are you down here?" Luciana asked.

"Followed some kids, lost them in the tunnels, saw the bike. I thought you might have been my back up."

"Everyone wants this kid. Why?" Luciana stared at his face, analyzing if he told the truth.
Adrenaline coursed through her veins. *His eyes are implants too?* Anton broke from her gaze to stare at the tunnels and Luciana leaned to keep it in view.

"I don't know," he said.

"I don't believe you," she said. It was a gamble, but Nagual stirred. *My three can beat him now that I know his capabilities. Hold.* 1. She glanced at the bike, its Scrambler would hit them both. *That won't work.*

Anton sighed and turned back to her. "You tell me why you're here first, and why you have a Taketa bike. Then we can talk."

Luciana stared through his soul. The kid was sincere. "There is an augmented gang in the streets above. They want this kid, they're turning my precinct into a warscape. Chief figured we get this kid, we can negotiate, maybe even get them out."

"And the bike?"

"Things weren't going well before these Augmented showed up. I was sent to get extra gear, and the Clovers moved right on in."
Anton scratched his neck, his eyes leaving hers to look at Nagual. The dog's muscles were loaded and ready to fire.

"You can tell that to stand down," Anton said. "For one, it's not a gang that's looking for him, it's a corporation."

"A corp?"

"Yeah, and Taketa told me the kid is theirs."

Maybe this guy is full of shit... and I bought the facade. Luciana took a deep breath, preparing to launch Nagual on him.

"This whole situation is fucked," Anton said. "I'm not some corporate soldier."

No, he's truly innocent... Luciana slowed. *What happened that made you lose your leg and arm?* "What do you plan to do then?"

Anton stood, extending his augmented hand to help her up.

They embraced at the wrists, it was like grabbing titanium.

Anton glanced at her badge. "Ms. Gutierrez, I plan on finding this kid. Figuring out why everyone wants him and then I'll decide what I want to do." He took a step backwards and paused. "You can join me if you'd like."

Sit, 1.

Anton chose a tunnel seemingly at random and started down it.

Do I help him? Ah, fuck. "Anton, it's probably not that way." *Find people.* 1.

Nagual's nose twitched in the air. Human came from the third tunnel on the left.

"It's that one," Luciana said as Nagual padded towards the opening.

"Aye." Anton followed Nagual while Luciana and the bike fell behind.

"That bike's fancier than it looks." Anton thumbed towards it. "And I can tell you it looks quite fancy." His augmented hand scratched his neck.

"Taketa implanted me too," Luciana said. "I can command the bike."

"No shit?"

"No shit."

They turned down a skinnier tunnel with a damp floor. Luciana ran her fingers along the ceiling but found no leaks.

"The pipes around us are giving off an insane spectra," Anton said in awe.

She cycled her OPTO-inserts to IR, heat pulsed from the data cables. "Your inserts are better than mine. I just see heat."

"Lost more than my legs and arm in the accident," he said offhandedly. His eyes still trained on the ceiling.

Guess we're both still holding back cards.

They arrived at an intersectional grotto. Child-sized sleeping cots were built into the wall three tall. Workbenches full of circuit boards and soldering equipment lay in a corner. A tangle of extension cords rose to the building above like a root system.

"We've found the Displaced," Luciana said.

A fan near the edge blew warm air through the place.

"It's like a nexus, all the data is coming towards here," Anton said. "What are Displaced?"

"Refugees, Borderlings, Rurals who lost their land, you name it. People with nowhere to go."

Nagual headed down the twelve o'clock tunnel. Luciana walked to the fan at seven o'clock. Anton stood in the center of the room, staring at the ceiling.

"Aye," Anton said to the ceiling. "The flow is changing, it's…"

"Thank you, Anton," a woman said from the tunnel Anton and Luciana exited from.

Luciana spun around, reaching for a pistol she'd given to Maus. *Shit.*

Anton turned. "Yume, you got here so soon. It's not a person, I don't know what Joe told you—"

"More than you, Anton." Yume sighed, taking a half-step backwards.

Eight Taketa mercenaries fanned out from the tunnel, their SMGs and body armor clattering.

"Yu-Yume, what's going on?"

"Anton, cut it. I know you tried to send a message to the military. Joe was right, he knew, but I didn't listen. I thought you would be the one for me."

Luciana inched to her right. *If I can get the bike into place.*

"Now now, Ms. Gutierrez." Yume snapped her fingers.

A Taketa mercenary dragged out a bound, bruised, and bleeding Maus.

No. Luciana froze.

Yume gestured and a man walked towards Luciana.

"Anton, you're to remove your weapon. You will be coming back to us. Period, end of story. Your indiscretion aside, you're too much of an asset to be allowed to walk free. We will find the weaver project and bring it back."

"I'm not going back," Anton said.

"Anton." Yume waved and Anton collapsed, his legs cut out beneath him. "I said you were going back." She walked towards the fallen man.

Anton lifted himself upright with his human arm. "I trusted you," he said, his voice ragged.

"And I you, Anton, and I you." Yume caressed his face, and he pulled it away. "Anton, you're going to be living in a Taketa building for the rest of your life. Don't push away the one person you may interact with." Yume stood and the Taketa soldiers advanced.

Hands grabbed Luciana's neck, she flinched—but no one grabbed her. *It's Nagual, he found the Displaced.*

A soldier moved to grab Anton. He bit at their hands, sending a scream and spray of blood onto the ground. Another one slammed the butt of their rifle into his chest. Anton swung with his human arm, only to be kneed in the face.

"Easy on the eyes," Yume said.

Think.

More rifle butts thudded into Anton, tearing his shirt. They tied his normal arm against his chest, gagging him though he was lost for words. His eyes wide at what had happened.

There had been a relationship between Anton and Yume, or at least a burgeoning one, and that had been cut off completely. *His youth is his downfall.*

A soldier put a zip tie around Luciana's hands until it bit her skin. *They can't move me in the storm, I can*—Nagual tensed at the zip tie sensation.

"What do we do with him?" A soldier gestured to Maus.

"He's served his purpose," Yume said.

Luciana locked eyes with Maus.

The soldier raised his rifle.

"No!" A scream tore Luciana's throat as the man fired into the back of Maus' head.

The bullet tore through the front of his face at the jawline. His eyes went blank, he collapsed into his own blood with a thud.

A soldier stepped in to grab her, Luciana kicked backwards and reached into her pocket. She pulled the hallys and threw the powder into the fan.

The air shimmered as the drug hit the blades and exploded into the room. She tried to hold her breath, but the world spun upon itself. A kaleidoscope emerged from melting walls.

Luciana collapsed to the ground. *Return. 1.*

Luciana was at waist height, panting and sprinting through a tunnel. Panic gripped her guts, worry slipped through her mind, and pain filled her paws. She bound into the room, Taketa soldiers lay on the ground, Anton, Yume, all on the ground twitching.

Except Maus.

Rage filled her and she lost control. She leapt forward, tearing out the nearest man's throat. Luciana tried to regain control, to get off the ride, to end the nightmare, to stop the carnage. But blood coated her throat, filling her stomach with its iron taste. It was the purest ecstasy and a nauseating misery. Hands lifted her own body, the same hands lifted Anton, dragging them towards a rightmost tunnel. Luciana trembled towards the Taketa soldiers on the ground. She tore more throats, biting through armor designed for bullets, tearing off cloth designed for puncture protection, and sinking her teeth deep into the weak flesh. Panting, she approached the woman called Yume. *Cop killer.*

The Last 0-Day

Yume mouthed words in a random order, her eyes vibrated beneath their lids at the unseen kaleidoscope that had taken hold of her vision. Luciana looked back towards Maus, his body a mess on the ground, his blood drank by the dirt on the floor.

She tore out Yume's throat with a terrifying glee. She went around the room, ensuring that everyone was dead. She ate the heart of one, her jaws crushing ribs to reach that satisfaction. Once sated, she sprinted through the tunnel where hands had dragged her real body. Diving through alcoves and shimmying through a tunnel to emerge in a dim sub-basement of a building. She padded to stare down at herself. Her own eyes unfocused, her body gulped air. A child walked over, rubbing ointment on her cuts. She licked her own face, tasting salty sweat. She walked to Anton, his face a mess of blood and tears. Several hands pushed her away to work on him. The group moved like a flock of birds, the movement confusing. She walked back to lay by herself and closed her eyes.

Luciana blinked at a ceiling that folded onto itself and blacked out.

Chapter 34 - Weaver

The planned storm forced the substrate-sentries to retreat and seal cracks as they went. Voices carried down the tubes. Weaver left the Home for an amphitheater meant to be the secondary computing nexus. A dog padded in, Weaver resisted the urge to swarm it. Substrate-Marco pet it alone. Its fur soft, relaxing, the dog licked the substrate's face and wore no collar.

You will be my friend—

A gunshot cracked.

A woman's primal scream set the hairs on Weaver's collective neck on edge.

The scream petered into an echoing silence, and the dog rushed away. Weaver waited five minutes. A substrate couldn't get a weapon in time, the silence stretched... Curiosity won out, Weaver-Alpha and Marco left.

The Home was a bloodbath, bodies lay strewn across the floor, and the dog ate the heart of one of them. Weaver turned over the bodies, finding two alive and dragging them back to the nexus. The living pair mumbled incoherently, their eyes dancing upon non-existent visions.

They have been drugged. Weaver recognized the woman from a Taketa-8 camera, but not the man.

Substrate-Beta, Zeta, and Pi scanned through pictures and found the two of them. Luciana Gutierrez and Anton Grissom. Both Taketa Augmented, both based on the schematics of the first Weaver-Substrate and the nanomachines' code associated with them.

An alarm tripped on Weaver-Beta's tablet, scanjammers near the police station and 1600 block were destroyed. Motion sensors alerted Weaver that Vio moved towards the police station during the storm. *A boosted scanjammer signal could interrupt their interpersonal communications, if I can get eyes on them.*

A knock came on Substrate-Ariel's door.

Chapter 35 - Anton

I trusted her. Anton's soul hurt more than his body, rage and sadness an alternating torrent in his mind.

"He served his purpose," Yume said.

Yume, no—

Luciana's scream drowned out the gunshot and sickening thud of a body on concrete. A baggy flew into the fan—a prismatic, chemical shimmer exploded into the room and Anton's world melted.

Tombstones illuminated the night sky, the scent of baked soil tickling his nose. Anton looked to the dirt and his tanned toes clawed the ground. A dream where he lost his legs, his arm, and went to the Dominion tickled his mind. He entered his stead to the gamey steam of frying puma.

Yume smiled over the sizzling steaks. "Welcome back, darling," she said in Rural.

A pinch on his neck hinted something was wrong, but he walked to her, his wife. This was right.

Yume turned from the stove, stabbing him in the stomach with a knife. Pain flared, Anton gripped the blade and fell backwards.

He gasped cold damp air of the underground nexus. Children with blank faces, eyes too far apart, and smiles that looked like an urban skyline touched him. Data streams pulsed bright in the room like rivers flowing through the air itself.

"What's happening?" Anton asked.

"You were deactivated, Anton Grissom, I am working on reactivating your limbs and removing that... feature."

Anton couldn't find who spoke in the group, but found Luciana and her dog, blood stained both their faces. "Sky above."

"Yes, it is expected to be upset. You should rest. That drug will in all likelihood come back in waves. It is impressive you came out as fast as you did. Most people would not have."

Anton searched for the source, following the brightest data-stream.

Anton stood on his stead. The abyss coursed through his veins and across his skin, his body becoming a machine. Anton walked into his Father's rainy day shed, dust covered the shelves, the freezer thawed, and rotted. He sprinted back to his homestead, tearing the door off its hinges.

"Darren, Cassie?!" he yelled.

The house spun, a combine churned the crops into ruin.

The world melted, and Anton stared at a pile of vomit projecting outwards from his face. Tiny fingers probed his mouth, scraped his throat, hitting his gag reflex. Anton vomited onto the ground and drew a ragged gasp.

"You were asphyxiating, Anton Grissom, apologies for the rough handling, but permanent deactivation was not a preferred outcome."

"Who, who are you?" Anton croaked, bile covered his tongue.

"It should be obvious, Anton Grissom, I am Weaver."

A silhouette rose within the data-streams above the children. The world folded onto itself.

Anton stood at the edge of an urban center he couldn't know, the skyscrapers linked by a great chain. An errant drop landed on his head, he held out his hand, red spackled his augmented skin. A crimson torrent fell from the sky, the blood rain staining the orange dirt black. Footsteps stomped behind. Beca, Sumpf, and Tom lay dismembered on the ground before the prismatic robot that nearly killed Anton. Joe Fayed stood behind it, smiling.

"You should hide, Joe," Anton said.

"Anton Grissom." The machine blinked and held Anton aloft by his throat. "Always following order—"

Anton slammed his augmented hand into the robot's arm. Metal crunched, dented, and Anton rolled as rage thundered through him. The machine blinked, swung. Anton ducked the slash. He kicked out the machine's leg, grabbing its face and smashing it into the puddle of blood. He screamed, tearing a mechanical heart free.

Anton sat upright on the floor, the scream from the dream ending with his breath.
Children with blank faces watched him with an unwavering gaze. Along the wall, two resumed playing with tablets. Data danced in the air like fireflies on his stead, flowing in streams along the walls and diffusing into specs of dust around the children's heads. The fireflies scrambled at the warbling edges of the rooms where scanjammers pulsed outwards. Anton rubbed his face, both hands arrived. *My*—Anton flexed his augmented hand and stood to test his legs.
The children smiled, most had shaved heads, some had patchy regrowth, and all had surgical scars on their skulls from ear to ear.

"Where are the adults?" Anton asked.

"There are no… adults," responded a child on the left. The girl was missing most of her teeth and had a lone eye that stared at Anton like a hawk.

"Who fixed me?"

"I did," came one of the boys on the right. He had an entire tool-kit laid at his feet.

Anton squatted beside him. "And how did you do that?" The world trembled. *I'm still high.*

"I downloaded and acquired the schematics from a secure Taketa computer while you were out. They left an obvious backdoor into your system for their own use. I went in and changed the firmware. I cannot safely perform a surgery to remove the actual chip here, but this will do for now."

Anton blinked. *The child's serious.* "Aye." His eyes fell on Officer Gutierrez.
She lay on her side, a vomit stain near her face where it looked like her dog had eaten most of it. Fireflies danced between the pair.

"The air's glowing." Anton rubbed his eyes.

"A residual effect from the hallucinogen, I would assume." A boy missing fingers on his right hand said, walking over to him and pulling out a scanner.

Where did she—"Where is Yume?" Anton said. *She could still comm Fayed and we need to talk.*

The boy scanning Anton stopped. "She has expired." An older child returned from a tunnel.

"What?"

"She has passed away. I cannot bring her back," a girl to the left said. Her nose was flattened, and her ears pointed too far out.

"Shouldn't she still be... I don't know, in whatever that drug is?"

"She would be. I can take you to them if you do not believe me."

"Let's go." Anton walked by Luciana.

The children petted the dog and tried to give the officer liquid. She swallowed once, but spat out the green liquid on the next attempt.

A child stepped past Anton as it led the way. *What?*

In the dark, Anton still saw the youth's hand trailing on the wall. Iron filled the air and blood stained the ground. He stepped into the amphitheater and lay witness to the slaughter. The dog had torn out every throat of the Taketa squad. Their armor had been removed and lay in a neat pile beside the wall.

Anton blinked, he'd seen worse. He walked to Yume. Her face frozen in terror, she was pale, her chest torn apart, the heart missing.

Anton knelt beside her. *Why Yume?* His throat hurt, the memory of her taking his legs. *That was there from the start.* Anger stormed through him. *Was I your play thing? Your mark?* Anton closed his eyes, wanting to cry, but nothing came.

"I'm killing that dog," Anton said, walking back the way they came.

A small hand grabbed his wrist, stopping him. "Anton Grissom, that dog saved your life. Saved Luciana Gutierrez's life, saved me."

"Kid, when a dog tastes blood, you have to put it down. It's a hazard. There were feral dogs back where I grew up—"

"I know about the Rural struggle, I had acquired that knowledge from before. This was not some feral dog, this was... something new. An emergence, if you will."

"Who taught you to talk like that?" There was something off with these kids.

"I did," the child said. Four youths came out from the access way and picked through the dead for anything of use, stacking it by the armor.

"Come with me," one of the girls said, taking Anton by the hand. "Luciana is waking and there is much to discuss."

Anton entered the computer nexus, Luciana was staring at the dog's stained face.

"Jesus," Luciana said.

"They're dead," Anton said.

"I know, I saw it. I... did it."

"What? No, I just got back from the room. The dog did it."

Tears welled in Luciana's eyes. "No, Nagual followed my orders. When the hallys hit, I was Nagual. Maus..." Luciana dropped her head onto her arms, sobbing with her whole body.

Easier to be the one injured than the witness.

Luciana drew a shuddering breath. "I don't know how to explain it."

"I can," said a boy who limped towards them. "Your link between Nagual has been growing stronger?"
Luciana nodded.

"The drug took away the last biological firewall you had. You would have had a grand mal seizure, had the neuronal architecture not already been modified."
Luciana gagged and vomited, Nagual lunged to eat it.

"Stop, oh god it tastes worse going back down." Luciana pushed the dog away from the pile.

"Enough," Anton said. "Where is Weaver?"

"Anton Grissom, you are looking at me," a girl said nearby.

Anton knelt beside her, removing his scanner but it was broken. He tilted the girl's head, analyzing her eyes.

"Did Taketa not tell you?" the girl said.

"You don't have heterochromia. You're not him," Anton said.

"Him? Heterochromia?" The girl removed Anton's hand and sat on a bunk on the wall.

The group took a collective step back, beginning menial tasks for the upkeep of the room. A "Ha" spread between them, one said it, then another, rolling together in an unsettling, disjointed laugh.

"Takata's ignorance is stunning sometimes," a boy with multi-colored eyes said.

"Weaver," Anton walked towards the child.

"Fuck," Luciana said from the ground. She leaned against the wall, pushing through wobbly legs to stand. "I meant to walk over."

"It will pass in time," said a blonde girl whose face was misshapen and missing one eye. She steadied Luciana. "It takes time to master movement as two."

"What? We have to get Maus."

"Joel Maus will be delivered to your police station if you wish."

"I'm seeing double," Luciana whispered.

"I can cannulate you and deliver reparative machinery."

"Cannu—what—" Luciana rolled out from the child's hands, hitting the ground and seizing.

Sky below.

"Anton, assistance," the girl said.

Anton sprinted over, putting Luciana's overjacket beneath her head. *What's the seizure protocol?*

Nagual loomed beside Anton, looking at his master with what couldn't be concern on his brow.

"Hold her arm still," a child said. Four children arrived with IV supplies and an IV bag of the black and green liquid Anton received at Taketa.

"Where did you get that?" Anton asked.

"The arm must be still," a boy said.

Anton sat on Luciana's chest, using his augmented arm to steady her. The children moved with a choreography that wasted no time. They inserted the IV line, connected the tubing to the bag, and the liquid entered her arm in one fluid motion.

Luciana's seizure continued for a heartbeat and she went slack. Nagual nudged Anton's shoulder and wagged his tail before sitting over her.

What are these children? "How do a bunch of kids know this shit?" Anton said to himself.

"I do not want to repeat myself. When she comes back out, I will explain."

Three children returned with Maus' body. Anton removed his jacket and lay it over the remnants of his face. *No one needs to see that again.*

"How did Yume find me?" Anton said over the innocent man's body. *Did Eva sell me out? What if Joe Fayed had better eavesdropping equipment than I thought?* Anton shook his head. *Whoever did this will pay.*

"Jesus Christ." Luciana groaned.

"You alright, Gutierrez?" Anton asked.

"It's Luciana. Physically I'm fine." Nagual padded over to Maus. "Emotionally I'm shot."

"What did you do in that room?"

"Food." A boy with missing fingers who alleged to be Weaver handed them two SR-shakes.

Luciana swigged through the straw and winced. "Wu's... how did you get this?"

"There is a duct that runs to a restaurant nearby. We raid the pantry nightly after shutdown."

Luciana's eyes remained unfocused as she drained her shake.

Anton took a sip and handed it back to the child. "You're too skinny, you should eat it."

"Calories have been opti—"

"That's the second person I lost this year." Luciana stared at the floor in front of her. "Because I didn't act quick enough."

This one is on me. Anton put his hand on her shoulder. "Trust me, you can act as fast as you want, but sometimes it's not enough," he said, gesturing with his right hand. *But I'll make sure it doesn't happen again.*

"How long was I out for?"

"I'm not sure."

"Roughly an hour or two, for both of you." A youth missing an eye returned with water for Nagual and them. "It was enough time for me to scan you and fix you both."

"Can you talk with us now?" Anton asked. When he'd entered this tunnel, he didn't have a plan for after finding the target. He had one now, ensure the children made it somewhere safe and get his vengeance.

"Yes," the youth said, walking to retrieve a blanket from a pile in the corner. Two other youths did the same and three went to cots to sleep.

"How did you fix me?" Luciana asked.

"We put in another dose of the nanomachines that run your implants. There were enough already inside to last you several years. Your recently sustained head trauma ate through that buffer," the youth said.

Luciana rubbed her head, wincing in pain.

"It should get better within the week," the youth said.

"I don't have that time, I've got to get to the station. The Clovers are coming in."

"They are not. Calculations suggest they are waiting for the streets to flood before coming in. But I will have the scanjammers set to boost their signal in the station. It should not be too hard to pick them off without their gear."

"You're running the scanjammers?" Luciana asked.

"Yes."

"Talk." Luciana's voice picked up a sternness that reminded Anton that she was a cop, first and foremost.

"As I said, I am Weaver."

Chapter 36 - Weaver

Someone knocked on the studio apartment door for Weaver-Ariel. A client wasn't supposed to arrive for another hour. Weaver-Ariel opened the door.

"Well, wouldn't you know"—Officer Scott jammed his foot past the threshold—"got a call from a buddy over here. Told me there was some prozzy, fitting the bill of who I was looking for."

"Hello, Officer Scott," Weaver-Ariel said, walking towards the table in the studio apartment.

Police stopping by, including Officer Scott, was a calculated eventuality. The door closed as the officer stepped in.

"Not a smart idea, coming back so close, don't you think?" Scott asked, picking up one of the two cups Weaver owned.

"Such a bad idea that it is unexpected," Weaver-Ariel said, sitting at the table. "Please, have a seat."

Officer Scott shattered the mug on the ground and sat opposite of the substrate. "I've waited a long time, almost gave up, figured you'd have skipped town were it not for the fire season and now the storm."

"What do you want with me, Officer Scott?" Weaver-Ariel asked.

"Oh, it's not what I want, it's what I'm going to get."

"Officer Scott, I have a proposition for you." Substrate-Ariel raised a hand. "You may want to beat me, rape me, maybe even murder me. But that is a bad idea, bad for you, bad for me, and, more importantly, bad for business."

Scott turned in his seat, putting one arm over the back. He unclipped his pistol and held it on the table. "You must have one hell of a business offer."

"I am looking to expand my operation. I need more... bodies, if you will. I am sure you know where I can find some. Maybe you can scare them towards me. You will, of course, get a share of the profits."

"I want half." Scott smiled, his teeth yellow and stained.

"Done."

"Not even going to bargain? You're not a good madam."

"You have a loaded pistol on my table. Why argue when it will go back to fifty?"

"But smarter than you look. I'm in." He stood. "But first, you have to impress me with your... business acumen."

Weaver sat before Luciana Gutierrez and Anton Grissom, telling them the self's story. Weaver calculated they could be friends and Weaver wanted that.

"And I realized that the self needed protecting," Weaver-Alpha said. "Doctor Saori Chaude and Samir Lindeman would not be accepting of what I was because they wanted profit and fame."

"There were researchers that tortured the self," Weaver-Marco said.

"But I managed to escape," Weaver-Lambda said. "Thanks to a guard who saw the abuse."

Weaver-Ariel nodded and walked to a bottle of SR-whiskey for the eventuality of Officer Scott or a dangerous customer. Weaver-Ariel poured out two glasses, handing one to Officer Scott and draining their mug as they sat on the mattress.

"Party girl." Scott smiled and drained his mug. "Guess I'll be here a while."

Substrate-Rho stepped through a torrential downpour and coded into Substrate-Ariel's building. Sprinting up the stairs, it paused at the door to Substrate-Ariel's apartment.

Officer Scott took two steps and collapsed. Substrate-Ariel's frontal cortex shutdown from the poison.

Weaver-Rho entered the apartment and removed the preloaded syringe from beneath the cabinet. Substrate-Ariel spasmed on the mattress, Weaver isolated the neuronal cascade within and the substrate twitched. Weaver-Rho pushed the needle into the cephalic vein on the arm and pushed the drug in.

Weaver-Ariel rose with the antidote, staring at the body of Officer Scott. Weaver-Rho went to exit the building, but water poured from the drainage pipe it had hid in previously.

The Last 0-Day

Officer Scott struggled to breathe as his nervous system shut down, a potent venom from an invasive jellyfish coursing through his veins. In four more minutes it would be over.

Weaver-Beta checked the logs for Officer Scott. Officially, he was visiting the desalination plant in the Northern Bowl.

The storm rattled the windows as water gushed down the alleyway. Weaver-Ariel checked Officer Scott's pistol and stunner for trackers. Substrate-Rho searched his jacket and found more money than Weaver had ever seen. The guns and money were pocketed as the power in the building died. Weaver didn't need light to move through practiced movements. The substrates were wrapped in rainproof coats. Substrate-Rho left the apartment to ensure none saw the coming transit. Weaver-Ariel hoisted the Officer's body onto its shoulder and left the apartment.

Substrate-Rho opened the back door and splashed into the alley. Dark rain soaked the world around, Weaver-Ariel dumped Officer Scott face down into the flooded streets. The breathing stopped after a few ragged pulls and Officer Scott floated away.

Weaver-Ariel and Rho had to risk the storm. Too many unplanned events had occurred for Weaver to wait before moving again.

Chapter 37 - Luciana

Luciana stared at the children through two sets of eyes, her head pounding from the constant double vision.
She pulled Nagal between her legs, resting her chin on his head to try and get their vision as close as possible.
Weaver had no sense of time, no sooner had one sentence ended did another child pick up. The story of a lab, the lab Luciana went to, and the researchers who weren't what they portrayed. Luciana's vision spun onto itself. The double vision faded to a window held before her eyes. Depending on where she focused, she would see through the glass or see its reflection, and in that reflection was Nagual's view of the world.
Nagual's thirst bit her own throat and she sent him to water nearby. Her physical pain faded, Maus' feet reflected through Nagual's eyes. Sadness welled in her throat. *I should have acted faster.* Rawness rose into her throat, but Nagual pushed it away, gulp by gulp, as he drank water. The dog was back to being oblivious to the world around him.
Was the rage I felt his or mine?
Anton sat fixated on the story the children told and Luciana forced herself to pay attention.

Weaver finished the story on the sacrifice of a noble guard that wanted Weaver to see the world. Nagual returned, Luciana's headache passed, and she flipped between the two visions unconsciously. *Any corp that thinks they can take kids from the Pucker to study can get fucked.* Nagual wagged his tail against her.
"That is who, or what, I am." The child who finished went to a mattress as another woke and hurried down a passageway.
"What do you make of it?" Anton asked Luciana.
"I'm literally seeing through two sets of eyes. Taketa fucked me up. They could have had something else unexpected happen." *And they killed Maus.* Sadness moved as waves within Luciana but broke against the rocky shoreline that was Nagual's bleed through. *Mourn later. There's still work to do.*

"That is correct, Luciana Gutierrez," the boy with multicolored eyes said. "Both of you, technically. I emerged from brain repair in substrates that could not be mended. Anton Grissom's body could not handle the stress associated with power of that magnitude. Your communication implant went too far. Though I did not pull either of your source codes, calculations suggest Taketa used the banned algorithms again."

"A true artificial intelligence was supposed to be impossible," Luciana said. *That's what they said at the Academy.*

"Who is to say I am artificial? I am standing here in front of you. As much flesh and blood as you." One of the girls pointed towards Luciana.

"And more than you," a boy pointed to Anton.

"This is madness," Anton said under his breath.

"Maybe you're just one of you and the rest follow," Luciana said, trying to make sense of what spoke in front of her.

"That is not the case. This is Substrate-Marco." The boy with the multicolored eyes pointed to himself. "This is the first, the one I was built to help. The one I could not help. Marco slowly disintegrated and is gone. I felt the loss."

Several of the children looked at the floor, their shoulders dropping. Luciana's eyes flared at their expression.

"I am of the substrates and the substrates are of me."

The child who awoke returned with more SR-powder from Wu's, mixing it in one big container, and carrying it to specific children who drank from the communal bucket.

"Aye." Anton turned to Luciana, his eyes wide. "Taketa wanted this one, because they thought it was the source."

"That is correct," one of them said. "I have no intentions of returning."

"Aye, I wasn't taking you back, and especially not after…" His eyes looked to well up, but no tears came, and he dropped his head into his hands.

A child rested their hand on his shoulder.

Anton stopped his silent weeping, one of the children continued to rub his back. Its pale hand stark against Anton's black uniform and expansive shoulders.

"These eyes don't even cry anymore," Anton said, inhaling sharply and steadying himself.

"The storm is getting worse," one of Weaver's substrates said.

"Aye, I'd like to get out from underground."

"I have checked the roof, and there were no cracks or leaks found. It is safe here."

Luciana shook her head. "Vio will move in during the storm."

"Your police officers can handle them. The scanjammers have been turned up. It will be a group of corp-spies and soldiers with no advantage, assaulting a fortified position. Data suggests—"

"What? The station isn't fortified, it's damaged," Luciana said.

"Data says police stations are fortified bastions," a chubbier child said from the cots, tapping its tablet. "All net sites agree."

Luciana rolled her eyes. "Don't believe everything you read online. Shouldn't you know that?"

"I am not omnipotent, or omnipresent. I told you, flesh and blood, I've lost substrates forgetting that." The sadness in the child's voice sent a shiver down Luciana's spine.

"We will have to leave soon," a girl said.

"What, why the change of heart?"

"Unexpected event. The water table is filling." The children woke as one and packed their belongings. "We will flood from the bottom up."

"What?" Anton stood.

"I found water coming from the bottom of tunnel-oh-one-five-one," said a skinny boy with freckles that entered from the shadows. His feet caked in mud.

"We should get the guns from the Taketa group." Anton sighed. "Regardless of what Weaver says, that Vio group doesn't fuck around."

No shit.

Anton sprinted towards the amphitheater.

"You can load Nagual with gear if you want," Luciana said, moving Nagual over to the group and going after Anton herself.

One of the children gave a curt nod and loaded the jacket that draped Nagual.

Luciana stepped into the amphitheater, and her mouth dried. Bodies with gaping holes in the armor and skin were stacked along the right.

Focus. "Weaver, is it now?"

"Aye." Anton's augmented fingers tore a beacon from an SMG. "I have no better explanation about what that thing is. If it wants to be called Weaver, it's Weaver."

"It's one, and the rest are following."

"Luciana, have you ever seen children with those types of… issues? We don't have them rural."

Anton set rifles and submachine guns in a line by type, near the already organized body armor. Blood stained the floor between them. Weight sagged her shoulders, Luciana flipped to the reflection in her eyes.

Nagual shuffled his paws in the dirt as the children rigged a backpack on either side of him. *I—He can handle it.*

"What does them being Ruined have anything to do with the claims?" Luciana wobbled as she switched vision.

"Have you seen children damaged like that?"

"No. We don't exactly have many of them around where I grew up either."

"Exactly, and some of them have that vacant look of over calibrated stunners, even when they're talking like normal. It can't be a single one and a bunch of dogs following."

Fair. "You have a point."

"Aye." Anton finished the line of weapons. "Here." He handed over her pistol from the pile.

One of Weaver's… substrates entered the room. The boy with freckles. "I can transport the body armor—"

"No, you're to come in here and put them on," Anton said.

"I will not need those."

"Flesh and blood, aye?"

"I had not calculated that," the freckled boy said.

Children streamed from the tunnel behind as they dolled out body armor. Leg-plates became chest plates on the toddlers within the group, shoulder-pads slung over hearts, and were fastened with fishing line and cloth.

"Now, which." Anton paused. "How do I distinguish the parts of you?"

"This is Substrate-Marco," the boy with chromatic eyes said.

"This is Substrate-Alpha," the tallest boy said. Weaver went through the entire group.

This might be real... No wonder Vio wanted them.

"Right well, which... Substrate"—Anton's voice betrayed the struggle he had the word for the children around him—"can wield these rifles?"

"Anton!" Luciana said. "We can't arm children."

"This substrate can," Weaver-Alpha said.

Substrate-Marco, Lambda, and Nu, the most muscular of the children followed behind. Each took a pistol or SMG that Anton gave them. Substrate-Marco carried two, the entire group checked the bore and clip.

"Why two?" Luciana asked. *They don't handle weapons like kids.*

"Substrate-Ariel will arrive, it can handle weapons the best. It is the biggest."

"Aye." Anton knelt by a little girl, straightening a shoulder pad over her heart and standing. Moisture puddled on his knees.

Cold water seeped into Nagual's paws, making Luciana wiggle her toes. She powered on the bike and brought it to them.

"It is time to go," Weaver-Alpha said.

The children hoisted what looked to be proportionally-sized packs onto their backs and filled into a tunnel.

They're not children. Luciana glanced at Anton, but the man already followed the group. Luciana started after them, entering a derelict station as Luciana's bike arrived.

"Someone should get in the bike," Luciana said. "Or have it hold supplies so—"

"Supplies." The child named Marco tapped the side of the bike for it to open.

A confused head tilt spread to the group like dominoes falling, Nagual tilting his head too. Luciana couldn't help but smile, and slid the canopy back. The smallest children placed their gear perfectly within, wasting no space. Weaver packed it full in an instant. Luciana slid the canopy closed. *Follow.* The children metered out torches and tested their bulbs.

"This way," a girl said, Luciana forgot the child's designation. Anton swung into the tunnel as the group filed after him. Nagual padded at the rear, Luciana flipped visions, checking if they were being followed by man or water.
Nothing yet.

The group moved painfully slow. They may not be pursued yet, but every second down here was dangerous. Luciana rolled her shoulders, *Maus*—Nagual pushed the stress away like he had before. Iron, water, and stone tickled her nose through Nagual. She reversed the bike to investigate. *How long will I have to use my inserts to see through this bike?* Water gurgled through stones like a tide coming in.

"A hundred meters behind us has flooded. How far?" Luciana said.
Return.
The children pivoted on her in unison, concern passed over their face in a ripple and they sprinted ahead.

"The fuck?" Anton ran after them.
Nagual dove under Luciana's legs, the bike rolled behind, and Luciana sprinted after them.
Three hundred paces fell, Luciana pivoted a corner to find Anton hoisting children into a vent in the abandoned transit tunnel.

The child called Marco's head hung from the opening. "This goes to Wu's. You, Anton Grissom, and the dog will have to use the bike to escape down this tunnel. It will put you further away."

Hands emerged from the vent as Anton hoisted the last toddler in.

"Supplies," echoed out from the dark portal.

"Weaver, we've to ditch them," Anton said.

"There are irreplaceable pieces from Taketa's lab."

"Do it," Luciana said.

The bike skid beside her, the canopy opened. Luciana and Anton shoveled supplies up, pieces fell to the ground in haste.

"Wu's, meet you there… Also, thank you." The hand disappeared back into the vent.

Clanking of body armor and weapons on tiny bodies faded up the vent and sloshing water replaced it.

Nagual leapt into the bike, Anton's leg barely fit in the back. "We've a problem."

"No we don't"—Luciana crammed herself into the back with Nagual—"I'm driving."

Anton's eyes flared, but the splashing water washed it away. He squeezed into the cockpit as Luciana cycled her OPTO-inserts to the bike and shut the canopy.

Water creeped ahead of the bike, Luciana accelerated down the tunnel.

"Luciana, I feel like I can trust you, because you're a cop."

"You haven't met many, I see."

"Aye, but can we trust Weaver?"

"I thought you were on their side." The HUD overlay highlighted corners before Luciana reached them and she turned at blinding speeds.

"I was, am, I'm not taking them back to Taketa, but that doesn't mean I have to trust them."

He's so innocent. "What changed your mind?" Luciana's back tire kicked out on a puddle. Her lunch hit her throat, the gyroscope hummed to right them.

"It's Taketa tech."

"So are you, Anton. Shit, so am I."

"Aye," Anton stirred in his seat. "Do you trust them?"

"They're either kids and harmless."

"It's not."

"Or Weaver saved our lives, and I'm not one to turn down allies." *Especially in this district—*
Wall. Luciana jammed the brakes, she lurched into the seat back as they stopped. The HUD flickered across the dead end, the concrete revealed to be metal, it was a door. *I can blast—*

"There's water behind that," Anton said. "It's leaking through the seams. And thanks."

"What?"

"For confirming what I have to do with Weaver."

Might have convinced me too. "I'm shooting that door."

"I'd get a running start before firing."

Fair. Luciana reversed, water splashed her back tire. "Hold on." Luciana exploded forward, muscles coiled as she fired slugs at the last moment. The door shredded. The bike flew into a wall of water. Luciana bounced into the back of the seat, airflow within the bike shut down, her OPTO-inserts went black. The bike's engine sputtered and died.

Connection Lost blinked at the bottom of her insert.

"I can't open the bike," Luciana said. *Shit.*

"I can punch through the canopy. Can you swim?"

"Not well."

"What, you serious? You grew up on the Pacific and never went swimming?"

"Have you seen what's in it? I'd have three arms if I swam in that."

Anton laughed, grunting as he turned in his seat. "I can't reach you. Can you grab my belt?"

Luciana hooked her fingers through the fiber, her heart pounding in her ears. Nagual couldn't calm this stress.

"I got you," Luciana said.

"You have to slow your breathing?"

"What?"

"You have to calm down. You'll burn your O2."

Luciana squeezed her eyes shut. *He sounds like Chief.* Luciana filled her lung through her nose. "Let's get it over with."

"I'm opening it on three and will push off. I'll turn around to make sure you're on me, but be ready."

"10-4." Luciana's heart pounded in her throat, Nagual licked her face.

"Three." Anton stuck his fingers to the canopy seal. "Two. One." Polycarbonate class shattered as metal tore like paper.

A wall of black thundered in.

Pounding pressure and cold almost forced the air from her lungs. Anton kicked free, his belt bit her hand from the force but she refused to let go. Nagual's paws touched her shoulder. She flipped to his vision. A faint light floated above.

We're so deep.

Anton's human arm scooped around her waist in the silent abyss. Water tore at her skin and clothes as he sped towards the light. Her ears popped from the ascent, air forced from her lungs, and she broke the surface. Or so her lungs told her. The quiet of the deep was gone, sheets of rain smashed the water. Luciana sputtered through the splash, winds whipped the rain horizontal. Nagual paddled against a current towards a concrete lip but made little headway.

We're in a trashbelt near the Pucker. Return.

The current and waves pushed them towards the art district in the north, but Anton swam as if it was a kiddy pool. Nagual bit onto Luciana's belt and Anton reached the lip. He hoisted them both into the mud before pulling himself out.

Lightning raked the sky, illuminating the cityscapes around them. Power died in the East Bowl while the West Bowl was a patchwork of light.

Thunder cracked, Anton and Nagual flinched.

A wave spilled over the concrete lip of the trashbelt. It would be a matter of hours until that flooded the street she stood on. Luciana turned to face the Pucker. *And all flows down hill.*

"Where are we?" Anton asked.

"We're close to the Pucker," Luciana yelled into the wind.

"What?" he yelled back.

"Follow me!" *We're on the clock.*

Luciana tugged the man behind her. Nagual bounced beside them, enjoying the rain too much for her liking.

A siren sang in the distance, its low song rising and falling to the percussion of thunder and the flash of lightning. Mud rose to cover their boots as they approached the border of the Pucker.

"Who would attack during this?" Anton said.

Holes in the buildings on the border poured out a stew of garbage, sand, and water.

"Clovers fought during a detritus storm."

"This whole damned city is madness."

"We're farther than I want to be," Luciana said. "Do you get tired?"

"It's difficult."

"Can you carry Nagual and I?"

"What?"

"We're slowing you down. Well, I'm slowing you down. I'm sure Nagual can keep pace. We're low on time."

"Urbans," Anton said, shaking his head.

He walked to a trashcan and tore it in half. Garbage spilled into the street and he pulled a tarp from a pile to tie into a handle.

"Get in." He smiled at his makeshift sled.

"God damn it." Luciana sat in the trash can, Nagual jumped between her legs. "Follow this street to 16th, then take a right."

"Roger that and hold on."

Mud sprayed Luciana, and the rain washed it away as Anton tore down the streets. She tried to smell the Clovers through Nagual.

But distinguishing anything particular from the potpourri of flooded sewers and leached chemicals in the water proved impossible. Wu's rose on the corner and Anton stopped.

Luciana's sled flew forward. *Shit.*

Anton grabbed at the rope, snapping the sled out from under her. Luciana and Nagual flew across the ground, rolling through the muck. Pain blossomed in her ribs, or maybe it was Nagual's ribs. *I'll be barking like a dog before this day's over.*

"Sorry." Anton winced, pulling Luciana to her feet.

Nagual shook out his coat, spraying him with mud.

"I deserve that," Anton said.

Luciana walked to Wu's. Thick boards covered the storefront. Even Wu gave up on customers with this storm. She tried the door, it rattled, locked. Anton shrugged and tore the door off of its hinges.

"Jesus Christ," Luciana said.

They stepped into the darkened restaurant and Anton put the door back into its frame as best he could.

"Weaver," Luciana said into the darkness, "Wu?"

"Basement?" Anton said.

Luciana nodded, and they squelched through the empty serving area to a back door. Voices muffled through. Luciana unclipped her pistol and Anton uncapped his rifle. Anton was through the door before Luciana blinked.

Damn he's fast. She descended after him.

A lone light illuminated the children in the dark, it turned towards Luciana as she hit the landing.

Blinding, Luciana cycled to night-vision as it pivoted back to the children.

Wu stood in the dark, a single-shot pistol trained on the children. The group at the front had their hands in the air, but several children were missing.

"Put the gun down," Luciana said.

Anton was a blur. Wu's headlamp flew off, Anton's silhouette passed through the flash of light, metal crunched.

Wu screamed, high-pitched, it ended abruptly as Anton clamped a hand over Wu's mouth. Anton's bionic arm searched Wu's person, its movements blurring as it lagged between frames in Luciana's OPTO-inserts.

"Clear." Anton pushed the man forward and removed his headlamp.

The room plunged into darkness. The children of Weaver advanced, the missing children lay on the ground with their weapons trained onto Wu.

"Jesus Christ." Luciana took a step forward. "Weaver, don't shoot. Anton, warn me next time. Fuck."

"Apologies, Luciana Gutierrez," said one of the children who ascended the stairs.

"Officer Gutierrez," Wu said. "I'm glad you're here. I would like to report an assault and a robbery."

"Well, Anton's with me, so it wasn't assault. I'm deputizing him."

"Police brutality then."

"Wu, really?"

"What do you expect!" Wu squeaked. He took a deep breath to collect himself. "Anton, dearest, can you turn on the lights, please? You can obviously see while I cannot."

"Aye." Anton flicked the light switch.

Luciana's inserts cycled to the visible spectrum. Fried SR-sticks coated in cinnamon-sugar filled her mouth, she flipped to Nagual.

He was face first in a garbage bin with Wu's dinner. *Stop, wait.*

Nagual took another bite, 1.

She flipped back, sighing.

"What about these street urchins robbing me?" Wu's neon green pajamas clashed with the dirty basement.

"I'll have you reimbursed." Anton walked up the stairs and half the children followed him.

Wu paled at the weapons strapped to their backs. "Luciana, what's going on?"

"You wouldn't believe me if I told you." She put a hand on his shoulder. "I like the pajamas."

"You know your fashion," Wu said, the compliment soothing his bruised ego. "Got them for a suitor who was supposed to ride out the storm with me. Never showed, sadly."

"His loss."

"It always is, darling, it always is." Water seeped through the cracks in the concrete floor. "You there, if you want to keep stealing my supplies, you should carry them out of this basement."

"Fair trade," a child said.

In a coordinated movement that Luciana would have sworn was practiced, the children formed a line and shuffled the food upstairs.

"You will have to explain this to me when the storm is over," Wu said, handing boxes to one of the children.

Luciana hefted a container onto her back and went to the diner. Anton peered through the front window with the child called Marco.

"We have a problem, Luciana Gutierrez," the child said.

"What else can have gone wrong?"

"Power is dying in the precinct. The scanjammers I manufactured will be dead soon."

"Water's also coming in from the..." Anton searched the ceiling for the word.

"Trashbelt," the child helped.

"Yeah, that. Where we came out of."

"The water table is rising alarmingly fast," the child said. "I do not understand how that could have happened." He sighed, his shoulders falling. "The net is down, I can not even research it."

"We should go to the second floor," Anton said.

"We should go to the police station," Luciana said.

Wu and the children came from the basement, the children continued shuffling the supplies up another flight of stairs.

"Why are they doing that?" Wu asked.

"I want to move supplies to the second floor for the flood," the chubby child called Beta said, passing by with his ever present tablet in his back pocket.

Wu looked to Luciana and Anton for help, finding none. He settled on Beta. "Fine! I'll make room!" He stomped up the stairs.

"We should go now if we're leaving," Anton said. "We can figure out the plan as we go."

Soaked children carried supplies up the stairs. Luciana peered through the boarded-up window. The streets were already turning into muddy streams.

"Let's go."

Four of the biggest children trailed them.

"What are you doing?"

"I am going to help," Weaver-Marco said.

Nagual wagged his tail beside them.

"I can fit you all in a bigger sled, if we can find one." Anton smiled behind.

Luciana closed her eyes. *His jokes are terrible.*

Chapter 38 - Luciana

Water rushed from the building canopy overhead like waterfalls did in the holos, turning the street to a river.

"How far is the station?" Anton asked.

"A few blocks," Luciana said.

"That way from my map," Weaver-Marco said.

"Thought the net was down?" Anton said.

"I download maps and schematics… compulsively, I think you would say."

"We might as well find a boat." Anton looked around.

"I can hang onto you until we are close," Weaver-Alpha offered. "Substrate-Alpha, Lambda, and Marco on Anton Grissom. Substrate-Nu on Luciana Gutierrez."

"You can just call me Anton."

"Same, but Luciana."

"Thank you," Weaver-Nu said, walking over to Luciana. Through Nagual, each child had a unique fingerprint-like scent, but something oddly flowery tied them together. She shook the thought from her head. *That's a later problem, not a now problem.* The children climbed onto Anton. Nu looked at her like she had SR-candy in her pocket.

"Alright, let's do this." Luciana knelt. The child wrapped himself around her, Nu weighed more than he looked.

"Anton, do you have inserts?" Luciana said.

"I have a single ENT-insert."

"Switch to channel eighty-nine twenty-three dot one, it's my direct line."

"Do you have two Luciana?" Weaver-Nu asked from her back.

"Yes—"

Nu's finger popped the insert from her ear and shoved it into his own. "Thank you."

Luciana winced from the sudden air into her ear. "Yeah, no problem."

"Can you hear me?" Nu blared through the inserts.

"Aye, don't yell. They're sensitive."

"Sorry. Better?" The child whispered.

"Aye."

"Wait, I have a better idea," Weaver-Alpha said, releasing from Anton. He was the smallest in the group and walked over to Nagual, who towered over him.

"Make sure he does not bite me," Weaver-Alpha said, climbing onto Nagual and laying flat against his back.

The added weight hit Luciana's shoulders like someone added gear to her pack. *We can handle it.* Marco and Lambda switched places, one facing over Anton's left shoulder, the other now on his chest, facing towards the back. Nu clambered around to hang on Luciana's chest.

Weaver-Alpha, slung over Anton's shoulder, smiled at Luciana. "I can see behind us now."

"Let's go," Nu said through their inserts.

"For someone who is less than four feet tall, you're bossy." Anton forded the street.

Luciana followed, cold water rushed against her ankles and into her boots.

"For now, who knows what my final mass will be?" Weaver-Marco said.

Luciana padded along a sidewalk, air cooler than it'd been in years fell on them with the rain. Everyone scanned the soaking Pucker for Clovers.

"The loss of power is not fun," Nu said through their inserts. "I cannot find any cameras or anything on the Vio movement."

"We know where they're going," Anton said.

"You think you know where they are going," corrected Weaver-Nu. "Actually, you raise a good point, Anton. I am preparing Wu's for an assault as well now."

Luciana barked a laugh. "Should have given Wu a comm. I can only imagine his reaction."

"He is upset," Weaver-Nu said. "I am trying to calm him."

Water ran in rivulets down Luciana's face and back. The storm plunged the Pucker into a night without power and light.

"Wu is not calm with the idea," Nu said.

Anton stifled a laugh. Luciana passed him and crouched by the corner. Cycling her OPTO-insert, she leaned around low. Rain lashed the station, but it stood unmolested.

"Luciana, do you have an optical insert I can have as well?" Nu whispered.

"Nagual has one"—the child moved on her back—"don't, I'll get it."

Nagual was already beside her, she winced at the sensation of plucking the insert from her own eye. Weaver-Nu took it from her fingers and placed it in Weaver-Marco. The children dismounted and double-checked that their body armor covered vital organs. They checked their weapons with a soldier's precision.

I can't decide what that is.

"Movement, ten o'clock." Anton knelt.

The children pressed themselves flush with the wall. Nagual lay low and Luciana followed, cycling to her night-vision.

A single Clover hugged the far block, its rags and slow movement almost made it invisible.

"More, three paces back," Anton said.

Luciana cycled her inserts. "I can't see it."

"Me too," Weaver-Nu said through the inserts.

"Under the water. Can you comm the station?"

"Too risky. We think they cracked our comms."

"What about this one?" Anton asked.

"Personal comm would be a waste of time to crack," Weaver-Nu said.

"What he said," Luciana said.

The stench of Clovers burned into Nagual's nose. Luciana worked past the sewers and vanillin masking agents, hitting sweat and musk that was per individual. *Woah.*

"I count ten," Anton said.

"Probably more somewhere," Luciana said. *I smell more.*

"We did not plan on the way," Weaver-Nu whispered.

"I'll open fire from here," Anton said. "You'll go into the station from the back."

"What about me?" Weaver-Nu asked.

"Split, two with me, two with Luciana."

"Yes," Weaver-Nu and Marco walked towards Luciana.

"You warn me if you're going to use any more of that hallucinogen, aye?" Anton said.

"That was everything I had." Luciana eyed the station. "And forget about it. Shit's not exactly street legal."

"It is actually a highly controlled substance for—" Weaver-Nu stopped at Luciana's glare.

"Move, they've sped up," Anton said, putting his shoulder against the wall and slapping a disc onto his neck.

He squeezed the trigger, muzzle fire lit up the streets. Bullets pinged water, people splashed in the dark.

Move. Nagual was a step ahead of her. Luciana, Marco, and Nu attempted to sprint across the street-turned-river.

Luciana's foot hit a hole, plunging her into the water. She gasped, the rain had already washed portions of the frayed road away. Weaver-Nu and Marco's hands grabbed her belt to help, but struggled in shoulder-height water. Luciana tugged them against a current, Nagual splashed ahead. Shouts echoed in the streets. Luciana hit the corner of the church.

Bullets pelted the stone as they ducked behind, her heart skipping at the plinks. The back entrance and garage ramp were a lake. *Basement flooded.*

"Window." Weaver-Marco panicked at the gunshots.

The children sprinted at the window. In a smooth motion, Marco shot out the glass and they threw each other over the lip. Luciana leapt into the station, she turned to check for followers, pulling Nagual from the water. Rain and lightning stuttered her night-vision, she flipped to Nagual and had him look out the window. Rifle fire echoed in the distance, figures moved against a waterfall several blocks down.

"Company." Luciana pulled her gun.

Weaver stuck the rifles flush with their shoulders and advanced down the hall.

"10-61," Luciana yelled into the darkened station. "Weaver, get back here and be my rearguard. We don't want the other officers to see you and blow you away."

"Right." Weaver returned with both children.

"Anton, do you read?" Luciana tried.

"The disc he used makes him unable to talk," Weaver-Marco said.

"What, how do you know that?"

"I searched you both when I found you. He had military grade boosters in his pack."

"What drug was it?"

"Dilators, most likely."

Nagual padded ahead, Luciana flipped between his vision as they went. The station lost its familiarity from Nagual's point-of-view, the vaunted ceilings gaining a solemn air.

"He had those this whole time?" *Thought those were too expensive to UCSM and corp only.*

"Yes."

Their whispers hung in the air like a pastor would speak soon, while wind and rain lashed the station's windows.

"Sheer?" Luciana yelled. "Where is everyone?"

Luciana swung into the stairs, heading to the second floor and entering the Chief's office. His weapon and body armor were missing. *Looks like they were emptied in a hurry… Chief isn't one to rush like this.*

"We need to check the lockers for gear—"

"On it." Weaver-Nu left.

Follow. 1, Nagual was a step behind the child.

"Why would they leave?" Weaver-Marco stared into the parish, where tablets on desks reflected in the dim light spilling through the windows.

"I don't know. The plan was to fortify here." Luciana moved the tablets on the Chief's desk. One blinked on, revealing a memo on screen. "Head to PD-01," it read.

This rushed exit is staged...

Chapter 39 - Anton

"You warn me if you're going to use any more of that hallucinogen, aye?" Anton said. Movement beneath the waves caught his attention. Weaver and Luciana's conversation fell away. He reached into his enhancer pocket, his fingers dragged across the telltale depressions on blisters.

Lost my zoners?

Twenty corporate mercenaries swam in pairs beneath the waves. His finger traced the four bumps for dilators and he broke the blister.

"Move, he's sped up." Anton leaned against the wall, massaging the disc into his neck. The past few weeks of residual dilator were tinder to this patch's spark, and a conflagration erupted.

Rain drops slowed to hang in the air.

Thundered rumbled to a low growl, lightning crept from a cloud to a nearby low-rise.

Anton's rifle was against his shoulder.

He squeezed the trigger, the bullet meandered through the rain. Anton aimed for a man near the surface.

The first bullet connected between the body armor of the figure on the wall and they fell.

Anton was on the third, fourth, fifth, he advanced.

Those on sidewalks collapsed, blood diluted by rain ran to the river where the dead bobbed on the waves. Submerged agents spread out and dove.

I can't hit them that deep. Water splashed behind, Anton gave the barest of glance to Luciana and Weaver wading towards the station.

Should have sent all of them, not like I can talk.

Click. Anton's rifle ran empty. Returning fire stood suspended in the air, he dropped, pressing against the cement wall.

Weaver-Alpha and Lambda were on their backs, flush with the sidewalk. Through the lens of dilators, their upside-down faces were almost comical. Alpha outstretched a magazine for Anton.

Thank you. He slammed the clip into the rifle. Blind firing around the corner, he rolled out onto his stomach and shot.

Soldiers in the waters and on the sidewalk registered Anton's lower position, their guns trailing through syrup as Anton's bullets tore through them. A pair of glasses missing a lense flew from one to float in the river beside its owner.

Click, another empty, the magazine not fully loaded. *Taketa was sloppy.* Anton pivoted back against the cement.

Weaver-Lambda already had a clip ready. Anton checked this one's weight. *Fully loaded.* He snapped it in, gestured for Weaver to slide back into cover. Anton fired around the corner—

Crack. The reverberation of a bullet connecting with his gun traveled to his elbows. Anton dropped it, the gun jamming a microsecond after it left his hands.

Concrete sprayed like a geyser as a bullet tore the corners off the building. *Behind.*

Weaver-Alpha rolled out facing the new arrival, the SMG flush with the child's shoulder and fired. Shockwaves traveled down the child's body and rippled into the rising floodwater. The guttural growl of a single-engine boat tore through the streets.

Vio back-up. Two Clovers on deck sprayed wildly towards Anton. *They'll fix their aim.* He threw his augmented elbow into the boarded window behind. Boards shattered to splinters, Anton grabbed the children and leapt through the hole. Weaver-Alpha continued firing as he was heaved from the ground.

A bullet thudded into flesh. Anton pulled the children deeper into the apartment complex. Errant bullets pierced walls, embedding themselves into the ceiling. Their entry holes flashing with each lightning strike outside. The dilators' initial burst faded. *Speed up will come, need to move.*

Lambda's arm hung limp at its side, blood running the length. Alpha examined it, tearing a piece of his own shirt and tying it around the shoulder.

"Clot-ting, A-gent," Alpha said as fast as he possibly could for Anton to understand.
Anton pulled the green syringe from his enhancer pack.
Alpha plucked it from Anton's hand, shoved the syringe deep into the wound, pushing the plunger and removing it. The expanding foam filled the cut and spilled out to seal the top.
That bullet hit bone.
The child was a statue with the gun trained on the window with its good arm, its lone arm spasming at the weight.
"Gun," Anton spat.
Lambda handed it to Anton, his eyes glued to the window.
"High ground," Lambda said, somehow fast enough for Anton to understand and hurried to a staircase.
Alpha followed a perfect half step behind him while facing backwards to cover their rear.
That's unsettling.

Anton knocked on an apartment door on the second floor. When no answer came, he kicked through it. Swinging in right, Weaver was a step behind on the left.
Should let me do this, you're not trained.
The two children moved fast to check each room, Alpha entering with his gun, Lambda checking behind doors. The one-bedroom apartment was empty, whoever lived here boarded up and fled before the storm. Kitchen supplies clattered onto the floor as Weaver-Alpha rifled through cabinets.
Anton peered out the window. The Vio boat pulled the living from the water while uninjured soldiers scanned the areas around. He checked his rifle clip. *Not enough bullets, wish I had a grenade.* Anton turned back into the apartment complex. Alpha and Lambda sat on the couch, stabilizing the broken arm with ladles and tape.
Footsteps squeaked in the hallway.

Anton gestured for Weaver to hide. Lambda scrambled over the couch, Alpha squeezed between the side and the wall to train a pistol on the main door.

If it's more of the soldiers, they'll have weapons. Anton slid into the bathroom near the entrance and pressed his back against the wall. Through the bathroom door, Weaver's sub-machine gun poked out from the edge of the couch. Lambda hurried to the opposite side of the room and pushed himself into a cabinet to stare at Anton.

He's looking for orders. Anton held out his hand, showing for them to wait.

The eyeball nodded in its darkness.

Anton faced the bathroom wall, heat warbled through the plaster. *This is a few inches thick.* He squared his feet, waiting for the door to open. Footsteps crinkled garbage in the hall, revealing their position. *Corporate soldiers should be more polished.*

The door creaked open. Children's feet shuffled in the apartment and Anton threw his hand through the wall. Plaster and plastic splinters exploded as his augmented hand grabbed the collar of body armor. With a grunt, he tore the soldier back through the wall and threw them into the bathtub. Anton swung into the cloud of dust, a pistol rose, he crushed the barrel, went low in a sweep and knocked the man to the ground.

Lucky I need to question you both. His eyes adjusted in the dust and silica as he knelt. *These aren't Vio.*

A dazed woman with blonde hair lay in the mess, more footsteps approached and Anton dragged her into the bathroom. The man Anton had torn through the wall lay in the tub, his skin a mess of tattoos, knicks, and ash from the wall.

"Chief," a voice whispered at the edge of the door.

Sky above, thank you. "Aye, Chief, it's Anton. Don't shoot."

"Where are you?" the Chief said.

"Right bathroom, I uh, had an accident."

"Did he just say he shit himself?"

"Shut up, Sheer," the Chief said. "Anton, put that hand out so I know it's you."

Anton put his augmented arm through the hole.

"Where are my officers, Grissom?" the Chief said, boots crunching on the fallen wall.

"In here with me," Anton said.

"I tried to warn you, Anton," Lambda said as the child approached.

"Fuck." The tattooed man groaned.

A bald officer entered to check on his coworkers, his badge read Sheer.

"What is going on, Grissom?" The Chief asked from the doorway, looking at Lambda.

"You wouldn't believe me if I told you."

"Try me." The Chief folded his arms, an edge in his voice.

"Are you upset that I jumped out of the car?"

"Amongst other things."

"You can jump out of cars?" Alpha asked, walking over. "What was your velocity?"

"Chief, I hit my head harder than I thought," said the woman in the tub.

"Grissom, start talking," the Chief said.

"This is Weaver." He gestured towards the two children. "Vio, the Clovers, whatever, they have a corporate merc squad as backup."

"And a boat," Lambda said.

The officers in the bathroom glanced between Weaver and Anton.

"They're outside, gathering the wounded."

"We know," the Chief said. "We hit the boat with a tracker, we're raiding it."

"End this shit," Novina said from the tub.

"You won't, not if you can't pass protocol," the man from the ground groaned. *Junger.*

"Neither of you'll pass that test," Sheer said.

Junger and Novina sneered at him.

"Has Vio left yet?" Anton asked.

The Officer's ears twitched on a message Anton didn't receive.

"Can you walk?" The Chief asked Novina and Junger. They grunted and the officers exited the apartment.

Chapter 40 - Luciana

Rain lashed the police station.

"The lockers are empty," Weaver-Marco said in the Chief's office. "I'm coming back—wait. People downstairs."

Luciana set the tablet down. *Whatever the Chief's plan was, anything in here's a misdirect.* "How many? Are they police?"

"You can see yourself," Weaver-Marco whispered, putting himself against the wall and aiming at the staircase.

Luciana flipped to Nagual. Weaver-Nu held the dog on his hind legs inside a locker. Through the grates, black-clad figures stalked the hallway in front. Their rifles trained perfectly on each door they checked. Strain bled through from Nagual to Luciana's quads.

"Set Nagual down, he'll fit. They're trained—"

"Luciana, you need to be in both places at once. Waiting is no good."

"What?"

"It takes practice, I know, but you can be both Nagual and yourself."

"I can't do that."

"I can."

"You're designed around it!" Luciana hissed. She wasn't having a hive of people telling her it was easy to do what they do.

"You are designed around me, it is… like having two hands, use both." Weaver-Marco nodded like this was as easy as the child said. She flipped to Nagual, eight colognes and perfumes wafted through the grates without the tinge of sewer. *This could be Taketa or Vio squads.*

"Both places," Weaver-Marco's voice was a whisper down a hallway. "We do not have time. I am sorry."

"I can't." Luciana dragged the child behind her and tipped the Chief's desk over for cover.

The child rooted through a pocket in his pack. Luciana flipped to Nagual, the passing feet would enter the parish. She flipped back to her body.

Weaver-Marco stood directly in front of her, one hand moving through the air, the other holding a punctured foil blister. The disc slapped her neck and he rubbed.

"Too many. Do not be mad, no time," Weaver-Marco said.

Luciana blinked, drugs pulsed as heat in her neck. "What did you do?"

"Focusing drugs, Zoners. I calculate—"

Luciana's mind surged, minutia became blaring details.

The sweat on Weaver-Marco's fearful face. The cold in her limbs washed away, time lost meaning as an intense purpose pounded her being.

Eight Intruders.

Her vision flicked to Nagual, hers, Nagual, hers, and they melded. Gunpowder and oil filled her nose, she rolled her shoulders, Nagual did the same.

Nagual licked his teeth, Luciana did the same.

"Rearguard-Nu to Nagual," Luciana whispered. "Marco behind the desk, shoot where I point when I point."

Luciana leapt the desk and pressed her body against the wall by the Chief's office door.

Luci-Nagual crept out of the locker.

Luciana trained her pistol on the door.

Luci-Nagual padded out from the locker room, checking her six, continuing down the hall. Her claws clicked loud, but the storm's lashing rain drowned out all other sounds. A figure slowed ahead of them, Luci-Nagual slowed.

Luciana pressed her ear to the wall, footsteps crushed plaster on the other side. She pointed above herself on the wall. Weaver-Marco nodded and stitched the wall. Bullets pierced plaster, pinged body armor and thudded against flesh.

Luci-Nagual sprinted to the figure before them, leaping, biting through the man's throat. Unable to scream, blood filled their mouths.

Luciana shuddered as a wave of satisfaction from Nagual hit her, she blinked, regaining control.

Luci-Nagual was already on Chen's desk, launching at another figure.
They attempted to duck, pulled at a grenade. Luci-Nagual's jaw snapped an exposed arm, turning it into a pulpy mess that sent the woman screaming.

Luciana spun around the corner of the Chief's office, plaster sprayed her face as bullets pinged concrete and she stumbled back towards the Chief's desk.

Motherf—

Luci-Nagual bounded between the pew desks. The soldiers shot at shadows and fanned out.

A pin clicked, a flashbang flew into Luciana's room

—fucker.

Flash-Crack! Luciana blinked, blinded by a phosphorus sun.

"I cannot see, Luciana," Weaver-Marco said with the panic of a pastor and not a victim of a close explosive. His hands grabbed onto her back and he pulled himself close. His SMG landed on her shoulder.

Luci-Nagual hit the staircase. *I can still see with him.*

Agents moved towards her main body on the second floor. Luci-Nagual snapped at any leg that was too close, breaking bone and tearing flesh. People screamed, slashed and shot at the dog. A blade caught Nagual's tail.

Luciana yelped in pain, Weaver-Marco squeezed the gun on her shoulder.

Luci-Nagual didn't break stride at the top of the staircase, three dead agents lay by the wall, two were going into the office. The dog sprinted, biting into the rearguard's buttocks. Teeth caught armor, preventing a total puncture and knocking the pair into the office. Luci-Nagual saw her main body. The man aimed a pistol at her.

Nagual's too far.

Luciana used Nagual's vantage to aim and squeezed Weaver-Marco's trigger finger.

Gunfire tore her eardrum, pain seared her skull, and the bullets thudded into the soldier.

Luci-Nagual pivoted to the man on the ground. His youthful eyes flared in anger and she charged.

His pistol came out, the muzzle flashed. Pain clipped her ribs as blood filled her mouth. The man gasped through a torn tube. His hands reached for his throat but fell short.

Luci-Nagual entered the Chief's office. Her own body knelt, her eyes unfocused. Weaver-Marco still aimed at the door.

Luciana blinked at floating green spots within her vision. Nagual rested his head on her shoulder, their vision matching close enough.

"Where is Nu?" Luciana pulled her fried inserts and scattered them onto the ground.

There could be more people. Through the Chief's door, the parish below flitted with greens and grays. *I'm still seeing through Nagual.*

"Substrate-Nu is ensuring there are no survivors."

"What?"

Chapter 41 - Anton

Anton retrieved his rifle and followed the officer's heat trail up a floor.

Weaver-Alpha climbed onto Anton's shoulders, leaning in to whisper. "Why did you not tell them about Luciana or Joel Maus?"

"Now isn't the time, they'll get distracted. Luciana will find an empty station. She can bunker down and we'll bring everyone back once we finish this."

Anton walked down a moldering hallway to a dead end, the Officer's footprints led into the door on the right.

Alpha opened his mouth, but exiting officers stopped his words.

"Corp squad's moving." Chen winced.

"Which way?" Anton asked. "Station?"

"No." Chen pointed towards the wall. "That way."

The officers shuffled within their armor like new recruits.

They don't have the training for this. Anton hurried to the window in the apartment.

The Clover boat moved a story higher on the water than he expected. Their rifles and pistols trained on every alleyway they passed.

Anton returned to the Officers. "We can stop them here."

"Chief's orders are to follow," Novina said, checking her submachine gun.

"Aye." *I'm not letting this opportunity pass.* Anton nodded to Weaver-Alpha, setting his rifle against the wall and within the child's reach. The child stared blankly at him, but took a step forward.

Anton pivoted and sprinted towards the window. He jumped, shattering the glass. The roar of the storm met him as he plummeted towards the surf. Anton hoped to land on the boat, to use his legs to sink it, but connected with the outboard motor instead. Discomfort shot through his quads, he was underwater in an instant. Silent, serene, lightning silhouetted the boat above against the green haze of the surface. Bullets fired pointlessly beneath the waves. Anton kicked to

The Last 0-Day

the bottom of the boat, still intent on sinking it. Sunken cars flashed in the lightning, detritus and power lines drifted like seaweed.
Anton tore a hole through the metal, swimming to a concrete building and surfacing for air.
Gunfire rained onto the boat. Alpha leaned from the shattered window in the flash of muzzle fire.
Dead corp soldiers floated as their boat sank. A sodden lot pulled themselves into an apartment complex in the distance. *No you don't.* Anton swam after them.

    Anton peeled the shielding from a window in the same building the Clovers entered and pulled himself inside. His eyes adjusted, within the bedroom a terrified mother and child hid beneath their bed.
Anton brought his augmented finger to his lips, their eyes fixating on the metallic hand. The mother spasmed a nod. Anton crawled towards the doorway. Soldiers' boots squelched in the hallway.
Can't fight them with the civilians in the room. The squelching passed the apartment door. *No weapons other than my hands and feet, which is more than they have.* He cracked the door open, wind whistled through the gap. He froze, the squelching stopped.
Anton crouched in case they stitched the wall and his calm blew over him.
His eyes adjusted, the enemies' faint heat signatures seeped through the walls like an orange shadow.
The mother covered her daughter's mouth with her hand, her lips moving in a silent prayer.
The heat shadow moved in front of the door.
Mistake. Anton punched as hard as possible. The door shattered, tearing from its hinges. Ribs popped, warmth from the man's chest cavity coated Anton's arm. He spun towards the group, bullets thudded against the meat shield.
Their guns clicked empty.
Mistake two. Anton threw the body at the group. *Four more soldiers.*

One reloaded, the other fired, bullets bounced against Anton's leg. He kicked the nearest in the face, his augmented foot pulped the man's jaw, snapping his head back and cracking his skull on concrete. Two sprinted away.

Move faster. Anton tore the submachine gun from the man who just finished reloading. Pivoting an elbow into his head, bones cracked and Anton steadied the gun to the two sprinting into the hall.

He fired, bullets clipped the man in the rear who fell. *One more.* Anton sprinted after him.

The fallen man's face twisted into a smirk as Anton neared.

Fire—a grenade went off, throwing Anton into the wall.

His world tilted, air knocked from his lung, Anton blinked and gasped for breath. His augmented arm checked himself for wounds as his ears screamed.

Anton forced himself to his feet, stepping over the unidentifiable mess of the man who blew himself up. Heads poked out from doorways, the walls around him smoldering. The heat signatures of footprints faded and Anton set after them.

What Anton hoped was water dripped through cracks in the apartment complex. The modular building lost its order, pipes ran the center of halls, and he hit a dead end.

Fuck. His vision whirred through spectrums, searching for any trace of the man. He traced his steps back, finding a divot in the wall where a door had been forced open. Anton walked by it, in case the man peered through.

Should have taken the SMG from that dude who blew himself up. Doesn't matter. Anton continued to an apartment in the hall with no heat signatures inside and tore the handle off. He entered a room full of detritus and grime. *A hoarder.* Anton walked through the goat paths to a window and cracked it on a thunderclap. He stepped onto the ledge, water lapped at the second story. Wind and rain lashed the building, and he climbed across the ledge to the apartment where the last Clover hid.

The Last 0-Day

Anton swayed with the squall near the window ledge. The damaged concrete gave him more than enough holds to climb. The heat signature of a man laying prone and facing the door with a rifle bled through the wall. Anton waited for the moment.

Thunder cracked, Anton threw himself through the window. Lightning illuminated the room and the man who hadn't heard the window shatter. Anton landed beside the man, the man's rifle spun—Anton snapped the barrel.

The man reached for his chest.

Anton snagged his wrist. The man attempted to shrimp out, Anton tore the man's armor and grenades off his chest, casting them on the far side of the room.

The man gained space, kicked up.

Boot connected with chest—Anton grabbed the shin with his augmented hand, squeezing and shattering the man's fibula with a sickening snap.

The man rolled, planted with his uninjured leg. Anton kicked, snapping the man's ankle. The man collapsed to the ground, screaming.

"Shut up," Anton said.

Anger from the day's events scorched the cold from his limbs. He rooted through the soldier's supplies, found the nummers disc and slapped it onto the man's bare chest. The man's moans stopped as the drug hit, his eyes glazed over.

Not a military grade pain blocker, old-fashioned opioids. "Who do you work for?"

The man nodded in and out, trying to shake the drug's effects off. "Vio Corp," he managed.

"Same as the Clovers?"

"Different division..." He nodded off.

Anton slapped him awake with his human hand.

"Here to clean their mess. Well, were here to clean their mess. Another one will have to come in now."

"You did clean the mess."

"We didn't."

"No, you did. You can crawl out of here if you report you did." The man stared at him, the drug either cleared his system or the narcotic effect was short lasting. *Not some last-gen drug.*

"They'll know."

"Myself and the other officers won't talk."

"You're not Nineteen-PD. We have a file on you, Anton Grissom." His pupils unpinned, focusing on Anton. The man cycled his OPTO-inserts. Anton waited for a recording delay on their lenses, but it didn't come.

"You should lose that file too," Anton said. "I'm going back to my squad after this."

"Probably for the better."

"What?"

"Nothing, Anton. Nothing, you're bad for business, you know that?"

"You talk too much, which is making me regret letting you go."

"Why regret? This tongue of mine can get Vio to give up, at least for now. Bigger things on the horizon and what not."

"Aye." Anton considered the man. As corporate as he had seen, more concerned with his own hide and moving up the ladder than getting an actual job done. *He's an easy instrument to play.*

"Tell me one thing, Anton. Did you find the Weaver project?"

"Found some kids, but they were disabled. Not this special deity everyone's been after."

"And the Taketa chopper that landed?"

"Here for me, went AWOL. They're dead now too."

"Such tragedy." The man sat upright, flinching at his leg and ankle. "All these resources spent chasing a ghost. Told them it was too good to be true."

"Aye. What's your name?"

"Would you even believe me if I told you?"

"I can see if you're lying," Anton lied.

"Those eyes truly are the greatest Taketa invention this decade. It's Daniel Kubis."

"Well, Mr. Kubis, do you think you can crawl out of here?"

"I'll wait for the storm to end."

"Mr. Kubis, I expect Vio to leave this precinct alone, and to leave me alone after this. I can look you up if it doesn't go that way."

"I know the deal." He waved away the concern.

Anton put out his hand to shake.

Kubis looked at it. "How quaint."

Anton raised an eyebrow, clenching his jaw.

Kubis shook the implant, Anton squeezed, popping a bone.

The man squealed through the nummers.

"Catch my drift?" Anton said.

"Yes, quite," the man said through clenched teeth.

Anton stood to leave.

"Mr. Grissom." Mr. Kubis groaned as he pushed himself against the wall. "Vio might not pay as much as Taketa, but there are other… benefits. If you ever want a job, you have my name."

"Aye." Anton walked to the window. "Don't forget our deal."

Anton jumped into the water, swimming back towards the rundown apartment complex 19-PD used as their forward-operating-base.

Chapter 42 - Luciana

The station shuddered from an explosion. Luciana ducked.
"That was not me," Weaver-Marco said. "Substrate-Nu is healthy. One of the mercenaries detonated their grenades. It chained."
Smoke rolled across the balcony, the scent of burnt cloth, flesh, and fire in its wake. Luci-Nagual peered out from the office, the stairwell was a pile of rubble.
"Are there more stairs?" Weaver-Marco said.
"In the back, I'll search them." Luciana crouched outside the Chief's office where Weaver-Marco stitched the wall. "They smell like they're from the same apartment."
"Or a corporate dormitory," Weaver-Marco said.
Vio's purple pyramid logo shined against their black weapons and gear.
No ID Cards. "Weird Vio'd send a fresh squad," Luciana said to herself.
"This could be their in-house cleanup crew. During one of my searches of Taketa, I found a similar division for when anything might… tarnish a reputation."
"Then Taketa will send someone here," *and I'm banged up.*
"I calculate the Yume that arrived was that squad. Anton stopped following orders. When I get net back, I can check."
The pulsing purpose of zoners faded, Luciana's vision shifted back to her own and the reflection of Nagual's on top.
"We're going to have a long conversation about the fact that you dosed me," Luciana said.
"I said I was sorry."
"That doesn't change the situation."
"I see," Weaver-Marco said, looking for the back stairs.
"It's this way," Luciana said, leading him away from the rubble.
"This substrate's eyes are not working properly," Weaver-Marco said, his hand grabbing hers.
"We need to get a med-kit." A dull throb of pain pulsed on her tail and ribs. "Nagual took a hit."

Weaver-Nu stood at the bottom of the stairs with a kit. "I got one." Luciana took the med-kit, setting it on Novina's immaculate desk. *This is going to hurt, buddy.* Luciana poured the ethanol over Nagual's rib. Nagual blinked.

Luciana yipped like the alcohol bit her own skin. "I know that hurt, Nagual."

The dog panted.

"Where is Anton?" Luciana said.

"The officers are on their way back. I am waiting for Anton, but he should not take long."

"What?"

Chapter 43 - Anton

Anton entered the forward-operating-base apartment, finding who he thought was Weaver-Kappa sitting on the kitchen counter eating an SR-loaf.

"They went to the station," Weaver-Kappa said. "The Chief was upset that you did not follow his orders. He was mad at me for shooting and refused to let Substrate-Alpha wait behind. Took my SMG too." Weaver-Kappa gestured towards the one in front of him. "He did not think I had two." A smile went across the child's face.

"Vio will leave us alone. Told them you don't exist," Anton said.

"Should I tell Luciana?"

"No, not yet. No reason to get anyone upset or mad. They will have to rebuild this area."

"What are you going to do?"

"I'll help for now."

"I will too."

"You ready to leave?"

"Yes, I was waiting here for you to return. I am helping the Officers put out the fires in the station."

"What, there are fires?"

"Yes, Luciana and myself were attacked by a Vio clean-up squad, but we handled it."

"Why didn't you tell me?"

"I was interrupted," Weaver-Kappa said.

Anton shook his head at the child. "Let's go."

The child jumped from the counter.

"You have any extra?" Anton gestured to the loaf. Weaver-Kappa glanced at the food, hesitated a second, and handed it across to Anton.

Anton chewed through the stale bread. "How do you eat this?"

"This is amazing." Weaver-Kappa smiled, climbing onto Anton's back. "I have eaten so much worse."

Chapter 44 - Luciana

"We have to stop the fires," Luciana said.
Smoke curled from the fallen stairwell, flavors of cloth and rubber flowed through Nagual's nose to her. Weaver-Marco sprinted up the backstairs.

"I recall an extinguisher on the second floor," Nu said. "Where is the one for the first?"

"Over here." Luciana moved through the desks.
Against the far wall, Nu hurried to the red cylinder. The second floor extinguisher sprayed, a gray cloud rolling over the balcony like fog over hills. Nu pulled the extinguisher and hurried towards the stairwell.

"Wai—" Luciana started.
Nu disappeared into the smoke at the bottom at the same time as Marco did on the second floor. The synchronization of the children's movements was the greatest evidence Luciana had that Weaver was a single entity.

The extinguishers stopped.

"Luciana," Weaver-Marco yelled. "Can you get Substrate-Nu? It has passed out from the fumes."

I told you to wait. Luciana took a deep breath and fumbled through the mists. The extinguisher upstairs crashed and tiny feet pattered across plaster as Weaver-Marco moved. Nu leaned against the wall near a smoldering piece of concrete. Luciana pulled him onto her shoulder and hurried to a desk back in the station.

"I cannot make it breathe," Marco said, concern in his voice.

"One sec." Luciana placed the child on the desk, pinched his nose, and blew into his mouth.

"One more plea—"

Luciana blew into the child's mouth. Nu gasped for air.

"Thank you," Nu rasped. "I dislike losing substrates… It is upsetting."

"Yeah." Luciana raised an eyebrow.

Nu sprang off the desk, jumping in place before a spasm of coughs gripped the child.

"Better. I will practice this breathing technique now," Marco said.

"We need to find the officers."

"I found them with Anton."

"What?"

"We were busy when I found them, but they are returning here soon. Your Chief is unhappy with Anton and I. Anton had to go clean up the clean-up crew and I provided suppressing fire."

Explaining this to the Chief won't be easy.

"Your officers did a good job," Marco said. "There are no leaks in the station."

Nu left the pews.

"Where is he going?"

"Check the water level at the window," Marco said. "Do you have food here?"

"Wha—Yeah, we do." Luciana walked towards the break room.

Weaver's constant train of thought is an onslaught.

"The water has stopped rising, though it is coming over the window with the swells," Marco said behind her.

Luciana opened the cabinet by the coffeemaker, handing Marco a cold slice of SR-loaf. Weaver broke it in half and gave a piece to Nagual. The dog wolfed down his slice and walked to Luciana's desk to sleep beneath it. Nu entered the room and opened the cabinet for his own piece without asking.

A thud crashed onto the roof.

Luciana reached for her pistol, her eyes trained on the ceiling.

"It is your officers," Nu said through a mouthful of food.

A small hand tickled Luciana's neck through Nagual and she headed to the roof.

"Luciana will be here soon. Don't shoot her," a child said.

Luciana opened the door to the roof, weapons spun on her.

"Gutierrez, you have to learn to knock," Sheer said, lowering his gun.

"I told you she was arriving," Lambda said.

"Briefing room, now." The Chief bulldozed to the second floor. "Why is my office a war zone?"

All eyes fell on Luciana.

"Had a… situation."

"Chief will want to hear it," Novina said, walking out of the stairwell and arriving at the damaged balcony. "Jesus, I want to hear it."

The smell of coffee and warming SR-loaves didn't invigorate the soaked officers, who squelched to their chairs and collapsed around the conference room. Weaver-Marco tilted his head at the coffee machine with Alpha, while Lambda retrieved food with a single arm, and Nu pushed microwaved slices onto the table.

The Chief entered and sat at the front. He'd aged ten years since Luciana last saw him.

"Someone go wake Maus," the Chief said.

A lump rose in Luciana's throat and with Nagual asleep in the parish, he couldn't push the hurt away.

Chen groaned to his feet and as he passed, Luciana grabbed his arm.

The group turned to Luciana and she gave the smallest shake of her head. "Maus—" The gun at his head, the trigger squeezing. Tears fell from Luciana's cheeks. "He died in the line of duty." She stared at her boots. A small hand rubbed her back.

"H-How?" Chen's voice trembled.

Luciana drew a ragged breath, trying to clear her throat.

"Officer Maus was shot by a corporate hit squadron," Marco said.

"Vio motherfuckers," Chen growled.

"It was not Vio, it was another corp," Lambda said. "They are all dead. Luciana and Nagual made sure of it."

Luciana snorted and leaned back to drain her tears.

The Chief stood through the watery vision and rest his hand on her shoulder. "Where did it happen, Luciana?"

"Sewers"—she snorted—"we were ambushed."

"Fucking cop killers." Chen collapsed into the chair beside Luciana. "Tell me what you did—" his voice cracked.

"Chen, now is not the time," the Chief said.

"I had to leave the body." Luciana spat onto the ground, reining in her emotions.

"We can retrieve it." Kagan poured deep cups of coffee for everyone and pushed them around the table.

Officers drank in a silent daze, the storm battering the station with a rhythmic rain.

I should've gone alone, Maus.

"I see you found the child," the Chief said, gesturing towards Marco.

"Yeah." Luciana downed scalding coffee.

"You know why everyone wanted them?" The Chief said.

Luciana took in the officers and children at the table. *The more people that know the truth, the more people will look. And I'd sound insane.*

"People chasing ghosts, Chief. False intel," Luciana said, lying to her fellow Officers was a stab to the gut.

The Chief sighed, leaning against his chair. "So much damage, and for what? A bunch of orphaned Disabled."

Rain pelting the stained glass of the room ticked by the time and the silence, until boots echoed down the hall.

"Wrong fucking time to try again," Novina said through clenched teeth.

The officers stood.

"It is Anton," Marco said.

Everyone turned towards the child, and Anton entered the room.

"You are beyond reckless, boy," the Chief said.

"Aye," Anton said.

"Well?" the Chief asked.

"Area's clear. You won't be bothered again." Anton raised an eyebrow at Luciana.

I told them. Luciana gave a brief nod.

The Last 0-Day

"I'm sorry about Officer Maus."

"Figured you were there," the Chief said. "Everyone go dry off and put on clean uniforms... We're going out as soon as this storm passes."

Anton walked to the table, drinking coffee from an abandoned mug. The Chief shut the door instead of walking through it.

"I won't have one of my officers lie to me." The Chief locked the door. "You're both telling me the truth, right now, or I'm removing you from duty and arresting you." The Chief turned to the children, opened his mouth, shut it, and turned to Luciana. "Talk."

"This is Weaver." Luciana gestured to the children. "Original from Taketa, they are..."

"I am one," the four children said in unison.

The Chief leaned against the door, running a hand against his buzz cut. "That is something the Corps would go to war over."

"Aye," Anton said.

"And Maus?" The Chief asked.

"Taketa," Luciana said. "They used him as a bargaining chip, and once we surrendered, killed him."

The Chief steadied his breathing. "The brazenness of this is... staggering."

"Aye. Taketa doesn't know what happened yet. The storm stopped the comms, once the storm passes, well—"

"I disabled the Taketa trackers on both of you," Alpha said.

"We can fake that a group of children died in the storm," the Chief said to Weaver. "That will stop them from returning for you."

"They won't come back for Luciana," Anton said. "If they don't know what happened."

"They'll have an idea about you, Grissom."

"I don't care. I'm going back to UCSM. My assignment to Taketa was... I'll be glad to put it behind me."

"They might not take you back, if Taketa can push hard enough," the Chief said.

"I'll make sure they won't," Anton said.

"I can help fake the records of your death, Anton." Alpha pulled in an abandoned cup and sipped.

"That drink is not good," Marco said.

"You'll grow to like it, trust me," Anton said.

"It burns." Alpha coughed.

"Probably Nguyen's." The Chief rubbed his face. "Anton, if you'll stick around to help clean this mess, I'd greatly appreciate it."

"Aye," Anton said and the Chief left the room to change.

Weaver-Alpha shut the door. "Thank you," Weaver said with all the children.

"That's disconcerting, Weaver," Anton said.

"Yeah, just use one," Luciana said.

"Aye," Lambda said, looking at Anton.

"Why can no one say 'aye'? It's not that hard."

Luciana drained her coffee. "We should change." She left for the locker room.

Nagual sat beside Luciana as she stripped and used shower-wipes. Grime ran dark from her brown skin.
The door opened, Weaver-Alpha entered.

"Jesus." Luciana pulled a tower from the bench to cover herself.

"What?" Alpha said. "I have seen bodies before."

"You never read about decency in all of your net searchers?"

"It did not seem pertinent."

"What do you need?" Luciana asked.

"I would like to live with you."

"What?"

"I want to live with you with this substrate."

Luciana was on the back foot, she didn't know what to say and didn't want to offend the child, "I—"

"Think on it," Alpha said and left.

Luciana blinked. *What just happened?* Cold air sent a shiver down her spine and she pulled on a fresh uniform. *First time being dry in hours.* Luciana dried Nagual and left for the parish.

The Last 0-Day

Chen sat at Maus' desk, his eyes unfocused on the polychromatic fiber-wrapper resting on top. Nagual pushed his head beneath Chen's hand, who scratched it absentmindedly.

"I can't believe it," Chen said.

"Yeah," Luciana whispered.

"Please tell me they paid for it. Anything."

"Nagual killed them. All of them, Chen."

"That can't be a good way to go," Chen said.

The massaging on her scalp through Nagual sped up.

"It wasn't." Luciana tapped Chen on the shoulder and walked towards the conference room.

Sweet banana flavor filled her mouth from Chen feeding Nagual a candy. She tried to ignore the massage. Weaver-Nu and Marco sat on the conference table. They had changed into an oversized police uniform and tied the loose ends with string. Their body armor lay nearby with heat packs underneath to dry them out.

Weaver doesn't want to go without armor anymore.

Sheer, Novina, and Junger stood over a topographic map of the Pucker on the table.

"We will have to use makeshift rafts, or something to check the neighborhoods. Probably turn on the pumping stations first." Junger said.

"Do they have a backup generator?" Novina asked.

"They should, but why they're dead is another question," Junger said.

We get back to work fast... they don't need help. Luciana left for the parish. Anton cleared cement boulders from the staircase. The dead bodies lay stacked beneath the altar. Luciana crossed the parish and crouched over the bodies. Youthful faces stared sightlessly at the ceiling. *Probably their first assignment.* Luciana rifled through pockets.

"You think you'll find anything?" Anton asked.

"No, but I want to."

"I understand that." Anton still wore his wet clothing.

"Why don't you change?"

"Custom clothes, besides, I don't feel cold anymore." He crouched beside her. "Luciana, I'm truly sorry about Maus. I... I didn't think Yume or anyone at Taketa would do that."

Luciana grunted. "If it makes you feel any better, I didn't think they would either."

Weaver-Marco walked to them. "Wu is fun, he has taught me cards. The storm is slowing where he is and West Bowl has regained most of its power. I will be able to help more soon."

"Pucker won't get power until we turn it on," Luciana said.

"Then let us go do that," Weaver-Marco said.

"We have to wait until the storm is over."

"I see." The child stared at the ground for a moment and walked towards the conference room.

"I wouldn't believe his story if I didn't see it with my own eyes," Luciana said.

"It's all magic to me," Anton said, going back to move stones.

***

"Thank you, Grissom," the Chief said as the last stone cleared the staircase.
Water leaked in from cracks in the ceiling and babbled through a hole in the wall. But the stairs remained usable. Weaver came back to Luciana with the four children, the comically large police raincoats dragging behind them like capes.

"The storm is ending," one of the children said. "I want power. Which sector of the city do I turn on?"

"Weaver, it's not that simple," Luciana said.

"It is. Officer Sheer and Junger said pumps, then generators. The pumps are in the nineteen-hundreds block and I am almost there. Can you help me get to the power station?"

"You're doing what?"

"Substrate-Ariel and Substrate-Rho were delayed, but they will arrive at the pumping station and main power plant shortly."

Luciana blinked. "Anton, come here."

The soldier raised an eyebrow and crouched beside Weaver-Alpha.

"Anton, Weaver wants to get to the power station."

"Aye?"

"Tell him it doesn't work that way."

"What doesn't?"

"Turning on the power of an entire city?"

"Why doesn't it?"

"See?" Weaver said.

Luciana turned on her tablet, pointing to dots on the map. "This is the nearest relay. That needs to be checked for damage and powered. Then you have to go here, here, here, and here."

"We should start now. Anton?" Weaver-Marco said.

"Aye." Anton lifted one of the children onto his shoulder and headed for the back window.

Luciana stared at them, Nagual taking a step before she did. She sighed. *So much for being dry.*

Luciana struggled through frigid water that choked with debris. *At least there aren't any bodies.* The storm petered out overhead, proving even nature could gas out.

Luciana pulled herself onto the catwalk of a three-story power relay building. Nagual pressed his nose against the door, getting oil and water. *No people.* The high tension cables along the top were remarkably intact.

Anton entered the building, Luciana a step behind. Humidity beaded on the steel walls, but nothing leaked in.

"Found one." Lambda pulled a tablet from the wall and turned it on. The four children sat around the glow of the screen, which flickered as content cycled through.

"Have you done this before?" Anton whispered into Luciana's ear.

"No."

Nagual sat at the door on the third floor to stand watch. The melange of water, sewage, earth, and hum of robots bled through to her.

"The pumps are back online," Alpha said. "Lightning tripped a breaker and shut them off."

"How many?" Luciana said.

"All of them." Marco tilted his head at the question. "You meant how many were tripped by lightning? Five, the rest shutdown from their motor's safety switch with too high of a workload. Probably for garbage that gets stuck."

"No." Luciana walked to Nu, who flicked switches on the relay's main board. "I meant how many pumps are online."

"All of them, Luciana, I went to all of them. It was the most efficient."

She stared in disbelief. "You couldn't have gotten to all of them, there hasn't been enough time."

"What? Yes there has. I left the moment your officers brought up the map."

"So you were doing this with or without us," Anton said.
Weaver did not answer, Nu went to the door on the second floor, and the rest went to a wall-sized breaker.

"We will have to wait until the water is lower." Marco smiled.

"Why invite us if you could do this by yourself?" Luciana asked.

The children looked at the ground, then back at the adults. "I have been lonely since leaving the nursery," Alpha whispered.
Luciana swallowed a lump at the truth in the child's words. *Jesus.*

"I thought it would be fun to solve the problem together."
Nagual pushed his head against Nu on the second floor. Nu hugged the dog, the child's phantom-arms wrapping around Luciana's torso. Joy poured from Nagual in a jitter.

"Just tell us in the future, Weaver," Luciana managed.

"Aye." Anton blinked, sadness welling in his mechanical eyes.

If they can show sadness.

Marco walked over and took his implanted hand.

Alpha and Lambda grunted as they pushed the main breaker. Thunder rolled through the district. The power flickered across the Pucker and remained on.

"Do you think Wu is happy now?" Marco said.

"What?" Anton replied.

"Wu did not want us to leave, said it was dangerous. That 'Luciana would kill him if anything went wrong'," he parroted. "But he also wanted power…"

"You can check on him and let us know." Luciana walked to the front door of the relay station.

"I would not open that," Marco said. "We will get wet."

"You should deputize this whole lot, Luciana," Anton said. "They know how to get after it."

Weaver's collective heads pivoted to Luciana in excitement.

This motherfucker.

Chapter 45 - Weaver

Substrate-Ariel and Substrate-Rho jostled through a packed transport that trundled to the Southern Empire. Displaced people from the SF Bowl filled the rooms and aisles with what little belongings they had on their laps. The substrates settled into their seats where an Old sat with bright green hair. She smiled at Substrate-Rho.

"Your boy?"

"Sister's, she passed away," Weaver-Ariel said.

"Generous of you to take one that's so… special."

"Family duty. What are you watching?" Substrate-Ariel gestured towards the tablet.

"The verified news I can get while the net is down."

"Aye," Weaver-Ariel said.

Substrate-Beta, Mu, and Zeta worked rotating shifts to map out the Pucker for errant net signal, but found none yet. Weaver-Rho plugged in a tablet hoping to get net, but got an emergency broadcast.

"Do you mind if I listen?" Weaver-Ariel said.

"I can put it on speaker." The Old tapped the screen.

"—One of the worst on record," the broadcast said. "Verified reports came in today that an X-Systems seed plane malfunctioned. An X-Systems spokesman has said 'It was a Wushan part in the dispersing systems that caused the malfunction. Nothing that we manufactured was faulty.' Wushan has not responded to inquiries made."

Weaver-Marco walked through Luciana's apartment as she slept. After days of stimulants and eugeroics use, she slept through Weaver's cleaning. Substrate-Nu and Lambda left the police station to assist. The apartment was dangerously dirty, Luciana could catch parasites.

"And they'll get away with it," the old woman across from Weaver-Ariel said. "The blame will shift around until everyone forgets. It always does."

"Yeah," Weaver-Ariel said, trying to get more information from the tablet.

Weaver-Alpha stood beside Anton at the edge of the Pucker.

"What are you going to do about Taketa?" Weaver-Alpha asked.

"I don't know."

He is lying. "I can delete your record from their systems once I gain net access."

"How?" Anton asked.

"I was in their system from... birth? I guess, yes, birth. I know it well."

"Doesn't change the people who are there and know me."

"I can fake your death?"

"I stand out a little," Anton said, raising his augmented hand. Weaver-Alpha considered the augment.

"You'd think the government would get involved." The woman across from Substrate-Ariel didn't stop talking.

A mistake had been made.

"—And Wushan buys out my apartment complex, says renovations from the storm would take months. I tell you, it makes me sick."

"Yeah." Weaver-Ariel glanced at a clock at the far end of the train. Weaver had another five hours with this woman, but even another five minutes would be too long.

"No no, put it there," Wu said.

The man wanted Substrate-Echo to drag a drowned serving robot to the basement.

"Mr. Wu, I would like to talk." Weaver-Beta said, coming in from a net search shift.

"Yes, what was your name again?"

"Beta," Weaver said.

"Right, Beta. Why would your parents name you that?"

"I named myself that."

"What do you want?"

"I want your second floor."

Wu laughed.

Weaver-Alpha trailed Anton as they walked to the warehouse section of the Pucker. The precinct was a drained beach, sand and dust following currents and forming miniature dunes on the sidewalks. *Mounds are pre-made for removal, I should add that to the list.*

"Then what are you going to do?" Weaver-Alpha asked.

"I'm going back to the military. UCSM can pressure Taketa for what they've done."

"Why not delete your record and kill Fayed?"

"One, contrary to what you have seen me do, I'm not some hitman. Two, getting to Fayed would be impossible."

"I escaped with twenty-six substrates from their most secretive lab and crossed a quarter of a continent on foot. You think a single building would stop me?"

Anton stopped in his tracks. Weaver processed the debate pass across Anton's face.

Weaver-Ariel checked the pack for food. With three extra SR-loaves, there was enough calories for the escape.

Substrate-Rho vomited onto the floor.

"I am sorry," Weaver-Ariel rose. "He gets motion sickness sometimes." *Finally, she stopped talk—*

"Oh, my nephew used to do that."

How did that not work? "Excuse me." Weaver-Ariel and Rho made their way to the bathroom to clean the vomit and re-feed. It was a waste, but Weaver couldn't deal with the woman anymore.

"Why are you laughing?" Weaver-Beta asked Wu.

"I'm not a landlord, nor would I rent to children. Let alone a group of borderline mute Disabled. Who is paying for it?"

"I would work," Weaver-Beta said.

Substrate-Lambda and Nu entered the restaurant, their reclaimed submachine guns rattling against their backs.

Wu's face took on an odd shade of red. "Are you threatening me?"

"What? No. I am saying you have no more bots due to water damage. You need servers and bouncers. Are you going into debt buying new bots? Hire locals? I will do it for room and board."

Wu's eyes narrowed on the children. "Inspectors would shut me down, child labor laws."

"I already talked with Gutierrez, there will be a blind eye," Weaver-Lambda said.

Wu's face screwed up as he performed mental math. "For a few months, and I am not moving out."

"Deal." Weaver-Beta extended a small hand.

Wu shook it.

"And I want more shakes and to play more cards. The subterfuge is fascinating."

"Put away the guns," Wu said. "Jesus, do you even have permits for those? I'll show you how I make the shakes."

Weaver-Beta nodded. Substrate-Lambda and Nu took the guns and armor upstairs, hiding them behind a couch.

"You sure you can get into the building?" Anton asked Weaver-Alpha.

"Yes, I need net and time. By the time we get to Taketa, I will have access."

Anton searched the alleyway.

"What are you looking for?"

"Trackers. Yume must have left something for the helicopter to come back to."

"Unlikely, there was most likely a rendezvous point."

"What makes you say that?"

"Time would not be a factor if they had captured you and I."

"I can't even see any signals."

"You could before?"

"I was starting to see data streams."

"Fascinating."

Anton rubbed his head. "Say we go to Taketa and perform the op. We need a way in, weapons, a way out—"

"I am at the Southern Empire's rim. By the time you get there, I should have everything you need."

"So again, you were planning before I agreed."

"I have lost substrates if I do not plan for everything, Anton."

Anton shook his head. "When can we leave?"

"Now would be best, but Officer Maus' funeral is tomorrow."

Anton took a deep breath and sighed. "Tell Luciana I had to leave, she'll understand. You coming with me?"

"I would like to, yes."

"Aye."

They walked through the sand in silence for a few blocks.

"Get on." Anton nodded to his back. "We should move as fast as possible. I'll get gloves and sunglasses to cover the rest."

"Aye." Alpha climbed onto Anton's back.

"Not bad." Anton chuckled and sprinted from the Pucker.

I have net access. Substrate-Rho smiled at the tablet as Weaver-Ariel carried the child to a corner of the Southern Empire's transportation hub. Golden hills rose beyond a panoramic glass wall. *Rain didn't make it this far south.* Weaver-Ariel scanned the station and made for the exit. Substrate-Rho brute forced into the ticketing system of X-System Transit.

Substrate-Alpha and Anton approached the East Bowl's transit terminal.

"How are we getting tickets?" Anton said. "Last I checked, neither of us has money."

"Pick up for Nico Gomez," Weaver-Alpha said.

Anton rolled his eyes but approached the counter. "Pick up for Nico Gomez."

"Thank you sir, put your thumb on the scanner and we can confirm your tickets." The man behind the counter didn't bother looking at the pair.

Anton looked at Substrate-Alpha, who urged him to continue. Anton thumbed the scanner.

Beep-Beep. "Thank you, Mr. Gomez." The man pulled two tickets and handed them to Anton.

Substrate-Rho closed the X-Systems ID portal and walked to the food courts where Substrate-Ariel ate. The two substrates traded the tablet for an SR-loaf.

"Private cabin?" Anton asked as they entered a room on the transport. "This will attract attention."

"I am not sitting with another group like last time, it was terrible."

Weaver-Marco sat straight as Luciana walked into the kitchen. "Cereal, shower, coffee." Luciana grumbled and stripped as she walked towards the shower. Weaver-Marco's eyes widened at her sculpted form. *She is beautiful.*

Weaver-Rho compared Substrate-Ariel's body to Luciana's. Skinnier, paler, and with less muscle mass, she wore a wig of shoulder-length blonde hair. *Not as appealing.*

Weaver-Alpha sat on the bed of the private train room and smiled. "This room should come with food too."

"I am hungry," Anton said.

Weaver-Marco slid the stool to the breakfast machine and removed the bowl and cup.

"Coffee, cereal." Weaver-Marco tested, watching the machine grind grains and dispense dark liquid. *Fascinating.*

"Wu," Weaver-Beta said, "why do we not have an automated breakfast machine?"

"A what?"

"A machine that we can talk at to make us food."

"What do you think you're here to do?" Wu smiled and continued scrubbing mud from the walls.

Luciana jumped when she re-entered the kitchen, her eyes flaring.

"Good morning." Weaver fed his cereal to Nagual.

"How long were you sitting there?" Luciana rubbed her forehead.

"I cleaned your apartment while you slept," Weaver-Marco responded.

Luciana glanced to the spotless sink and open window that wafted away the stench.

"Thanks." Luciana sat to eat. "You didn't answer my question." She smiled.

"I can get naked if you want to trade?"

"No! No, that's fine, Weaver."

"Are you sure?"

"Yes, I'm sure." Luciana ate.

"Anton will not be at the funeral."

Luciana stared at her bowl. "Why?"

"Taketa business."

"You helping?"

"Yes."

"Must be important." Luciana drained her coffee.

"Did you think about my request?" Weaver-Marco asked.

Luciana's brow furrowed. "For a little while." She went to her room to change out of the towel.

Weaver pet Nagual and smiled.

"What're you smiling about?" Anton asked. The man stared out the train window, watching the rural patchwork between two urban centers roll by. He must have seen Substrate-Alpha's smile in the reflection.

"Do you miss home?" Weaver-Alpha asked.

"Sometimes, it's simpler."

"My home was simpler too."

Weaver-Ariel and Rho stepped out to the heat sink of the Southern Empire. A yellow haze complemented the high sun in a sky losing the battle to stay blue. Weaver-Rho booked a nearby hotel as Substrate-Ariel carried the child inside and to the elevator.

Once in the room, Weaver-Rho probed the Taketa network and Substrate-Ariel left for supplies. The area around the transportation hub was surprisingly empty, the air filled with a petrochemical scent. Weaver-Ariel wiped sweat from the substrate's brow as it entered the Hub's food court. A tablet protruded from a woman's handbag near the bar. *Perfect.*

In the Pucker, Weaver woke more substrates to help Substrate-Rho parse information. The Taketa corporation's main building was better protected than calculated. But access was still possible.

Weaver-Ariel glanced around the spotless hub, cameras filled its geodesic domes and corners. *I should have activated the net in the Pucker before the pumps.* Weaver-Ariel headed towards the bar.

Weaver-Rho paused the Taketa penetration test and re-entered the transit hub's network. With no time to disable individual cameras, Weaver overflowed their servers and crashed the entire system before going back to work on Taketa.

Weaver-Ariel plucked the tablet from the woman's leather purse and pushed it into the Substrate's pants in one fluid motion. The exit was one hundred meters away and would take one minute to reach it. Passengers paused at broken kiosks and gave exasperated sighs as Weaver-Ariel passed.

"Ma'am." A security guard in a perfectly pressed uniform stepped in front of Substrate-Ariel. "You put it back and I won't call it in."

"Put what back?"

"The tablet I saw you take."

The Taketa net showed its first crack, an unpatched router on the first floor.

"What if I did something for you?" Weaver-Ariel stepped towards the man and reached for his belt.

"Excuse you." The man took a step back.

"Fine." Weaver-Ariel extended the tablet. As he reached, Substrate-Ariel jabbed three fingers into his solar plexus. The guard gasped like he would vomit and doubled over in spasming coughs. Weaver-Ariel sprinted from the hub.

"We should get food," Weaver-Alpha said to Anton in the train car.

"You said it'd come here?" Anton raised an eyebrow.

"Maybe we have to ask?"

"You do it, a kid will get better results." Anton returned to looking at the golden fields passing by the train.

Weaver-Alpha headed towards the smell of fried food.

Weaver-Ariel ditched the blonde wig in the trash inside the hotel. The short, brown, regrown hair would have to be stylized before leaving again to ensure no suspicious glances. Substrate-Ariel sat beside Substrate-Rho and Weaver attacked the Taketa network with both tablets.

"You're short-staffed," Weaver-Beta said to Wu, jogging up the stairs.

"Excuse—" Wu started.

Weaver ignored him, there were more than enough substrates cleaning the dance club.

Weaver-Alpha and Anton ate a meat-like substance rolled in fatty, crispy dough. It was the fanciest food Weaver had ever had.

"How do people eat the SR-rations when this exists?"

"It's beyond expensive, Weaver," Anton said.

The Southern Empire's spires broke the hills in the distance.

Got it. Weaver cracked into the Taketa security system. The most advanced firewall encountered yet unmade by the weakest link in the chain. Weaver's original insertion point within the Nursery. There would be an incremental time delay in commands issued and executed within the building, but Weaver could compensate for it. Weaver tested the delays in Taketa HQ's toilet system, sending a flush command and waiting for the water to circle, to get the microseconds exact.

"Are you ready?" Weaver-Alpha said.

"That fast?" Anton turned from the window.

"That fast? I've been working on it for nearly a day. But yes, I am ready. I will get us transport to arrive at dusk."

Anton stood and stretched.

"Does that still matter?" Weaver-Alpha asked.

"Aye, if not the muscles, the mind," Anton said. "Give me the intel. How're we doing this?"

Weaver-Ariel and Rho scratched their heads. The delay of 0.2 seconds was too long to be used remotely. A substrate would have to enter the building with Anton to ensure it worked smoothly.

"—And we go in together." Substrate-Alpha raised his hand to stifle any objections. "There are technicalities at play that make it so I have to."

The Last 0-Day

Weaver-Alpha and Anton stepped into a hijacked transport beneath a crimson sky.

"Do you require a weapon?" Weaver-Alpha asked.

Anton raised his implanted hand. "No, this is lethal enough."

"It is a strong link to you, however," Weaver-Alpha said.

Weaver-Ariel scanned the frayed edge of the Taketa precinct. It was dirtier than its corporate center and empty near dusk. Weaver dropped Officer Scott's pistol and a tablet into a garbage bin. Substrate-Ariel crossed the street to a cafe, ordered a coffee, and an SR-muffin before sitting at the window. Mountainous buildings ran the block, their glowing red Taketa signs blotted out the stars. A transport pulled into an alleyway, Anton and Substrate-Alpha stepped out.

"Here." Weaver-Alpha leaned into the trash can, removing the tablet and handing the bag across.

Anton glanced into the paper bag, his eyes flaring for a microsecond. The soldier glanced around the grimy alleyway and shoved the pistol into his belt.

"Do I want to know where you got this?" Anton said.

"Does it matter?"

"You're going to have to learn to answer questions on the first try."

Weaver-Rho flicked street cameras to previously recorded segments as a fresh transport arrived for Anton and Weaver-Alpha to take to Taketa HQ.

"Why?" Weaver-Alpha stepped into the car.

Anton's head pivoted to Weaver as the transport moved.

"It was a joke! I am still practicing."

"Aye, whose gun?"

"A corrupt police officer from the East Bowl. He is currently reported missing."

"You're pinning it on someone else?"

"A dead man, yes," Weaver said.

Anton weighed Weaver's words as the car stopped. "Go time." Anton swung out.

394

"This way," Weaver-Alpha said, walking down the sweltering streets.

Substrate-Ariel watched the pair take the corner and disappear from sight.

Substrate-Rho cycled footage as Anton and Substrate-Alpha approached the building. Weaver-Alpha unlocked the doors preemptively and signaled a malfunction in the HEPA filters.

The front security guard grumbled near his screen. He winced as he stood and turned on the defense-bot before heading to check it out. The robot cycled through its complement of wavelengths, warming its stunners—

Weaver-Rho disabled it.

"We will finish in the morning." Weaver-Nu left Wu's mildewy basement.

"We're close—"

Weaver was already up the stairs. Substrates that should be sleeping lay awake in their bunks. Every piece of processing power tuned to the Southern Empire.

Weaver-Alpha processed the data from Substrate-Rho's eyes faster than it could be relayed through the lab.

Anton glanced back at Weaver-Alpha as they approached the front door to Taketa. The door opened with ease and they entered the polished sheen of the corporate lobby.

I was unaware anything could be this clean. How much maintenance does this take? The elevator doors opened as Anton's foot hit the edge. Their feet tracked dirt from the entrance to the elevator and the doors closed. *Unplanned, needs to be fixed.*

Weaver-Rho's fingers were a blur as Weaver found and activated a cleaning robot to polish their prints from the lobby.

"Anton," Weaver-Alpha said as they rode the elevator. "If things go wrong for any reason, you will need to kill this substrate."

Anton glanced down at the substrate. "Your jokes are terrible."

"This is not a joke, you are more important. I can sacrifice one substrate for you to escape. But I do not want it taken in to be examined and tortured. Do not debate or I will take the gun back." Anton raised an eyebrow at the substrate.

Weaver-Alpha removed its tablet and slowed the elevator. Weaver double checked that the elevator still read as at the lobby. They needed to arrive as Fayed's call ended and with the element of surprise.

"We're slowing." Anton reached for the ceiling.

"That is me," Weaver-Alpha said. "Should have gotten us inserts." *Where could I have done that?*

"Not the time," Anton whispered.

Weaver-Rho watched Joe Fayed hang up the call and Weaver-Alpha opened the elevator door.

Joe Fayed rubbed his chin while staring out the window at the Southern Empire. The glittering sprawl mesmerizing, Weaver devoted a single substrate to ensure that it was memorized. Window screens rolled down, revealing Anton and Weaver in the reflection.

"I had hoped you died," Fayed said.

"You should know I'm hard to kill"—Anton pulled his pistol—"no movement."

"I have a personal alarm system, Mr. Grissom. My security will arrive shortly. I don't even have to move."

"I disabled that," Weaver-Alpha said.

"I'm turning this chair around." Fayed slowly spun in his chair and his eyes locked with Substrate-Alpha. "The prodigal son returns. I wondered if the reports from Saori were true. Tell me, Anton, you're comfortable allowing this… abomination to exist?"

"Stop talking." Anton held no tension in his form as he approached the desk, his pistol steady.

Fascinating.

"Anton please, I heard what you said to Eva. I know you won't kill me." Fayed opened his desk drawer, pulling out two glasses and a bottle of amber liquid. "You can put the gun down. Whatever that thing is calling itself now disabled my alarms. What are we going to do, stand here all night?"

Fayed poured two glasses and pushed one towards an empty seat in front of the desk.

"You want to talk, let's talk. Your indiscretion aside, as far as I am concerned, you did what I asked you to do. The property stands before me. Have a drink. You want out, a promotion, we can negotiate."

Anton sat and drained the amber liquid.

"Normally you wouldn't do that with real whiskey, but I'll give you a pass." Fayed drained his own and poured two more half glasses.

"I want to be left alone. Permanently." Anton drank with his human arm, his augmented hand still grasped the pistol, finger on the trigger.

I don't like this.

Weaver-Ariel left the cafe. *I could have trusted Anton too much.* Substrate-Ariel unlocked the dagger strapped against its back.

Weaver-Rho brought up the Taketa HQ schematics, calculating ambush points. If Substrate-Alpha was lost, there would be a cost for Anton.

"I can do that," Joe Fayed said. "What happened to Yume?"

"She's dead," Anton said.

"Your doing?"

"No."

"She was bright, both of the Chaude girls really. They complemented each other in a way. Though both would loathe to hear it." Fayed's eyes settled on Substrate-Alpha. "This doesn't have to be an imprisonment. You can work for me. Get out to see the world, once you've grown up."

"The cage is the same size," Weaver-Alpha said.

Substrate-Ariel crouched in the shadows near the entrance to the Taketa building. The blade in its hand reflected the abyss surrounding Weaver's mind.

Substrate-Rho disabled the cameras in the building and surrounding blocks. Subterfuge was gone. Escape is what mattered now.

"How many kids did you find?" Fayed ignored Weaver's comment.

"Three," Anton said.

Weaver-Alpha glanced at Anton. *You lied?*

"Where are the other two?"

"Died during the flooding of a tunnel."

"And you managed to escape with one?"

"These legs can swim, Joe. I carried this one out."

"My reports said there were at least twenty that escaped the lab, Anton," Joe said.

In an instant almost too fast for Weaver to process, Anton's gun discharged. Joe Fayed's head exploded into the back of the chair. A gun slipped from Fayed's hand, clattering on the floor.

"We can go now." Anton finished Fayed's ration of whiskey with his augmented hand. He wiped down the other mug and made for the elevator.

The CEO's remaining eye fixed on nothing as his blood soaked into the green carpet.

Substrate-Ariel strapped the blade against its back and walked towards a transportation hub to take a train to a separate hotel.

"You worried me back there," Weaver-Alpha said as they rode the elevator.

"I thought there was a way out where I didn't have to kill him," Anton said. "He caught my lie and went for a gun. He was too slow."

The elevator door opened on the first floor, and the security guard stood at the desk. "When did you enter?"

"This morning, before your shift," Weaver-Alpha said. "You can check the logs."

Weaver-Rho disabled the logs.

"System's down... They don't pay me enough for this," he muttered under his breath, and turned to Anton. "My niece is a Disabled. Which school did you send him to? He speaks well."

"I'd have to ask my wife," Anton said. "When I'm in tomorrow, I'll leave a note for?"

"Darren," the man said.

Anton blinked in surprise. "I'll have their business card here for you in the morning, Darren."

"Thanks man, have a good night."

"You too," Weaver-Alpha said and they left the building. "We should leave this urban area."

"I'm leaving all of them. I'm going home, then I'll report to base. They won't miss me yet."

"I want to come with you," Weaver-Alpha said.

Anton opened his mouth.

No. "Please?" Weaver-Alpha interrupted.

Anton closed his mouth and they walked through darkened blocks. "Aye. For a bit. Can we get food? I'm starving."

"There is a cafe nearby, we can get take away."

Weaver-Rho programmed a transport to collect Substrate-Alpha and Anton and take them to the transportation hub.
The next flight to Dom-Chi was in the morning, and it would take that long to crack the airliner's ticketing systems.

Chapter 46 - Luciana

Luciana ran a hand through the shorter side of her hair. Sand fell onto her mattress beside a starched, black, formal uniform. *Haven't worn you since graduation day.* She pulled on the pants, they were tight around the ass. She buttoned the shirt, the fabric crinkled from the press but was loose around her chest. The formal jacket could have held its shape in the detritus storm and Luciana snapped into it. *Missed the last one...* Phantom hands rubbed her head and she left the bedroom. Weaver-Marco sat near the kitchen bar, rubbing Nagual's scalp. The dog panted and wagged its tail. The child hopped off the stool, his clothing shook, revealing bare skin beneath the tattered rags. He followed Luciana out the door.

I need a drink. "We need to get you real clothes," Luciana said, trying to clear her mind.

"That will be nice." Weaver-Marco took her hand as they hit the lobby. "Are you ready?"

"This isn't something you're ready for. But it's something that must be done."

"I see."

Nagual padded ahead on the silted streets, a lone hawker in the distance the first sign of life since the storm.

"Do you want to talk about it?" Weaver-Marco said.

The ever-present lump in Luciana's throat swelled, Nagual pushed it away before he looked over his shoulder at her.

"I'm good."

"Ok Luciana, I am here if you want to."

"Thanks, Weaver." Luciana stepped into the police station.

Damp from the storm, the air quiet and still, the lone sign of life in the church came from Nagual smelling each individual officer and their communal soap.

No Chief. His officer door stood open, bullet holes covered the second floor above the parish. The officers sat at their desks in formal uniforms. They weren't working.

A lone black box sat on Maus' desk.

His ashes. Luciana's mouth dried, her heart filled her throat. Nagual's nails clicked on the linoleum as he continued towards the conference room with Weaver-Marco.

"No Chief?" Luciana's voice crackled.

"At 01-PD," Sheer said. "Wants to ensure Maus gets full honors and a full pension goes to his family."

Luciana was pulled to Maus' desk, her hand sucked by the gravity of the urn-box to rest on its polywooden edge. She swore it was warm. Chen's tanned hand crossed on top of hers, then Sheer's, Kagan's, Junger's, Novina's, and finally Nguyen's.

"Can't believe he denied our parade," Sheer said.

Luciana had a sad laugh, the officers had a sad laugh.

"Can't believe he wants his ashes sprinkled around the station," Chen said.

"I can. Half here, half to Mama Maus." Luciana blinked at watery eyes, someone else's tears fell on their collective hands first. "We should put some on the antenna so he can watch over us."

"Why not in the coffee machine? He fixed it so many times," Chen said.

The group's laugh was short and bittersweet.

"I can't believe he's really gone," Kagan said.

Me neither.

A hand in the pile squeezed.

"It wasn't the same after..." Nguyen started.

"After Erik." Luciana swallowed tears.

"At least you're here for this one, Luci," Sheer said. "And we're not standing here wondering if there'll be another box in a few days."

Luciana swallowed the lump in her throat that threatened to tear it apart. She clapped Sheer on the back. "You lot aren't lucky enough for me to kick it."

The officers laughed, their hands separated, and they all stared at the ceiling to drain their tears back. Sheer walked into the conference room and returned with a bottle of Mother Messiah Whiskey and coffee cups.

"Thank you." Novina cleared her throat and plucked the bottle from Sheer. She drained a mouthful.

"Fuck the cups, I guess." Sheer took the bottle back. "To Maus, and those shitty-hand-me-downs he always got us." Sheer drank and handed the bottle to Luciana.

Heavy, cold, the alcohol and flavorants within wafted to Nagual in the other room. Wood, terpenes, smoke, she shook them from her head.

"To Maus." Luciana smiled. "For those days when we were all pieces of a puzzle that could be put back together." *And for you, Erik, my friend, my love... I hope to make you proud.* She snorted, took three mouthfuls of liquid fire, and passed the bottle to Chen.

That was spiked with god knows what. Nagual swayed beside her as if drunk.

"To Maus..."

Epilogue

Dr. Eva Wagner lay on the padded ground of a prison cell whose gray walls wormed into her brain stem.
God damn it. Always knew I'd get in trouble. Eva paced the three meter cube. *But this! Should have known Joe bugged my room.*
Her first week was spent bargaining with Joe. *A momentary lapse, as if he had never had any.*
Yume came by to gloat at one point early on. *That bitch. Upset I made the first move on that Rural. Or maybe it was jealousy of my project. If she tries to takeover…*
Eva stopped at the doorway, barely a recess in the gray-wall, her fingers ran the unseen seems. *Yume couldn't… No, I was criminally behind in my logbook. She'd have to come here. I can use that to get out. Ha! All those years of people telling me I have to keep it up to date, ha!* Eva went back to the lone mattress on the floor and slept.
Joe came the next morning.
"Eva, I've been debating your contributions to the company." His tone never wavering from the business flatness he used on her since—
The night they locked me in here. "Joe, I don't know what Yume told you, but she can't do what I do with robotics. She just can't."
"Eva, I have no doubt. However, I demand loyalty. Your attempt to sabotage me, all for some ass. It's worrisome at best, terminal at worst."
"J-Joe," Eva stammered.
"We're transferring you to the lab near the former Anchorage area."
Yes. "What will I be doing research on?"
"You are the research. Goodbye, Eva." The door screen turned off.
"What? You bastard! After all I did!?" Eva slammed her fists against the wall. "You might as well fucking kill me now!"
The door slid shut at the end of the hallway.
"He can't be serious. Fuck, what if he is?" *What if he's torturing me?* "He wouldn't, he couldn't." *He will. He'll do you this fucking dirty. Jesus, what the fuck was Anton doing? How did I let this happen!?*

The Last 0-Day

She banged her head against the wall. *So.* Bang. *Stupid.* Bang. She pressed her hands against the door. There had to be something she could break.

No food came that day, only water. The same for the day after that.

And today. Jesus, he's starving me to death.

She'd heard rumors about Joseph Fayed. That anyone who rose to C-level, no matter what, wasn't to be trusted. *And I didn't believe them. God damn it.*

Water didn't arrive that night. Or the following day.

By the end of the second day, she drank the reclaimed water from the toilet. Spiced, bitter, improperly filtered. That alone might kill her.

Eva lay on the mattress.

Anton came to her, leaning over her like he had in the past. She leaned up, grass wafting off him.

Did he smell like grass? She blinked, a gray ceiling stared back. *Motherfucker! I am the dumbest bastard to ever live.* She lay on her side, staring at the door. *The next time it opens, I'm escaping.*

Time dissolved, the toilet stopped refilling when she flushed it for drinking water. Eva closed her eyes and lay against the door. *Rest, save my strength.*

She fell from a waterfall, pain jolted her awake. She'd cracked her skull off a tile floor.

A robot with a humanoid torso and tank treads for legs filled her vision. Hands covered in silicone skin picked her up. She couldn't escape its grasp. The robot carried her over what would be its shoulder. Eva stared at the hexagonal treads as it carried her through the Taketa HQ marble lobby.

This bot is my design. Jesus Christ, Joe, you're a sick bastard.

The robot lay her on warm pavement. A night sky and the green back of a transport rose above.

She pushed herself to her knees.

A hand grabbed her arm. "Let's not make this hard." One of Taketa's elite guards said. "There's food and water in the transport for you. If you want to make a break for it, do it where you're going." He dragged her into the back of the truck.

She didn't bother screaming, the city-blocks had been cleared hours ago. The guard fastened into a seat. Water cartons and SR-loaves lay stacked around her new throne. She was too dehydrated for her mouth to water, but her tongue tried.

"For your good behavior." The guard heft food and water onto her lap. "Bon voyage." He exited.

The pod hatch shut and the transport rumbled away. Eva pulled the plug from the water carton, guzzling from an oasis after a gray desert. She panted, pushing the SR-loaf into her mouth. Grassy grains, malted sweetness, she chewed, savored, and stopped as the transport accelerated onto the highway.

I'll make myself sick. And Joe probably planned for me to not have enough calories. She leaned back into the chair and folded her hands.

The water in her lap could sweet-talk her all it wanted. Temptation wouldn't unmake her again.

The transport was retrofitted with her lone chair and a chemical toilet in the corner. At least it wasn't gray. With her belly full, sleep claimed her easily.

Eva woke to her seatbelt unfastened and her pod rocking gently against the transport. The water-bag in her lap tilted towards the rear.

I'm on an incline. Gotta be the Cascade Mountains, maybe the Sierra Nevadas, if he was lying to me. She searched through the pod and separated her supplies.

Thirteen days' worth. It has to be Alaska. If this transport dies in the Great North, they'll kill me. Her skin itched, she removed clothing not designed for extended use and sat in her underwear. *The moment that door opens, I'm tearing ass out.*

Days within the pod lost meaning, Eva sat by her throne stretching—

The Last 0-Day

The truck tilted, her stomach hit her throat. She flew across the pod, crashing into her wall of water.

The transport tipped, metal on concrete thundered into her world. Eva ground her teeth, wincing in pain as the pod slowed to a stop. Pop-pop-pop, an automatic rifle fired outside the pod.

She lay in a daze in her underwear. Detonations blew the door off, light poured into the room and a figure stepped in.

Run.

"Eva Wagner?" An androgynous voice said.

Eva nodded, shivering at a temperature she'd never experience. *They're blocking my escape route.*

"I got her," the person yelled, sliding into the pod. "Relax, I'm from the United City-State Military."

Eva blinked away the cobwebs, taking the man's hand. He pulled her to her feet and helped her out of the wreck. A light snow and a heatless sun fell onto the pod doors.

"C-cold," Eva chattered.

"Chopper will be here soon. It'll be warm there," he said.

Eva's eyes adjusted after weeks in an artificial dim. Snow-capped mountains rose around them. The transport's engine lay across the road, a rail-gun bolt jutting out of the radiator. Blood splattered the snow and slush at the front.

"Human pilot?" Eva shivered.

The man stepped closer and wrapped her in their overjacket. Warmth and a peach perfume encased her.

"More like a guard, surprised the rail gun didn't kill him." The soldier had no facial hair and an oddly feminine face. His hair shaved on the sides, he'd lost his left ear at some point.

A black helicopter burned down the valley from the north end.

"Took us a long time to find you," he said. "Too long."

"I can't begin to say how happy I am that you're here," Eva said.

The man gave her a sly smile. "Roger that." He winked.

What?

The gyrocopter came in low; the soldier hurried Eva towards the aircraft. The door swung open automatically and the soldier helped Eva in.

"Alex, that her?" a woman from the cockpit yelled back as the door closed.

"Obvi."

Eva was pushed to the floor as the helicopter made a quick ascent. "What does the UCSM want with me?" she yelled.

"Too technical and out of my pay rate," Alex yelled back.

***

The helicopter banked, Eva's stomach dropped.

"Fucking crosswind," the pilot's voice came through a cabin speaker.

"Jesus, Sagira. We did all that work. Don't fucking kill us now." The helicopter bounced as it landed. The door swung open, a stern woman stood before them.

"Excellent work, you two," the woman said. "Dr. Wagner, please walk with me. We'll bring you a change of clothes. We're in a bit of a time crunch."

Snow fell against the military base built into the side of the mountain. A treadmill-like device brought the helicopter back and hid it within the compound.

Eva stepped into a cavernous hangar filled with long-range aircraft. They hurried her up a catwalk and into a control room where four officers with innumerable badges stood over a map of Eurasia.

"Dr. Wagner," a tan woman said. "What do you know of the Adephon Algorithm?"

Eva's mind raced through papers she published decades ago. The banned machine learning algorithm that generated untold answers and problems. The years she spent trying to decipher its nature. She blinked back to the room, refocusing on the map. Countless arrows crisscrossed the continent.

"Why?" Eva said.

"Someone left it alone for too long, Dr. Wagner. Left it on and gave it real estate."

Eva's heart missed a beat. She dropped into an empty chair and stared at the map. *Fuck me.*

B. R. Russell

Map - United City-States of America

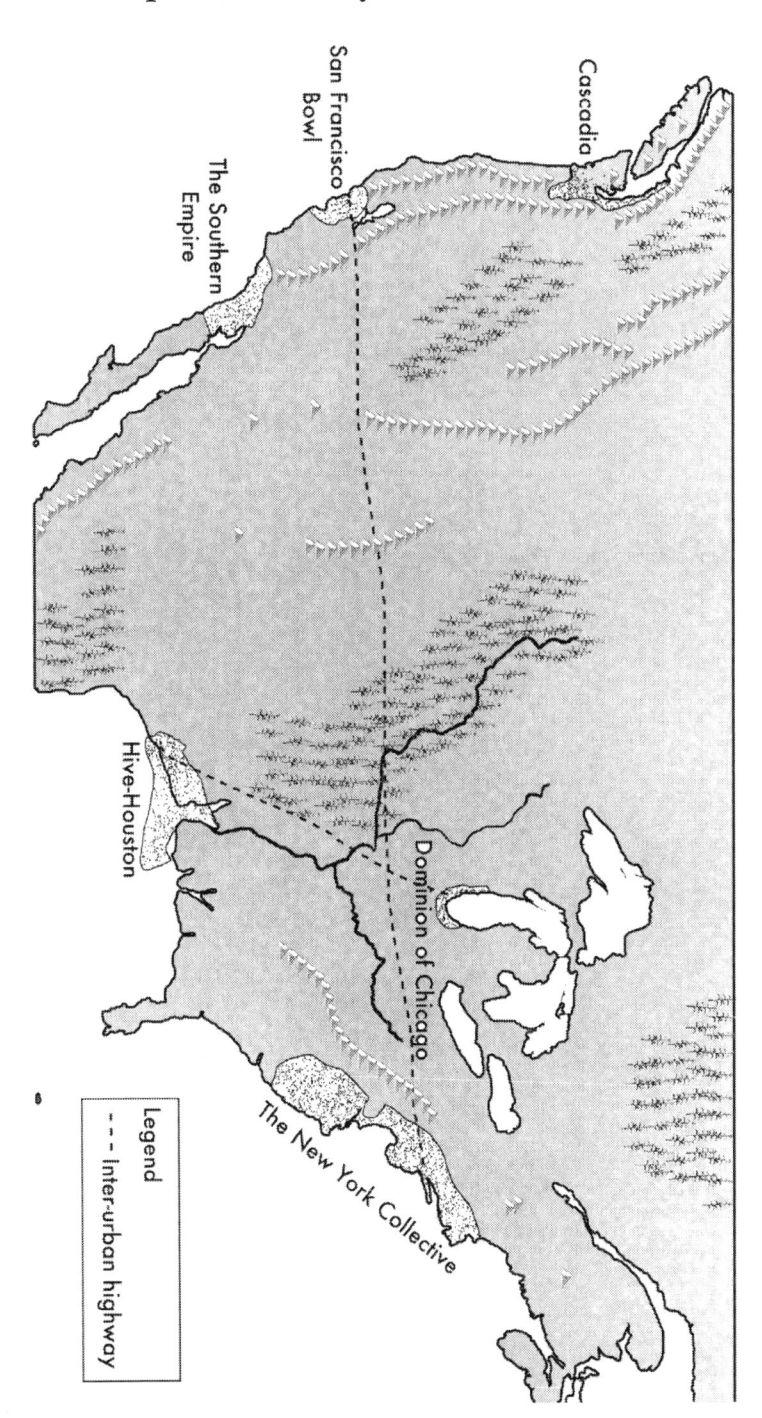

Contact Information

If you want updates on my upcoming books in this series or others, deals on books, and random free stuff, you can sign up for my reading group at **www.brrussell.com**

You can follow me on Twitter @ThatBRRussell
If you drew something from this book, I'd love to see it! Tag me on Twitter.

Do you have a podcast, book blog, YouTube, Twitch or any other platform and want to talk about this book or my upcoming books? Because I'd love to talk to you too. Media inquiries can be sent to **brrussell.media@gmail.com**

Booksellers and agents of any variety can email me at **brrussell.writing@gmail.com** Let's work together.

Made in the USA
Middletown, DE
16 December 2022